THE Thrill OF THE CHASE

THE Thrill OF THE CHASE

NEW YORK TIMES BESTSELLING AUTHOR
LAUREN DANE

CONTENTS

Author Note

Hey there, all you lovely reader friends!

Way back in 2006 I got an idea that I knew I couldn't sell to the publisher I had been with at the time so I took a chance on a new publisher and a new editor with my small-town contemporary romance.

Twelve years later, the Chase Brothers series has been reissued with Carina Press, but with the same beloved editor, Angela James, who continues to kick my butt and make me a better writer.

I've done very little to change these books. Some grammatical stuff here and there, but though I like to think my writing has come a long way in those intervening dozen years, I wanted to keep these the way they were. The heart of the stories is unchanged. The heart of this group of friends and family is unchanged.

The Chases remain a personal favorite of all the books I've written and it's always a pleasure to see them reach new readers even now. If you're a new reader to the series, welcome to Petal! I hope you enjoy your stay. If you're returning, welcome back!

Either way, I'm glad you're here.

Lauren

Giving Chase

Chapter One

Friday night in Petal. Half the town—that is, those citizens sixty and under—were gathered inside The Pumphouse seeking refuge from the rain and enjoying three-dollar pitchers of beer and burgers. The crowd noise was so loud, whatever song playing on the jukebox was indistinguishable. Still, Maggie, Dee and Liv sat at their usual table—the one by the window—so they could watch the goings-on. They'd sat there, every Friday night, for the last four years. It should have seemed mundane, boring, but it was the time when each of the friends got to reconnect after a long week and it was a bright spot instead.

But the usually happy Maggie sighed into her beer before taking the last drink and setting her empty glass down on the table.

"So, I finally broke up with Sam. It's definitely over."

With an inelegant snort, Liv tried to catch the server's eye to order another pitcher. "Maggie, honey, it's been over for at least a month now. You just haven't been willing to admit it to yourself. And heaven knows our manners were too good to break it to you." It was Maggie's turn to snort at that.

Stifling a grin, Liv continued. "Anyway, he's an ass. He's been an ass since the fifth grade. You're too good for him."

"Way too good for him. He needs a momma, not a girlfriend." Dee's nose wrinkled in disgust.

"Well, the problem is this town is just too damned small! Who've I got to choose from? And let's keep it men between twenty-two and fifty who aren't married, living with his mother or gay." Maggie handed a five over to Patrick for the beer and began to pour out for everyone. "Keep the change, sugar." She winked, getting a cheeky grin in return before he turned and headed back through the crowd to the bar.

"It really is a shame he's gay. He looks as good going as he does coming." Dee's voice trailed off as she watched him disappear into the crowd.

"Yeah, a shame for our team." Liv sighed. "But you know, you're failing to mention the hottest real estate in town. How about one of the Chase brothers?"

Maggie snorted. *Yeah right.* Those boys were mouthwateringly handsome. Tall, broad, boy-next-door gorgeous. The women of Petal had been lusting after them since preschool.

"Sure, why not! But no. I'd rather have Brad Pitt, he's about as available, although I suppose I'd have to fight Angelina for him." Maggie rolled her eyes. "Liv, *everyone* wants those boys. Even if a girl like me could catch their attention—I have no desire to be a notch on someone's bedpost. Maybe I just need to lower my standards. Roger Petrie has been asking me out for years. Maybe I should say yes. After all, he has a job, lives in his own home and has all of his teeth."

Liv and Dee burst out laughing. "Yeah but he's creepy! I mean, he's got like, what, fifty cats and a goat living *in* his house?"

"On the other hand," Liv said, breathless from laughing, "an animal lover can't be all that bad."

"Question is, how much of a *lover* is he? I mean, he sleeps with the goat!" Maggie's words dissolved into laughter.

"*Eww!* Time to change the subject. You don't need to lower your standards, Margaret Elizabeth Wright! There are plenty of decent men in Petal. You just have to be patient." Sweet as she was, Dee didn't know she said it in that way women do when *they* have a boyfriend.

"And what do you mean, *a girl like you*? Are you suggesting that those Chase boys are too good for you? Because you are dead wrong. My God, Maggie, you're beautiful! It pisses me off that you can't see it. I blame your mother." Liv shook her head as she looked at her oldest friend.

Petite and blessed with fine, almost delicate features, Maggie had a head of gorgeous strawberry blonde hair. She usually wore it in a tight knot at the back of her head but when she let it free, it hung past her waist. Tortoiseshell glasses often hid the big amber-brown eyes fringed with long lashes. Hell, Maggie was pretty when she looked like a buttoned-up schoolteacher. But Liv knew Maggie had a knockout figure lurking under those clothes and itched to cut and style the hair, get rid of the glasses and show a bit of skin.

"Liv, those Chase boys are out of my league. Men that handsome and, well—manly—don't notice high school history teachers." And she had to admit that they were all so powerfully vital and masculine that it intimidated her.

"Speak of the devils…" Liv nodded her head and the three turned to watch the Chase brothers stroll into the bar. In fact, every single woman—and even the not-so-single ones—noticed the four impossibly handsome brothers.

"My, my, my. Those boys sure are fine." Maggie's gut tightened at the sight.

"Yepper." Liv fanned her face with a napkin.

"Mm-hmm." Dee nodded.

Once they'd disappeared into the back where the pool tables were, the women turned back to their conversation.

"Go on, Dee, tell us about Arthur. We know you want to." Every Friday night Dee did a weekly "Arthur is so wonderful" update.

Arthur Jones was Dee's boyfriend. One of the good guys. They were planning a wedding for Valentine's Day.

"He planted a magnolia tree in the backyard earlier this week and put in an arbor with yellow climbing roses. Three of them because you know, we've been together three years. He's so sweet."

Smiling through the sudden lump in her throat, Maggie stood and patted Dee's shoulder. "Yeah, he is." She stood up. "I'll be back. I have to make a pit stop."

It didn't used to bother her so much that she didn't have someone. Dating around was fine. Fun even. But lately, Maggie had begun to want the kind of love and connection that Dee had with Arthur. She wanted someone to make breakfast for. Someone to plant flowers with and take long walks hand in hand at the lake with. She now knew she was missing something and she wanted it.

On her way back from the ladies' room, she heard Patrick call out that their order of chili cheese fries was done. With a wave to thank him, she moved to grab them and save him a trip. Three steps from the kitchen window area someone slammed into her. Knocked sideways, the platter of gooey fries flipped over, dropping with a *splat* on the side of her blouse and down the leg of her pants.

"Hey! Watch where you're going!"

Maggie spun around, astounded at the tone. "Me? Did you just bark at me? You're the one who bumped into me! You made me drop this food all over my clothes and the floor. Last time I checked, it's the person walking backward's job to watch out." Looking up, and then up some more, she came to the insanely gorgeous face of none other than Shane Chase.

"You were in the middle of the aisle," he growled at her, arms crossed over his chest.

"It's the walkway, dumbass! It's called that because it's where people *walk*." Unable to stop herself, she used a very slow voice and her heart sped a bit as his jaw clenched at her tone. And then her inner bitch wanted to snicker. Instead she couldn't resist. "Facing *forward*, I might add." This guy took the cake! A little bit of good looks turned him into a self-righteous jerk.

Narrowing his eyes, he leaned into her personal space to intimidate her. But she refused to step back. She did work with teenagers every day after all. And the man was acting like a big baby. "Did you just call the sheriff a dumbass?"

"No, I called *you* a dumbass. The dumbass who wasn't watching where he was going and slammed into me and then yelled at me, the dumbass who has *no* manners—I'm calling *that* guy a dumbass. That you happen to be a cop is not relevant. Although one might expect a cop to actually act with civility and basic manners!" She huffed. But the impact was not as impressive as she'd hoped given that he was nearly a foot taller than she was. And all that distracting hard muscle and really nice smell. Why did a jerk like him have to smell so good she wanted to lean in and take a bite? It'd serve him right if she did. Shaking her head to dislodge the question about what he may taste like, the fog cleared a bit and she found her mad again.

"She's got you there, Shane." Kyle Chase approached, smiling at her apologetically. "Are you all right? That cheese stuff is pretty hot. Did you get burned?" He handed her some napkins but she just looked down at herself. If she tried to wipe it with the napkins the gooey mess would just get worse.

At least one of them had manners. He probably tasted good too. Stifling a smile she unclenched her fists and stepped back. "Thanks. It just stung a bit but my pants took the brunt. But I've got to go and get out of these clothes." Swinging her head to glare at Shane, she noted he was still glowering, only this time at his brother. "And you! I have sixteen-year-old boys in my class who have more manners. Take a civility training class or something." She harrumphed and spun around to stalk back to their table.

"Oh my God! What was that all about?" Liv handed Maggie her purse and raincoat.

"That moron Shane Chase slammed his gargantuan body into me and made me spill chili cheese fries all over myself! And *then* had the *nerve* to yell at me like it was my fault! Dumbass! I have to go. I'll talk to you two later." She tossed some money on the table.

"Now who's the dumbass? We're coming with you. I have plenty of takeout menus at home. Let's go." Liv got up and Dee followed.

The three women headed out together into the evening, grousing about Shane Chase and his abominable manners.

"Well, that was really special, Shane. You were awful to that little woman. Happy now? Or do we need to go and search out some old ladies we can knock over or steal some candy from toddlers?" Kyle egged his brother on as they played pool in the back of the bar.

"She called me a dumbass!"

Kyle smirked when Shane missed the shot.

"That's because you are one. You rammed into her, made her spill food all over herself and then instead of apologizing, you yelled at her. You're lucky all she did was call you a dumbass. She had quite the vicious gleam in her eye." Kyle lined up his shot and missed.

"She's cute for someone so small. I don't think I ever noticed that spark behind those glasses and those stuffy shirts. I've seen her around town but who is she?"

"Maggie Wright. She was in my year in school." Matt looked up mildly before leaning back down to take his shot. "She's a teacher at the high school now. History I think. Clearly a real menace to society." He rolled his eyes as he straightened and grabbed his glass.

"Sarcasm doesn't suit you, Matt. You're too pretty. Anyway, she's a rude little woman." But Shane's voice didn't sound so sure anymore.

"*You're* rude, Shane. Mom's gonna kick your ass when she

hears about this—and you know she will. Petal being Petal, I bet the story is weaving its way across town right this very moment," Marc taunted. "I don't envy you Momma's wrath but I can't wait to see it."

Maggie was up to her elbows in dirt, planting primroses when Polly Chase rolled up and got out of her car.

"Maggie? Honey, is that you?" Polly click-clacked up the front walk. The woman was a sight to see. She was not even five feet tall but that was the only thing small about her. A head of heavily lacquered hair stood several inches high, matched only by the spiked heels on her feet and a handbag bigger than a small country. All of this fit in the late 1970s Caddy she drove around town like a menace.

And her presence was big too. Polly Chase was the town matriarch. Her family was one of the oldest in Petal and her husband's just as old. Both the Chandlers and the Chases had a hand in the building and governance of Petal for five generations. When Polly married Edward Chase thirty-five years before, it had been the ultimate marriage.

Still, Maggie had always thought Polly, who sat with her on the Historical Society, and Edward, an attorney in Petal, were very nice people. However, seeing how rude her oldest was, she began to wonder.

Standing up, Maggie took off her gardening gloves and tossed them on the walk. "Yes, Mrs. Chase, it is. What can I do for you?" As if she didn't know. "Why don't you come on in? I was just going to get myself some hot tea. Would you like a cup?"

"Oh that would be perfect, shug. Thank you." Polly followed Maggie into the large house that belonged to her parents at one time and now was hers.

"Please, sit down and I'll get the water on." Maggie swept into the large kitchen and lit the burner under the teakettle. While she waited, she prepared the teapot, measuring the loose tea, spooning it into the mesh ball. Hanging it into the pot she turned and put a few oatmeal cookies on a pretty plate.

Steeling herself, she took a deep breath before going back into the living room a few minutes later. She put the tray down on the coffee table and sat across from Polly.

"It'll need steeping for another three minutes or so. Would you like a cookie? They're fresh-baked."

When Polly had taken a few bites of the cookie, Maggie poured her a steaming cup of green tea. "What can I do for you today, Mrs. Chase?"

"Honey, I heard what my boy did to you last night at The Pumphouse. I'm just mortified! So naturally I wanted to come by and apologize. Because it also came to my attention that he failed to do that on top of everything else."

Softening at the sight of Polly's distress, Maggie leaned across the space separating them. Reaching out, she squeezed the other woman's hand. "Mrs. Chase, please don't be upset. Whatever Shane did, he did on his own. You have nothing to do with it. I'd never think that."

"Honey, you're too nice. Now I'm just embarrassed. They weren't raised to talk to anyone that way, much less a woman! Don't think I haven't been on his tail all morning. He's managed to avoid me so far, but mark my words I'll find him before the day is through. And when I corner that rat, you can be assured I'm gonna tan his hide!"

Maggie stifled a laugh at the picture of Polly spanking her nearly thirty-year-old giant of a son, badge and all. "Well if it's any consolation to you, Kyle did come over with some napkins and asked me if I was all right."

"Oh he sang like a bird when I got out to his work site this morning. He's a good boy, Kyle. Always treats people with kindness." Polly smiled with pride. "They might be big, giant boys but they're *my* boys and I'm still their momma. I heard you called Shane a dumbass."

Maggie blushed fiercely. "I'm sorry. I shouldn't have, it wasn't nice but he was just really obnoxious and I lost my temper."

Polly burst out laughing. "Honey, it sounds to me like he *was* being a dumbass. You don't have to apologize to me. They get it from their daddy you know." She gave Maggie a wink.

After tea and cookies and a discussion on the next historical society function, Polly excused herself. "I have to run now, Maggie honey. Rest assured I'll wrangle that boy into doing the right thing. Thank you for the tea and cookies." She gave Maggie a big hug and teetered on her spiky heels back down the front walk, giant handbag in tow, and sped off.

"You and I have a double date." Liv stood on Maggie's doorstep several hours later.

Automatically, Maggie opened the door to let her in. "What?" Maggie took in the garment bag and the big train case in Liv's arms and tried not to panic. God only knew what her best friend was up to.

"Jeezus, Maggie, get the freaked-out look off your face. I'm not going to kill you. Our dates are Shaun Stadey and Alex Parsons. I was shopping at the Piggly Wiggly earlier today and they asked if you and I had a date for the Homecoming Picnic tonight. Of course I told them they'd be filling the bill. And now you're getting a makeover. No argument. I brought some clothes by, too."

"A makeover?" Maggie's eyes moved to the train case and big garment bag. "No way! Liv, do you remember what Toots looked like when you got finished with her? I'd give you one of my kidneys but you don't have the best record with makeovers. Anyway, I have to get out to the car wash with the kids, I just came home on a break."

Unmoved, Liv stared for a long moment. "Okay, but Maggie, Toots was a dog and we were eight. So shaddup. And no, you don't need to get back to the car wash. It is pointless to try and think of ways out of this. Dee and Arthur are over there now and doing just fine. You know how much that freaking precious Arthur loves kids. Honestly, sometimes don't you think he's got to be a pod person or something because he's so perfect?" Liv hustled Maggie up the stairs and into her bedroom.

Maggie couldn't deny herself a guilty snicker and then sobered up. Well, she tried anyway. "Aww, leave poor Arthur alone. He's a nice guy in a sea of asshats. And Dee, being a pod person herself, deserves someone equally as nice. Plus, he's kinda hot in a very nerdy way, dontcha think?"

One perfectly manicured eyebrow rose along with the corner of one side of Liv's mouth. "Whatever. In any case, there is no excuse for you not to let me do this." Liv laid the bags on Maggie's bed, unzipping them with military precision.

Stepping back, she glanced from the clothing to Maggie and back again several times. "Okay, clothes for tonight. Alice let me have a few things from her store to bring over here for you. They're all really cute and it would only be a couple hundred bucks and I think you should buy them all. But, I'm willing to leave you alone for a week if you buy at least one outfit. Come on, I know they'll all look great on you."

Despite her amusement at Liv's hard sell, Maggie broke out in a nervous sweat. "Didn't you just tell me how beautiful I was on Friday? Why do I need a makeover?"

"You *are* beautiful, Maggie. But these clothes will fit you. You've got a great body but you never let anyone see it because your clothes are all at least a size too big. This stuff isn't tight or slutty, it's just modern and it'll flatter your figure.

"A trim and style of your hair will frame your face. You don't need those glasses tonight because I'm driving anyway. Oh, and by the way, I made you an appointment at the eye doctor for Tuesday. I'll meet you there. You need new frames that better fit your face. Contacts would be nice too, don't you think?"

Cripes, the woman was a steamroller! Maggie eyed the door, considering her chances for escape. Liv caught it and shook her head as she stepped in front of it, blocking Maggie's way.

"Don't even think about it."

Maggie knew by the set of Liv's face that she wouldn't win this one. She sighed and Liv grinned, sensing imminent victory. Still she added a few things to sweeten the offer. "Sam will be there. Probably with some skanky date. You know you want him to see what he's missing. Better yet, Shane Chase will be there too. Let's show that dumbass what's what."

Unable to hold it back, Maggie let her grin spread over her face. "You play so dirty!" But she was already looking through the stack of clothes on her bed. She had to admit the stuff was really cute. Liv did have good taste for a girl who used grape Kool-Aid to dye a dog's fur back when they were kids.

Liv's eyes sparkled as she pulled out a dark blue scoop-necked blouse and a denim skirt. "I like these the best. You have great legs. Not that anyone would know since you always wear those long teacher skirts. And ugh, worse, the mom-waisted pleated khaki pants. Pleats! Oh the agony of watching any woman under eighty wear pleats!"

Maggie burst out laughing at the look of disgust on Liv's face.

"To go with it, those cute boots we saw in the window of Radison's last week."

"But I didn't buy those boots, remember?"

"Yes you did. You can pay me back later." Not bothering to look up, Liv pulled them out of the bottom of one of the garment bags and put them on the floor. "It'll be perfect. The skirt is the perfect length and the boots will come to the top of your calf. Well, what are you waiting for? Try on the whole outfit."

"If I do this will you stop setting me up and trying to make me over?"

"Well, I hate to point out that if I do this, I *will* be making you over. But I promise to not try again for the next six months."

"I'll take whatever I can get. Fine, hand me the clothes. But I'm wearing my glasses. I'm not gonna be blind just to look cuter."

Liv grinned and handed the outfit over to Maggie. Once Maggie had undressed, Liv shook her head in amazement when she saw Maggie's underwear. "Girl, you're something else. Look at those undies! I always forget that you're wild beneath the clothes."

Fighting a blush, Maggie smiled. "What? A girl needs pretty undies." She looked down at the forest green, lacy, high-cut panties and the matching demi-bra. Pretty panties and bras were somewhat of a weakness for her. She had drawers full of the stuff.

"Girl, you're a mess of contradictions. Now, get those clothes on."

Once changed, Maggie looked down at the outfit and back at her reflection in the mirror. Liv had been right. The clothes weren't tight but they showed her figure. She looked pretty. The skirt came to just below her knees and the boots weren't too high-heeled that her feet would be dying in half an hour. She tugged the bodice of the blouse up a bit, it showed more boobs than she normally did. "Liv, jeez, you can see my boobs."

Rolling her eyes, Liv clucked her tongue. "Now, shug, don't exaggerate. You can see your *cleavage*, big difference. Even at that, it's just the very top of your cleavage. I promise you it doesn't look slutty or even daring. Wow, I'd forgotten that you had breasts with all those buttoned-to-the-chin shirts you wear beneath the bulky sweaters."

"Janie is the sweater girl. She's the one with the great figure."

Startled, Liv gave Maggie an appraising look up and down. There were moments when Maggie revealed another small, but bone-deep wound her mother and sister had laid on her and it broke Liv's heart.

"Mags, you've hidden your light under a bushel for far too long. You look so pretty dressed up like this. Jane Marie is not the only pretty sister. Stop letting her mess with your head." She motioned to the chair. "Come on now, let's get the rest of you done."

Putting a drape around Maggie's shoulders, Liv loosed Maggie's hair and wet it down. Quickly and efficiently, she trimmed about four inches, layered it to free the curls and cut the front to frame Maggie's face. The weight gone, the pretty strawberry-blonde hair was a riot of curls.

After the application of some goop to hold the curl and wall out the frizz-inducing humidity, Liv opened up the train case.

With artful application of subtle colors, Liv emphasized Maggie's giant amber eyes and put a shine on her full lower lip. Maggie didn't need a lot of makeup and would have been uncomfortable in it anyway. Finished, Liv stood back and surveyed her work. Impressive. The mousy schoolteacher was gone. In her place, a pretty, fey-looking woman with long legs and a nice bosom. Not bad for a few hours' work.

Cocking her head, Liv met Maggie's eyes in the mirror. "Look at yourself, Maggie." Moving away, Liv changed her clothes and finished getting ready while Maggie just stared at herself in the mirror.

For so very long she'd only looked at herself in the mirror long enough to put her hair back. That wasn't her place in her family. The shock that she could be something else, *someone* other than the smart one in the Wright family, hit her. Tears burned her eyes for a moment until she blinked them back. "Wow, Liv."

If Liv saw the tears she ignored them. Just one of the million reasons Maggie loved her. "Instead of saying, *I told you so*, I'll just say that you look fabulous. In fact, we need to go clothes shopping! Or you could just keep the outfits I brought over *and* we could go shopping. You can show me where you get all those fancy panties." Liv winked.

Maggie fingered the colorful clothing in the bags. "Well, maybe. I mean, looking at myself right now... I think that I much prefer this me."

"Hon, you're the same you. Clothes and a haircut don't make you into a different person. But these clothes do allow the world to see more of how gorgeous you are on the outside. Everyone already knows how beautiful you are on the inside." Liv paused a moment. "I don't want you to feel I didn't already think you were beautiful. Inside and out, even with those ugly-assed schoolmarm clothes. You're the most beautiful woman I know."

Maggie stayed silent for long moments as she swallowed past the tears in her throat. Her emotions seemed to have chosen that moment to run riot. "It's just that you've always been the gorgeous, glamorous one. Dee's the sweet, pretty one and I was the smart one. It feels weird to see that I can be the pretty one, too. Heck, sexy even."

Arms encircled her from behind as Liv hugged her. "Aw, shug, your mom sure did a number on you. Yes, your sister is a beauty but she's not the only stunner in the family and on the inside, she's a troll."

"Janie's tall, blonde and married with two perfectly gorgeous children. She never looks unkempt. Her house is a freaking showplace and her husband adores her. She's perfect."

"Bleah! You want to be blonde like Janie? We'll get you some of the same blonde she has, it's out of a bottle. And beyond her looks what does she have? You're good and kind and smart and funny. You give back to this town and those kids. Honestly, sometimes I want to smack your momma for making you think that just because your sister was in pageants that you're not as good. Well, I'd like to smack her for a whole host of reasons but that's neither here nor there now. Now, we have a picnic to get to, let's go."

Chapter Two

Petal's Homecoming Week festivities were a major happening. Everyone from three months to a hundred and three came out to at least two of them—the picnic that set off the week and the football game against Crawford High.

The picnic was held down at the park, on the shore of the lake, and the evening ended with fireworks. The entire town came out to eat themselves silly on barbecue, homemade ice cream and peach pie. As traditions went, it was one of Maggie's favorites.

Maggie had to admit, the attention Alex Parsons paid her was wildly flattering. When they'd approached he'd given an almost cartoonish double take as he'd realized who she was. He seemed nice enough and he certainly had no problems being on a date with her. It was really nice to have a man so clearly attracted to her. His arm casually circled her shoulders as he guided her through the park.

Stopping at the top of a rolling hill that led down to the water, Alex turned to her. "How about right here to spread the blanket?" The spot would provide a perfectly unobstructed view of the fireworks and was close but not in the path of the tables heaped with food.

"Perfect." Maggie helped spread out the large blanket. Straightening, she suggested that the guys stay to guard their spot while she and Liv went to grab the food.

"You sure you don't want us to do the food run?" Alex asked.

"No, that's okay. Maggie and I can get in and out quicker. Anyway, all of the old ladies love Maggie and will give her the royal treatment."

Blushing, Maggie couldn't deny it. After all the years she'd been volunteering and taking meals to the folks at the retirement home and senior center, they did love her. And she loved them too. They'd become her family in many ways.

As she walked away, Alex watched her with a dreamy smile on his face. A woman like Maggie would make a wonderful wife and mother. There'd been so many others, women he'd thought were the right one. Could Maggie be it? He didn't quite dare allow himself to believe he may have finally found her.

"Who's that?" Intrigued, Kyle stared at the redhead in the skirt walking past them toward the food tables. He loved the way she moved, graceful but a little shy. That long curly hair was gorgeous. Hell, *she* was gorgeous. Was she visiting town? He recognized the dark-haired woman as Olivia Davis, the mayor's secretary.

Chase men did not fail to notice beautiful women and the other two looked up as well.

"Oh my lord, that's her!" Marc burst out laughing.

"Her who?" Shane craned his neck to get a better look and blanched. "Oh no, it's the teacher."

"And it looks like she caught you drooling, too. Listen, why don't I go over and apologize to her for you, I know how much you don't like her." Kyle realized he was only halfway joking.

"I owe it to her. I was a jerk." Muttering to himself, Shane shoved himself past his brothers and stalked toward Maggie.

Catching sight of Dee and Arthur, Maggie waved them over.

She pointed toward their blanket. "We're over there with Alex and Shaun. We just came to grab food."

"I'll come with you two. Arthur, can you take our stuff over there? I'll be back shortly, with extra potato salad." Dee smiled sweetly and Arthur kissed her nose before loping off toward the blanket.

Dee turned back to Maggie and gave her a once-over. "My God! Girl, you look gorgeous!"

"It's all Liv, I had nothing to do with it."

"Shaddup. I cut your hair and helped you pick some clothes. I didn't give you a kidney or anything." Liv waved her comments off.

"Don't look now, Maggie, but I do believe the big bad sheriff is drooling," Dee murmured.

They didn't even bother to pretend not to look as Liv and Maggie turned in unison to look in his direction.

"Oh and look, he's coming over here." Liv smirked.

"Great, and the whole town is watching. Is the man incapable of doing anything without making a scene? God, this is going to get back to my mother, I know it." Maggie blushed scarlet as heads turned to take in Shane's progress toward the three women.

Coming to a halt before them, he stood, hands on his hips. Maggie had to crane her neck up to see his face. What a surprise, he was glowering. *Did the man have any other facial expression where she was concerned?*

Frustrated anger coursed through her. "Yes? Did you fall getting out of your car and have come to yell at me for it? Or wait, let me go and grab some food and you can crash into me and spill it. I know! Gas prices are my fault right?" Maggie narrowed her eyes at him.

Anger flashed in Shane's eyes. "No. I came to apologize but I can see that you aren't ready to hear it."

"That's right, turn it around on me. Make it my fault *again* that you didn't do the polite thing last night. Gee, you think that because you are so good-looking that you get a free pass?"

Ohmigod, did I just tell him I think he's good-looking? She groaned inwardly.

"What's your problem anyway? Are you just naturally cranky?"

"Me? *I'm* cranky? You take the cake, buster. If you'll excuse me, I have a picnic to attend with my *friend*." Maggie's teeth were clenched so tight her jaw ached. She, Liv and Dee snorted and turned and walked as one toward the food tables as if Shane didn't exist.

"Smooth." Kyle approached, watching her as she walked away.

"What now? I came to apologize and she started in on me before I could say a single word."

"Shane, you're a giant. You stand at least a foot taller than the woman. You stalked over here with that look on your face and glared down at her. Of course she felt threatened! You are aware you're physically threatening right? It's one of the reasons you rarely get challenged as a cop. So if the bad guys won't take you on you think she's immune? And you do have a history of intimidating her."

Kyle's eyes wandered again to Maggie. Watching as she chatted animatedly with her friends and the women handing out heaping plates of food. "You know, she cleans up pretty nice. I had no idea."

"No."

"Huh?"

"I recognize that tone, Kyle. A woman like that is trouble. There are plenty of beautiful women in Petal. Stick with one of those." Shane's glower was back.

Kyle laughed heartily. "Hmm, you're sounding a mite jealous, Shane. You looking for a bit of trouble? If so, I'd be happy to stand back and let you at her."

The two of them watched as the women walked back to their

blanket. Alex got up and went to help with the plates of food she'd been carrying and then helped her down to the ground.

"Uh-oh, looks like someone else got to her first. Who'd have thought that little schoolteacher with the conservative blouses and the bun would look like that underneath?"

"I stole Melissa Harken from Alex Parsons back in the eighth grade. I don't see why I can't snatch our pretty schoolteacher from him." Matt strolled up with Marc. The grin on his face made it obvious he was deliberately goading Shane.

"Yeah, right. And that would be before or after you admit to all of us you have a thing for Olivia?" Kyle winked at Matt who laughed.

"Yeah. Well. Anyway. I don't think it would be very hard to push Alex out of the picture."

"No one is snatching anyone!" Shane turned away, stalking back to their blanket, grumbling under his breath.

The other three broke into laughter. "Uh-oh, this one has gotten under his skin big-time," Kyle said. "She is a pretty little thing, isn't she?"

"Hot is more like it. Damn, look at those legs. It's always the quiet ones." Of all the brothers, Marc was the one who seemed to revel in female attention the most. He watched Maggie with a sly smile. "How come I never noticed her before?"

"You're three years younger than we are. Plus, she's not the tight-jean-wearing, belly-button-ring kind of girl you usually chase." Matt turned to find Shane back at their blanket, drinking a cider and staring in the direction of Maggie Wright. "We'd better get back over there before he pops a vein."

In marked contrast, Maggie was having the time of her life. Alex Parsons was a nice guy and it was a treat to have a man pay that much attention to her. And when Alex leaned over and kissed her quickly on the lips—just a peck really—Sam walked by with his new girlfriend. He'd nearly fallen over himself as he'd done a double take. It wasn't like she wanted him back, but it was nice for him to see what he was missing.

"So, Alex, how do you like working at the library?"

"Oh, well I don't think I ever imagined being a librarian when I was a kid. But I do love it. The job here was a stroke of luck really, I'd been trying to decide whether or not to go to grad school and I got the offer." He shrugged. "But I found out that I love it. I may still go back at some point but for now, I'm really happy where I am." Alex took her hand in his. "It's really great to turn young people on to books, knowing I'm opening up new worlds for them. I bet it's like that for you as a teacher."

Maggie's eyes lit up. Teaching was her great passion. "It is. I'm so lucky to have two tracks. The advanced placement history class is filled with kids who are very disciplined, high achievers. They want to be there. God, the work they produce is amazing! They're a joy to teach. My other class is just your everyday sophomore history class. There are so many kinds of kids in it. Some are just biding time until they drop out, some just barely scraping by. But my favorites are the ones who start out bored and then I introduce something that totally excites them and they become history buffs." She felt shy suddenly as she'd revealed something so important to her. "I know it's goofy but I love it. Last year, I took my AP class on a trip to Washington, DC, and I think that they were more excited than I was to see the Constitution and the Declaration of Independence."

"Are you cold?" he asked Maggie when she'd shivered a bit.

Maggie stood up. "A bit. It started out so warm. I just need to run back to the car to grab my jacket and an extra blanket to wrap us up in."

"I'll come with you," Alex said, standing with her.

"Okay. Thanks." She gave him a smile and caught the keys Liv threw her way. Maggie liked the way he held a gentle arm around her waist as they walked. Not too much, just enough to let her know he wanted to touch her.

After grabbing her jacket and the extra blankets, Maggie

locked up. Turning back around, she ended up nose to nose with Alex.

"You smell really good." Alex's warm, cider-scented breath caressed her face. He tucked a wayward curl back behind her ear.

"Thanks. That's why I wear it back."

Alex took her chin gently between his fingers and tipped it up. Slowly, he brought his lips to hers. He was warm and gentle and the kiss only lasted a few short seconds. Maggie blinked up into his face and smiled. He hugged her quickly before walking back to their blanket.

Back on the hill, Alex sat behind her, pulling her into the warm shelter of his body. Wrapping the fleece blanket around them both, he left his arms encircled about her as well. Warm and content, Maggie leaned back against him and they watched the sky for the fireworks.

Afterward, it was with regret that Alex helped pack up the blanket and their possessions. He didn't want the date to be over. He didn't like the idea of having to say good-night to Maggie. He'd liked seeing that she was cold and then taking care of her. She needed someone to take care of her. He could see that. He also knew she was a lady and he wanted to take it slow to show her that he appreciated that.

Back at the car, Liv and Shaun kissed quite deeply at the driver side door and Alex burned with embarrassment and anger on Maggie's behalf. Maggie shouldn't have to be exposed to that sort of thing. But clearly Olivia was her friend and had way too much influence on Maggie's life. After they'd dated awhile, Alex would know how to best deal with Olivia's bad influence and help Maggie make better choices with her friends.

With an internal sigh, he smiled at her instead and held her door open. "Can I call you, Maggie? I'd like to take you out again."

"I'd like that." She dug out a pen and some paper from her

bag and wrote out her phone number and handed it to him with a smile. "I had a really nice time tonight, Alex, thank you."

He leaned over and kissed her again, still gentle and brief. He wanted to show her what a total gentleman he was. She gave him a small wave and got into the car and finally that slut Olivia stopped kissing and joined her.

"That went well, didn't it!" Liv said as they drove away. "First of all, Shaun is a great kisser! Second of all, did you see the double take that Sam gave when he saw you with Alex? Man that was perfect. Lastly, did you notice Shane Chase staring at you all night like he was a hungry wolf and you were a T-bone steak?"

"Yes, I saw Sam and yes, it was quite satisfying. Alex is a nice kisser—no fireworks—but I did feel like he was taking things slow. He asked if he could call me again and I said yes. Lastly, no, I did not notice Sheriff Dumbass looking at me. Boy, is that man sour!" And incredibly handsome and he smelled as good as all those Chase boys seemed to. Including Kyle. A man with a goatee was so sexy. One with a uniform, the other with a goatee! Whooee.

The next few days were hectic as the school year wore on toward midterm exams and the homecoming game approached. Still, not so busy that when Alex called Maggie couldn't find time to have dinner with him Wednesday night at El Cid.

The dinner with Alex was nice. He was attentive and smart and he loved many of the same things she did. Their conversation was lively as they discussed books and travel and history. Still, Maggie couldn't quite shake the odd feeling at the base of her spine at times during the evening. It wasn't that he ever did or said anything wrong though and Maggie was sure she was just trying to talk herself out of a nice guy as self-sabotage.

At her front door she turned to him with a smile. "Um, would you like to come inside for some tea?"

Grabbing her hand, he brought it to his lips and kissed it.

Moments later he pulled her close, holding her against his body. "If I come in, I'll want to never leave and I think that's moving a bit fast for you."

"It's not that I don't like you. I do. But yes, it would be a bit too fast for me." Still, she didn't make any move to stop him as he lowered his lips to hers for a kiss. This one more passionate than sweet and he held her tight for a few long moments afterward.

"Good night, Alex. I had a lovely time." Placing a hand in the middle of his chest, she moved him back from her gently.

"Would you like to go to the homecoming game with me on Friday night? Then maybe go out for a drink and a bite afterward?" He admired how much of a lady she was. He liked that she was saving herself just for him. His sweet Maggie.

"Yes, I'd like that. Dee, Liv and I all meet on Fridays at The Pumphouse. It's an after-Homecoming tradition for us, too. Arthur will be there and I'm guessing Liv will have a date but I don't know who. Shall we meet them there afterward?"

"I like Arthur. He's a good guy and I think Shaun is planning to ask Olivia." He mentally ground his teeth at the thought of Olivia but smiled instead. "Shall I pick you up at six then? I'll bring the seat cushions and the blanket?"

She smiled and he was glad he'd let her know how much he liked taking care of her.

"Okay, I'll be here." With a last look, she went into her house and he walked to his car and went home.

Alex led Maggie up the steps toward an empty spot on the bench seats, at the stadium. She looked so pretty in jeans and boots with a deep green turtleneck sweater. Instead of the bun, her hair was loose in back, held by a headband. Having it down in back left the pretty color around her face, making her eyes seem larger. He liked that she'd kept the glasses. Liked that she was lovely and modest, too.

Wanting to be sure she was comfortable and warm, he placed

the two seat cushions on the cold aluminum bench and sat down next to her. He grabbed her hand and held it in between his own.

After a while, Maggie stood up. "I'm going to go to the ladies' room. Shall I bring us back some stuff to snack on?"

Alex smiled at her thoughtfulness. "Sure. Some hot chocolate and some licorice."

"I'll be back in a few minutes then."

When Maggie exited the restrooms she saw Shane Chase waiting there and eyed him warily.

He held up his hands in the universal sign of surrender. "I mean no harm, I promise. I wanted to apologize to you for how I acted. At The Pumphouse last Friday and then Sunday at the picnic, as well."

Narrowing her eyes for a moment, Maggie let out the breath she hadn't realized she'd been holding. "Apology accepted. I'm sorry if I jumped to conclusions at the picnic. I'm usually not that big of a bitch."

"I do seem to bring out the best in you." He chuckled. "For such a little woman, you sure pack a mean punch." His smile melted her insides. The man was just flat-out handsome. Perfect, white teeth. Chocolate-brown hair that was just a bit too long in the back and looked really soft. But his eyes were startlingly blue. Like the blue of a cloudless summer day. Her stomach fluttered just looking at him.

"I did not punch you! But you would have deserved it if I had." She raised an eyebrow. "But according to Cecelia Wright, that's not what ladies do. We bake and butter wouldn't melt in our mouths. Oh, and know how to embroider. Too bad I can't embroider or know how to keep my mouth shut. I can bake though." She snorted. *I just snorted!* Horror roiled through her.

Instead of being disgusted, he threw back his head and laughed, a deep rich rumbling sound. "Embroidering is overrated anyway, Margaret. That is your name, right? I'm Shane Chase by the way. Otherwise known as dumbass." He held out his hand for her to shake and she pinked a bit. His grip was gentle but sure.

"I was getting rather fond of thinking of you as Sheriff Dumbass. You were being one, you know," she mumbled and he laughed a bit more.

"So my mother, brothers, father and half of the town have said."

She laughed at that. "Yes, I'm Margaret but most other people call me Maggie." She looked around him toward the stands. "Thank you for the apology, Shane. I need to grab some snacks and drinks before heading back. The game'll be starting soon."

"Oh, of course. It was nice to meet you, Maggie. Glad we cleared the air. See ya around." With a wink and a grin, he put his hands in his pockets and strolled away whistling.

Was that disappointment she saw in his eyes or wishful thinking on her part? *Probably just gas*, she snorted to herself.

He certainly was something else. In truth, she'd never met someone with that kind of sheer masculinity and sex appeal before. It left her a bit breathless. Still, she couldn't help but watch his ass in those snug jeans as he retreated back toward the stands. And she didn't feel one bit guilty about it either.

When she got back she handed out the armful of goodies she'd purchased. "Were the lines long?" Alex put the blanket back over her lap once she'd sat back down.

"Oh, no, not really. I just saw someone I knew and started talking." She blew on her hot chocolate.

Alex frowned. "Oh. Well, I was worried, Maggie."

The sharpness of his tone brought her head around to look at him with surprise. Her mouth opened to issue an automatic apology but she clicked her teeth together to stop it. The more she was around him, the more proprietary and paternalistic he became. It troubled her and she doubted she'd be seeing him again after the night ended.

As they filed out after the game, Shane caught her eye and

she waved, smiling as he waved back. Alex noticed and shot an angry glare at Shane.

In the car, on the way over to The Pumphouse, Alex started in on Maggie about it. "I saw you flirting with the sheriff."

She winced at his tone. Definitely wouldn't be seeing him again after the date ended. Red flags flew all over the place at his behavior.

"I wasn't flirting. I waved at him. I ran into him briefly tonight and he apologized for something he did last week. I saw him as we were leaving the stadium and I waved. If you notice, I waved at his mother and father, too."

"You're with me. You don't need to talk to other men." Angrily, he parked the car and got out, leaving Maggie to process her shock and discomfort over how he'd just acted.

They walked into the bar and went to their table. But before they sat down, Maggie swallowed her insulted fury and stopped him with a hand on his arm. "I want you to know it makes me uncomfortable that you talked to me that way, Alex. I haven't done anything wrong."

The rigidity in his posture loosened as he shot her a sheepish smile. "You're right. I'm sorry, Maggie. It's just that you're so beautiful and I really enjoy being with you. I got jealous. I apologize."

Relieved that he wasn't going to flip out, Maggie smiled back wanly, still uncomfortable with his behavior. "Apology accepted. Oh look, it's everyone else." Just wanting to get the rest of the evening finished, she waved at her friends.

The place was packed, more so than usual and Maggie didn't fail to notice when the Chase brothers and their dates came in about half an hour later. Still, she wasn't going to let Alex control her so when Shane nodded his head to her in greeting she smiled back and sent him a brief wave. She felt Alex tense up but he didn't say anything.

But later when Shane got up to go to the men's room, Alex excused himself and walked back there.

"Hey, Chase, you need to leave Maggie the hell alone." His voice was an angry hiss and it echoed from the bathroom walls. Maggie was *his* damn it. His and no one else's.

Shane turned around to stare at him, eyebrow raised. "Oh, is that so?"

"Yeah, that's so. She's mine, Shane. Back off."

"Huh, well here's the thing, Alex, I waved hello at her, twice. I didn't kiss her or anything. Now, just between you and me, I like her. I think she's a nice woman with a lot of spark. I'm thinking of asking her to dinner sometime but I certainly wouldn't do it when she was on a date with another man."

"She's too good for you. Maggie Wright is a lady and she needs a man to take care of her. You're a dog. You're slime and you don't deserve a special woman like her. I'm telling you, she's mine, Chase, and you're upsetting her with your unwanted attentions."

"Um, I don't think so. From what I understand, you've gone out with her a few times. Sorry but that does not a girlfriend make. I had a girlfriend who cheated, I certainly know the difference. In any case, if that's how Maggie feels, I'll certainly respect that. If I hear it from her. Now if you'll excuse me, I have a nice cold beer to get back to. Have a nice night." Shane walked past Alex and out the door.

Alex stormed back to the table and put his arm around Maggie. "Alex, I need my arm to eat." She shrugged him off. He glowered at her for a moment and he saw the fear in her eyes—just a flash—before she went back to eating her cheeseburger.

He knew he'd moved too fast as he took her home. She sat against the door and wouldn't look at him, avoiding small talk. He had to win her back. Had to show her how well he'd take care of her.

"You don't need to walk me to the door," she said as she got out the moment he stopped the car. "The porch light is on, I'll be fine."

He got out quickly and went to her side. "Don't be silly. It's late and dark. And I like being with you, Maggie."

At her door she unlocked it but stood directly in front of it, blocking his way. "Well, good night, Alex."

Moving in for a kiss, he felt her stiffen and tried to show her how much he liked her but she pulled back and put a hand between them to push him back.

She was right of course. He shouldn't maul her on her front porch. What if her neighbors saw? He needed to protect her reputation. She was important in the community and people looked up to her. As her husband, he'd need to always keep such things in mind. "I'm sorry, let's take this inside, shall we?"

"I'm really tired, Alex. I think I'll pass on any company. Thanks for the game and dinner." She took a step back, fumbling with the doorknob directly behind her.

He exhaled sharply. She held herself away from him and that was not all right. But he had to let her know he was there for good. She was just worried he'd love her and leave her. "Fine. I'll call you later. You know what, Maggie? You're my girlfriend, right?"

Her eyes darted around until finally coming back to look at his face. "Um, well, no. We've dated, yes, but to my mind, that takes a lot longer than a few dates."

"Good night, Maggie." He turned and walked away from her without another word before she could say anything else.

Moving into the house quickly, Maggie locked the door behind herself. She also threw the dead bolt. Her hands shook. He sat in her driveway for several minutes more and finally pulled away. With a sigh of relief, she sat in a heap on her couch.

After the nausea passed, she went through the house and checked to make sure her doors and windows were locked as she replayed the evening in her mind. The way he spoke to her, held on to her all the time—it was really frightening and totally inappropriate. It'd started out sort of nice but went right to patronizing, clingy and then outright scary in really short order.

No more dates with him, that was for sure. No, when she got up the next day she'd talk to Liv and work out a way to break things off that made it clear she wasn't interested but also didn't make things worse.

Chapter Three

The day started out pretty darned good when she was down-town picking up ingredients for the banana bread.

Distracted as she shopped for baking supplies, Maggie was walking down Main Street when she literally bumped into Shane.

"Sheriff Chase, you seem to make a habit of knocking into me." Her flirtatious laugh died in her throat as she looked up his body and into his face. Try as she might, she couldn't ignore the tightening in her stomach at the sight of his khaki-colored uniform stretched tight across his muscles.

"You're a menace, Miz Wright." He laughed back. "Tell you what? To make up for crashing into me, yet again, why don't you buy me a cup of coffee and a cinnamon roll?"

Unreality slid into her. Did the man just ask her for coffee? Still, she managed to hang on to her flirty tone. "All right, if it's that or go to jail, I suppose I'd better bribe you."

They walked the two blocks to the Honey Bear Bakery. "Why don't you grab a table and I'll get the drinks and cinnamon rolls?" Maggie waved at an open corner table.

Shane blushed. "Oh no! I was just kidding. I'll buy."

"Nope, not this time. It's my treat. Now go on, get a table, I'll be over in a sec." Maggie made shoo motions with her hands.

He hesitated for a moment and she could see him wrestling with how he could wrangle his way into paying but he soon gave up and sighed. "Fine. I'll get us a table."

At least being alone at the counter and getting the giant rolls and steaming cups of coffee to the table without spilling gave her the chance to concentrate on something other than the fit of his uniform and why in the world he'd be interested in her to begin with. But eventually, she arrived at their table and had to unload the tray and sit down.

"You know, when I went away to school, my dad would mail me these cinnamon rolls at my birthday and holidays." The pleasant memory of her father cut into the happiness she'd been feeling.

"That was nice. Sounds like something my mom would do."

"Your mother would bring them herself." She laughed, thinking about Polly Chase and that mile-long car of hers.

He chuckled. "You know her pretty well then."

"I happen to think your mother is an amazing woman. So old-world in many ways but she always surprises me with how modern she is. I have to laugh every time I hear the click clack of those heels coming down the hall when the Historical Society meets. Everyone stops messing around and waits patiently and quietly until she comes in. Every time she does the same thing—slams that massive purse of hers down on the table, gives her hair a primp and flops into the chair."

"According to my father, she started out with a tiny purse back before she had me and it's gotten bigger over the years. We all thought that when all of us moved out and it was just her and Dad again, it would get smaller." He shook his head. "But I swear she needs the car just to cart the purse around."

Maggie burst out laughing. "She came to my house you know—to apologize for you."

"She's the ultimate meddler but her heart is in the right place."

"Hey, don't complain, you could have Cecelia Wright as your mother." She winced as it came out, more bitter than she expected. "Oh God, never mind, that just sounded awful."

"How about this? Why don't you let me take you to dinner tonight and you can tell me the whole story?"

Her eyebrow went up and a smile played at the corner of her mouth. If she'd been watching herself from a distance she wouldn't even have suspected her stomach had just run riot with butterflies and she had a mental picture of herself doing the somersault of joy.

"Hmm, well, I'd love to do dinner but I'll skip the whole my-mother-doesn't-understand-me story."

"How about a movie afterward?"

"Okay." *Okay? Yeah, soooo casual.* She snickered mentally.

"I'll pick you up at say, seven? Do you like Italian? We could go to Vincent's and then, um, I've seen the action flick at the Orpheum but there's a double feature at the drive-in, would that be all right?"

"Are you trying to get me to make out with you at the drive-in, Shane Chase?" Apparently, aliens had taken over her body. Flirty aliens with nerves of steel. She hoped they'd stay until he left or she'd die on the spot.

He turned pink and laughed. "You've caught me!" He gave her a grin, white teeth making him look a bit wolfish. "But of course you know I'm a total gentleman now that I took that civility class you recommended."

She threw back her head and laughed at that. "Okay. I live on the corner of Fourth and Magnolia." She stood up. "I need to finish my errands. It was nice sharing a cup of coffee and this nine-thousand-calorie cinnamon roll with you. I'll see you tonight." He walked with her to the sidewalk and they each headed opposite ways. She hoped the smile he had on was half as big as hers.

Still, she continued to grin like a fool back at home and mixing the bread. She was pretty impressed with the way she'd held it together and stopped herself from jumping up and down squealing with delight.

Her good mood held on until she noticed that she had some messages. Playing them back, a sick feeling replaced her happiness. There were six from Alex. And he'd already called twice before she left the house to start with. Each message she listened to got more intense. The way his voice had started off calm and friendly but turned into something like a sharp snarl on the last message sent a cold chill down her spine. Especially the part where he ordered her to call him immediately and chided her for being gone without letting him know her whereabouts.

It had to end. She'd decided that the night before but she wanted to do it face-to-face. Freaked as she was, she didn't want to stop seeing him via voice mail, that seemed cruel. Picking up the phone with trembling hands, Maggie called him back but ended up leaving a message that she wanted to talk to him.

She ran the loaves of bread over to the retirement home. She sucked it up and stopped by her parents' house and Janie's as well. Best to just get that out of the way. As it happened, she had enough of an emotional high from her afternoon and upcoming date that the visits weren't too bad and she escaped as quickly as she could.

Back at home, she called Liv and begged for her help to get ready for her big date.

Liv showed up breathless and eager less than five minutes later. "I can't believe you didn't call me immediately! Let's go and get you an outfit while you tell me every last detail."

Liv pushed Maggie upstairs and made all the right noises as Maggie told her about the afternoon coffee with Shane as she got dressed.

With her usually curly hair blown out straight and captured in a headband, the pleated skirt and sweater made Maggie feel vibrant and sexy too.

"Very collegiate and sassy. Damn I'm good." Liv looked her work over with a critical eye.

"I know, without this I wouldn't be going out with a man like Shane Chase at all."

"Maggie, you need to stop this. You're still you. I told you before, it's not like I turned you into something you weren't. So I added a bit of sparkle. Shane Chase has been mooning after you since that night at The Pumphouse. A night you were covered in chili cheese fries and had your hair in a bun."

Ducking her head, Maggie hid her blush. She knew it was true but it was hard to overcome what she'd been told all her life. But she was too old to let her mother still make her feel inadequate. Taking a deep breath she stood up straight and held her head up. "You're right. Thank you. He's going to be here any minute. I'd better go downstairs. You going out with Shaun tonight?"

"No, I'm going out with Tom Maddox, he's picking me up in an hour. I should get home now. Speaking of Shaun, what's up with Alex? What crawled up his ass last night?"

"Oh my God! I forgot that I hadn't told you about this yet." Maggie related the whole story of how Alex had acted the evening before as they went downstairs.

"Major red flags are waving with this guy, Liv. He's seriously creeping me out. He called me eight times today! This guy is seriously not right."

"No shit. Why didn't you tell me? You shouldn't have even let him bring you home last night. You could have slept at my place."

"I know. It just kept getting worse and worse and it wasn't until I was sitting here in the dark, wondering if all my locks were working that I realized how truly freaked out I was. Anyway, the little voice said get away and so I am."

"Well, that's a good idea, Maggie." Liv frowned. "Never ignore the little voice. Be extra careful around him, okay? You call 911 and then me if he comes around. You know you can come over any time if you're feeling scared, too. You have a key for a reason." Liv kissed Maggie's cheek. "But for now, have a good time and I'll see you at brunch tomorrow. I expect a full report!"

Grinning as she watched Liv jog down the block that separated their two houses, Maggie saw Shane's truck pull onto her street. She ducked back into the house to check her hair and lipstick and grab her coat.

She opened the door as he walked up onto the porch and she wasn't quite sure where her breath went. He seemed to steal all the oxygen from the area where he stood.

While she tried not to gawk, he looked her up and down and smiled. "Wow. You look beautiful." He reached out to touch her hair. "I like the curls but this is nice, too. You can see all of the different colors of red better this way."

She blushed. "You're really good at that. Thank you. You don't look so bad yourself, Sheriff." Dark denim jeans hugged his long muscled legs. A black-and-gray sweater brought out the blue in his eyes and contrasted the color of his hair. Man, he looked so good she wanted to grab him and jump on him.

One corner of his mouth rose. "Thank you, Maggie. Shall we then?" He indicated his truck with a tip of his head and she nodded. He helped her into his ridiculously large truck and they drove to Vincent's. They shared small talk on the way over. Maggie was surprised by how easy he was to talk to.

Heads turned as Shane led Maggie to a dark table in the back. But she soon forgot the scrutiny as they ordered. Dinner was good, conversation came easy and they finished and took off to get to the drive-in before the show started.

Shane parked toward the back as his truck was so high and big it would have blocked the view. He pushed the bench seat all the way back and moved away from the steering wheel and into the center. Bringing him very close to her.

"I brought a blanket. It's been getting so cold in the last few days. I would have brought beer but you know, being the sheriff means I can't do illegal things, even when they'd be fun. I did bring snacks, though." Reaching behind the seat into the rear cab, he pulled out a sack of chocolate, Red Vines and some bottled water.

"You think of everything, Shane Chase." Maggie moved in a bit closer. It was very nice to be there beside him.

The double feature, two action movies with Bruce Willis, was entertaining. It didn't matter that the audio wasn't that good if you could see things blowing up. It was easy enough to follow the plot. By the middle of the second movie Maggie had snuggled up against Shane's body. Her feet curled under her, his arm around her shoulders, she felt utterly lazy and warm—and very turned on by the way he felt against her. It had been a year since she'd slept with anyone. She'd dated but none of them were people she'd wanted to sleep with. Shane Chase brought a level of physical desire into her life that she wasn't sure she'd ever felt before.

"Shane?"

"Hmm?"

"I do believe you promised something regarding making out?"

He looked down at her, surprise on his face. She blushed as the surprise heated into something more. "Never mind. I can't believe I said that out loud. It's the sugar. I need to stop eating sugar, that's all there is to it."

"No way. You said it," he murmured, moving his head down to her, "and I aim to hold you to it." A gentle hand at her chin tipped her face to his just as his lips reached hers. Electricity sparked between them, firing her nerve endings to life.

He tasted so good she had to have more. Coming up to her knees, she moved to get better access to his lips. His growl of approval vibrated down her spine and he pulled her to him tightly.

The kiss deepened as his tongue swept out, tracing the curve of her bottom lip before taking it between his teeth and nipping it. She sighed into his mouth as desire roared through her. She didn't recognize the sound of need that came from deep inside her but he matched it when she sucked on his tongue.

Those big hands caressed her back, leaving tingling, heated flesh in their wake. She wanted them on her thighs, sliding higher, wanted them palming the nipples that throbbed to be touched.

When one of his hands slid up into her hair and fisted, violent shivers racked her. So much need, she felt like she was drowning in it.

He'd been moving his hands down her back to her ass when his phone rang. Stiffening, he pulled back from her lips ever so reluctantly. "I'm sorry, that's my work phone. I have to get it."

Too desire-stunned to speak, she nodded her understanding.

"Chase," he grunted as he answered.

She watched as he went into work mode and the gentle, sexy face turned serious. Straightening her clothes, she sat back down on the seat and reached to turn off the audio so he could hear better.

"Hang on, let me get something to write on." He grabbed a pad and pen from his overhead visor. "Go," he ordered and began to scribble information down on the pad. "Yeah, I'll do it." Sighing, he snapped the phone shut.

"I'm sorry, Maggie, but I have to go on a call. I'll drop you home on the way." Apology was clear on his face as he moved the seat back into place and slid back behind the wheel.

"Don't be sorry. It's your job." She admired her ability to not sound disappointed. She certainly didn't want the man to feel guilty about being a cop. "I had a really good time tonight. Thanks for dinner and the movies."

"How about the making out?" He gave her that wolfishly wicked grin—the one that sent a ball of heat straight to her gut—and she laughed.

Before too long they'd navigated out of the parking lot and were on their way back toward her house.

"That too." She tried not to grin so wide her face would split open. He made her feel giddy.

"So, did I pass?"

"Pass what?"

"Muster. As in, am I second-date material?"

"Ask me and find out."

"Maggie, can I take you out again? Like say, for ice cream on Tuesday night?"

"Ice cream, huh? It seems you've found out my secret. Throw something sweet at me and I'm putty."

He pulled up in her driveway and started to get out but she patted his arm. "No, go on your call, I can walk to the door."

He rolled his eyes at her before getting out and walking around the car to help her down. "It's not so urgent that I'd just throw you at your door." At her door he kissed her quickly. "I'll see you Tuesday then? I'll pick you up at seven."

"Okay, be safe," she called out and waved at him as he drove away.

Maggie walked into the restaurant where she met Dee and Liv for brunch every Sunday and her smile was apparent from across the room.

"So?" Liv asked before Maggie had even finished sitting down.

Maggie looked at both her friends. "So, it was great. We had a lovely dinner and then we went to the drive-in. We watched most of both movies, had a major, *major* kiss but then he got a work call and had to go. He did ask me out again. We're having ice cream on Tuesday."

"Oh my God! Of course you said yes." Dee grinned back at Maggie.

"Of course she did!" Liv waved her hand as if it were a done deal. "So, is he a good kisser or what? Details, Maggie, we want details."

"Duh! I tell you I've been dreaming about kissing Shane

Chase since I was in the fifth grade and he was in the seventh. It was better than any of the times I kissed my pillow, I can tell you that."

"Dreamy. It's so romantic, Maggie. You've got the man you've always wanted." Dee sighed.

"I don't *have* him. I'm dating him. Big difference, especially to a man like Shane Chase. I need to remember that superhot lust is not the same as love." Maggie shrugged. She had a tendency to wear her heart on her sleeve and she knew Shane Chase had warning signs all over his very delicious body.

Liv nodded. "I'm glad you said it. It's good to remember that, Maggie. Sam was a dolt but Shane is big-league because he's a player. Not in a bad way, he's not a mimbo, but he's not a one-woman man either. And he's one of those men who's sort of overwhelming with all that testosterone rolling off him. It's really hot, but heck, it would fry my circuits, too!"

"I know. And I feel like a total hoochie for saying this, but I want to have sex with him. I don't think I've been this horny. Ever."

"You're the farthest thing from a hoochie that I can think of. Jeez, woman, you haven't had sex in a year! And this big old hard-bodied studmuffin strolls into your life. What woman wouldn't want to have sex with Shane Chase?"

"Hey, if I didn't have Arthur, I'd totally agree. But I do agree with the assessment that Shane is a nice boy to play with but he's not the kind to set up housekeeping. You're old enough to eat dessert first every once in a while, Maggie." Dee laughed and turned to Liv. "And how was your date with Tom?"

"It was all right. I'd give the date a six and a half out of ten. Speaking of Chase brothers, I bumped into Matt this morning. He's gotten even better looking since high school."

"Yes indeed. He's grown into his looks." Dee waggled her eyebrows.

"Certainly doesn't hurt that he works with his body a lot as a firefighter."

"I've contemplated setting my back deck on fire to get him over to my place," Liv said around a mouthful of waffle.

They all laughed at the idea of Liv in her backyard with lighter fluid and a negligee on, waiting for Matt Chase to arrive.

"Why don't you just ask him out?"

"Nah, he's the kind of guy that needs to be in the lead."

"Hmm, well, I'll have to think of something to bring the two of you together," Maggie said thoughtfully.

"Don't you dare mention this to Shane!" Liv actually colored at the idea.

"Why not? Oh my God, did you just blush?"

"Because! Jeez, I'm not desperate, Maggie! I can trap a man without having you tell Matt's brother that I like him. That's so eighth grade."

"I guess a Halloween party at my house and a game of spin the bottle is out then?"

They all laughed at the memory of the Halloween party that Dee had at her house when they were in the ninth grade. "That was my first official French kiss. Andrew Johnson, in Dee's mom's broom closet. Good times," Liv said dreamily.

"Yeah well look what you did to him, Liv, he's gay." Maggie laughed. "Clearly you were too much woman for him and it spoiled him forever for the rest of us.

"Seriously, Liv, I'm on it. I'm going to think of something because let me attest that a taste of Chase is worth the work." Maggie waggled her brows suggestively and the laughter started anew.

Across the room, Matt and Kyle Chase ate their brunch while they watched the women laughing at their table. "What do you suppose all of that is about?" Kyle couldn't stop himself from looking at Maggie Wright. *Damn*, he liked the way she looked when she laughed. But his brother liked her first and so he backed off. There were rules about this sort of thing.

"Looks like trouble but the kind of trouble a man enjoys in the end." Matt sipped his coffee.

"So what did Shane say about their date last night?"

"I haven't seen him yet. Maggie looks pretty glowing though."

Maggie looked over and saw them. Smiling, she waved. The other two looked around and waved hello as well before huddling together, the laughter starting again.

"Hmm." Kyle grinned. "I do believe we're the object of some female giggling, Matt. I think I like it."

"Hell, Kyle, I *know* I like it."

When the women left they waved again. Kyle enjoyed the view through the big front windows as the three women walked together down the street.

Alex melted back into the doorway of the hardware store so he wouldn't be seen. Someone had to watch over her.

He'd wanted to get Maggie alone but she was always with her damned friends. Or with that jerk Shane Chase. Oh he'd seen the man pick up *his* fiancée the night before. Saw the kiss when Maggie returned. But she did not let Shane in. His Maggie was still saving herself just for him. And Shane Chase was just a momentary distraction. Alex would make sure of that.

Olivia and Maggie decided to grab a bite at The Pumphouse before Maggie's ice cream date with Shane.

Arriving a bit early, Maggie saw Matt Chase across the street with Johnny Prentice. She gave a friendly wave hello and they returned the greeting with a few shouted hellos.

Still smiling as she turned back toward the door, she bumped into Alex. Fear slithered through her as she realized she hadn't even seen his approach.

Shit. She really hadn't wanted to deal with him that night. She'd tried to call him to arrange to see him face-to-face to break things off. But he hadn't returned any of her calls. It wasn't like she was avoiding the issue but she certainly didn't want to have the discussion in public in the middle of the sidewalk.

"Hi, Alex." She gave him a wary smile, not at all liking the look on his face.

He grabbed her arm in a grip so tight she winced. "Hi, Alex? Is that all you've got to say?"

"What the heck are you talking about?" Her voice rose as she struggled to get free.

"The way you can't help but talk to every man you see. I told you, *you're with me*. You don't need to talk to any other man. Are you trying to make me jealous, Maggie? You don't need to play games. All it's doing is really pissing me off. I don't like my woman to act that way."

Still keeping a tight grip on her arm, he steered her into The Pumphouse. That grip was the only thing that prevented him from getting slapped as she tried to get free and keep her balance.

"What the hell are you talking about? I don't need to talk to other men?" she demanded through clenched teeth. "Let me go this instant!"

"You heard me, Maggie. You're my girl, I don't want you all over other men like a slut." He hissed and his grip on her arm tightened and caused her to gasp in pain.

Hearing the words, she stilled for a moment. Fury replaced the fear. "You did *not* just call me a slut!" Her eyes narrowed at him. "And I said—Let. Me. Go. Now or I'm going to kick you in the junk!"

By that point, the conversations around them had gotten quiet and for the second time in a few weeks, she was the subject of attention at The Pumphouse.

Noting that they were being watched, he let go and she took the opportunity to move away from him. But he stepped closer, filling the space between them. "You don't need to be hanging all over other men."

"I *waved* at them. I didn't flash my boobs at them or blow a kiss. I waved hello. But even if I had, *you* don't get to decide what I need to be doing, Alex."

He grabbed her arm again and moved her toward her usual table. "You're making a scene. Sit down." He shoved her into the booth.

Her eyes widened at that. "In the first place, you will not touch me ever again or you'll draw back a stump. In the second place, you need to get a hold of yourself right now, Alex. No one talks to me this way. You don't own me. Hell, we've only gone on three dates."

"You don't tell me to get a hold of myself when you're the one acting like a whore!" he said in a stage whisper.

"What?" Grasping the water glass on the table, she dashed it in his face, taking his moment of surprise to push him back and scoot out of the booth. "I know you didn't just call me a whore! How dare you!" She pushed up into his face, seemingly undaunted by the fact that he was several inches taller than she was.

Liv and Dee came rushing in with the Chase boys right behind them. For a moment, they all stood and looked in the direction of the fracas. Kyle's face turned so red it was purple. He and his brothers together with Arthur stalked over.

"How dare I? You're a tease, Maggie Wright. You come on to every man you meet and now you don't like it when you get called what you really are." The viciousness in his voice made her skin crawl. He was like a completely different person. Reaching out, he grabbed her arm and yanked her to sit back down.

Shane stalked forward and grabbed Alex's wrist, squeezing tightly until he blanched and let go of Maggie. "You need to let the lady go now, Alex," he said in a voice that was low and threatening.

"Are you all right, Maggie?" Kyle had moved around Shane so he could kneel in front of her. Slowly, he reached out and took her hand.

"That asshole called me a whore!" Maggie fumed but she knew her trembling was so bad that anyone looking could see it.

"I think you need to leave the premises, Alex, before I have to arrest you for assault." Shane moved so that he stood between Alex and Maggie.

"Oh, so you can fuck her then? This is all about you getting into her bed isn't it?" Alex's voice broke, he screamed it so loud. Incensed, Maggie jumped up to get in his face but Kyle grabbed her, his arms around her waist, murmuring into her ear.

"You bastard! Don't you ever call me or contact me again."

Shane dragged Alex to the door and tossed him bodily outside. "You're lucky I'm here as the sheriff today, Alex. If I was just here as Shane Chase you'd be spitting out teeth right now. Now you leave her alone just as she's asked or you'll be asking for a world of hurt." Shane glowered at Alex and turned back into The Pumphouse.

Olivia and Dee spoke softly to Maggie, trying to calm her down. Shane approached and put a hand on her shoulder. "Maggie, are you all right?" he asked, concern evident in his voice.

Kyle looked at the staring crowd. "Okay, folks, I'm sure we don't want to upset Maggie any more so let's just get back to our beers and burgers."

"Thank God you came in when you did. What made you come in?" Maggie asked them gratefully.

"Matt saw you bump into Alex. He thought it looked like Alex had grabbed you. I was walking up the street with Kyle, Matt called out to us and we all came over. I'm sorry I didn't stop him sooner. What happened, Maggie?"

"I don't even know really. I was walking in here and saw Matt and John across the way and I waved. I turned around and bumped into Alex. I said hello and for whatever reason, it set him off. He started freaking out about me waving at Matt and John. He said I was acting like a slut, that I was his girl." She rubbed her arm where he'd grabbed it. "Then he grabbed me, twice, and shoved me into the booth and called me a whore. That creep called me, Margaret Elizabeth Wright, a whore! I should kick his sorry ass for that." On the outside she was livid but she burned with humiliation.

Kyle's face darkened. "Are you hurt?"

She shook her head. "I might have a bruise on my arm but other than that I'm just pissed off."

"Would you like to press charges, Maggie? It's assault you know." Shane knelt on his haunches in front of her.

"No, I don't ever want to deal with him again." Her bottom lip was trembling.

"Come on, let's get you home. I have some time left on my shift." He looked to Kyle. "Can you run her home? Just go through her place?"

"It's not a problem. Really, don't go out of your way." Maggie chewed on her lip.

Kyle smiled gently at her. "Don't worry about it. It's not out of my way at all. And it's certainly not a chore to ferry a beautiful woman around town." He reached out to her to give her a hand that she took gratefully.

Liv and Dee hugged her and told her they'd call her the next day. "Do you want to stay with me?" Liv asked.

"No, Liv, I'll see you tomorrow, I just want to go home and take a bath and go to sleep."

With a gentle guiding hand, Kyle nodded to everyone and took her out to his car.

On the way to her house he stayed quiet, letting her pull herself together. She appreciated that space. She wasn't ready to talk about it any further at that point.

When he pulled into her driveway he got out and came around to help her get out. "I'm going to come in, Maggie. Just to do a quick check. I don't think there's a problem but let's just be safe. All right?" He took the key from her and unlocked the door.

"You think he might be here?" Nausea rolled over her at the idea. She'd always felt safe living alone, now she didn't.

"No, darlin', I just want to be safe." His voice was soothing as he reached in to turn on the light before walking into the foyer. "I'm just going to look around. I want you to stay here while I do. I'll be right back."

Leaving her there, trying to set aside how scared she looked, he walked through each room of the house. He checked window seals and locks, closets, doors and under beds. No one else was there or had tried to get in and he was pleased to note that her locks and other security were in good shape.

"It's all right," he called out, coming down the stairs. The scent of her bedroom was burned into his memory. Rain and vanilla. And the sight of her panties, folded in silky piles on her dresser, had made him clutch his chest. The knowledge that the woman wore silky, lacy thong underwear in every color of the rainbow haunted him.

The woman was involved with his brother. His brother who hadn't bothered to call yet to check in.

"I know it sounds weird but I'm suddenly hungry. Care to see what I've got in my fridge? I know I need some food to go with that scotch I'm going to drink."

He didn't want to leave. "Sure. Sounds good." Following her into the large kitchen, he sat at her comfortable, worn table.

On her tiptoes, she reached up into a cabinet and pulled out a bottle of scotch. "Why don't you do the honors?" She put the bottle on the counter. "I'm going to see what we've got to choose from." Turning quickly, she opened the fridge and began to examine the contents.

In companionable silence, Kyle poured them both two fingers of scotch, breathing in the smoky scent. He handed her a glass that she quickly drained and held the glass out to be refilled. With one eyebrow raised, he poured more but she merely took a sip and put the glass down and continued to work.

He went back to his place at the table and watched her as she moved through her kitchen. She pulled out vegetables, rice, some chicken and started preparing things. "How does chicken and rice sound?" She poked her head around the refrigerator door to ask.

"It sounds really good. Are you sure you wouldn't rather get takeout? Or be alone? I don't want to impose."

She grinned at him. "Hey, it's no problem now that the scotch has kicked in. I'd love to cook for you as a thank-you for coming home with me."

He laughed. "Okay then, lay it on me. Can I help?"

"Nah, I've got it down to a science."

And so he watched her as she moved with efficiency around her kitchen, chopping and sautéing. They made small talk but he let her lead, not pushing her to fill in every moment of the silence. He could tell she was still processing the events from earlier.

With a start, he realized he wanted to know her more. Wanted to spend time with her. And God, did he ever want to kiss her. He'd known he had an attraction to her but this was more.

Kyle knew in his gut that Shane would fuck up. He was of two minds about it. The mercenary side of him wanted Shane out of the way so he could take her out. Freely express to her just how much he enjoyed her company. But he also knew a woman as sweet as Maggie would be hurt when the inevitable happened and he hated the thought.

So he put his feelings away and decided that fate would out in the end. He had to step back. He didn't like it, but brothers had rules and he would not betray that.

After dinner he walked to her front door. "Are you going to be all right? He's wrong, you know," Kyle said quietly, touching her chin.

A lump formed in Maggie's throat, words couldn't get past it.

"You didn't do anything wrong. You're a good person, Maggie. A kind, beautiful woman. Alex is twisted, broken. This is about him, not you."

Swallowing her tears she nodded. "Thank you. Thank you so much for saying it. I'll be fine. My doors will be locked up tight and I have no problem calling 911 if I have to."

He smiled and leaned in, kissing her forehead. "If you need anything, you can call me. I'll talk you through or come over, whatever."

"That's very sweet. I appreciate it."

"Good night, Maggie Wright."

"Good night, Kyle Chase."

Maggie cleaned up the kitchen, grateful to have something to do. Leaving a few lights on downstairs, she trudged toward her bathroom and took a long hot shower. With a butcher knife, her cell phone and a baseball bat all within reach.

It might have been an overreaction but she was alone and you got to overreact when some creep attacked you.

Clean and warm, she crawled between her sheets and left her bedside lamp burning. But as she lay there, it wasn't Alex she thought of, or Shane, it was Kyle.

He'd been so gentle with her, so kind and funny and considerate. On top of being marvelously handsome, he was such a beautiful person on the inside. She really liked his company.

For long moments, there with her eyes closed, she imagined that his attentions that evening had been more than a man helping out a woman in distress. He'd seemed attracted to her but that couldn't be right. It was absurd enough that Shane was attracted to her, there was simply no way that *two* Chases were interested in her. And anyway, she was dating Shane, she should be thinking about that.

Yeah.

Maggie had to admit that she was slightly bothered by the fact that Shane hadn't really checked in with her after the incident at The Pumphouse. Not that night when he was supposed to have taken her out and only one brief phone call in the week after. It was an effort but she reminded herself that they were just casual and that she'd be a brokenhearted fool to get attached. That way lay pain and anguish.

So she'd told herself until Friday night. She and her friends sat at their normal Friday night table, drinking beers and talking when she saw Shane walk in the front door. Her heart skipped a beat and she smiled at him. A smile that quickly faded when she saw he was with Kendra Fosse. Tall, blonde, regal Kendra. Maggie turned back to the table quickly.

"What?" Liv looked toward the door. A frown marred her face when she sighted Shane and Kendra. "Maggie, I'm sorry, hon. Don't worry about it. I was thinking that we should go and kick up our heels at the Honky Tonk tonight. What do you say?"

Dee nodded, standing up and throwing some money on the table. "Sounds good, I haven't danced in forever. Let's go!" She tugged on Maggie's arm and got a smile and an eye roll. Still, she thought it best to leave and allowed them to pull her out the front door.

In the back room, Kyle saw Shane's entrance with Kendra and Maggie's reaction and subsequent retreat. "You are some piece of work, Shane," he murmured as Kendra walked past them to hit the ladies' room, probably to apply more hair spray.

"What?"

"What? Jeez, you said you were going out with Maggie, right?"

"Yeah? So? It's not like we're serious. I like her and all but I'm not planning to marry the girl." Shane's voice was gruff. Kyle knew it was just to hide how freaked his brother was about being hurt again like he'd been with Sandra. But at the same time, it was bullshit that his brother protected his heart by being an asshole.

"I never made promises, Kyle. Stop making me out to be the bad guy here. I honestly didn't remember about her being in here on Fridays until I was already through the door. I'm not trying to hurt her."

"Oh, okay. I was under the impression you had a thing for Maggie. My bad. I didn't know she was just the next in a long line of women you toy with and move past because, God for-

bid, you actually allow yourself feelings about any of them."
Scowling, Kyle took his shot.

Matt snorted in disgust at his oldest brother. "I think I'm
going to go. I'm meeting the guys over at the Honky Tonk." He
finished his soda and stalked out.

"Wait, I'll come too. Friday night's a good night at the Tonk.
Lots of lovely ladies to dance with." Marc followed with a laugh,
pointedly ignoring his oldest brother.

Kendra came back and draped herself over Shane's arm,
looking bored. "Are you going to play pool?" she asked, a tiny
bit of a whine in her voice.

"Yeah, you want to play?"

She looked horrified at the very idea. "No, why would I want
to do that? The sticks are used by everyone. Eww."

"They're called cues," Kyle said under his breath and shot
yet another ball into the pocket. He couldn't help but think that
Maggie would have jumped at the chance to play with them. He
imagined those big whiskey eyes glittering with delight after
she'd sunk a ball.

Kyle cleared the table of the solids and put the cue back into
the slot on the rack. "I think I'm for the Tonk, too. Nice seeing
you, Kendra. Shane."

"You want to hit the Honky Tonk, too?" Shane asked her.

"Sure," she said, looking bored still. "At least they have a
better quality of mixed drinks there."

Maggie was glad she'd let them drag her to the Tonk. Instead
of moping about Shane and gorgeous Kendra, she was kicking her heels up and dancing the night away. The Dixie Chicks
were coming over the sound system and she had Ryan Jack-
son's fine body guiding her along the floor effortlessly. Okay,
so he was as married as the day is long and his wife put him up
to dancing with Maggie so she could rest her feet but he made
her laugh and she was having fun.

"Maggie, do you want a drink, sugar?" Ryan asked, having to yell in her ear.

"That sounds good, my legs are tired!" She laughed as he spun her off the floor and back toward their table and his wife who had her shoes off and her feet up.

It took a few seconds to register that Matt and Marc were there with Darla as well. "Oh hi."

"Hey, Maggie. You sure were tearing it up out there." Matt said it with an easy smile and she relaxed a bit.

"Nah, it was all Ryan. Darla let me borrow him a bit."

Drinks had arrived and they'd all fallen into an easy back and forth, talking and laughing, when Kyle, Shane and Kendra came in. Marc waved at them and they started toward the table.

"Uh, I should go and find Liv and Dee." She moved to stand but Matt put his hand on her elbow to stay her.

"They're both out there dancing." He nodded with his head and waved at the other women who saw and waved back.

"Oh."

"Stay awhile and visit, Maggie. Chuck's not showing any sign of letting Liv get away anyway." Darla laughed, not knowing why Maggie wanted to run and hide.

Kyle came and sat down next to her, giving her a warm hello. "Hey there, shug. You owe me a dance tonight." He stood up again. "In fact, why don't we hit it now?" He bowed slightly and extended a hand and after a brief hesitation she took it, never once looking at Shane.

"All right then. But remember excessively tall men have much longer legs than small women. Which means you'll be dragging me all over the place if you go too fast."

"Do I look like I don't know how to take it slow with the right woman?" he said with cheeky innuendo in his voice and she rolled her eyes.

"One of these days I need to meet your father to see if he's as full of it as you four are."

Kyle laughed as he led her down the steps and onto the floor.

He twirled her once and into a slow two-step as the tempo of the Martina McBride song came on and slowed the dancers down.

"You all right?" he asked her when they were away from the table.

"What do you mean?" He was so close to her it was hard to concentrate.

"Shane isn't a bad guy you know. He just got screwed over pretty severely a year and a half ago by his fiancée. Turns out she was sleeping with his best friend. Ran off with him a week before the wedding. Ever since, he's guarded his feelings with women—never goes out with them for longer than a few weeks."

"I really don't care. I have no say in what Shane does. I just went out with him officially once and chatted with him a few times. I'm just dating him casually, I know that. It's not like I have a vested interest in him or anything." Even she didn't believe it as she said it.

She liked Shane Chase, thought she might have been the one to settle him down. But okay, she knew it now. Knew it truly was just a casual dating relationship and she could do that. She was an adult woman after all. Liv did it all the time. There was no reason why she couldn't enjoy herself with people and date around casually.

Kyle smiled. *God, she was so genuine and in way over her head.* "Ah, Maggie, you're too sweet for this game. You're a wonderful woman but don't count on him coming around to that. He's not ready to let himself really care about anyone just yet. I'd hate to see you get hurt. I just want you to know this up front, to protect yourself."

"I appreciate the advice, Kyle." She ruthlessly tamped down the sinking feeling that he was right. At the same time, Kyle's arms around her made her feel warm and relaxed. The flesh just under his hand at her back tingled a bit. Maybe Alex was right, maybe she was a slut.

"If he wasn't my brother, I'd ask you out myself." He tried to sound lighthearted but it was the truth.

"Please don't."

"Don't what?"

She stopped and pulled away, turning to escape him and the dance floor. He followed, catching up quickly. Reaching out, he grabbed her hand to stay her but she jerked it away and ran for the back deck. Sighing, he followed, catching up with her in the much quieter, much cooler, night air.

"You want to tell me what the heck you're talking about? Don't what?" He hoisted himself up to sit on the wooden railing of the deck so that he could face her.

Throwing one hand up in frustration she sighed. "Don't pity me and throw a few false compliments my way because you feel sorry for me."

He was still confused. "I don't pity you and they aren't false compliments."

"Please! My God, you don't think I have mirrors at my house? I know what I am and I know what I'm not. I'm not Jane Marie, I'm not Kendra. I can't compete with that. But I sure as hell don't want some kind of pity thrown at me because Shane has gone back to his regular diet of tall, gorgeous women. It's okay that I was an aberration. I shouldn't have expected more, it's my own damned fault."

Kyle sat in stunned silence for a few moments. He didn't know whether to laugh or cry. This woman was so beautiful and so special and yet, she thought a vapid, shallow woman like Kendra, or worse, her own sister, was better than she was.

Grabbing her hand, he brought it to his lips. "Sugar, I can't believe you think you have to compete with any other woman. I don't believe you do have mirrors in your house. If you did, you'd see a beautiful woman looking back at you and it's clear you don't. Honey, take it from me—a lover of women—you are absolutely, positively gorgeous. I am not throwing pity at you. Honestly, the only thing that's keeping me from grabbing you and kissing those beautiful lips is the fact that Shane is my brother."

Sighing, she ran her hands through her hair and over her face. "I can see you need an example. I was a virgin until I was twenty-two. My first year of graduate school. I went out on dates sure, but no one ever showed any passion toward me. Like a lot of grad students I had an advisor. He was so nice, so attentive. He loved to read what I wrote. Praised my work, paid attention to me as a person." She hesitated and then continued. "No, as a woman. He made me feel sexy and desirable. The first time he made love to me was in a hotel room in Atlanta. We were there at a symposium. He was gentle and sweet and he took his time. We continued to see each other throughout that entire year.

"My family came out to see me, my mom and dad and Jane Marie. It was a pretty big deal. The first and only time they ever visited me, actually. Anyway, I'd invited Charles over to dinner at my apartment to meet them all. He came and was his charming self. My mother and dad went out for a walk and I thought I would too. Janie and Charles said they would stay back and have coffee. It was a lovely early spring day but at the last minute, I decided that I'd skip the walk and go back home. When I let myself back into the apartment, I saw that Jane Marie and Charles were on the couch."

Her eyes blurred, lost in the memory. "They were having sex. Her perfect pleated skirt up around her waist and his slacks on the floor. I just stood there for a moment, not understanding at all, you know? My mind just wasn't registering what the hell was happening. Anyway, I stood there until I felt sick and then I quietly and slowly backed out of the room like I was never there.

"I confronted him later about it and he told me that he'd never imagined that a girl like me would have a stunning sister like that and what did I expect? I never said anything to anyone else about it. It was a good lesson for me about things. And you know? I was a fool to ever pretend that any Chase brother would think I was worth more than a few amusing dates and maybe a quick fuck." She hugged her arms around herself.

"My God, Maggie. What a bitch your sister is! What a calculating bastard your professor was." He moved toward her but she backed up.

"I have to go. Please don't say anything, I've never told that story to another soul." She spun on her heel and stalked back inside to the table. Still refusing to look in Shane's direction, she grabbed her coat and purse, pleaded sick and pretty much dashed out the door.

Kyle started to follow her out but Shane came up behind him, grabbing his arm. "What is going on?"

Shaking Shane off Kyle glared at him. "It's none of your business, Shane." But it was too late, as Maggie sped out of the parking lot.

Shane showed up after school on the next Wednesday. "Hey, Maggie, you have time for dinner?" he asked smiling.

Maggie looked at him, dumbstruck. Fine, if he wanted a casual thing she'd give it a try but there was no way she'd be some last-minute drop-in date. "Hi, Shane. No, I'm sorry, I have plans. Perhaps another time," she said casually.

"Oh. How about tomorrow night then?"

"Fine. Pick me up at seven." Keeping a smile on her face, she walked past him to her car.

She didn't have plans of course so she stopped by the bank and asked Dee to have dinner with her.

"Honey, what do you think you're doing?" Dee asked as they munched on pizza at Maggie's house.

"What do you mean?"

Dee made a disapproving sound and frowned. "Margaret Wright, being dishonest is not who you are. Don't lie to me and don't lie to yourself. I know you and Liv think I'm some silly virgin but I know enough to see you're in over your head with Shane Chase."

"What do you mean!" Maggie challenged. The truth stung.

"Oh, don't be stupid! Honey, you are more than good enough

for him. He's the one who isn't good enough for you. You know what I mean. You are not the kind of woman who can do a casual affair. It's not part of your makeup. I'm not talking down about women who can do it. But I've known you your whole life—you're not one of them. Your heart and head are too connected. You're only going to end up hurt because Shane Chase cannot give you what you want and deserve. Listen, it's still early, I can tell you like him but it's not that deep yet. But this is a dead-end street. Shane Chase is a dead-end man. You cannot save him."

The eyes she turned to Dee made Dee's heart ache. "I'm fine, Dee. I can handle it, I promise."

Dee sighed and squeezed her hand. "You know where to find me when you need me."

Shane knocked on her door precisely at seven and looked delicious as usual. He looked up and back down her body, with a slow sexy smile. "You look gorgeous, Maggie." He bent down and stole a quick kiss. "Ready?"

"Sure."

They went to The Sands, just a normal small-town diner. She felt so comfortable with him. He was attentive and charming but neither mentioned the incident with Kendra.

"Hey!" She slapped at his hand as he attempted to steal a fry off her plate. "Get your own fries, buster."

"You won't share them? Not even with the sheriff?"

"Hell no!" she said, eating the last fry with relish.

He leaned over and placed his mouth over her ear. "Can we go back to your house, Maggie? I'd really like to be alone with you."

His warm breath on her ear and his confession sent shivers down her spine. "I'd like that." No sooner had the soft words left her lips than he'd yanked her up, thrown money on the table and they hurried out to his truck.

Once they were inside her house and on the couch he looked

down at her with a grin. "I've wanted this since you spun around and started getting in my face at The Pumphouse that night. And definitely since I had to leave you on your doorstep after the movies."

Leaning up, she nuzzled his neck. He smelled good, his skin was warm. His head fell back against the couch. She really liked the moan he made when she nibbled his earlobe and then down to the hollow of his throat.

"But you never noticed me before. Back in high school you dated girls with flashy bodies and perfect clothes." She looked up at him with a grin.

"I think we established that I was a dumbass. I'm an idiot for not noticing you but your attitude is what turned me on first." With a low growl, he brought his hands down her back and around to cup her breasts. Her breath caught as his thumbs moved up to flick over her nipples.

Her head tipped back for a moment as she enjoyed his touch. After a bit she moved so that she was looking into his eyes again. Slowly, he leaned her back onto the couch, settling himself into the cradle of her thighs.

His lips found the hollow of her throat and she arched, grinding into him.

"God, I love this," she sighed.

And he froze.

He sat up quickly and reached for his coat. "I have to go. Thanks." He rushed toward the front door.

"Wait! You're leaving?" she asked, incredulous.

"I have to get to work first thing." She barely understood his words he said them so fast, not meeting her eyes.

She wished she could crawl into a hole and disappear.

"I'll call you," he mumbled as he let himself out.

"Don't bother, asshole!" she yelled out, but heard the door slam as he scurried out like the rat he was.

Chapter Four

The next night, the three of them sat in their usual booth. "And he left scorch marks in my front hallway he ran out of there so fast!"

Dee and Liv had looked at her, incredulous, as Maggie told them the whole story.

"I didn't say I loved *him*, I said I loved *it*. I mean goodness, we were making out on my couch. It felt good!" She tossed back yet another beer and motioned to Patrick to bring them a fresh pitcher.

"I don't understand. What an ass." Liv's face showed her anger and concern for her friend.

"Me neither but I'm done. What does he think? That he can throw a burger at me and get a cheap silent screw? God, he made me feel so stupid!"

Dee winced as she squeezed Maggie's hand in sympathy. Both Liv and Dee froze, looking toward the door, and Maggie knew that it was Shane. She slowly turned around and saw that he was there with Kendra. *Again.* This time his arm was around her and she was nuzzling into his neck. He saw her and didn't even flicker recognition in her direction.

For a moment her mouth hung open and tears stung the back

of her eyes. "Don't!" Liv whispered urgently. "Don't you let him make you cry, Maggie! He's not worth your tears."

She turned to face them. "I can't believe how stupid I've been," she whispered back and wiped at her eyes. "Okay, I could accept that we weren't serious. But the way he just ran out like that and just now? My God, he makes me feel like nothing."

Kyle saw Maggie wipe at her eyes, after she'd stared, hurt and dismayed at Shane. Shane who'd unbelievably looked through her like she didn't even exist.

Matt and Marc saw it too. "Shane, what the hell is wrong with you? You're really going to blow something that could be so good because of Sandra?"

Expressionless, Shane stared back at him.

"Whatever, man, I never thought I'd see you act like such an asshole. You don't deserve her," Matt spat out as he swept past and toward the front of the bar.

"What is he talking about?" Kendra asked.

"Who knows?" Shane knew, but he couldn't afford to deal with that. He had to make a clean break and it was better for both of them if he did it harshly but quickly, like ripping a bandage off all at once. He could not let himself care for Maggie. If she hated him, that would never be a problem.

Matt walked over to Maggie's table and sat down, talking quietly with the three women. Kendra snorted with derision. "Why would a man like Matt waste his time with that woman? She thinks she can put on some new clothes and let her hair down and compete with the real women of Petal?" Her mouth twisted viciously. "Janie might be worth it but not that bookworm."

Kyle stared at them both, mouth open. "You are one stone-cold bitch, Kendra." Disgusted, he threw his cue down on the table. "And you are not the man I've always thought you were." He shook his head at Shane and walked past them to join Matt at the table with Maggie and her friends.

"What did he just call me?" Kendra's pretty face was pinched.

"Maggie is a friend to *some* of us. We don't appreciate people saying nasty things about her." Marc looked at Shane and narrowed his eyes, looking away sadly before heading off as well.

"Hey, Maggie," Matt said as he approached the table and sat down. "Listen, I just…"

Shaking her head to stay him, Maggie held up a hand. "Please. Don't. It's not your fault. It wasn't like he and I were serious or anything. I was just mistaken about him being a nice person."

Kyle strolled over then and sat next to Maggie. "Hey, Red. My brother is an asshole. Please don't judge the rest of the Chase men by his actions."

Maggie stood up. The tears were right there but she'd be damned if she'd give Shane Chase the satisfaction of seeing them. "I have to go." She shoved at Kyle until he moved. Liv and Dee stood as well.

Liv handed Maggie her coat. "Let's go to my place. I stopped at the package store yesterday and I have a big old bottle of Jose Cuervo Gold just waiting for us. Heck, let's get some pizza delivered. I've got a few DVDs I've been meaning to watch, too. I'm pretty sure one of them is *Thelma and Louise*." She and Dee each grabbed one of Maggie's arms.

"Thanks, guys," she tried to say lightly to Kyle and Matt but her voice broke and she shook her head hard to keep them from saying anything. "I'll see you later." The tears sprang to her eyes, bottom lip trembling as she hurried out.

Kyle looked at Matt, scowling. "I can't believe Shane made her cry."

The next weeks went by in a blur. Shane hadn't even bothered to call to apologize or even to say he didn't want to see her again. She supposed that was the message he sent by going out with Kendra.

But she'd be damned if she'd allow that asshat to chase her away from her own life or make her feel bad for thinking that she deserved to be respected by her dates. So she held her head up high and continued her Friday night Pumphouse-with-the-girls dates. Of course, he'd shown up with women. Different ones each Friday but at least Kendra was gone. For the most part, Maggie just made it her mission to pretend he didn't exist.

She bumped into Matt at the bank and they'd chatted for a few minutes. She also ended up sitting on the same bench as Kyle and eating lunch once at the park. He talked her ear off and was friendly and jovial. Admittedly, she found him wildly attractive. But he was way off the menu. It still didn't stop her from thinking of him or sneaking looks at him on Fridays when they were in the back playing pool.

Her life moved into a new stage. One where she was proud of herself for not letting Shane's actions get her down. For a long time, she'd let people run her over. But no more. From that point on, Maggie realized she had every right to be treated well. She put the Shane incident behind her and she'd moved on.

One thing that did bother her was seeing Alex lurking around her neighborhood several times a month. She did her best to ignore him but she had to admit it did scare her slightly. He usually was doing something that she'd been able to explain away to herself—jogging, riding a bike, that sort of thing—but he still gave her the creeps.

Halloween came and went and Maggie worked in her garden all day the first Sunday of November. She tore out the old beds in the side yard and finished installing the raised beds she'd begun to build during the early fall. After getting her spring bulbs in the ground, she trimmed her climbing roses and fertilized her grass and trees. By the end of the day she'd cleaned out her yard and felt like she'd cleaned out her life. It felt damned good.

Sore but pleased with a very hard day's work she showered before retiring to her back porch with a novel and a cup of hot tea.

"Wow, you've done some major work here."

She turned and saw Kyle Chase standing there, hands in his pockets. He looked so handsome it took her breath away.

"Idle hands and all of that." Her words were wary, even as her pulse sped at his presence.

He grinned and raised one hand in a casual wave. "Now that I've said 'hey,' you gonna invite me up there for a cup of tea? You're a Southern woman after all—it's hardwired in your genetic code."

"Tea?" She began to lose her battle against a smile.

"No. Unfailing courtesy, even when you don't want to be courteous."

Laughing, she put her book down. "Come on up and sit, then. I'll go and get another cup." Motioning to the couch she disappeared into her house.

With a secretive smile of his own, Kyle made himself at home on the small couch gracing her back sun porch. As a landscaper, he knew just exactly how much work she must have done to make her yard look so great. Somehow, knowing she was such a hard worker only made him want her more.

Within moments she appeared again, carrying a tray with a steaming mug of tea and a plate of muffins. She bent to put it down on the low table in front of him.

He smiled, grabbed the tea and breathed deeply, letting the heat from the cup warm his hands.

She motioned to the plate of muffins. "Blueberry muffins. I've been baking for the retirement home. Have one, they're still warm."

The porch was enclosed and had a fireplace at one end that sported a warm blaze. The popping of the wood accompanied the soft clinking of his spoon against the mug as he stirred in sugar. She looked comfortable and beautiful as she sat, curled into her chair.

"These muffins are criminally good," he said around a mouthful. Hot damn, was there nothing this woman wasn't good at?

"Thanks." Her smile faded as she got down to business. "Okay, niceties out of the way. What brings you here, Kyle?"

"I don't know." He hesitated. "Yes I do. I wanted to see you."

She narrowed her eyes at him. "You wanted to see me?" she repeated blankly.

"Yes. Maggie Wright, I wanted to see you. I can't stop thinking about you. I should you know, but I can't."

She sat utterly still, staring at him for a few moments. Pleasure warred with panic inside her. She couldn't deny she'd been attracted to him from the start. But she kept telling herself he was out of her league and also related to someone she'd dated, however briefly.

"You should what? What do you mean?" Her voice was careful.

Leaning forward, he sat his mug down, wiping his hands on his jeans nervously. "I mean that I can't get you out of my mind. Your lips, your beautiful amber eyes. God, the way you smell—rain and vanilla. Is it a perfume or do you just naturally smell that way? Your skin, it's like milk. That dusting of freckles across the bridge of your nose, it makes my hands itch to want to run a finger over them. Your smile, you're so genuine, Maggie. It's a very appealing total package. And I can't stop thinking about you."

She closed her eyes slowly and put her head down. "Please don't do this. I can't take it."

He came to kneel in front of her and slowly raised her face to his with a hand on her chin. "Don't do what?"

"This! Damn it! You heard my story that night and now you feel even sorrier for me. You had to get on your white horse to come over here to try and make me feel better."

He brushed his lips along hers and she stilled again as his taste warmed her. "First of all that was way over a month ago. I don't feel sorry for you, Margaret Wright. I feel something else for you. I want you. I want to get to know you better. I've tried not to think about it because of Shane. But since that night when he made you spill those fries, I've been crazy about you. I've gone out with a dozen women since then to try and push you out of my mind and it hasn't worked.

"The story you told me about your sister and the professor, it did change things but not in the way you think. It made me realize just how stupid I was being for letting you go because of Shane. Especially when Shane was such an ass. Life can be about taking chances and finding really great things and yes, failing sometimes. Or it can be about wondering *what if* because you never dared to try. Now see, I look at you and I kick myself because I was willing to say *what if* because of Shane. And damn it, he doesn't deserve you." His eyes looked deeply into hers. Her heart quickened but not out of fear. Instead she let go and fell into his gaze.

"No more, Maggie. I want you. I don't care what Shane thinks at this point. I would have come earlier but I wanted to give you some time to deal with how he treated you. It was about the hardest thing I've done in my life so far, watching you and wanting you but waiting. But as far as I'm concerned, Shane's loss is my gain. Give me a chance to show you that not all Chase brothers are bad. Let me get to know you, show you who *I* am."

Maggie looked at him and she felt her heart open back up, just a tiny bit. "I don't know. What about Shane? He's your brother."

"What about him? Are you in love with him? If you are, I'll back off, but only for a while because I'll be waiting for it to wear off. If not? Well, I've talked with Matt and Marc about it, to get their opinion on the matter and they're under the same impression I am. If Shane wants to continually close himself off because of an ex-fiancée, the rest of us should be able to follow our own hearts."

Maggie eyed him warily. "Love? I went out with him a few times. No, I'm not in love with him. I liked him and he made me feel like less than nothing. It was cruel and I have no clue why he acted the way he did. Ex-fiancée or not, he was a total jerk. Contrary to what he may have thought, I knew what our situation was, I wasn't looking for a ring, for goodness' sake!" She rolled her eyes at Shane Chase's giant ego.

"But I don't want to cause any problems between you two, either. Plus, Kyle Chase, why are you interested in me anyway? How do I know you aren't just doing this out of some kind of sibling rivalry thing and will lose interest in a few days?"

"First of all, I'm going to be totally honest with you. I've never actually pursued a woman before. They always come to me. That should show you a bit about how interested I am. I like you. You intrigue me. You're beautiful and sweet and funny and a hell of a baker. Why shouldn't I be interested?

"Second of all, I have no need to compete with Shane over women. Pool? Sure. Baseball? Oh yeah. I would never use you like that." He drew a fingertip down her cheek. "Let me in, just a little bit. Get to know me. Let me know you. Come on, let me court you, woo you. I've never wooed before, it should be fun."

"I've never been wooed."

"See? We'll both learn something. Let the woo begin." He grinned and she smiled hesitantly. "We'll take it slow, Maggie," he whispered and kissed her softly, his lips featherlight over hers.

Her body tightened, moisture pooled between her legs, her breasts grew heavy and her nipples hardened. All from a kiss. Wow, he was good.

Breaking the kiss, he leaned back to look into her eyes. "Your lips are softer than I'd imagined. And I've been imagining, a lot."

She had to clear her throat twice before she found words. "So um, this wooage? Does it mean casual dating, as in we'll be seeing and sleeping with other people? I've come to understand and accept that I'm just not the kind of woman who can do the casual each-of-us-seeing-other-people thing. I'm not cut out for it. I know it's against all of the hot guy dating rules to discuss such things but I just want to get things crystal clear up front."

"Hot guy dating rules?" His grin was cocky and she narrowed her eyes.

"Yes, as in guys who look like you and have their pick of every beautiful woman who comes their way."

"And those rules are different from the non-hot guy rules?"

"Are you making fun of me?" One eyebrow slid up slowly.

"Yes," he said, starting to laugh.

She put her hands on her hips and glared at him, but she was sure she lost the effect she was going for when her lips slid into a smile.

He stopped, leaning in to give her a quick kiss to attempt to appease her. "Sugar, wooage—at least in my own hot guy dating rule book—does state that there will be exactly two people in the relationship. You and me. No one else. You're different from the other women I've dated. And that's a good thing," he added quickly. "I have no desire to share you."

"Let's just say that I agree to this. How are we going to deal with Shane?"

"I'll tell him myself. No need for both of us to do it. Shug, I don't want to be mean and I'm not trying to hurt you for my own gain but has he even called you since your last date?"

"No. The ass ran out the door and never called me again. Whatever, I'm past it now." The hurt had passed but the humiliation and the anger still burned deep and pushed old buttons.

"I don't think he meant to disrespect you. Hell, I love my brother and he's a good person but ever since Sandra, he's been like this with women. I think anyone that he truly likes is someone he'll push away right quick. I don't know why I'm saying all of this, it only makes him look better but he is a nice guy, he's just wounded."

She touched his cheek with a finger and smiled at him. Wounded? She'd love to wound him herself, *the asshole*. Instead she took a deep breath and let the anger go. "No, I'm glad you said it. I have a major concern and it's not how I feel about Shane. It's about making problems between two such very close brothers."

"Let me worry about that. I'll tell him when I see him in an hour and a half. We have family dinners each Sunday, you know."

"God, your family is going to think I'm a major slut." She cringed and he began to laugh anew.

He laughed and laughed and then laughed some more. *If she only knew the women I'd dated in the past!* He saw her narrowed eyes and changed his mind, glad she didn't know. He kissed her hand. "They won't. They know you. My mother thinks you are the best thing since hush puppies. Secondly, Maggie, I've dated slutty women, they know the difference, as do I."

"Oh God, again! So not only have you dated gorgeous women but slutty ones, too? How can I compete?"

He stifled another laugh. "Sweetie, how many times do I need to tell you? *You* are a gorgeous woman. Plus, why on earth would you have to compete against slutty? I mean, it's fun and all when you're young and carefree but slutty is in my past."

"It is? Because although it seems like I'm a slut for seeing two brothers from the same family, I'm not, I've not been intimate with very many men, less than you can count on one hand."

He caressed her face and ran his thumb along her bottom lip. "Hell yes, it's in my past. And I know you're not a slut, Maggie. I never thought that. Now, if every once in a while you wanted to *play* at being slutty." An eyebrow rose and he grinned. "Yes indeed, that would be mighty nice. But I've recently developed a terrible yen for gorgeous redheads who bake cookies for seniors."

Sweet heavens, the man was irresistible. "Awfully sure you'll get me into bed aren't you?"

"Oh yeah," he purred. Putting his hands at her waist, he pulled her forward on her chair and into his body. Sliding up to her back, the heat of his palms spread languid desire through her body as he brought his lips to hers. He tasted like tea and blueberry muffins. His tongue swept into her mouth like it belonged there and she actually mewled with pleasure at the sensation when it slid along hers in a sensuous caress. Gone were the teasing, hesitant kisses he'd given her earlier. This was the real thing. Soft and hot and he clearly knew his way around a kiss. She wondered what that mouth would feel like against her pussy and her clit throbbed in approval.

His skin was hot to the touch and so very hard. Letting herself go, she moved her hands, stroking her palms across the muscles of his wide shoulders and back. She couldn't touch enough of him and moved to touch the bare flesh of his neck and slid her hands down his back a little. He groaned softly into her mouth.

"Oh," she said softly, her head lolling back when he moved his lips to kiss the hollow just below her ear. The edge of his teeth nipped her earlobe before he pulled back.

Slowly opening her eyes, his smile made her pulse speed up. The man was sex on legs. Shane who?

"Well, my, that was definitely worth waiting for. Damn, Maggie, you taste good."

She blushed and he cocked up the corner of his mouth into a sexy grin. "Can I take you dancing on Wednesday night?"

"I love to dance."

"Good, it's a date. I'll pick you up at seven so we can grab a bite first and then head over to the Tonk afterward."

"All right."

He stood, drawing her up with him. "I have to go to dinner at my parents' house. I wish I could stay and smooch on you for another five hours or so." He sighed and then leaned down to kiss her again, thorough and quick. Enough to leave the weight of his lips tingling on hers.

"Have a nice time. I'll see you Wednesday." She watched as he quickly headed down her porch steps and into the yard. Yep, the man looked good going too.

* * *

"Shane, I need to talk to you." Kyle came into the living room where his dad and brothers watched the game.

"Yeah?" Shane said, distracted by the television.

No one made a move to leave. Kyle sighed and caught a thumbs-up from Matt.

"I just wanted to let you know that I'm going to be dating Maggie."

Shane looked at him blankly for a moment, eyes blinking slowly. Then, a red flush crept up his neck. *"What?"* he bellowed, jumping to his feet.

Kyle looked at his brother but didn't react. He'd seen it before and he stayed calm because he was in the right. "I'm now dating Margaret Wright. I've just been with her at her house. She and I are going dancing on Wednesday. I've thought about this long and hard. I've liked her from the start but I backed off when you showed interest. However, since you have decided to treat her so badly, I figure all deals are now off."

"I'm dating Maggie, Kyle."

"No you aren't. You *dated* her and then you hurt her. You humiliated her and made her feel used. I waited six weeks for you to fix it and you haven't—" Kyle shrugged "—so too bad for you. Hell, Shane, you didn't even have the decency to call her and apologize for the way you treated her the last time you saw her."

"Or the way you acted when you brought Kendra into The Pumphouse," Matt added.

"You too?" Shane turned to him.

"I happen to really like Maggie. She's a nice woman, Shane. You made her cry. You didn't have to see her anymore, but instead of treating her with respect, you toyed with her and then you tossed her away. You didn't show her any kindness at all." Matt shrugged.

Edward looked at his sons and shook his head. "Is this true, son? Did you treat her as poorly as it sounds?"

"She knew it was just casual. I like her but she had to push it."

"How?"

"When we were kissing on her couch, things got a little… heavy. And then she told me she loved it. I don't need any love, damn it. I just wanted to go out on some dates and have a casual thing. She pushed it and I had to back off, for her sake and my own."

Kyle's face hardened with anger. "You dated her, made out with her and ran for the door and never called her again because she said she loved being touched by you? No! How dare she say that! My God, what a man-eater she is! How dare she compliment you! Jeez, now that I know all of the facts, I'll be sure to run the other way." The sarcasm in Kyle's voice hung heavy in the air between them.

"Tell Dad the rest of it. How you've paraded other women in front of her and looked right through her like she didn't even exist. You could have just said you didn't want to see her anymore. But you set out to make her feel like nothing. I hate that you let Sandra turn you into such a prick."

"Son, I can't believe you'd behave in such a way," Edward said, interrupting before anything physical could erupt between his sons. He frowned at Shane. "In any case, it sounds to me like you'd broken up with Maggie before Kyle expressed an interest in her. I don't see what the problem is with him dating her."

"I don't want him dating her!"

"Why? You say you don't want to be with her, that you had to back off. You haven't called her in six weeks and I know you've been dating other women in the meantime."

"Because. Why are you taking his side anyway?"

"Because is not an acceptable reason, Shane. I'm taking Kyle's side because you have treated the girl shabbily and you yourself said you wanted to back off. I don't see why you should be bothered if your brother is going to take her out."

"What if I still want her?"

"What if, what if," Edward said with an agitated wave of his hands. He leaned forward. "Maggie is not a thing! She's not a toy you can hold back until you want to play with her again. She's a person. A person who deserves respect. I surely have raised men who love women but I have not raised men who treat women the way you've treated Margaret Wright. Shane, you know better and you should be ashamed. Let her go, son. Why hurt her any worse? As long as Kyle treats her well and respectfully—which he'd better or his mother will have both your heads—why not let it go? You get your freedom and he gets to date a woman he likes."

Shane leaned back in his chair, defeated. "Fine, Kyle, but if you hurt her I'm going to stomp on your neck," he growled grouchily.

Kyle's anger drained away. He wished like hell that Shane could get past what Sandra had done. "I like Maggie an awful lot. She's relationship material and that's what I've offered her. I intend to honor that promise."

"Kyle Maurice Chase a monogamous man?" Marc held his hand to his chest in mock disbelief. "Well, this ought to be good. Don't mess it up because I find Miss Margaret Wright to be enchanting. If you mess it up, she'll never give me a chance."

"Not a chance, monkey boy," Kyle growled. He looked toward Shane. "Are we okay? She was very worried that this would set us against each other. I promised her that we weren't competitive over women, just pool and baseball."

Shane sighed. "Yeah, but don't mess up like I did."

"Not a chance, I'm way smarter." Kyle stretched as he winked. Rolling his eyes, Shane continued to glower.

Chapter Five

Maggie hadn't told Liv or Dee about her date with Kyle. She didn't want to have to face their skepticism over the whole thing. Liv would no doubt make some loaded comment about brothers sharing women and Dee would just give her one of those patented sweet Dee looks.

She stood in front of her closet door for at least forty-five minutes trying to decide what to wear. Four outfits later, she finally chose a pair of low-slung jeans, her cowboy boots and the bronze shirt that had a bit of a shimmer to it. It had three-quarter sleeves and buttons such that a small sliver of her belly would show along with a bit of cleavage. Still, not too much of either.

Searching through her jewelry box she decided on the leather choker with the piece of turquoise that Dee had given her for her birthday a few years back and her silver hoop earrings. It was simple and not more glitz than she'd feel comfortable with.

Pulling a few strands of hair from her face, she twisted them and pinned them back from her face with pretty clips. The barest bit of makeup, a touch of Chanel No. 5 behind each ear and between her breasts—not that he'd be going there, no matter how tempted she was—and she was good to go. Except for the nervousness that threatened to make her stomach riot and turn itself out on her bedroom floor.

She jumped when the doorbell rang. He'd shown up five minutes early. Taking a deep breath she opened the door and her breath was gone.

Where Shane's looks were rough and almost savage, Kyle's were beautiful. He still had brown hair but it was more blond than chocolate. It was longer than Shane's, too. Kyle's eyes were a beautiful green, like the ocean on the day after a storm. His skin was golden from working in the sun all day. He was tall but rather than his older brother's six and a half feet, Kyle towered at just under six feet. Tall—especially in comparison to Maggie who was an inch shy of five and a half feet—but not so tall she got a neck pain to look into his face.

And what a face! His nose was perfect, almost Roman. Full, sexy lips were framed by a mustache and goatee. Crisp blue jeans clung nicely to long legs and a body-hugging red shirt showed off his upper body nicely. He was long, lean and mouthwateringly good-looking. She stared at him, speechless for a few moments.

When she opened the door he almost fell to his knees. She was there, hair cascading around her face, just a hint of makeup, lips shiny. Her shirt was snug, breasts clearly outlined by the soft material the color of autumn leaves. Something about the shimmer of it brought out the highlights in her hair and made her eyes smokier. The thick leather choker around her neck was very, very sexy. A creamy expanse of skin peeked from between the waist of her low-slung jeans and the hem of the shirt. For a short woman, her legs were quite long and capped off with some seriously sexy cowboy boots.

"Wow," they both said simultaneously.

"Jinx." She grinned. "You look really handsome."

"Ma'am, I'm just here to fight off the men who'll mob you for looking as sexy as you do."

Before they left for dinner, she gave him a brief tour of the house. Kyle was impressed with the work she'd done herself.

"You've done a heck of a lot of work, Maggie."

"Thanks. This house wasn't the most pleasant place to grow up at times. I feel like each time I do something to make it more my own, I chase some of that away."

"I'm gonna want to hear that story."

"Oh, it's not good for digestion. On the other hand, your momma is something special." She grinned at the image of his flamboyant mother. "She's one of a kind. You're lucky to have her."

"Don't I know it." He laughed and motioned toward the car. "Shall we go then?"

"Absolutely."

He opened her car door and she got in. "You know, you don't have to open my door for me. I'm a big girl."

He looked at her and laughed. "Believe me, I've noticed. But you do know my mother, right? If she even caught wind of me not opening your door she'd hunt me down. She's been known to come out to my job sites or my office to lecture me or inter-rogate me about my brothers. Secondly, I just want to take care of you a bit, part of the whole wooing thing, you know. I know you're capable of doing it, I just want to spoil you a little." He gave her a smile so sexy that she swore she could smell her insides boiling from the heat.

Taking a deep breath, her hands gripped the edge of the seat to keep herself from jumping on him.

Stifling a smug smile, he raised a brow, satisfied he caused such a response in her. "How does steak sound? I'm really in the mood for it today. The Oak Room's got a pretty varied menu if you don't want steak, though."

"The Oak Room sounds just fine, Kyle." Truth was, she'd always wanted to go there on a date and had never had the chance. It wasn't fancy really, it was *the* meeting spot for folks her age in Petal.

At the side of his car, in the faint light of the restaurant, he leaned down to kiss her. She stood on her tiptoes and he bent his knees—they fit well. "You taste like strawberries," he murmured against her lips.

Warmth bloomed through her at the contact. "Flavored lip gloss." Her eyes were still closed as she replied. Still savoring the moment. With a small smile, she wrapped her arms around his back and brought his mouth back down to hers again for another kiss. She didn't know why she felt so wanton with him, she just did. There was something explosive about their chemistry.

Chuckling, he obliged her, his mouth covering hers, sucking her bottom lip in between his teeth and laving the sting with his tongue. A breathy moan of delight escaped her.

His hands slid to the small of her back and brought her body against his tighter. Damn it she tasted good. She felt right against him, in his arms. Her soft sounds of pleasure tightened his need for her. His cock was rock-hard. He had to tamp down his impulse to roll his hips, grinding into her as he reached down to grab that stellar ass to pull her up and over him. He broke off before he lost that thin shred of control, not wanting to paw her in a parking lot.

Putting his forehead to hers he got his breath back until he was able to speak again. "Let's go inside, Maggie." He took her hand in his own and led her into the restaurant.

She felt out of place immediately once they got inside. Practically everyone there knew Kyle—servers, managers and patrons alike. The women eyed him appreciatively and looked at her speculatively. She recognized many of the people but many were from the crowd she'd never been included in. Suddenly, it was like high school and she hated the way it felt.

Kyle felt her tense up and, once they were seated at a small table, he scooted his chair nearer to her own. "Is everything all right, darlin'?"

"Fine. I'm just hungry." She smiled at him, relaxing at his

nearness. He looked skeptical but she didn't elaborate so he let it drop, sticking close.

The server took their order and brought over a glass of wine for Maggie and a beer for Kyle. He held her hand, running his thumb back and forth over her knuckles. He couldn't get enough of touching her skin.

"So, you had a story to tell. I want to know about you. About your family."

She shook her head and put a hand up. "Oh no, we don't need to go there. Tell me about your family instead."

"Uh-uh. It's your turn. We've already talked about Polly Chase. Let's hear about Cecelia Wright. Come on, please?" He fluttered his lashes at her making her laugh.

Sighing, she took a drink of her wine and a bolstering breath. "Okay, the truncated version, then. Cecelia Bradshaw was Miss Georgia. Before that Junior Miss Georgia. She was also homecoming queen two years running, the Magnolia Festival Queen, and a whole host of other titles that she'd be happy to tell you all about any old time you wish. When Cece was nineteen years old, she met the son of the man who owned the largest orchard in the county and of course, Tom Wright was immediately and forever in love with her. They married at twenty and moved into the house I live in now.

"Cece has one tall, regal, golden haired daughter who is married to the quarterback and has two adorable children and they live in a brand-new home over in Cherry Hill Estates. That daughter keeps a spotless home, always has perfect hair and makeup, and bakes cookies and embroiders. Butter would not, and never has, melted in Jane Marie's mouth. Janie, as you know, followed in Cece's footsteps and was homecoming queen and Magnolia Festival Queen and a host of other pageants that my mother would also be happy to talk to you about.

"Now poor Cece has another daughter. This one is not tall, is not beautiful and hated the very idea of pageants. No, poor Cece's youngest child liked—gasp—books! Not just books but history. Of course Cece's suffering went even deeper when her husband would brave her wrath to occasionally nurture this child's love of books and history.

"Luckily, this daughter went to college and graduate school out of town, only returning for holidays and continually disappointed her beautiful mother by not bringing home a quarterback, heck, not even a defensive end. Worse, said short, bookish daughter with the red hair—*Margaret, you can have a variety of hair colors these days, darling, why don't you let me make you an appointment at my salon*—became a teacher! Are you aware how much money teachers make? Are you aware that that daughter will never marry an appropriate man if she hangs around a school all day?

"Doesn't this all sound like I should be on some daytime talk show? It sounds bitter but honestly I'm not hindered by it. I've moved on and Cecelia Wright is a nice enough woman. I was just not what she expected. Anyway, now you know the whole sordid tale and you should feel free to run for your life."

Enraged and utterly shocked, Kyle's hands balled into tight fists. Why on earth would any mother act like that? Cece Wright should be proud to have a daughter as wonderful as Maggie. That she didn't treasure Maggie made him sad.

"Honey, I'm not running anywhere and you know what? Red hair—your red hair—is incredibly beautiful and downright sexy. Plus, I love history and my house was always filled with books. Heck, you'd probably know that working with my momma on the Historical Society Board. Oh and I voted for Amylynne Jessup for homecoming queen."

"Oh my, you flatterer you." She laughed. Relief moved through him as he saw the strain leave her face.

"I thought that was you," a female voice said. Kyle and Maggie both looked up to see Janie standing there.

"Hey, Janie."

"Maggie." Janie nodded her head at her sister and then looked to Kyle, her face breaking into a smile. "Hi, Kyle. What are you doing here?" Janie looked at Kyle as if Maggie weren't even there.

"Are you asking me?" Kyle was surprised and appalled at the way she barely spoke to her own sister. Of course, given the history he just heard, he shouldn't have been.

"Yes of course. Who else would I be asking?"

"I'm here on a date with Maggie. We're having dinner. What else would I be doing?"

"On a date with Maggie?" She sounded incredulous.

"Why do you sound so surprised, Janie?" Maggie asked with an arch of her eyebrow.

"I, uh, well I just thought that Kyle was a bit out of, well, not from your crowd."

"My crowd?"

"You know, Kyle and I moved in different circles. You weren't exactly in the popular crowd."

"High school was ten years ago, Janie," Kyle gritted out, wanting very much to be done with her.

"She means to say that you're out of my league, Kyle. Isn't that right?" Maggie asked, eyes narrowed in a way that Kyle had come to notice meant she was getting hot under the collar. He liked it, made him want to bend her over something and fuck her.

"Of course not!" Janie's claim was utterly unbelievable, especially as she rolled her eyes.

"Well he is. But for some reason, he likes me, go figure."

Kyle put his arm around the back of Maggie's chair and looked up at Janie. "I do like Maggie very much. Moreover, Jane Marie Campbell, I had no idea you were such a snob, and toward your own sister. I'd have thought that out of all the people in Maggie's life, you'd certainly be a fan. Your sister is a beautiful, intelligent and strong woman. Hell, she's out of *my* league."

"Hardly. I'm sorry, I'm not trying to be mean or anything, but Maggie knows more than anyone what her limitations are. How she managed to go out with two Chase brothers in a few months, well, I can't begin to imagine." She made it sound like Maggie was some two-bit whore.

"My limitations?" Maggie snorted, choosing to ignore the last comment for the moment.

"Well at least you're smart and pretty enough. And now look, you even have a good-looking date. But you aren't pageant material and you weren't popular and this is not your kind of place. I'm just saying what's true."

Kyle's mouth dropped open in shock. "You are truly the rudest woman I've ever met and you've been shamelessly bitchy to your sister. I think *you're* jealous, Jane Marie. Now, if you'll excuse us, our food will be here any minute and you are ruining my appetite."

Janie spun around and stalked off without another word. He turned to Maggie and shook his head in disbelief. "My God, Maggie, has she always been like that?" No wonder she had issues about her looks.

"She comes by it honestly. It's nothing my mother hasn't said a thousand times."

He didn't even know how to respond to that. Their food came and luckily, he was able to joke, tease and coax her into a better mood and they ended up enjoying their dinner.

"Let's go, gorgeous. I can't wait to get you out on that floor and show you off."

She snorted, following him outside into the fresh, Janie-free air. Truthfully, she hadn't felt this good in a long time. She'd never stood up to Janie like that before. She knew she'd hear from her mother about it, but it was worth it to see Janie's face scrunch up like she'd sucked a lemon when Kyle sent her packing. Maggie hoped she got wrinkles from it.

The Honky Tonk was packed. Wednesday nights were buck beer and two-dollar well-drinks night. Cheap booze was always an incentive to get out and dance and listen to music. She and Kyle had a beer and a shot and hit the dance floor. He was really a good dancer and despite the height difference, they seemed to fit well together. He twirled her gracefully and even managed to sneak in a few quick kisses while they were dancing.

After six songs he pleaded exhaustion and dragged her to a table. Matt and Marc were there with some friends who all greeted them happily as they came over to join them.

Matt reached out and pulled a corkscrew curl straight and let go, watching it spring back into place. "I've wanted to do that since fourth grade," he said, laughing.

"I know, it's the bane of my existence. It's why I wear it in a bun so much."

"Bane? My God why? Your hair is fabulous. I know women who go to the salon to get expensive perms and still can't get hair like yours." To underline his point, he pulled another curl with apparent delight.

Maggie grinned at him and Kyle slapped Marc's hand when he reached over to try it. "Hands off," he growled.

Maggie was stunned. He actually acted jealous.

"Hi, Kyle, let's dance." Lyndsay Cole sidled up to him, stopping just short of rubbing against him like a cat in heat.

Maggie shot her a look of annoyed anger. It was obvious that Kyle was there with her. Hell, he was sitting with her chair between his thighs, holding one of her hands.

"Lyndsay, do you know Maggie?" Kyle asked smoothly, moving away from her touch and even closer to Maggie.

Lyndsay looked over at Maggie for a quarter of a second and back to Kyle. "Yeah. So anyway, how about that dance?"

"Lyndsay, I'm here with Maggie. I'm *with* Maggie. She's my only dance partner."

"Her?"

Annoyed, Kyle sighed. What was with the women of this town anyway? He was beginning to get a very good understanding of Maggie's inferiority issues. He realized he had to find ways of working through them with her. "Of course her. Who else?" He turned his back to Lyndsay and kissed the nape of Maggie's neck but he felt her stiffness. "Darlin', shall we dance?"

"You know, I'm tired. I think I'd like to go home." Her voice was so small, it squeezed his heart.

He turned her face to his gently. "Don't let her get to you." He said it in no more than a murmur.

"I'm not. I really am tired," she lied. She realized then that it would be like this every time they went out. He'd gone out with a lot of women, all of them pretty and popular like Lyndsay and Jane Marie. Maggie was so far out of their league that she'd never find a way to fit into his life.

He narrowed his eyes at her. "Maggie, don't run off on me." He meant more than just her wanting to leave the Tonk. "We're having a good time. My brothers and friends are all happy to see you—to see us. To hell with what people like your sister and Lyndsay think." He could see she was skittish, probably thinking up reasons why they couldn't be a couple and he wasn't about to let that happen.

Standing up he grinned down at her. "Come on, it's a slow number, at least dance close with me before we go." He put on his best little boy pleading face and she relented, holding out her hand for him to take.

Once on the floor he pulled her tightly against his body. Head resting on his chest, his heart beat for her. The citrusy scent of her hair wafted into his face, teasing his senses. Her body fit against his, soft against hard. His arms tightened around her and he smiled against the top of her head. It would take some work to get past her defenses but he knew she'd be worth it. He could kick Shane's ass for making things even worse. But then again, if Shane hadn't been such a fool, Maggie would be in his arms now instead of Kyle's.

The slow song faded and a fast number came on. Smoothly, Kyle kept his hold on her, easing her into a faster dance. Maggie hesitated a moment but relented and let him keep her on the floor.

"You're smooth, Chase." Her smirk of amusement made him chuckle and twirl her into a dip. He laid a series of kisses down her neck while he had her extended over his arm and delighted in her laugh.

"It's all been practice for the time when I had you to work on."

Grinning, she looked into his face. "Lord, you are so full of it." He righted her and clutched his heart in mock dismay.

Laughing, they walked back to their table where, thankfully, Lyndsay had left. "I really should be getting home. I have to be at school by nine tomorrow morning."

"Oh all right. I'll take you home but only if you promise to come to my house for dinner on Friday night. That is *after* your drink with the girls and my pitcher and pool with my brothers. I wouldn't want you to flout tradition, after all. We can leave from The Pumphouse for my house at eight thirty. That should be enough time for me to trounce them all at pool and for you to gossip with Liv and Dee."

"Oh all right," she said with mock annoyance, echoing his earlier words, but it was ruined by the grin she couldn't suppress. He made her happy.

"Good answer, now your carriage awaits, princess," he said, bowing.

"Night, Maggie," Matt said, kissing her cheek.

"Night, guys." She waved at them. Marc stood up to give her a kiss too but she saw Kyle raise an eyebrow at him. Marc burst out laughing and blew her one instead.

"What was that all about?" she asked him as he drove her home.

"Marc's a skirt chaser, he likes your skirt."

"If you say so. I'll remind you that I've lived in this town my entire life and the only Chase brother who's ever really spoken to me before two months ago was Matt."

"Hey! I've talked to you here and there."

"*Excuse me, miss, you dropped your book*, doesn't count. We're from totally different worlds, Kyle. Surely you can see that."

"What I can see is that in high school—back ten years ago for me and what, eight for you? What I can see is that we ran in different crowds but heck, I was two years ahead of you anyway. You went to college right away and then grad school. I started my own landscaping business. If you'd yelled at my brother before that night I'd have surely noticed you. Okay, so I didn't really notice you before that night but once I did—once I got to know you a bit—I saw what I'd been missing."

She sighed, putting her forehead against the window.

"Maggie, stop trying so hard to find things wrong with being with me. I know you're skittish after Alex and then dumbass Shane, but I'm not them. Let me show you that."

She turned to him, giving him a small smile. "I'll try."

He took her hand and kissed the knuckles. "Good."

When they got back to her house she sat bolt upright. "What the hell?" She yanked open her door before the car had even come to a full stop, heading toward her front porch at a dead run.

"Wait! Damn it, Maggie, wait!" Kyle yelled as he put the car in park and jumped out to catch her and grab her arm.

She stared at the broken front window and "WHORE" written in red paint across her front door. "Who would do something like this?" Her voice was a taut whisper.

Kyle held her tightly against him. With his free hand, he pulled his cell phone out and called Shane who agreed to rush over immediately. But not before admonishing them not to go inside.

"Sweetheart, let's sit in the car out of the wind until Shane gets here," he said softly. With gentle hands, he guided her back down the driveway to his car, holding her while they waited for Shane.

"Jesus, Maggie, I'm sorry." Shane arrived shortly and walked up to her front door, surveying the damage with a wince. Another officer was there with him and appeared to set about looking for clues or evidence or whatever cops did.

"We're going to talk to your neighbors to see if anyone saw anything. Right now, I want to go into the house to make sure it's clear, all right?" She nodded, handing him her keys and his eyes tangled on Kyle's arm wrapped around her shoulders.

"Maggie, why don't you stay with me tonight? I have a guest room and I'm near the high school. Your windows are broken out, it's not safe." Kyle brushed his lips over her temple.

Before she could say anything, Matt and Marc pulled up. Throwing the car into park, they rushed to where she and Kyle were standing. "Oh shit, Maggie! Are you all right?" Matt looked agog at the door and what was written on it.

"Alex," she said in a hoarse whisper.

Shane came back out of her house and spoke to the other officer before coming back to them. "Maggie, it's clear inside. There's no one there. There's a brick on your floor. It's probably what they used to break out your window. It landed on your coffee table so the glass there is broken, too. Matt, can you and Marc get those windows boarded up?"

"You bet," Marc said.

"There's wood in my garage from when I was drywalling." Her voice was flat, emotionless, as she struggled to process it all.

Matt squeezed her arm and he and Marc walked past her and toward the garage. Before too long, they were hammering boards over the broken-out window.

"Maggie, you think Alex did this?" Kyle asked.

"He called me a whore at The Pumphouse that night and he went off on Liv once at the market, saying the same thing. I've never been called a whore in my whole life other than by him." Tears rolled down her face, she bit her bottom lip to keep it from trembling.

"I'll go and check him out, ask him a few questions. Listen, can you stay with someone tonight? Even with the windows boarded up it isn't as safe as it could be." Concern was clear on Shane's face.

"She's going to stay with me," Kyle informed him.

"No. I'm not leaving. I will not let this chase me out of my own home," she said angrily before walking past them both and into her house.

Kyle looked at her, annoyed, and Shane glowered. "You need to convince her to leave." Shane's voice was gruff.

She returned with a bucket of cleaning solvent and a big scrubbing sponge. She dragged on rubber gloves and set to scrubbing the horrible word off her door.

"Not gonna happen," Kyle said in an undertone. "Find who did this, Shane. We can't let her be terrorized like this."

"I will. If it's Parsons I'm gonna stomp him."

"Don't. Don't get fired. Arrest him, then I'll stomp him later."

Shane laughed with cruel promise and walked back up to the porch where she had succeeded in removing the W and most of the H. "Maggie, please call me. Any time day or night if you need anything." He lowered his voice. "I'm sorry I was such a jerk but please trust me to protect you right now. Let me be your friend as well as the sheriff, all right?"

She nodded her head, not taking her attention from the scrubbing. "Thank you, Shane."

"Why don't you let Matt and I do that, sweetheart? We've finished with your windows. Go on inside so that you can call the glass shop. They can get out here first thing to replace them." Marc gently took the gloves off her hands and put them on his own and took the sponge. "Go on, baby." And she nodded.

"Thank you."

Kyle squeezed Shane's arm and followed Maggie into the house. "Maggie? If you won't stay at my house, let me stay here. I promise my intentions are purely to help, no ulterior motives. Please? I'll be worried about you if you stay here alone."

Before she could answer, Polly Chase came through the door

and pulled Maggie into her arms. Even at eleven on a Wednesday night, her hair was in its usual bouffant and her spiky heels were on those tiny feet. "Honey, you're coming over to my house right now. No arguments!"

Maggie looked at all of them—Shane talking to her neighbors across the street, Matt and Marc who had just finished scrubbing her front door and had boarded her windows, Kyle who stood there looking worried for her and now Polly. In the last half an hour she'd gotten more comfort and love from the Chase family than she'd had from her own over her entire life. It hit her like a blow to the chest and she began to sob in earnest.

Polly smoothed a hand over her hair, crooning motherly soft words. Kyle looked worried and helpless. His mother locked eyes with him. "Kyle, go upstairs and pack a bag for Margaret."

"I can't impose on you," Maggie choked out, shaking her head. "I'll be all right." She'd always been. She'd taken care of herself most of her life.

"Kyle, do as I say. Margaret, you aren't imposing. I'm a mother, it's my job. Let me help, sugar. Let us help." She didn't ask if Maggie wanted to stay with her parents. Polly had seen the way Cecelia Wright treated her youngest daughter and the father seemed pretty disinterested. She knew that Maggie had no one to help her other than her girlfriends and the Chases. "On second thought, Kyle, come take over for me. I'll go grab some clothes for Maggie. Goodness knows what you'd pick for the girl to wear to work tomorrow."

Kyle looked at his mother thankfully and pulled Maggie into his arms, rocking her slightly while his mother click-clacked up the stairs.

"It's the last door on the left," Maggie called out.

"You see how useless it is to oppose her will?" Kyle asked with a smile on his face and was relieved to see Maggie smile back at him. "Resistance is futile, Maggie. My mother is tougher than any Borg."

Polly came back downstairs and led them all out the door.

"Kyle, why don't you drive Maggie over to our house? I'll meet you all there."

Kyle nodded and helped Maggie into his car. He watched her carefully out of the corner of his eye on the way to his parents' house. "I won't ask if you're all right, I can see how not all right you are. I know my family is a bit overwhelming but we mean well. Let us in, let us help."

"I…" *don't know how.* "I'll do my best," she said instead.

He pulled up in front of the house and helped Maggie inside. "Come on, baby. I'll get you settled in the guest room. Which by the way, is my old room." He raised his eyebrows suggestively and she allowed herself a laugh.

He put her overnight bag on the bed. "Why don't you take a shower and get changed? Come down afterward. There'll be hot cocoa and there's no saying no. My mother will only come and drag you down."

She nodded and walked into the bathroom at the end of the hall, a dazed look on her face. He stayed there in the doorway until he heard the shower turn on.

"Did you tell her to come down for cocoa?" Polly asked as he entered the kitchen, throwing himself in a chair with a heavy sigh. He watched his mother rattling around starting to heat the milk and took comfort from it.

Kyle grinned at Matt and Marc, already sitting at the table. "Yes, Momma. She's taking a shower first. I told her to come down and that you wouldn't take no for an answer." Standing quickly, he hugged her and kissed the top of her head. "Thanks for taking her in. She needed a momma tonight. I don't think the one she has fits the bill."

"Cecelia Wright is a cold fish to that girl. I never understood it," Polly said with heat.

Shane walked in as Maggie came down the stairs wearing sweats and a T-shirt. Polly saw her bare feet. "Oh no! Honey, I forgot to get you some slippers. Matthew, go and get her a pair of socks to keep her feet warm."

"It's okay, I'm fine." Maggie held out a hand to stay Matt.

Matt just laughed at her and jogged out of the room. He returned in less than two minutes. "Here, sugar, put 'em on or she'll do it for you."

"Thanks." Maggie looked up at Shane as she pulled the socks on. "Well? Any news?"

"We've arrested Alex Parsons. He had a bucket of red paint sitting on his back steps. The fool still had it under his fingernails."

Nausea roiled through her and she felt light-headed in disbelief of the situation. "Why? I only went out with him three times! We never got more serious than a kiss. I don't understand why he hates me so much."

"Well, I don't think it's hate. It gets worse."

Kyle moved his chair closer to Maggie's, reaching out to grab her hand.

Maggie paled. "What?"

Shane sighed. "He had pictures of you. *Hundreds* of pictures of you. Some of them were taken of you at the school, working in your yard, some were of you in the house. And there are ones he clearly used a telephoto lens with. You're, um, naked in some."

She put her head down on the table, rage, shame, and mortification fought within her. She wasn't sure she could even begin to process it all right then. "I've seen him in my neighborhood a lot. I just tried to ignore him."

"He had some of your stuff too, Maggie. He must have broken into your house to get it."

"Stuff? What stuff?" She looked up at him.

"Um." He scratched the back of his neck. "Underwear, bras, nightgowns."

She groaned. It just kept getting worse. "He snatched my

panties? Naked pictures of me? The whole town is going to hear about this. I'm going to have to move."

"You'll do no such thing! You have nothing to be ashamed of, Margaret!" Polly said sharply. "Honey, he's the pervert. Why should you be embarrassed?"

"Are you kidding me? Jeez Louise! Not only does some freak totally violate me and my home but I'm going to look like a slut when this is all over. I'll probably lose my job."

"You look like no such thing, honey. How could you think so? He's the one who fixated on you. People know you. No one who knows you could ever believe such a thing."

Maggie scrubbed her hands over her face. "They're going to see one guy that I dated taking pictures of me naked. And that I've dated two other men since, both brothers. You don't think that makes me look a tad bit loose?" Just saying it made her want to dig a hole to crawl into.

"It makes you look like you have good taste! I'll tell you one thing, Shane and Kyle are two of the five best-looking men in this town. Why shouldn't you have dated any of my boys?" Polly lowered her voice and pushed a curl out of Maggie's face. "I've known you since kindergarten, Margaret Wright. You're a good, honest, upstanding woman. There's nothing loose about you."

Kyle smiled at his mother over Maggie's head. She'd already taken Maggie into their family as one of their own. Whether Maggie liked it or not, Polly had extended her family's protection to her. No one would be making any cracks about Maggie in the presence of any Chase.

"What's going to happen to Alex?" Maggie asked Shane, still red-faced but looking slightly less mortified.

"He's being booked for vandalism. The window people will be out at your place first thing and if the cost of replacing the windows is over five hundred dollars we'll charge him second-degree. After the underwear thing, we'll charge him with theft as well. I can't say that we'll be able to charge him with breaking and entering, depends on whether or not he admits to getting into your house to grab your stuff."

Edward Chase entered the room and patted Maggie's shoulder. "Hey, sugar. I sure wish our first meeting could be under better circumstances." He smiled gently before sitting down at the table. "I've heard most of the story. If you can believe it, Alex called and asked me to represent him! I declined of course, conflict of interest for me. Anyway, he's got Larry Dickerson from Riverton coming out. Larry's a decent sort. I think you should go first thing and see Judge Benson and request a temporary order of protection against Alex. I'll come with you. If you like, I can talk with the district attorney and see if she'll make an order of no contact part of any sentence Alex gets. It's pretty standard in a case like this."

"You're all being so nice to me. I don't know what to say, thank-you doesn't seem to be big enough." Her face heated and tears threatened to return.

"Don't say another word, Margaret. It's what you do for the people you care about. Now, get that hot chocolate into you. Are you hungry? I can make you a sandwich." Polly patted her shoulder.

"I'm hungry," Matt said.

"Me too," Marc echoed.

"Yeah, I could use a ham sandwich. Do we have any of that ham from dinner the other night left over?" Kyle asked.

"If we do, can I have extra mustard on mine?" Shane grinned.

Edward smiled at his wife and looked back at the tiny woman his sons had made part of their family. "I'll go out into the garage and grab some milk from the big fridge."

"I'm not hungry. I think I need to lie down. I have to be at work at nine."

"I think you should call the principal and let her know what's going on. Take a personal day. You have a busy morning ahead of you. You'll have to see the judge and make a statement and press charges down at the station."

"Good idea, Shane. Why don't you call now?" Kyle asked her.

She sighed. "I'll call from upstairs. I need to call my home-owner's insurance agent and make a claim too."

"I'll walk you up," Kyle said.

Maggie stood up and put a staying hand on his shoulder. "That's all right. I know the way." She looked at him and the rest of the family. "Thank you all so very much. Good night."

Kyle kissed her hand and looked up into her face. "Good night, sugar. I'll see you in the morning."

She nodded and went up the stairs into the guest room and closed the door behind her.

She called Ellis Mason, the principal of Petal Senior High, and told her what happened and that she'd be out for the rest of the week. Mason was shocked and sympathetic, urging Maggie to take all the time she needed to and to call if she needed any help.

She called her insurance company and put them in contact with the glass company and gave them the case number as well.

She dialed Liv's number and dumped the whole story on her, sobbing.

"That perverted bastard!" Liv fumed. "Don't worry about the pictures, chances are this won't even go to trial. I'll even forgive you for not telling me—your best friend since the third day of kindergarten—that you were dating Kyle. Are you sure you don't want to stay here?"

Maggie laughed, wiping her face on the hem of her T-shirt. "Who knows if I'll be dating him after this whole mess. Jeeza-lou, this says *issues* from about five miles away. I appreciate the offer of a place to stay but I'm fine. I'm going back home tomorrow after my windows get replaced. Will you call Dee for me? I'd hate for her to drive by and see the boards and not know what was happening."

"You bet, dollface. Are you going to call your family?"

"No, what's the point? Anyway, I'll be hearing from my

mother soon enough, I told Janie off tonight, or rather, Kyle did. She'll run straight to my mother with it."

"Okay, you must tell me the whole story very soon. I may be able to wait until our Pumphouse date but not a moment more. Now, go to sleep and call me if you need me."

Maggie hung up and snuggled down into the bed. It was indeed Kyle's old boyhood bedroom, the bed smelled of him. She drew it around her, letting herself be comforted by that.

Downstairs, Polly placed a platter of sandwiches on the table. "I can't believe all that girl has gone through."

"Well, I just hope Alex pleads out. A trial would suck for her. I'm not even sure the pictures would get out. They may not be admissible. But the scandal would hurt her. Doesn't matter that Alex is the one who did wrong." Shane spoke around his ham sandwich with extra mustard.

"Enough people saw the incident at The Pumphouse and I'm sure Liv would be happy to testify about his comments at the market, too. I'm betting that some of Maggie's neighbors saw Alex lurking around the neighborhood as well. I'm hoping that the evidence is such that Larry just advises him to take a deal. He most likely won't even do time, just a fine and anger management." Edward sighed.

"He won't even go to jail for that? After he terrorized her and broke her windows?" Marc said, outraged.

"I doubt it," Shane said. "Even if they did have a trial and he was found guilty, he'd still probably only do two or three weeks. The court will see it as he didn't hurt her physically. And of course he'll promise to never do it again. He's a librarian, they'll want to go easy on him. They'll see him as a positive influence in the community."

"Does he have any priors?" Edward asked. "I find it hard to believe that he would suddenly obsess over one woman like this. This kind of stalking behavior is usually a long-term thing. I'll have one of the investigators I work with do a bit of checking with Alex's old girlfriends."

"Good idea, Dad. I know he doesn't have any priors here in Petal. I ran his information myself when we booked him."

"He went out of town to college. UGA if I recall," Matt said.

Shane picked up his cell and dialed the station. He spoke to the officer on duty, telling him to check to see if Alex had a criminal record either at the university through a grievance system or in other cities.

Chapter Six

The next morning Maggie woke up, getting ready quickly. Her hair up in a triple twist at the nape of her neck made her feel sleek and classy and a bit untouchable. She silently thanked Polly for packing professional-looking clothing when she unzipped the garment bag. Choosing a black skirt and a cream-colored blouse and some black pumps, she checked herself over in the mirror one last time before leaving the room. Chin up, she headed downstairs.

"Good morning, Red." Kyle came out of the kitchen to greet her. He kissed her quickly and gently on the lips and then placed another kiss on her forehead. "You look nice. Momma's got breakfast just about done. Come on into the dining room."

She walked into the dining room and saw that Edward was already there dressed in a suit and Matt was there too. "I thought you two lived on your own?" She asked Kyle.

Edward laughed and went back to his newspaper.

"We do. But I wanted to take the day off to help you, to be with you. My loser brothers are here all the time to scrounge free food from Mom."

Touched, she reached out and squeezed his hand. "You took the day off for me? You didn't have to do that."

He brought her hand to his lips. "I know I didn't have to, I wanted to. Now sit down. You want some coffee?"

"That would be nice, thank you." She sat, looking to Edward. "Mr. Chase, what time should I go to see the judge?"

"Edward please, darlin'. And I'll come with you. He does ex parte motions at ten thirty on Thursdays. I've had my assistant get the paperwork filled out—what parts you don't have to do, that is—and we'll swing by my office to finish them first. We can leave here by nine thirty. You can ride in with Kyle. I'll need my car later."

"Don't I need to fill out a fee agreement or something?"

"Honey, this is not something I'd charge for. You're like a part of our family! I wouldn't dream of charging money for it."

She shook her head. "Edward, I can't let you do that. You're providing professional services and guidance to me. It wouldn't be right to take advantage of that."

Kyle narrowed his eyes at her as he put a mug of coffee in her hands. Damn but she was independent. He wasn't worried though, if Edward Chase could handle Polly, he could handle Red.

"I would be insulted if you pursued this any further." Edward looked down at her face, putting on his uber father mask, throwing in a bit of lawyer for effect.

Maggie didn't know what else to do or say. She didn't want to insult the people who'd helped her so much. When she got home she planned to make a huge batch of her lemon almond scones and some blueberry muffins and deliver them to Edward's office. She'd bring extras to the house as well. "Thank you for your kindness," she finally said, admitting defeat.

"Any time, sugar." Edward smiled and went back to reading the paper.

At the courthouse, the judge heard two minutes of her story before issuing the temporary order. It helped that one of the witnesses was the sheriff. "The papers will be served to Mr. Parsons at his home address. I understand he is currently out on bail."

"Thank you, Your Honor," Maggie said and they walked out into the hallway. Once out of the judge's hearing she turned to Edward. "He's free? They let him go?"

"I hadn't heard yet. Apparently so."

Shane stepped forward then. "He made bail a few minutes ago. He's home on his own recognizance. I'll have the papers served immediately. I need you to come to the station now so we can take more of your statement."

"How could they just let him out? He broke my windows! He wrote that stuff on my door. He has...pictures of me! The man is a panty thief!"

"I'm sorry, Maggie, it's not up to me," Shane said gently.

"Well this is just bullshit!" she hissed and the men around her were taken aback by her language but hid their amusement well.

"I'm sorry, sugar. This is the way of it, sometimes." Edward patted her shoulder. "I'm going to leave you in Kyle's able hands. I have a hearing to get to. I'm your attorney so if you need help, you call me right away, all right?"

"Thank you so much." He probably couldn't have any idea how much he'd helped her but she hoped she could make it up to him somehow. Even if it took her ten years.

He kissed the top of her head and was off with a wave to his sons.

"Kyle, you don't have to babysit me. I know you have work to do."

"That's why it's so cool to be the boss. I'm not only going to stay with you, but when I take you back home, I'm going to install some motion-controlled lights for you."

She thought about arguing but saw the set of his mouth and let the idea go. He was just as stubborn as she was. Instead she gave him her thanks and sent some silent thanks of her own out for having such good people in her life.

Back at her house, Maggie cleaned up the inside while Kyle installed the motion detectors for the lights. From his vantage on the ladder, he saw a Lincoln pull up to the curb out front. A tall, blonde woman got out and stalked up the steps and into the house. An open window was right below where he was working and he heard the entire exchange.

"Margaret, where have you been?" the woman called out as she walked in through the door.

"Hello, Mother."

"I tried calling you all last night but you didn't answer. Nice girls don't stay out all night, you know. Think of how the town will talk. Were you with some man? Oh never mind, silly question. Anyway, I got a call from Jane Marie about the deplorable way you treated her last night. Your jealousy of your sister has made you mean-spirited. She can't help that she's prettier than you are and has a handsome man. You had no right to take it out on her."

"Oh, I see, so automatically, whatever Janie says is true? That's right, why even bother asking for my side of the story." Kyle heard the hurt in her words.

"You cannot be trusted over your sister."

Hearing all he could take, Kyle walked around and up the steps and into the house.

"For your information, Mrs. Wright, Maggie wasn't home because her house was vandalized and windows were broken out. She stayed with my mother and father until the glass could be replaced."

"Are you the contractor?" Cecelia looked at him haughtily until recognition lit her eyes and she sent him her thousand-watt beauty queen smile. "Wait, you're a Chase aren't you?" Her eyelashes fluttered in the presence of such a handsome man and Maggie rolled her eyes.

"No, ma'am, not the contractor. I'm Maggie's boyfriend, Kyle Chase." He held his hand out to the vile woman.

"Boyfriend? *You?*" Cecelia started laughing as if it were the funniest joke she'd ever heard.

Kyle cut off her laughter. "Moreover, and I don't mean to

tell tales out of school, but I think you should know that it was Jane Marie who was a very nasty woman last evening. Maggie and I were having dinner, minding our own business when she came over to our table and was deliberately hurtful to her sister. Maggie did nothing more than defend herself. I'm the one who asked Janie to leave us alone." He put his arm around Maggie's shoulders and wished he could toss Cecelia Wright right out of the house.

"Margaret has been jealous of her sister's superior looks her whole life. Margaret never ran in the popular crowd or got elected homecoming queen and she couldn't stand it that Jane Marie was. Jane Marie is simply superior and Margaret needs to accept that once and for all."

Fury and hurt coursed through Maggie. And then, clarity and calm. She was done letting herself get treated that way. By anyone. "That's a lie. I was happy for her. If she could actually stop being so nasty to me for a few days, she and I got on quite well. I'm still happy for her. I just no longer choose to be spoken to like I'm an ugly stepchild."

"What are you talking about?" Cecelia looked shocked that Maggie would dare to defend herself.

"The way you've spoken to me my whole life, Mother. As if I could never quite make the grade because I didn't look like you and Janie. It's quite an achievement to win pageants and I'm happy and proud of both of you. But there's more than one kind of achievement in life. I graduated second in my class at college and first in graduate school. I had full-ride scholarships for all six years. I have a good job. I have nice friends, a good life. Mother, why can't you just accept me for Margaret and not as someone who isn't a carbon copy of you?"

"The boyfriend thing is new." She eyed Kyle up and down.

Leave it to Cecelia to focus on that instead of everything else. Maggie sighed. "First of all, I've dated since I came back to town to teach four years ago. If you had ever bothered to ask me about my life, you'd know that."

"A bit of a makeover I see. Now if you'd just go blonde you could really look good. Although I must admit that even Jane Marie never landed a Chase brother."

"Don't talk about him like he's a grade of meat."

"Darling, he's much better-looking than you are. You must be doing something right. Maybe I underestimated you."

Kyle exhaled sharply. "Ma'am, I was raised by Polly Chase to never be rude to a woman but in the last day, between you and your oldest daughter, I've been put to the test something fierce. Maggie is beautiful. She's funny and smart as all get-out. She's compassionate, strong and generous. How dare you talk to her like she's not?"

Cecelia Wright's eyes opened wide. "Margaret, are you going to let your young man speak to me like that?"

"Hell yes, Mother. Goodbye. Oh and I do so appreciate you asking if I'm okay after my home was vandalized last night."

Cecelia Wright gasped and stormed out of the house.

"Oh my God, Kyle Chase." Maggie turned to him, lips in a tight line, hands on her hips.

"I'm sorry, Red. I didn't mean to be rude but I couldn't believe how she was talking to you."

Maggie threw her head back and laughed. She laughed and laughed until tears ran down her face and she had to sit down right in the middle of the floor. "Oh my lands! I've never seen her with that look on her face, I hope it freezes." She gasped out her laughter.

A smile cracked Kyle's worried face. He joined her on the floor and pulled her onto his lap. "Girl, you are something else," he murmured into her hair.

"Question is, what exactly is something else?" she asked, looking up into his face.

"Something special," he said softly, leaning down to kiss her upturned lips. "Something sweet," he added and nibbled on her chin. "Something sexy." She tipped her head back to give him access to her throat and he kissed down to the hollow there.

"Mmm. That's nice."

He looked down the line of her body, over the curve of her breasts, down her stomach, her small hands fisted in his shirt. "Yes, very nice." God he wanted to see her naked. To feel her bare flesh against his own. To taste her.

Maggie laughed then, a low, sexy sound. This woman was trouble. She made him want to jump inside her skin. Wanted everyday memories like going camping and working in the yard. Yearned to hear her voice, smell her skin. See if she had freckles anywhere else.

For years he'd avoided such trouble, liking the single life very much. But Maggie Wright was the best kind of trouble he'd ever been in and he wanted to gorge himself with more.

Trailing the tips of his fingers down her belly he traced circles around her navel, slightly easing the hem of her blouse up. She shifted then and ran her fingers through his hair, dragging her fingernails lightly across his scalp. "Oh God, please touch me. I need your hands on me," she whispered.

"Hey, girl! You in there?" They both jumped at the sound and Kyle reluctantly sat Maggie up, smoothing her shirt down.

"I'm sorry," she whispered and he laughed and shrugged. "In here, Liv," Maggie called out, having to clear her voice.

Liv walked into the living room and saw them both getting up off the floor. "Whoops! Sorry. I can come back later."

"No, I need to finish installing those motion lights, anyway." He turned and kissed Maggie's nose and whispered, "I'll get back to where I was later on."

"You'd better." She smiled at him and watched him walk out of the room.

"Well," Liv said with a grin on her face.

"Yeah, turns out I had the wrong Chase brother to start with but now that I've corrected my mistake things are much better." She snorted, starting to laugh.

Liv tossed her bag into a chair and crossed her arms, looking at her friend. "So what happened with Alex? By the way, I'm parched. Can I get some tea?"

"Yeah, come on through." Maggie motioned her into the kitchen, giving her the basics on the way. "They let him out on bail today. He's home! I can't believe that. Oh, and they're charging him with possession of stolen property for having ten pairs of my underwear, three bras and a teddy, a bustier and a silk robe. It was my favorite robe, too! I thought it was at the dry cleaners. It's not like I can wear any of that stuff again, God only knows what he did with it all."

Both women shuddered in disgust. "Eww. What about the pictures?"

"What about them? Apparently he didn't do anything illegal. Any pervert can set up and, using a telephoto lens, shoot you taking a shower. Ridiculous. You can bet I'll keep my curtains closed up tight. Hell, I even safety-pinned them closed because a few of the pictures were shot between the gap where the two panels didn't quite meet. Though they do go toward making him look like the perverted stalker he is so we can use that in the protection order hearing."

"I feel guilty, he seemed so nice."

"Don't feel bad, Liv. How could you have known? He was a nice guy for a while."

"So tell me about the fracas with Janie last night." Liv's eyes lit up as she drank her tea.

Maggie spilled the entire story to Liv.

After first being shocked, Liv started laughing at Kyle's response. "I knew that boy was a keeper! Has hurricane Cece been here?"

"Of course. She starts in on how she's been trying to get a hold of me and how nice girls don't stay out all night. Kyle comes in and tells her I've been vandalized. She actually flirted with him and then he tells her he's my boyfriend and she laughed like it was a joke. Liv, she told me that my word couldn't be trusted over Janie's and that I was jealous because she was superior to me." That sliced into her gut.

Liv looked like she saw a pile of steaming dog doo. "Your mother is awful. She's a crime in thirty states."

"I stood my ground, Liv. For once in my life I defended myself and it felt great. Kyle defended me, too, which was very sweet. Poor ol' Cece ran for the door looking like she needed some more Botox. I hope she and Janie get five new wrinkles from this."

Unashamedly listening from his ladder outside, Kyle nearly burst out laughing.

"You know, Liv, the Chase family showed me more love and concern in half an hour than my mother has my whole life. You should have seen them all here last night. Every single last one of them helped me. Matt and Marc boarded my windows and then finished scrubbing my door off. Polly showed up and ordered me to stay with them. At their house she made me hot chocolate and Edward appointed himself my attorney. Today he came to court with me. Shane took my report personally and has kept me updated on everything and Kyle has been with me the whole time. He took on my insane evil mother and sister."

She stopped for a moment, tears choking her voice. "It's just that I've been alone for a long time. I've had you and Dee and all but if my knee got scraped I got a lecture about being clumsy. Polly Chase is the kind of woman who would've cleaned it off and blown on the skin while she put hydrogen peroxide on it. They're all so wonderful and I'm horribly frightened that Kyle's feelings for me will wear off and I'll be alone again. Only after having been a part of their world, it'll be really lonely." Her voice had gone to nothing more than a whisper at the last admission.

Liv held back her own tears and hugged Maggie tight. "Girl, you always, always have me and Dee. And I think you should give Kyle a chance. By your description of his actions, he's in it for the long haul—the good, the bad and the ugly. Anyway, why quit now? You've already been in their world, it's not like you can erase it."

"Oh, Liv, last night it was so clear that I'm in way over my head. At The Oak Room everyone knew him. It was filled with people who never spoke a single word to me in high school. Everywhere we go women stare at him blatantly. Lyndsay Cole came on to him right in front of me! Even after he told her he was with me. How can I compete with that?"

"Maggie, you have got to stop this. You're nearly twenty-seven years old. How long are you going to let your mother and sister do a number on you? You don't need to compete with the Lyndsays of the world. You're better than they are anyway! Take a real look at yourself, please. You underestimate yourself so much! That's why you dated men like Sam for so long. You made a comment a while back about lowering your standards— sugar, raise them. You deserve it. Let yourself be happy. Let yourself be with Kyle Chase. You won't die if it doesn't work out. But imagine if it does."

Kyle leaned against the wall of the house, under the window, trying to process all he'd heard. He had to launch Operation Make Margaret Wright Know What a Goddess She Was, and he had to do it right away. Listening to her talk about her mother and sister, about how she felt last night among people he'd moved with for years, he felt bad. He needed to look at his own life a bit. He saw how shallow Jane Marie and Lyndsay were and wondered how many others in his circle were like that.

He pushed himself to standing and finished the last bit of installation for the lights and tested them. He was walking around the front of the house when Shane pulled up.

"Hey, Shane." He walked over to meet his brother's approach.

"Hey. Listen to this, Alex Parsons has four prior no-contact orders on file. Seems that he had quite the way with the ladies back in college. I also talked with Dad's investigator who spoke with two women here in Petal who've had such bad experiences with Alex they were afraid to file police reports."

"Well, well, well. What a bastard. What does this mean then, for his case?"

"I passed it all on to the prosecutor's office. They contacted Alex's attorney. He's going to plead out."

"At least she won't have to testify or face him in court," Kyle said. "Let's go and tell her."

Shane nodded and they went in. Liv gave Shane a dirty look but smiled at Kyle.

"What's happening with the case?" Maggie asked, handing each of them a mug of hot tea and pointing their attention to the platter of scones.

"He has a criminal history of stalking women, Maggie. He's got four protection orders taken out by women at the UGA. He also apparently has a bad history here in town. He made a plea deal today. He'll officially sign it in court next Wednesday if the judge agrees, which he will. He's agreed to a permanent no-contact order—he has to stay five hundred feet away from you at all times, can't contact you, and he's promised to not take any pictures of you. He'll have to pay for your windows and take anger management classes and have counseling."

"And how much time will he have to serve?"

"He won't be serving any time at all."

She froze, blinking quickly. "*What?* The man broke into my house and stole my panties...for God's sake! My favorite robe— I bought that robe in Milan and I can't ever bear to touch any of it again. He took pictures of me without my knowledge or consent, he manhandled me, broke my windows out and wrote an offensive word on my door and he doesn't serve any time? Worse, he's got a history of this and he gets away with it again? It's no wonder those other women didn't come forward. But oh well, I suppose I got what I deserved and all, being a woman who dared to go out with him and then you, oh and don't forget Kyle too."

"I'm sorry, Maggie. If it were up to me he'd be in prison for years, you know that. But the court doesn't view his crime as that serious and they'd rather take a plea agreement than prosecute because it's cheaper and easier. If he violates the protection order—which you'll have granted as a permanent order because he's agreed to that as well as the no-contact order—you'll have double protection."

"Oh well, I'm sure that piece of paper will do a fine job! Oh and now I can't even use the library because he's there."

"This conviction will go on his record. He'll have to get help. Maybe he'll truly get the help he needs."

"Oh, his permanent record, I'm sure he's shaking in his boots! And help? Bully for him. But. What. The. Fuck. About. Me? Huh? What do I get out of this except for broken windows and a twitch every time the wind blows a branch against a window?"

Liv gasped, not because she found the word so horrifying but that she'd never, ever heard Maggie use it. Kyle had an amused look on his face.

Shane looked at his brother, annoyed. "What?"

Kyle turned and looked at Maggie. "Get mad, Red! Who is this asshole to terrorize you? Who are these judges and attorneys who're going to let this guy off? Who is your mother to treat you like crap? Who is Jane Marie to treat you so badly when she's a nasty cheating liar? Aren't you sick and tired of it all? Don't you deserve better than that?"

"*Yes!* Damn it, I do! I'm a good person. I volunteer. I'm a teacher. I treat people right and look at what happens."

"Look what happens when you don't accept anything less than the respect you deserve, Maggie," he said softly, running the backs of his fingers down her cheek.

Realization dawned. "You trying to teach me a lesson, Kyle Chase?"

"Sure am." He folded his arms over his chest with an aura of authority. "You may not be able to make the court system punish Alex for this. Not in the way you want, but damn it you can make sure that everyone else in your life treats you with respect and on your own terms."

"Like my mother."

"Yeah, and your sister."

"And women like Lyndsay," Liv added.

"Definitely," Maggie added, looking dangerous.

"And me," Shane said. He sat down on the couch and looked up at her. "I owe you a big apology. I'm sorry I didn't just have the decency to say I couldn't see you anymore to your face. You deserved better than me shoving Kendra at you like that."

Maggie looked at Shane for a long silent moment. Panic ate at Kyle when he understood that he was falling hard for little Miss Red. If she still had feelings for Shane he didn't know what he'd do.

She took a deep breath. "Apology accepted. Shane, you know, I didn't expect you to propose or anything. I understand you've been hurt badly but not every woman is like your ex. There's someone out there who you can make a future with. But if you keep running and closing yourself off at the first thought of actually having feelings for someone, you'll die lonely. Don't do that. Underneath that gruff exterior, there's a really special man."

Maggie looked over at Kyle. Smiling, she held out her hand for his. Relief rushed through him but he pretended that he'd never been worried at all.

"In the meantime, Shane, if you ever hurt a friend the way you hurt Maggie, I'll kick you right in the junk." Liv's eyes were ferocious as she said it and Shane crossed his legs.

Maggie's phone rang and she grabbed it. It was Polly.

"Hi, honey. Are any of my boys over there with you now?"

"Yep, Shane and Kyle. You need them?"

"I just wanted to invite you to dinner. You can tell them to come too. I'm making smothered pork chops, mashed potatoes, salad, corn bread and I wasn't gonna bother baking after you sent those delicious scones and muffins over."

"Thanks, Polly, that's so kind. I don't want to impose on you two nights in a row."

Kyle narrowed his eyes at her. "Is that my momma?"

"Yes, she's inviting me to dinner and she says you two can come, too."

"What's she making?" Shane asked.

"Smothered pork chops."

"Tell her I'll be there," he said immediately.

"You and I will be there in half an hour." Kyle's expression didn't leave room for argument. "Oh, and wait, let me talk to her." Kyle grabbed the phone she held out. "Momma, you got room for one more?"

"Of course I do. Who else is coming?"

"Olivia Davis, the mayor's secretary. She's Maggie's best friend and she's here right now."

"Good, she's a pretty one. I'll put her between Matt and Shane. See y'all soon then."

Kyle hung up and looked back at them all. "Olivia, my mother would love for you to come as well. I promise you an excellent meal. Plus, well my family can be a bit overwhelming so it'll help Maggie to have you there."

"That and there's never an objection at our house to another beautiful woman," Shane added.

"Flattery and pork chops when all I was gonna do was eat a Lean Cuisine? Hmm, I think I'll have to choose the pork chops."

"Okay, but let me change. I have dust and glass shards on this skirt." Maggie bounded up the stairs to her room.

She changed into a pair of soft jeans and a fleece sweater and came back downstairs. "I sure like watching you go up and down stairs," Kyle murmured as he captured her waist, pulling her to him.

Smirking, she kissed him quickly as they headed out to the car. "Glad to be entertaining."

Maggie felt immediately at home when she walked inside the Chases' home. Within moments she'd garnered hugs and kisses from everyone, although Kyle scowled at Marc who just laughed.

"You all know Olivia?" Maggie introduced her friend.

"Yes," Matt answered immediately. "You'll be sitting next to me tonight."

Maggie smiled. It looked like with a little help from Polly, Maggie was able to get Matt and Liv together after all.

"You got any other hot friends, Maggie?" Marc asked.

"Sorry, Marc. You've dated most every woman in Petal. Dee is lovely but she's engaged. Everyone else you've probably gone out with."

Kyle laughed at that one until Marc took her hand and kissed it. "Except for you, sugar." He winked.

"My goodness, you boys are a menace." Maggie blushed and Edward laughed as he led them all into the dining room.

The food was, as advertised, completely delicious. Maggie watched, amused as Matt and Liv hit it off. The brothers argued about the Braves' chances for the next season while Polly and Maggie talked about the upcoming auction for the Historical Society.

After they'd eaten and cleaned up, Kyle put his arm around Maggie. "Well folks, I'm going to get Maggie home. Matt, can you please give Liv a ride home? She rode over with us and I want to stop by my place for a minute to pick something up."

Matt perked up. "Of course, no problem. I was hoping to stay for dessert though. Liv?"

"Are those Maggie's lemon almond scones I see?"

"Oh, yes. She brought them over earlier today."

"Then I'll definitely stay for dessert." Liv got up and hugged Maggie and whispered, "Tell Kyle I owe him one."

Once they were driving, Kyle reached out and grabbed Maggie's hand. "I wasn't trying to get rid of you, Red. I was trying to get rid of them. I thought that it might be nice to stop by my condo to get some coffee ice cream. Maybe watch a movie. What do you say?"

"I say, I love coffee ice cream!"

Kyle's condo complex was on the south side of town and had

a series of small streams that led into a large man-made lake at the center. Kyle's two-story town house was on a little spit of land that looked out over the water.

He pulled into the attached garage and took her inside through a side door. Maggie had to admit she was impressed. The living room and kitchen opened up to the second floor. Pretty maple hardwood floors gleamed and ceiling fans circled lazily, moving the air. It was tastefully furnished and reasonably neat.

"This is really nice, Kyle."

"Want the grand tour?"

"Sure."

He showed her through the first floor, through his office and the living room and nice-size kitchen.

The upstairs featured a guest bedroom and attached bath and a large master suite with windows overlooking the stream and lake. Hues of sage green and sand gave the space a cool and relaxed feeling. His bed, on a low platform, dominated the room. Maggie couldn't help but stare at it for long moments.

"Wow, this is beautiful. Puts my bedroom to shame."

"I thought the same thing when I saw your bedroom. It's so warm, so you."

She turned to him and he looked at her without saying anything for several long moments.

"Red, we should probably go downstairs now."

"Yeah."

Neither of them moved.

Reaching up, Maggie unzipped the front of her sweater. It exposed her skin to just above her belly button. *Oh my God, did I actually just do that?* She panicked but then realized that it was done and she may as well ride it, or him, out. It was time to take her life into her own hands and live it.

His lips parted and he looked at the small vertical slash of skin exposed through the open zipper.

Maggie turned and walked into the hallway, leaving her

sweater unzipped. She went down the stairs and heard him follow her. Calmly, she sat down on his couch, turning to look at him when he joined her. His pupils were huge, his breathing shallow.

He pulled her close. "What are you up to, Red?" His voice was a lazy purr and suddenly, she felt a bit like prey.

"Nothing, it's just a bit warm," she said breathily. His nearness affected her, sped her heart. Warmed her from the inside out.

The corners of his mouth tugged up. "Are you teasing me, Red?"

She shook her head slowly. "I'm promising you."

"Good lord, woman. You trying to kill me?" He nuzzled her neck.

"Uh-uh." It came out slow and soft as her head lolled back to give him more access. "I'll need you later. Or now."

"Are you saying what I think you are saying?"

She sat up and laughed. "Sheesh, Kyle, I know you've slept with like a hundred women. Haven't any of them teased you? Or am I doing so poorly at it that you don't get it?"

"There's the Red of my dreams. I love it when you go all sassy on me." He pushed his face into her cleavage and breathed her in. His goatee tickled the sensitive skin there and shivers of delight and anticipation broke over her.

"I was hoping you meant you wanted to make love. But I wanted to be sure because I respect you so much. I just don't want to push past where you're willing to go."

She leaned over and pressed her lips to his ear. "Kyle, can you respect me while you're inside me? Because I really—and I mean really—need you to fuck me." She knew she was blushing but it felt so good to say what she'd been thinking.

She saw the shiver run down his skin and he moved to look into her face. "Do you know how sexy you are? I don't know that I've ever wanted anything as badly as I want to make love to you." Standing up, he held out his hand to her and she took it. Hand in hand, he led her up the stairs to his bedroom.

Closing the door behind them, the rest of the world felt far away. While she stood and watched him, he pulled out some matches and lit the candles that ringed the room.

"They're new. I bought them thinking about how you'd look with the candlelight flickering off your skin."

"Dude, you say the best stuff. You're so getting lucky." Smiling, she grabbed hold of her zipper and pulled it all the way down, separating the two halves as she slid the sweater from her body completely.

He blinked a few times. "Damn it, woman, you're gonna kill me. Just full of surprises, aren't you?" With a grin, he reached to turn off the overhead light. "Yeah, just what I thought. You and candlelight—a very sexy combination."

"*I'm* sexy? Kyle Chase, do you look in the mirror very often?" Maggie went to him, reaching out to slowly unbutton his shirt. She gloried in the feel of his skin as she slid the shirt down his arms and off. The warmth of his body and the scent of him hit her face. She closed her eyes, leaning in to take a deep hit of him.

Drowning in hormones she stepped back to take a long look at him. His upper body had the long lean muscle of a runner or a cyclist. He was hard and packed but not bulked.

"Dear lord, you're beautiful." Leaning back toward him, she flicked her tongue over one of his nipples, delighting in his hungry moan. The heated salt of his taste set her taste buds on fire. She wanted more of him. All of him.

Needing to touch him, she slid her palms down the muscled plane of his abdomen. Her fingers tucked just inside the waistband of his jeans, tracing around the edge and the sensitive skin there. Getting down to business, she unsnapped each of the seven buttons there. Every pop seemed so loud—vibrating off her spine as she uncovered a bit more of his body.

Kneeling to help him step out of his jeans and socks, she

looked up, thrilled when she saw the inescapable evidence of just how much he wanted her—how much Kyle Chase wanted Margaret Wright.

"Now there's a picture to last me many a cold and lonely night," he murmured, looking down at her kneeling. Heart hammering in his chest, he reached down to caress her face. Every nerve ending in his body lit when she rubbed a velvety cheek along his thighs. Her fingers and nails grazed down the backs of his legs, kneading the muscles of his calves.

Her caresses came back up his legs and into his boxer-briefs to cup the hard muscle of his ass. Grabbing the material, she pulled them down, leaving him totally naked to her view. He should have felt exposed. But instead heat spread through him at the sight of the greed in her gaze.

She'd intended to stand back to look at all of him but the heated velvet of his cock called to her and she didn't want to resist. Instead, she grabbed him in her hands, holding him so that she could take him into her mouth. Her tongue slid over the bead of semen that pearled at the head and his taste burst through her.

"Holy shit, Red," Kyle stuttered as his hands fisted in her hair.

She hummed her appreciation around his cock and continued to taste him. Her nails lightly scored over his balls and he sucked in a breath. "This is going to end before it begins. Come on, Red, stop for a minute."

She sat back with a kiss to the head of his cock. And then one more because she needed him so much. With a sigh of longing she took his hand and let him help her stand. She stepped back so that she could look her fill at him. And she could have done it for ages, he was so handsome.

"Red, come here. You undo me with the way you look at me. I want to look at you now." Kyle's voice had gone husky and she heard the strain in it.

Taking the two steps to get to him, she put her hand on his

stomach and slid it down, taking his cock into her fist. Moaning, he arched into her hold. She looked down at him, hot and hard, avarice on her face and he laughed.

"You're good for my ego, Red." He ran the tip of his index finger down her skin and over a pouty pink nipple. The material of the bra was sheer and embroidered with leaves of all colors. "Pretty." He popped the catch between her breasts and slid the bra down her arms. "I love front-closure bras. Best. Invention. Ever."

She looked up at him with a smirk. "Seen your fair share of them have you?"

"Oh no." He put his hands up in surrender and shook his head. "That's not a question I'm even going near. It's an unwinnable woman dead-end question like does my butt look fat in this."

"No way! The answer to that question is always no. Anyway, you brought it up." A grin won over her face.

"My answer is it doesn't matter. No other woman in the universe matters but you."

"Good one. More than enough to get me into your bed."

"We do try," he murmured. "Now, I was in the middle of something before you interrupted me, Red."

"My apologies, sirrah. Pray do continue." She bowed in a mock curtsy.

He laughed, picked her up and laid her on his bed, putting her hands up above her head. "That makes a lovely picture." Leaning down over her, he placed a reverent kiss on the tip of each nipple. She sighed happily.

He smiled while his clever hands made quick work of her jeans. The underwear was a match to the bra. "You had this sexy stuff on under all of those conservative clothes all the time didn't you?"

"Pretty underwear is an addiction. Some people buy shoes, some people buy expensive wines. I buy lingerie and books."

"That's an addiction that I am fully willing to enable, Red."

He gave her a lascivious smile, pulling the small scrap of material down her legs. When she was totally naked, he paused to slowly drag his gaze up the length of her body. "You are so beautiful, Maggie."

And she was. Hair spread out over the coverlet, a flush of passion on her face, breasts heaving, long legs moving a bit restlessly under his gaze—amazing. "Oh," he whispered, moving his face closer to her. "Look at this. It looks like someone shook powdered cinnamon here." He ran the flat of his tongue across the dusting of freckles on her shoulders. "Tastes better than cinnamon though," he murmured.

She squeaked at the contact of his warm tongue. He chuckled and flicked the point of his tongue on a path south to her breasts. "Now these, Red." One of his eyebrows rose as he snuck a quick look up at her and then back to her breasts. "I had no idea that breasts so pretty existed under those blouses you wore buttoned up to your chin. Not that I haven't spent a lot of time in the last few months thinking about them." He circled a pebbled nipple slowly with one hand and mimicked that with his tongue at the other.

Arching her back, she pressed her breasts closer to his mouth. She tried to reach for him but he was too long-waisted. Moaning in frustration, she shoved at him, pushing him onto his back.

Moving to kneel between his thighs, she ran her hands across the muscles there, down his calves and back up again. His stomach was flat and she traced the bands of muscle up to his chest, which also bore a mat of blond-brown hair.

His nipples were cinnamon and deliciously sensitive. Moving her mouth to him, she licked over the flat ridge of each. Shuddering, his hands fisted in the blankets as she followed the licks with the edge of her teeth.

Sitting up, she looked at him some more, trying to decide what to touch next. His face was masculine and defined but still beautiful, the kind of face that still looked handsome at seventy. He watched her through gorgeous green eyes fringed with lashes any woman would love to have.

After raising her finger to her lips, tapping it as if she were trying to make a decision, she moved to slide her hands over work-hard biceps and powerful forearms. Her lips kissed the tips of each finger on his large hands. His neck was long, chin bearing a cleft covered in that sexy goatee. She traced the tip of her tongue over his lips across to his jaw and up to his ear-lobe for a quick nibble.

"You're killing me," he groaned out and she laughed.

"Let me see what I can do about that," she murmured, kissing her way south. And then he heard nothing but the blood rushing in his ears as she lowered her mouth over him. His body jerked at the intensity of the sensation. He whispered her name and his hands went to her head, caressing her scalp.

Looking down and seeing the mass of red curls spread over his stomach and her sweet ass swaying in the air as she went down on him nearly drove him over the edge.

"Baby, please, stop, I want to be inside of you. I want to look up at you as you ride me, Maggie," he whispered hoarsely. The smile she sent him made his cock jump in anticipation. "There's a condom in my pants pocket. Over there on the chair near the foot of the bed." She nodded and crawled down to the end of the bed and reached out, grabbing the pants and rifling through his pockets until she found it.

"I won't comment on the fact that you had one in your pocket, Kyle." She smirked as she ripped the foil packet open and rolled it on him. She moved up to straddle his thighs, smiling sexily down at him.

"And I won't comment on how spectacular you looked bent over getting my pants—except to tell you that your pussy is so pretty and to promise you that I will be getting that view again soon. Only with my cock deep inside you. As for the condom, a guy is dead without hope. What if we'd been driving out by the lake or something and we'd wanted to make love? Badda bing, badda boom, I had a condom and we could have done it. Oh dear God…" His words ended on a gasp as she slowly slid down onto him, encasing him in her very tight, very hot pussy.

She moved, taking him into her body inch by inch and pleasure drove up his spine. He looked up at her, surprised at himself. Woman on top had never been a real favorite position for him for sex. But watching her—lips slightly parted and wet from her licking them in concentration and desire, her eyes glazed, lids at half-mast, breasts gently moving as she did, the patch of auburn curls meeting his brown-blond one—he reconsidered. She was so amazing that it made his stomach hurt. He grabbed her hips, his own rising to meet hers and he slid in that last inch or two. A sigh broke from both of them as he seated himself fully inside of her.

The embrace of her pussy, the way she squeezed him and fluttered around his cock was fantastic. So much so, he needed to still for several moments to rein himself in. "Sweet heaven, your pussy feels amazing, Maggie. I don't think I want to leave it."

His words shook her down to her very core. The raw need in them, the way he'd laid himself so open and vulnerable to her got to her in ways she'd never even imagined.

She had to take a deep, steadying breath. Orgasm was very close and it felt like every single nerve in her body was firing and shouting with joy. This was something more than great sex. More than physical. This was deeper. She swiveled her hips experimentally and his eyes flew open wide and he groaned.

"Oh, I see you like that." A throaty laugh bubbled from her and she did it again, this time tightening her inner muscles around him.

The truth was that at almost twenty-seven, Maggie had only had sex—well, intercourse—with three men. Now four. She wasn't very experienced. Adding up even the four men, she'd actually only done it ten times total and it'd been a year since the last time. Although if the other times had felt this good, she didn't think she could have withstood a year-long break. She felt vastly inexperienced next to Kyle but he made her feel like it didn't matter to him at all.

"I like everything you do, but that was quite exceptional. Do it again," he said in a hoarse voice as he brought his hands up to cup her breasts, kneading them and rolling her nipples between agile fingers.

Her head lolled back, arching her back, bringing a change in her angle over him. This brought his thrusts even deeper into her. Swiveling at the same time he rose to press into her brought a gasp from both of them. The intensity of the contact was immense. One of his hands slid down her belly to her pussy where he gathered her honey up to her clit, slowly circling it as she rode him.

Suddenly her back went straight as electric pleasure rode through her, bringing climax in its wake. She moaned his name once before losing speech as the erotic assault pulled her under.

The rippling and pulsing of her pussy around him, combined with her cries of pleasure, pushed Kyle over with her. The muscles on his arms corded with exertion as he moved her body over his own while the flush of her climax crept over her skin.

After what had to be one of the most intense orgasms of her life, she went boneless, collapsing onto him, utterly unable to move. Gently, he rolled her to the side and pulled out of her and she whimpered at the loss of contact.

"I need to deal with the condom, Red. I'll be right back." He jumped up to run into his bathroom and came back quickly, sliding into the bed next to her, pulling her into him.

They must have fallen asleep because the candles were almost burned down completely when Maggie opened her eyes. One of Kyle's legs was thrown over her thighs and his arm was curled around her. She lay there for a few minutes, enjoying the way he felt against her body, his breathing against her hair, the anchoring sweetness of his fingers threaded through her own. She felt totally satisfied. Physically and emotionally.

After some time, she craned her neck to look at the clock. Seeing the time, she sighed.

"Hey, Red." Kyle stirred as he awoke and kissed her thoroughly.

"Hey. Sorry I woke you. It's after two. I should probably go home."

He tightened his grip and burrowed his face into her neck. "Why? I like you right where you are. You're so warm and sweet. You smell so good. Plus, it'll be a lot easier to have sex with you again if you're actually here. Naked."

She smiled. "Well isn't it against the rules to have me stay over?"

"Which rules are those? Is this from the mysterious hot guy rule book you referenced the other day? I must tell you, Red, you need to stop worrying about all these supposed rules."

She socked him playfully. "Don't make fun! I'm not good at this. I don't know how to do it."

He looked at her, his lascivious grin back in place. "I don't know about that, Red. It felt like you knew how to do it pretty darn well to me."

"That's not what I was talking about and well, if you must know, that was only the eleventh time I've ever done it. I know it seems like I'm easy, but that isn't the case."

"You're a natural then. And I've told you before, you don't seem easy, not by a long shot. You're wonderful." He chuckled but his soul roared with satisfaction. Only eleven times? He loved that about her. That she was a natural sex bomb turned him on immensely.

"Easy for you to laugh, you're an ace at this."

"Thanks for the compliment. I'm glad you think so."

She sighed in frustration. "You're deliberately trying to confuse me and yank my chain."

"No, I want you to yank mine." He wiggled his eyebrows

and she dissolved into laughter and he kissed the tip of her nose. "Maggie, I *want* you to stay the night. I *want* to wake up with you in the morning. I don't have a rule book. I just go by what I feel. This is all new to me too, you know. You're the first woman who's ever slept in this bed. I'm not normally a spend-the-night-with-me kind of guy. I told you, I'm wooing you, Margaret Wright."

She snorted and snuggled back into him. "In that case, I've got to tell you that wooing has totally exceeded my expectations. By the way, I have the day off tomorrow. Are you going back to work?"

"You temptress! I do have to work, but I can do it from my office downstairs. Why? Are you actually opening up enough to spend the day with me?"

"I thought we could at least have a nice breakfast."

"And lunch and don't forget I'm making you dinner. You did already agree to have dinner with me. I think you should just stay in my bed all day, naked. I'll bring you anything you need, including me."

She cracked a smile. "I like you, Kyle Chase."

He sobered and kissed her, a bare brush of his lips across hers. "Oh good, 'cause I like you too, Maggie. A whole hell of a lot."

"Enough to cough up that coffee ice cream you lured me over here with?"

He burst out laughing. "For a tiny little thing, you sure eat a lot."

"I have a fast metabolism."

He sat up. "It sounds good. Let's go." He pulled on a pair of sweats and she grabbed what she thought was her shirt but it was his. Moving to put it down and look for her own shirt, he startled her when he put a hand on her arm. "No, put it on."

She pulled on his shirt and buttoned it up. Of course, she had to roll the sleeves a few times and the hem came to her knees but shivers ran down her spine when she caught him watching her with that lazy cat look of his.

"Damn, this will change the way I feel every time I hear Keith Urban sing 'You Look Good In My Shirt.' You look so good that I want to throw you right back down on the mattress and climb between those thighs of yours."

"Later, I want ice cream," she said and it ended on a squeal because he lunged at her. She ran past him and down the stairs laughing.

He dished up two bowls of ice cream and they spread out a blanket on the living room floor, watching a movie while they ate. Or they watched the beginning of a movie anyway.

Kyle took her bowl and put it aside. "Done eating?"

She cocked her head at him. "Well, since I allowed you to take my bowl without protest, I'd say yes."

"Good. Because I'm not done eating." His lips curved up and she gasped as he pushed her back onto the blanket. Making quick work of the buttons on her shirt, he pushed it off. She looked up at him, watching his eyes as he devoured her with his gaze. Smiling like the Cheshire cat, he reached out and brought his bowl over.

With a yelp, she nearly shot up off the floor as he drizzled ice cream over her breasts. But soon that yelp became a moan as he licked up the sweet liquid with the flat of his tongue. The cold ice cream followed by the heat of his tongue gave her gooseflesh.

"Hmmm, where else would this ice cream taste good?" He raised an eyebrow as he spooned it down her belly and over her thighs.

She watched him as he licked his way down her belly and over her thighs. He pushed them open. "I need my hands, Red. Hold yourself open for me so I can lick all of you."

Her breath caught but she did as he asked.

His cold tongue licked up through the folds of her pussy and around her clit and she couldn't resist rolling her hips.

"Sweeter than ice cream and I can eat it in any weather," he murmured against her.

Her hips rose up involuntarily and she whispered his name. "You like that, Maggie?" he murmured and flicked his tongue over her clit. "Damn, but your pussy is sweet. Sweet and wet." He pressed a finger deep into her and shuddered as the walls of her pussy gripped him. "I like that you're so slick for me."

She was beyond a place where she could form the words to tell him how good he felt there between her thighs. All she had were whimpers and breathless sighs as her head slowly moved from side to side. The muscles in her thighs and abdomen began to tremble as orgasm approached.

When he hooked his fingers inside her and found her sweet spot she rolled her hips and cried out. The pleasure was sharp-edged, nearly too much to bear.

"Yes, Maggie. Come for me, honey," he said just before he slowly sucked her clit into his mouth, grazing his teeth over it just slightly.

In a rush of intense sensation, her climax drowned her as her very cells exploded in heat and light and pleasure. Wave after wave shuddered through her in a seemingly endless pattern. Wringing her out, flooding her mind and body.

He continued, not stopping until he'd pushed her into another aftershock orgasm and she sobbed with pleasure and the intensity of feeling, finally pushing his head away and begging him to stop.

Afterward, his lips on hers tasted of sugar and ice cream and her.

Chapter Seven

The next morning, Maggie opened her eyes and saw that she and Kyle were lying on his living room floor with a blanket thrown over them. She stretched with a wince. Man, that was some workout. Each of those aches was well earned and she planned to enjoy the memory of the night before with each and every protest of her muscles.

She sat up slowly and finally noticed that he'd been watching her. She made a mental shrug. It was too late to be embarrassed now, he'd seen her, *had her*, in many combinations just a few hours before.

He pulled on a corkscrew curl and let it go as his brother had done. "Matt was right. That is fun." He did it a few times more.

She raised an eyebrow at him. "Finished? I need a shower and all of my stuff is at my house."

"You're not leaving here. At least not yet. You can wear my shirt with your jeans until you go home to change. I'll even lend you a pair of my underwear."

"Which will hang to my knees." She snorted and then remembered what had happened to her own favorite pairs of underwear and shuddered with revulsion.

"Why the shudder? Do I disgust you?"

"It's not you. I was just thinking about underwear and then about my underwear that got stolen. And that's just icky. I feel the need for some retail therapy."

"Retail therapy?"

She turned to him, eyes widened. "You don't know what retail therapy is? I thought you were an expert on women?"

He threw back his head and laughed. "I thought so until I met you. Now I think that I was an expert on bimbos and I'm woefully uneducated about real women. So teach me."

She gave him a smug smile. "Good answer. Anyway, retail therapy is shopping. It's what some women do as a pick-me-up when they're down. Although in this case, I'm not down in the traditional sense, things are going pretty well for me right at the moment." She looked at him and fluttered her lashes. "No, I need to exorcise a demon. A nasty perverted rat bastard demon named Alex who came into my house and pawed through my panties and stole every single pair of my favorite ones."

"Let me do the work I need to, it should take me about an hour and a half or so. Go home, get showered and changed, bring us back some breakfast and coffee and then you and I are going panty shopping."

"You? A man? Wants to come shopping with a woman? For clothes?"

"Ah, but not for clothes, not for skirts or shoes." He shuddered. "For lingerie. And that, my love, is a whole different story. Any time you want to shop for silky underwear, I'll gladly accompany you." *Did I just call her my love?* He thought about it for a second and realized he wasn't panicked about it the way he would have been if he'd said it to any other woman. Of course, he never had said it to another woman.

Ohmigod, did he just call me my love? She panicked and then realized after a moment that it felt totally natural. "I'll warn you, I have very discriminating tastes with respect to lingerie. I go to Atlanta for it."

"Good, we can get lunch there." He stood and helped her up,

swatting her behind as she went up the stairs to grab her pants and the rest of her clothes.

"I can't wear your shirt, it's cold out. My pullover is much warmer." She pulled on her jeans without underwear and a slow sexy smile broke over his face.

Grabbing the pullover from her hands, he turned and pulled something out of his closet, tossing it at her. "There. It's wool. Very warm."

She pulled it on without a bra and had to fold the sleeves up a few times. It smelled like him and felt heavenly against her skin. It was huge on her but it was warm and he looked like he was going to devour her.

"My sweater and no bra, I feel like it's Christmas morning! I just want to bend you over something. All those alpha male instincts are aroused."

Of course, that wasn't the only thing aroused. The man could really talk a good game. He made her tingly just listening to him and he wasn't even really trying.

Grinning, he walked her out. "Oh, you don't have your car. I drove." He reached over and grabbed his keys off the table at the entry hallway. "Take my car. That's my house key, just let yourself back in when you're finished. I'll get to work now. Don't forget to bring back coffee and breakfast."

He kissed her silly and fought a smile as she got into his car and had to adjust the seat forward. He opened the garage door for her and stood there as she pulled away.

Maggie's house was fine when she got home. No broken windows, nothing taken that she could see. Checking the locks one last time, she headed up to take a long hot shower to work out the kinks in her muscles from the repeat performances on the living room floor at two thirty in the morning. Catching sight of what looked like carpet burn on her ass, she giggled as she toweled off. Who'd have ever thought that she, Maggie Wright, would get rug burn from oral sex on Kyle Chase's floor!

Quickly drying her hair, she got dressed, put on a minimal amount of makeup and went down to check her messages and with a smile, got back on her way.

She stopped off at the café and placed an order for two deluxe breakfasts with pancakes and smoked ham to go and headed back to Kyle's place. When she unlocked the door and turned back to grab the food she'd set down, he was there, smiling at her. Taking the bags from her hands he dropped a kiss on her forehead.

"Hey, Red, set the coffee on the table. I'll bring the food, plates are already out." He started opening containers and popping things in his mouth.

"Knock it off. Sheesh, you're a hound dog in more than one way. I don't take kindly to my potatoes being purloined."

"Me? A hound dog?" He grinned as he sat down next to her and she started filling their plates with the huge amount of food she'd brought.

"I got two deluxes with ham. I hope you like ham." She knew he did of course, remembering his request for a ham sandwich from his mother a few nights before.

"I love ham, and eggs, and potatoes and toast and pancakes. This is perfect." He put three small chunks of potato back on her plate. "To replace what I stole."

Snorting, she speared them on a fork and ate them. "Don't think I'm too proud not to eat them. I love potatoes."

He laughed. "Roger that. You were gone two hours."

"You said you had about an hour and a half of work to do. I thought I'd leave you alone to do it."

A woman who willingly gave him space? "I missed you. I thought you could help me in the shower." He grinned wolfishly.

"Maybe later," she said dryly and tore into her breakfast.

"I'm beginning to see that it's dangerous to come between you and your plate."

She gave him an annoyed look and took a bite of his toast.

* * *

The hour-and-a-half drive to Atlanta and back with Maggie was quite enjoyable. Kyle couldn't get over how funny and vivacious she was. How he could have had a woman like that right under his nose all these years and not noticed was beyond him.

And there was no denying how enjoyable it was to sit and watch her finger lacy and silky panties and bras for the better part of an hour either.

He'd sat in the store, a pile of lingerie on his lap, hiding his erection as he thought of taking each piece off her. With his teeth. The thought of all of those silky scraps lying against her bare skin made him so hard he had to move a few times to keep from injuring himself. As it was, he was sure there would be imprints of the rivets from his button fly on his cock.

He dropped her off at her place with several bags of things he couldn't wait to see her wearing. Running inside, he checked to be sure the place was okay and made plans to meet her at The Pumphouse later on.

She walked in the front door of The Pumphouse at precisely seven to find Dee and Liv already there with a pitcher and chili cheese fries. After some quick hugs and kisses they got down to gossip.

"So? You were going to tell me about last night with Kyle?" Liv sipped her beer.

"Oh my lands! You know, I go for a year without any sex and when I break the dry spell it's with Kyle. The man is so unbelievably sexy that I'm all fluttery just thinking about it. Thing is, with Kyle, it's so much more than sex. I mean, we laugh all the time. He's so smart and kind. It just feels like we've known each other for a very long time. The sex was astounding. I'm talking ice cream coffee in the, um, small of my back at two in the morning, astounding."

"You go! Speak of the stud himself, he just walked in with Matt," Dee said, and Liv and Maggie both turned around.

Kyle saw her and a big grin spread over his face. It mirrored the happiness that spread, warm, through his chest. He
promptly went to her side, bending to kiss her. And it wasn't a
quick peck either. He couldn't just take a small taste. He pulled
her into his body and set his mouth to hers in a kiss that stole
her breath. He wanted to mark her, take up her every thought
the way she did his.

When she put her arm up to go around his neck, he saw a
flash of the lace edging the pink bra. Oh yeah, the one with the
teeny matching thong. His cock throbbed at the memory. And
at the memory he'd be making with her later on.

"Hey, Red. See, pink does work on redheads," he said softly
as he pulled away and kissed the knuckles of the hand that had
been around his neck.

"Hey, Kyle." Her blush matched the tremor in her voice. He
loved that he made her feel that way.

"Hi, Matt," Liv said with a grin.

Matt smiled sexily at Liv. "Hi, Liv. Dee. I'd ask how you
were, Maggie, but since Kyle hasn't shut up about you since he
picked me up from work, I already have a good idea."

Maggie blushed. "We've got more gossip to dish here and
Shane is scowling and tapping his watch at you so you'd better
get over there. I'll see you at eight thirty."

"You bet, Red." He kissed her again and sauntered back to
the pool room with a wave at her.

"Oh my God. You two give off more heat than a transfer station. Holy cow!" Liv fanned herself with her hand.

"How did the night end with Matt, anyway?" Maggie asked
Liv to change the subject.

Liv sighed. "He's a perfect damned gentleman! He took me
home and we talked in my driveway. I asked him in for coffee
and he told me he had to work!"

Maggie wrinkled her nose. "He did? Well, I know he's sweet
on you. Maybe he really did have to work. I'll do a bit of snooping. Totally subtle, I swear!"

"So how are things with Arthur the stud?" Blushing furiously, it was Liv's turn to change the subject.

"Good. He put new floors in the hall bathroom and the pantry, they look so nice. We had sex on our deck, outside!" Dee said the last bit in a whisper.

"No way!"

"Well it was dark and we were under a blanket on the glider but still, it felt naughty."

"Woo, Arthur," Liv said grinning. "I'm glad you two are getting some. I haven't had any in a month. Since my last date with Shaun."

"A month! How do you survive?" Maggie said sarcastically.

"Hey, I like it regular! When I was with Charlie, we had sex at least once a day. Since he and I broke it off, it's been catch as catch can. I tell you, Matt Chase looks so good I could eat him with a spoon." She looked wistfully back at the pool table where the Chase brothers were playing.

"They're so beautiful," Maggie said, smiling.

"Yeah huh," Dee agreed.

"Oh, is that Lyndsay?" Liv asked.

Maggie looked and saw that indeed Lyndsay Cole was undulating her way over to Kyle. "No way, girlfriend. Kyle wanted me to get mad and demand respect? This is day one." Standing up, she made her way back to the pool room.

"Hi, Kyle. Why don't you buy me a drink? I promise you'll get lucky." Lyndsay sidled up to him.

He stepped away. "Hi, Lyndsay. No thanks. I told you, I'm with Maggie." He took his shot and missed as he saw Maggie stalk over looking like a gloriously angry fairy.

"Maggie?" Lyndsay looked confused.

"Yeah, Maggie Wright. As in me."

Lyndsay turned around and made a big show about looking down at her but Maggie stood her ground and narrowed her eyes at the other woman.

"You must be joking. Did you lose a bet or something, Kyle?"

Maggie just looked at the other woman, her arms crossed over her chest. Kyle took his shot and made it. Kissing Maggie's neck, he took his next shot, sinking it as well. He totally ignored Lyndsay. He normally would have hated any kind of showdown between women over him but he was utterly turned on by watching Maggie mark her territory. And it was good for Maggie to stand up for herself.

"Be on your way, Lyndsay, he's not interested." Maggie made shooing motions with her hands and Matt laughed.

Lyndsay snorted. "Please. You think you can hold a man like Kyle?"

"Seeing as how you never had him to begin with and I have him now? Yeah. In any case, if things do go bad and we break up, you're free to take a shot at him then. Unless and until that day comes, back off. Kyle is taken and your feelings about that are irrelevant."

Kyle put his arm around Maggie and pulled her into his side.

"Whatever. You can't hold him for long." Lyndsay flounced off in a huff.

Maggie said something unladylike under her breath and Kyle threw back his head and laughed. He kissed her until she was breathless and led her back to her table. "Thanks for defending my honor, Red."

"Mmmm," she replied and he walked back to the pool room chuckling.

"Way to go, Maggie!" Dee and Liv grinned at her.

"I have to confess, being an uppity woman is really fun. I can't believe I've missed out all these years. I do have a lot of ground to make up!"

Liv laughed and gave her a thumbs-up.

"So, Arthur and I are hosting Thanksgiving dinner at our house this year. My parents and his are coming over, as well as his brothers and their wives and my sister and her husband and kids. You two are welcome to come."

"I'm going to go to my sister's in Crawford. I promised last year."

"I don't know what I'll do. Usually, I'd let myself be guilted into a day of agony at Cece's house of pain but I think I'm going to decline this year. I'd rather eat a frozen turkey dinner than subject myself to any more from them."

"Well, as long as you know you're welcome at ours. But from the looks of it, you'll be eating turkey and watching ball games at the Chase household." Dee seemed convinced but Maggie looked dubious.

At eight thirty the pool game broke up and Kyle stopped at their table. He held out his hand with a bow. "Are you ready, darlin'?"

She smiled and took it. Turning around she leaned down and hugged her friends as she said her goodbyes.

"Oh hey, you coming to the Grange tomorrow?" Dee called out as they got to the door.

"Oh, is that tomorrow night?"

Every year, the weekend before Thanksgiving, Petal had a community dance at the Grange that also served as a fundraiser and food drive for the local food pantry and soup kitchen.

"You aren't going to any dance without me, Red. I have two tickets already. In fact, the whole Chase family does it every year. Please do me the honor and come as my date?"

"Well, when you put it like that." She kissed his nose. "I guess I'll see y'all there," she said to Liv and Dee.

When Kyle got into the car he turned to her. "I told my momma that I'd bring her over some milk and butter. Is that all right with you?"

"Do I mind if you do a sweet helpful son thing? Of course not."

Kyle laughed. "You don't understand Polly Jean Chase, Red. She's probably got three gallons of milk in the giant refrigerator in the garage and at least two extra boxes of butter as well but she wants to see you. To monitor this thing between us."

"Ah, to make sure I'm treating you right?"

He laughed again. "No, sugar. To make sure *I'm* treating *you* right."

They stopped by the Piggly Wiggly and took the groceries over to the house. Polly pulled them both into a big hug and stuffed a cookie into Kyle's hand.

"Momma, I'm taking Maggie back to my house to make her dinner, I don't need this."

"Eat it, Kyle Maurice Chase. You need your strength." Polly looked to Maggie and smiled. "Oh and, Margaret, I wanted to let you know we expect you at noon."

"Noon? For what, Mrs. Chase?"

"Polly, honey. And for Thanksgiving dinner of course. In fact, if you want to come earlier, we have breakfast at eight."

Kyle looked amused as he devoured the cookie he'd protested so vigorously minutes before.

"Um, are you sure I won't be imposing?"

Polly put her hands on her hips and squared her shoulders. Kyle, recognizing the stance, took a step back and watched. "Honey, you're dating Kyle. That makes you one of us. I'll be cooking a turkey and a ham, it's not like a bitty scrap of a girl like you eats that much." Kyle wisely kept his snort to himself.

"You're the first steady girlfriend that we've had in this family since that bitch Sandra broke Shane's heart. You don't think I need another woman here in this sea of testosterone? Besides, I like your company."

"Thank you. I'm sorry if I seem ungrateful. I'm happy to be invited, I like being here." How could she say, *It's just that I didn't grow up in the most normal of households and I'm only learning now how to interact with families that aren't as messed up as my own*? It was just too embarrassing so she just smiled. "Can I help cook?"

"Oh no, honey. My sister will get here the night before. She and I'll get up early to start everything. Just come when you want. I take it you'll be coming, then?"

"Yes. Thanks so much for inviting me. I insist on bringing dessert, though."

"I can't argue with that. I've been eating your baked goodies for years."

"Good!"

"Have we passed inspection yet? It's getting late and I want to get Maggie fed."

"Of course! I'll see you both on Thursday then."

"You'll see us tomorrow at the Grange," Kyle said.

"I forgot that was tomorrow night. Well, I'll see you both then. Night, sugar." She kissed Kyle and then Maggie.

Kyle chuckled the whole way to his place. After trying to ignore him, she finally gave in. "What are you laughing about?"

"You, trying to fight off my momma. She's determined to make you one of our own. You can't fight it. I don't want you to either."

Back at his condo she sat and drank a beer while she watched him prepare the salad that would go with the lemon chicken he'd popped into the oven. He looked good there. Proficient and able.

She hadn't said much since his last declaration in the car. In her mind she'd gone back and forth but she couldn't deny it anymore and she didn't want to. Screwing up her courage at last she put her beer down and took a deep breath. "I'm not going to, you know."

"Not going to do what, Red?" He turned to look at her, a smile on his face.

"I'm not going to fight it anymore. I like your family. If you're truly comfortable with me at events and dinners, I'll come when I'm invited."

Putting his knife on the cutting board, he came to kneel at her feet. "I love for you to be with me and my family. This is all rather new for me you understand. I've never, ever had a steady girlfriend but I'm not freaked out like I thought I might be. I don't know, it just seems—" he paused, searching for the right word "—right. Being with you seems right. My family loves you." He stopped and swallowed. "And I'm, well…quite frankly, on my way to loving you, Margaret Elizabeth." He shrugged. "Now if six months ago someone had said that I'd say that to any woman without a gun to my head or without feeling faint, I'd have laughed. But you seem so right to me. I hope I'm not freaking you out."

She reached out and pushed a lock of his hair out of his eye. "I'm not freaked out. I have my moments of insecurity where I wonder why a man who looks like you is interested in me." She shrugged. "But I've decided that I don't care. And okay, so there's a bit of residual strangeness about the whole Shane thing. But I love being with you. You make me happy. You make me laugh. You accept me on my own terms. It feels right to me, too."

"I thought the Shane thing might bother me but last night, when we were together, it didn't. And anyway, I get to see you naked and sweaty. He never did. I shouldn't feel smug about that but I do."

Unsuccessfully stifling a smile, she shook her head in amusement. "Well, sick as I am, I'm sort of flattered by that. I suppose we're made for each other then, huh? Look, the thing with Shane was totally dumb. It wasn't anything and it wouldn't have been a blip on my life radar if he hadn't acted like such an ass at the end. But it's over and done and I don't sit around and wish things had gone differently. You don't hold yourself back, I don't hold myself back. This is more. Intense and deep, special."

"I'm sorry he hurt you. Thing is, if he hadn't messed up, you'd be with him right now instead of me so I can't feel bad so much about the outcome. As for how it is between you and me? Yep, it's special." He leaned forward and kissed her lips. "Can you spend the night tonight?"

She nodded. "I like waking up with you. I've never woken up with anyone before, it's very nice."

"Me either. Before you, Red, I was the guy who left. Not the moment he came or anything so crass. But shortly afterward.

I like having you here. I like hearing your voice and smelling you in my bedroom."

Maggie liked that very much. "I like being here, too. I do need to do some yard work tomorrow though, so I need to go home in the morning."

"Well, you know that your boyfriend's a landscaper right?"

"I'd heard something about that, yeah." She laughed.

"Well, why don't I help you? We can go over to your place and do whatever yard work you need doing. I can spend tomorrow night at your house. That is, if I'm not rushing."

"You aren't and yes, I'd like that."

Dinner was excellent, Kyle was a very good cook. After they'd cleaned up the kitchen together he turned and her pulse sped to see the look in his eyes.

"Maggie, I need you. Right now." Her mouth dried up as she watched him stalk toward her. He was overwhelming in that moment and it thrilled her. One-handed, he pulled the fly of his jeans open and hers with the other hand.

Making quick work of getting naked, she stood there frozen against the force of his needy gaze. She found herself backed against the wall in the dining room. He dropped to his knees and her stomach clenched.

"I want to taste you," he murmured and spread her open with his thumbs. "Thigh on my shoulder." It wasn't a request. Complying, she leaned back, putting her weight against the wall. A gasp ripped from her lips as his mouth closed over her pussy.

One of her hands gripped the doorjamb and the other sifted through his hair. She cried out when two of his fingers pressed deep into her and turned to hook, stroking her sweet spot. A gasp of his name when his teeth scraped gently over her swollen clit.

"Mmmm. You like that." He couldn't see her enthusiastic nod so she pushed his head back into place and ignored his chuckle.

The tip of his tongue drew circles around her clit over and

over until her legs shook so hard she could barely hold herself up.

"Oh God, please. Kyle, please."

"Please what?" He looked up at her and one eyebrow slid high.

"Pleasemakemecome!"

A third finger joined the other two inside her and he moved back into place. His tongue drew through her pussy, sliding back and forth through her folds until he got back to her clit. And he stayed there. Insistently, relentlessly flicking over her with a featherlight but consistent stroke. On and on until her climax bloomed and exploded over her with such force she flung her head back, smacking it against the wall behind her.

Muscles still jumping she found herself bent over the table. She heard the crinkle of the condom wrapper as he widened her thighs. Gripping the side of the table, she braced herself as he thrust into her to the root in one long stroke.

"Told you, you made me want to bend you over something. Holy smoke you're so hot it drives me crazy," he murmured and began to thrust deep, over and over. Her nipples hardened against the cool, unyielding surface of the table.

She'd never been taken in such a spontaneous, raw way and it thrilled her to her very core. That she made him feel so out of control that he had to bend her over the kitchen table and have her right at that very moment was wildly exciting. His desire of her elevated her. Made her feel like a goddess. To be the focus of such regard, such intensity, made her tremble and sweat.

Kyle looked down at the feminine curve of her spine, before arching back to watch his cock disappear into her body only to withdraw, covered in her honey. Damn but he wanted her. In every way, in every place he could imagine. He'd never desired a woman so deeply before. She affected him on such a primal level that it should have scared him. But all he could feel was the way the hot, wet flesh of her pussy embraced him.

Sucked at him even as he pulled out and welcomed him again as he thrust back deep.

"Damn it, Maggie, you feel so good." His head fell back as orgasm took over his muscles and he came deep inside her.

He pressed a kiss to the back of her neck and carried her upstairs to his bed. He went to sleep knowing that the woman curved against his body would be that way for the rest of his life.

By the time they arrived at the Grange the next night, most of the Chase family was there and had scored a table. Her heart warmed at the genuine enthusiasm they greeted her with. All the brothers told her to save them a dance and Kyle scowled and rolled his eyes at them.

"You know, Liv should be here too." Maggie's tone with Matt was casual and she was delighted to see his face light up. "I knew it!"

"What?"

"You *are* interested in her!"

He sighed and then grinned in resignation. "Yeah, I've had a crush on Olivia since high school."

"For heaven's sake, why didn't you kiss her the other night? Or at least go inside?"

"I've been kicking myself for that ever since then. I really did have an early seminar that next morning. I want to give her the time and attention she deserves."

"Oh good! I'm relieved to hear it. Of course, she's my best friend and has been since the third day of kindergarten, so I'm totally biased—" she gulped in a deep breath before continuing "—but I can still tell you that she's just the most wonderful woman on the planet."

"I doubt it, Red. I know the most wonderful woman on the planet and she's not Liv Davis." Kyle kissed her freckles and heat bloomed as she blushed.

"Lord. I hope that's not catching," Marc said of the two of them. "It's nice for you two and all. But Kyle has been a happy-go-lucky bachelor all of this time and he's so obviously gone over you, sugar, it scares me."

"It'll happen to you too, you know. When it's supposed to." Kyle's smile was smug.

"Maggie, fancy seeing you here."

Maggie turned in the direction of the cold voice and saw Janie and her husband Rick, and their parents, Cece and Tom Wright.

"Janie, Rick, Mother, Daddy. Hello," Maggie said tightly. The look on her mother's face told her it wasn't going to be a pleasant conversation.

"Hey, honey." Her father bent down to kiss her cheek. "Sorry," he whispered into her ear. She braced herself for what was coming next.

"I had no idea you'd actually have a date for this but as you're here I'll go ahead. Since you've decided to be so mean and jealous of your sister, you're no longer invited to Thanksgiving dinner. Perhaps if you spend the day thinking about how you can be a better sister, you can come to Christmas dinner." Her mother's voice was so cold it hit Maggie like a slap and she winced.

Rick looked distinctly uncomfortable as did Tom but neither man said anything.

Maggie just sat there for a moment as she pushed the pain away and gathered her strength and self-respect. Inhaling deeply she looked her mother straight on. "If that's how you feel, Mother. Have a nice evening."

"Wait just a darned minute, Cece Wright!" Polly stood up and came over to Maggie, putting a hand on her shoulder. Kyle held her hand on the other side.

"Yes, Polly? I suppose you're going to butt in?"

"You can keep your snotty comments to yourself. Maggie's coming to dinner with our family on Thanksgiving, where she's loved and appreciated. Christmas, too. If you refuse to see what an exceptional daughter you have, well, you know, I've always wanted a daughter, what with four boys and all. You should be ashamed of yourself."

Maggie could feel the Chases build a protective wall around her. Shane stood on the other side of Polly, Matt on the other side of Kyle. Edward and Marc were on the other side of the table but had stood as well.

"Margaret should recognize her betters. She needs to accept that her sister is prettier and more successful than she is and stop being so bitter about it," Cecelia snapped.

Maggie had had enough. She stood up. "Mother, you don't know anything about it. I am *not* bitter that Jane Marie is pretty! I don't know why you keep saying that, it simply isn't true. But pretty isn't everything! You treated me, my whole life, like nothing else mattered but pretty. Well what about when pretty goes away? What about when pretty only is on the surface? What about when she's like you? Pretty on the outside but cold and heartless on the inside?

"I told myself that if I could just do well in school that you'd appreciate me. That if I behaved and never got in trouble you'd love me, but it never happened. When I was nine and you told me that you wished you'd never had me because I left you with a C-section scar, I tried to tell myself that you didn't mean it that way but you did. And I understand that now. I accept you for the monster you are, Mother."

Kyle looked at his family and they all bore the horrified look he had. This woman told her child she wished she'd never had her, because of a scar? She'd just told her child in front of others that she wasn't as good as her sister because she wasn't as pretty?

"How dare you talk to Mom like that!" Jane Marie spat out. "You're jealous of us both. Jealous of what we have!"

"This is so ridiculous I wish I could laugh. Janie, I'm not jealous of you. I am happy you are lovely and have a nice husband and a good life. I won't, however, let you or anyone else make me feel inferior anymore. I'm done with being the family scapegoat. You all enjoy your night and Thanksgiving dinner."

Janie grabbed Maggie's arm then and towered over her. "You think you can hold a man like Kyle Chase just by opening your legs for him? I was a virgin on my wedding night. Too bad you can't say the same thing." The ugly words came out in a hiss.

Maggie looked at her sister, shock clear on her face. And then she narrowed her eyes. Kyle knew what was coming so he sat back and waited.

"How dare you say that to me, Jane Marie? You of all people. You sure you want to go down that road? Rick isn't the only one of us who knows that's a lie," she said in a voice so quiet and low that it made the hair on Kyle's arms stand up.

"How dare you say that! I was a virgin. You are just, again, jealous that you can't get a man to marry you or even to date you without putting out."

Maggie sighed. "Okay then, why don't we give old Charles a call, shall we? You remember him right? My old grad school advisor who was also my boyfriend? You know, the man who rucked your precious pleated Anne Klein skirt up around your waist and fucked you on my couch while you thought I was out on a walk? Don't sell your bullshit about being a virgin to me, Jane Marie. I saw your legs wide open, *to my boyfriend*, so I know the truth."

Jane Marie paled. "You…you saw? You knew and never said anything?"

"What could I have said, Janie? How could I have conveyed how betrayed I felt? I mean, my whole life people told me how much prettier you were, I convinced myself that you were. That I couldn't hold a man if you were after him too. I know a lot better these days. I'm a different person now."

"What is she talking about?" Rick asked.

"Now all of you go on and have a nice evening. I've said all I needed to say and I feel ever so much better. Just think, now you can have the family you always wanted, Cecelia. Since you already pretend I don't exist, it shouldn't be hard."

Maggie turned her back and sat back down between Kyle and Polly, who both hugged her tightly.

"Don't come crawling back when he dumps you," Cecelia spat out and they all moved off.

"Oh good lord. Who needs a drink?" Edward drawled.

Maggie raised a hand and he took it and kissed it. "You got it, baby girl. One stiff bourbon. Be back in two shakes."

Shane sat down as did Marc. Liv, Dee and Arthur, who had heard the whole thing, came over as well. Liv and Dee pushed in and each hugged her tightly. Polly looked over them at Kyle and her eyes were shining with unshed tears.

"Good for you, Maggie. You should have said all of that a long time ago. I'm proud of you. By the way, how could you not tell me that Janie slept with your boyfriend?" Liv said.

"I don't want to talk about it anymore. Not for a while. I can't or I'll lose it and I don't want to. More and more people are showing up and I just can't face being the focus of yet another town drama."

"I'm sorry, sweetie." Liv sat down in an empty chair, conveniently next to Matt. Dee and Arthur sat across from them on Marc's other side.

"Here you go, sugar." Edward put the bourbon in her hand and she downed it in three big gulps. His eyes widened for a moment and he laughed and put the one he got for himself in her hand as he exchanged it for the empty glass.

"I think you and I need a dance, Red," Kyle said.

She stood up, knocked back the second bourbon and set the glass down, looking back over her shoulder at Edward. "Thanks. I feel much better now." He winked at her and watched as his son took her out to the dance floor, wrapping himself around her protectively.

"Our boy is falling in love with that little spitfire," he said to his wife, who'd come to sit next to him.

"Yes, I think so too. It's nice. She's special. I can't believe her family. My goodness, how awful to tell a child you didn't want her. To compare her to the other child and say she's lacking."

Kyle looked down at Maggie and felt a protectiveness he'd never felt toward anyone other than his family. He felt possessive and full of admiration for the woman in his arms. "Baby, I'm sorry about all of that."

Maggie was snuggled into his body and she just shook her head, not wanting to talk. When the slow number ended he led her back to the table where luckily everyone had moved on to another topic.

"You hungry, Red? Wait, stupid question. You want me to grab you a plate?" Kyle teased.

"No, I'll come with. You'll steal my food if I don't guard it," she said.

"Never come between Red and her food," he told his family.

Despite the beginning of the evening, the rest of it was quite enjoyable. Maggie danced with every male Chase including hers, at least twice. She laughed with her friends and ate at least three platefuls of food. She saw Kyle talking to the DJ and then come back toward her, looking like the cat that ate the cream.

"What are you up to, Kyle Maurice Chase?"

"You know my darkest secret now." He gave a quick look toward his mother. "My great-grandfather was named Maurice. I narrowly escaped it as a first name."

She chuckled and then cocked her head as a slow number came on. One that she and Kyle had danced to at the Honky Tonk and later, had made love to. "Raining on Sunday" by Keith Urban.

"I'm beginning to think of this as our song. Care to dance with me, Red?"

She nodded and he led her out to the floor, pulling her snug against him. With a satisfied sigh, he kissed the top of her head before laying his cheek there.

* * *

Back at her house he drew her up the stairs to her room. "Let me love you, Maggie. Let me show you how special and beautiful you are," he murmured.

"I'm yours, Kyle."

He grinned. "I'm a lucky man." He picked her up, gently putting her on the bathroom counter.

Watching her in the mirror he reached around to unzip the back of her dress. She shrugged out of the top of it while he pulled the rest of it off. Her nearly bare ass sat against the cool counter, her nipples tightened in her sheer bra.

"You look good, Red." He popped the catch on the front of the bra and her breasts came free. He chuckled. "Now you look even better."

She grinned at him, looking into his face. "What is it about being nearly naked when you're fully dressed that turns me on so much?"

"That's a coincidence. It turns me on, too." One-handed, he pulled his pants open and his cock sprang free.

A gasp broke from her lips as he pulled her ass to the edge of the counter and she caught a glimpse of the flutter of colorful silk as he tossed her panties over his shoulder. The crinkle of the condom wrapper made her body tighten in response.

His fingertips brushed through the folds of her pussy, making sure she was ready. "God damn, so wet. Always so wet and ready for me."

"Yes. Oh God, pleasepleaseplease, I need you, Kyle."

"Yes, Red. On the way." The fingers at her hip dug into her skin as he entered her hard, in one thrust. "Yesssss," he hissed softly.

She wrapped her legs around his waist and turned her head, watching them in the mirrors. Saw a woman she didn't recognize, small and sexy as a fully clothed man fucked into her. Watched that woman arch to take him in deeper. Listened to her pleas and orders.

"So beautiful. You're so damned beautiful, Red. Look at yourself. See what I see every time I make love to you." He met her eyes in the mirror. "Sexy. Those long legs wrapped around me. Your eyes, hazy with pleasure. Lips, shiny wet." He leaned in and nipped her bottom lip between his teeth, causing her to gasp. "I love the way your breasts move when I'm inside you. Love the way your pussy is so tight that it hugs my cock. You have no idea how hot you are deep inside. It drives me crazy. Sometimes during the day I'll be working and it'll come over me suddenly—the sense memory of your pussy, clutching me, fluttering around my cock like it's doing right now, just before you come."

He wet his fingers in her mouth and reached between them to find her clit, swollen and slick. "I want your orgasm, Red. Show me how gorgeous you are when you come."

Her eyes blurred as her breath caught. Endorphins flooded her as she came, eyes still locked with his in the mirror.

"Oh, yes. That's the way." He groaned as his own climax shot from the balls of his feet straight into her body in wave after wave until he could no longer stand. They stumbled back into the bedroom together, collapsing on the bed.

She fell asleep fairly soon and he covered her with a blanket before getting up to take his clothes off. He watched the easy in and out of her breath and wanted to kick the crap out of anyone who hurt her or made her feel lacking in any way.

The next morning they made time for breakfast together before each left for the day.

"Your mother invited me to your family dinner tonight, Kyle," Maggie said as she put a mug of coffee in front of him.

"Good. I'll see you at six then." He flashed that sexy smile.

"Are you sure? I don't want to barge in or anything. And I… well, I don't want you to get tired of me, seeing me every day."

"Red." He hooked an arm around her waist, pulling her to his lap. "I am not going to get tired of you. I like seeing you with my family, they like you. I enjoy being with you. We talked about this. I thought you were okay with it."

"I thought I was. Are *you* sure? There's an awful lot of drama in my life these days. It annoys me, it must really annoy you."

He sighed. "Sugar, I know how much of a number your mother did on you but you have to stop letting her influence you. Believe me, if I want some space I'll say so. But I want to be with you. Do you want to be with me?"

Silently, she nodded her head. Afraid to say anything because if she did, she knew she'd blurt out that she loved him.

"That settles it then. I'll see you at six tonight."

That night, she stopped by the grocery store to buy pecans and corn syrup for the pecan pies she was going to make for Thanksgiving and some lemons for the tartlets she wanted to try. On her way out she saw Alex Parsons come in and fear gnawed at her. He watched her warily and when it was clear she was leaving, he went back toward the dairy section.

She ran home and put away her groceries and changed, putting her hair back with a loose clip. Once she'd arrived at the Chases', Marc came out as he saw she was walking up the front steps. "Thought I'd grab my hug and some sugar out here. Kyle's crazy-jealous." He gave her a kiss on the temple as he chuckled.

Grinning, she shook her head at his cheek. Once inside, Kyle saw her and got up to give her a hello kiss. "I saw that brother of mine out there, I suppose he accosted you."

"A girl doesn't tell tales," she said before going into the kitchen to say hello to Polly where she helped set out the food on the dining room table.

"Boys! Dinner is ready," Polly called out and they all came in rapidly. Edward held out Polly's chair and Kyle held out Maggie's. He settled in next to her and within minutes, plates were filled and people had eaten enough to take the edge off and begin talking.

"I saw Alex today," Maggie said quietly.

Shane looked up at her with serious eyes. "Where?"

"At the market. I was leaving. He was coming in. He waited to see which way I'd go and then went in the opposite direction. I hope that means he's going to obey the court order."

"Did he say anything to you?" Kyle asked.

"No. He barely even looked at me, thank God."

"If you see him again and he doesn't leave or it looks like he's come to bother you, call the cops immediately. I assume you have the order with you? We'll get you the permanent ones after Tuesday when he'll be back in court," Shane explained.

"Yes, I keep it in my purse. I have one in my car, at work and at my house like you said. By the way, I'm coming to court on Tuesday."

"Why?" Kyle asked.

"Because, I want to see it. To be able to speak if I can and to be sure that nothing else happens. It's bad enough he's getting away with it, I want to be sure he has to do all of the stuff I was told he was going to."

"Maggie, honey, why don't you let me go instead? I'm your attorney. I'll speak on your behalf if necessary." Edward looked concerned.

"Listen, I know I'm small and all but darn it, I won't hide from this. It happened to *me*. I want to witness it to its conclusion. I want those pictures back, with the negatives, so I can destroy them myself. I want my clothes back, too."

Shane sighed and looked wearily at Kyle, who just rolled his eyes and shrugged. "Fine, Maggie. But, Dad, I think you should be there too, just in case."

"I'll be there as well," Matt and Marc said at the same time.

"Me too," Polly said.

"Of course I will," Kyle added, squeezing Maggie's hand.

She tried not to cry—she'd been doing it so much lately—but she failed. "I'm sorry! I swear to y'all that I'm not usually so weepy. Anyway, thank you all so much. Honestly, I just don't have words to express just how much I appreciate all you've done for me."

"Well, certainly a bit of cherry cobbler will cheer you up!" Polly winked and passed the large pan around the table.

At nine that night, a very weary Maggie said her goodbyes and Kyle walked her to her car. "Red, do you want to stay the night at my place?"

"I do but I shouldn't. I have to go into work early tomorrow to get some more work done. I want to have all sixty-eight of my students' term papers read and graded by Tuesday because we have Wednesday, Thursday and Friday off school. If I go back to your place, I doubt I'll get much sleep." She grinned at him.

"Okay, but have dinner with me tomorrow then. I'll pick you up at your house at six and we can grab a pizza."

"You drive a hard bargain, Kyle. I'll see you then."

He bent down and captured her lips and as always, after one of his kisses, she felt slightly woozy, like she was drunk from his touch.

Chapter Eight

She'd finished the papers by the end of the day and put them in her locked cabinet and went home. Only to find her father waiting for her on the porch.

"Daddy, what are you doing here?" she asked, unlocking the door and letting him inside. "I have a date, he'll be here in half an hour."

"Oh, honey, I failed you," he said.

"Yes, you did," she answered honestly. She gestured to the sofa and they both sat. "You see, I used to think that you did your best. That you tried to make up for how she was with our trips and the small indulgences you gave me but now I think that you just tried to duck your guilt. It's not right, but it's over."

"I'd like to say that I had no idea that she was that bad or that she didn't mean to be as harsh as she was but I'd be lying. I made bad choices. I loved your mother something fierce. I loved her beauty and I made a choice—her over you. It was wrong and that love I had for her has slowly tarnished and died over the years. I don't even recognize myself anymore, Maggie. I used to be such a strong man. I used to be a leader. I've run our family business for my entire adult life! People look up to me, trust me to take care of them and their families and they shouldn't because I couldn't even take care of my own."

She sighed. "Listen, Daddy, if anyone can trust you to take care of them, it's your employees. You've always done right by them. As for what you've become as Cecelia Wright's husband, I can't say. That's yours to deal with."

"I'm filing for divorce, Maggie."

Shock froze her in place. "What?"

"I stood there and watched your mother and sister castigate you in front of a room full of people. I said nothing. When I heard you say your mother told you she wished you were never born, I felt the last bit of love I had for her die. I failed you but I cannot stay with that woman another day. I've moved out. Edward Chase's brother is handling the divorce. The papers have been served."

"I don't know what to say."

"Don't say anything. Just let me try and prove that from now on, I can be a better father. Let me take you to dinner. I know you can't on Thanksgiving because you'll be with the Chases. How about Friday?"

Words escaped her as she thought about it. She should kick him out and never speak to him again but she couldn't. She loved him. The part of her that was the little lonely bookish girl whose daddy took her to Philadelphia for her birthday because she so loved history—that part of her wanted to recognize what a big step he was taking. "All right. Let's do it early though. I have a longstanding thing with Liv and Dee and I meet them at seven every Friday night."

He smiled and squeezed her hands. "Thank you so much, sweetheart. How about you and I meet up at El Cid at five?"

"All right. What are you going to do for Thanksgiving?"

"Darlin', you're such a sweet girl. Thank God you take after my mother. I'm going to your aunt Delia's for the day. You enjoy your beau and his family. I'd like to get to know him better, he seems like he cares for you."

"I do, Mr. Wright, and I worry that you might hurt Maggie."

Maggie and her father turned to see Kyle walking into the room. He leaned down to kiss the top of her head and sat on the arm of the couch next to her. "I knocked but you didn't hear me. I was worried so I let myself in," he told her.

"Kyle, this is my daddy, Tom Wright. Daddy, this is Kyle Chase."

Tom Wright stood and held his hand out to Kyle. "Young man, I'm here to beg my daughter to give me another chance to be a better father. I've left my wife. Your uncle has taken the case. I'm fortunate, because Maggie has agreed to let me try, starting with having dinner with me on Friday. Would you like to come as well?"

Kyle shook his hand and nodded solemnly. "I would, sir. If Maggie is willing to give you another chance, I can as well."

"I'm staying with your aunt and uncle for a while, until I find a place. You call me there if you need me. I'll see you on Friday." He nodded and walked out.

"Are you all right?" Kyle sank down next to her on the couch.

"I think so. I'm just stunned. My father adored my mother, literally. He said that the way she acted Saturday killed the last bit of love he had for her. My mother is going to be insanely angry about this."

"Who cares what your bitch of a mother thinks, sweetheart? Don't give her the power to hurt you ever again."

"I won't. I'm done. Now, I need to change. I'm sorry that I'm not ready." She jumped up and ran upstairs and changed quickly and came back down.

"You're quick. I don't have to ask if you're hungry." He grinned.

She socked him in the arm and he laughed, pushing her out the door and to his car.

After dinner, leaning against the car, Maggie smiled up at Kyle as he rubbed a wayward curl between his fingers. "By the way, one of my students said you were hot and gave me a way-to-go today."

He chuckled. "That so? Well I'm glad we're on the gossip circuit, it should stop anyone from trying to poach you."

"Me? Okay, buster, if you say so." She snorted and turned to kiss the fingers holding her hair. When she turned back to face him, his eyes had gone a much deeper shade of green, almost the color of pine trees. Her breath caught.

"Maggie, let's go back to my house. Or your house, I don't care which. I want to touch you, make love to you."

She felt the heat pool in her belly and she nodded—rendered speechless by the want in his eyes.

They were closer to his house and so they went there. Once inside, he grabbed her hand, leading her to his room. Moving to him, she pressed her face into the flesh of his neck, his warmth and scent lulling her. He picked her up and carried her over to the bed, gently laying her down.

Quickly kicking off her sneakers and yanking her sweater off, she was unzipping her jeans when she looked up to see Kyle already naked and looking down at her with intense heat.

"Oh," she whispered when he pinned her in his gaze.

He gently moved her hands and pulled the rest of her clothing off himself before lying down beside her. They both let out a gasp when bare skin caressed bare skin.

"You feel so damned good, Maggie. I've never wanted anything this much in my life," he whispered as he strummed his fingers through her pussy, making her even wetter than she already was. "I feel that every damned time I touch you. Keep thinking that it has to mellow a bit but each time I see you, I want you so bad it hurts. And when my fingers or my cock finds your pussy, you're ready for me, always so ready for me. It turns me on so much that you want me so badly." His voice was hoarse.

Her heart pounded in her chest. She reached back for the

box of condoms he'd put in the drawer underneath his bed and grabbed one.

"Stay there," he murmured and she stopped, her head hanging off the bed. Pleasure rocked through her when his mouth reached the humid flesh of her pussy. Closing her eyes, her hands hung above her head, touching the carpet beneath the bed, still holding the condom.

The blood rushed to her head as the sensation built. His tongue speared into her and then up and around her clit. Over and over as his hands at her hips held her steady. She barely recognized the sounds coming from deep inside her as he slowly devastated her with his mouth, loved her. He built her up slowly and gave her no place to hide as the climax slammed into her.

He dragged her limp body back up onto the bed and took the condom from her hands. Dimly she heard it rip and her eyes opened in time to see him roll it on his cock.

"I need you, Red." And without any delay, slid into her welcoming body and shuddered at the intensity of it. "Man oh man do you feel good," he murmured, his lips against her neck.

Wrapping her legs around his waist, she rolled her hips up to meet his thrusts. The heated flesh of her pussy parted around him and then grasped, pulling him back into her body just milliseconds after he'd pulled out. Each thrust into her body felt like homecoming.

He moaned her name and braced his weight on his elbows to look down into her face. She gazed back up at him, open, totally open. Nothing existed but the delicious friction of their joining, of her silky thighs cradling his hips, of her heels digging into the flesh of the small of his back. Her eyes deep and luminous—like amber in candlelight—held only him. In that moment Kyle realized he was no longer falling in love with Maggie, he was already there. She owned his heart.

At that realization he came, waves of pleasure rolled through him as he poured into her. He put his face into the crook of her neck and breathed her in. "I love you, Maggie," he whispered as the last of his pleasure flagged and he slumped beside her.

She turned onto her side and peered into his face. "What did you just say?"

"I said I love you, Margaret Elizabeth Wright." He looked into her eyes seriously.

"Oh, that's what I thought you said," she replied and then got silent.

"Is that all you have to say?" he demanded sulkily. He'd never said the words to a woman he wasn't related to and she had nothing to say back?

"No."

"What?" He knew he sounded sullen but he was worried.

Noticing her fine tremble, he felt bad for upsetting her. But then she finally spoke. "Oh God, I'm so glad. I love you, too. I was so scared that it was all just me." The words came out in a gasp as if she'd been holding it inside desperately.

Relief flooded him as he hugged her close. "Thank God! I've never told a woman that before and here I was thinking that my first time out I'd totally bombed. God, Maggie, I love you so much it makes my chest hurt. I think about you all day and when you aren't with me, all night. I can't get enough of you. Not just the naked sweaty writhing you but the total package."

"I thought I'd die after I left you last night. I just wanted to give you some space but then I couldn't sleep. I tossed and turned all night long."

"I *told* you I'd tell you if I needed space, Maggie. I need *you*, silly woman."

She snuggled into his body and smiled against his flesh. "I actually should go home, I have no clothes here and I need to work tomorrow."

"No way, Red. I'll come with you and sleep at your place. I have a job at the Bluebird Inn, it's closer to your house anyway. I've realized I hate sleeping without you. I love that little body tucked into mine. I tried putting a pillow there last night but it was no good."

"It's nice to know I'm better than a bag of feathers," she commented dryly.

"Oh yeah," he agreed and rolled out of bed to grab a change of clothes and some toiletries.

Maggie watched him gather his things with a smile. So damned handsome and he loved her. She sighed happily. "You know, you could bring an extra few changes of clothes and leave them at my place, just in case."

He looked around at her. "Yeah? That would be all right?"

"More than all right," she said and he came back over to her, dropping a kiss on her lips.

"Okay. You should do that too. I mean, bring some stuff over here."

"I like the idea of my panties in your drawer and some of my clothes in your closet, just in case a skank like Lyndsay comes over."

He rolled his eyes. "I told you, I rarely brought women over here, Red. But I like the idea of your panties in my drawer, too."

"Better in yours than Alex's," she commented with a grin.

He looked at her askance and then laughed. "I'm glad you can laugh about it."

"What else can I do? I'm all cried out. Anyway, you make me feel like laughing instead of crying."

"Good. Now let's get over to your place and I'll make you moan instead."

"You've got a deal!"

They promised to meet at the courthouse later that afternoon as they'd left the house.

When she got there, her nervousness abated when she saw Kyle and Edward waiting for her on the front steps. Waving, she climbed the stairs to meet them. Kyle stiffened up and a red flush broke over his face. Edward reached out to hold his arm, shaking his head once. Alarmed, Maggie turned around to see what he was so angry about and saw Alex walking up the steps behind them. His attorney put himself between them and Alex and ushered him inside.

"Kyle, cool down, boy, or I'll make you wait out here. Maggie, darlin', are you all right?"

Taking a deep breath to brace herself, she nodded. "Yes. Let's go in, I'm ready."

Kyle took her hand and they followed Edward into the courtroom where the rest of the Chases, Liv and Dee were already seated. Smiling at them all gratefully, she and Edward moved past them to a more forward row. Kyle stayed at her side, her hand still tucked in his even as they sat down. Shane came in through an interior door and sat down away from them all. Of course he was there as sheriff but he caught Maggie's eye and smiled at her reassuringly.

The judge addressed the prosecutor and Alex's attorney before approving the plea agreement. Alex asked permission to address Maggie and the judge looked at her. "Ms. Wright, do you assent to Mr. Parsons addressing you?"

She leaned over and asked Edward if it would affect the protection order, which the judge had just made permanent, and the no-contact order and he shook his head no.

"Yes, Your Honor, he may address me."

Alex stood up and turned toward her and Kyle squeezed her hand.

"Maggie, I'm truly sorry for frightening you and for the damage I did to your home. I won't bother you again. I'm getting help in my counseling and I hope that someday we can be friends again." He sat down and looked at his attorney.

Maggie just sat there. Be friends with him? Was he out of his mind?

"Very well, is that everything?" the judge asked.

"No, Your Honor, there is the matter of the stolen property belonging to Ms. Wright, and the photographs and negatives that he agreed to turn over. We have not received these items." Edward stood and addressed the judge, back straight, and Maggie felt in good hands.

The judge turned a steely gaze to Alex and his attorney. "Well?"

The attorney whispered to Alex, who began to argue with him. "Your Honor, Mr. Parsons has left these items at home and will forward them to Ms. Wright by the end of the week."

"No!" Maggie said urgently to Edward. "I want those pictures and my underthings back today! He promised."

"Your Honor, Mr. Parsons has known he had to turn over these items since he made this agreement last Thursday. My client is understandably upset. Not only has Mr. Parsons terrorized her and vandalized her home but he possesses intimate items belonging to her and has taken photographs of her, without her knowledge or permission. We are prepared to wait while a police officer escorts Mr. Parsons to his home to retrieve these items posthaste," Edward said calmly but firmly.

The judge looked at Alex and then to Shane. "Sheriff Chase, can you or one of your men escort Mr. Parsons to his home to retrieve these items? Which, by the way—I have difficulty understanding why he was given them back after he was arrested to begin with?"

"Yes, Your Honor. I can send Officer Spence right now. The items were given back to Mr. Parsons by mistake, included in the inventory of his personal items when he was released from jail."

"Do it then. Mr. Parsons. You have half an hour to produce *each and every one* of the items you agreed to in the plea agreement. If a single item is missing—a single photograph or negative—I will send you to jail for a week on contempt charges. Do I make myself clear? We will recess until two fifteen, at such time you had better be back here and in full compliance or I'll toss your butt in jail."

Alex nodded and Shane spoke quietly to his officer and he

escorted Alex outside. Maggie shook with anger. When the judge walked out she turned to Edward. "He did that on purpose! He was going to try and get away with keeping all of that stuff. He's not sorry at all."

"I'm going to wring that bastard's neck," Kyle ground out.

Maggie put a restraining hand on his arm. "No. It's what he wants. It's better if we just get on with our lives and pretend he doesn't exist."

"Maggie's right, Kyle. He'd press charges and you'd be the one in jail," Matt said, having come to join them once the judge had left the courtroom.

"Then you all can protect Maggie." Fury still coursed through him.

"I don't need protection, Kyle, I need you. I don't want him to win anything else. Please."

Shane approached. "Hypothetically speaking and all, if I were, as the sheriff, to hear any threats against another citizen, I'd have to get involved." He looked directly at Kyle. Kyle nodded at him quickly, scowling. "You did a good job, Maggie."

"You sure did. You kept focused and remembered to address me instead of the court directly. The judge is on your side here," Edward said, patting her shoulder.

They sat and waited for Alex to come back and twenty-eight minutes later he did, holding a large box that Shane took possession of. "Let me do the inventory, Maggie. You don't need to see it."

She rolled her eyes at him and grabbed the box. "No, let me." She shooed them all away and asked to use the jury room. She wouldn't give Alex the satisfaction of seeing her upset.

"Sweetheart, please let me come in and help you." Kyle's words were softly spoken as he brushed a lock of hair out of her face.

"No," she whispered back, caressing his cheek. "I appreciate you wanting to be with me, I really do. But this is just too much for me to share with you. I plan to burn all of the pictures in my fireplace tonight but I want to make sure everything is here. I can't wonder whether he's got copies or not or I'll go mad."

Kyle nodded and kissed her forehead.

"Liv, Dee, can you help me please?" she asked and both women nodded and went with her into the jury room.

All of her underwear and other lingerie were there and they moved it with a pencil rather than touch it and put it back into the plastic bag. The pictures were deeply upsetting. She counted each one and then Dee and Liv matched with a negative. Maggie knew how bad it was when Liv didn't even make a crack. She was horrified knowing her most intimate moments were most likely seen by half the police force. The other ones were just creepy, knowing that Alex had watched her do her laundry and go grocery shopping.

"They're all here. Let's go out and tell the judge." She put the lid back on the box and her head up high and they all went back out where the judge was waiting.

"Is everything there to your satisfaction, Ms. Wright?"

"Yes, Your Honor."

"Mr. Parsons, if copies of any pictures you took of Ms. Wright show up, I'll throw you in jail. You're lucky that you haven't had to beat off the concerned men of Ms. Wright's life over this incident. I am going to be keeping an eye on you due to your prior history of harassing and stalking women. Keep your nose clean and keep away from Ms. Wright. Do I make myself clear? If she is somewhere that you come upon, it is up to *you* to leave. If she comes into a place you are, other than your workplace or your home, it is still up to *you* to leave."

Alex nodded, keeping his eyes down.

"Then get out of my sight." The judge banged his gavel and the doors were unlocked for the next case.

"I have to go back out to my job site, Red. Why don't you go home with Momma? I'll pick you up there when I'm done."

"No, thank you. I need to get rid of all of these pictures and the other stuff. I can't bear knowing it's out there."

"I don't want you home alone."

"Listen, I have to get back to my life. I can't be afraid. I won't be afraid of being in my own home."

He sighed and kissed her gently. "I love you, Red. I'll come by after work. Please lock your doors."

"I love you, too. See you later, thanks for being here."

She turned to the rest of her friends and family who were dumbstruck at hearing Kyle say he loved her.

Kyle laughed. "What's the matter? You think she's too good for me?"

"Hell yes," Matt said and Marc laughed.

Polly started sniffling and gave Maggie a big hug. "Honey, you call if you need anything all right? You are a brave, strong girl."

"I'll have someone drive by every once in a while, Maggie, just to check," Shane said. He patted her on the shoulder and she smiled back at everyone.

"Thanks, all. I'll see you later." She kissed Edward on the cheek and Kyle walked her to her car and watched her drive away.

Shane walked up behind him. "That should be me, but if it can't be, I'm glad it's you."

"You don't have the guts to let yourself love, Shane. You'd better find them or you'll end up alone. I'm sorry, Shane. I love her and she's mine. That you fucked up and she fell into my lap is a sad thing because I love you and you're my brother and all. But man, a woman like her, she's what I've been waiting for my entire life." He turned and looked at his older brother. "Deal with it, Shane. I don't want you to be alone. You deserve what I've got." He squeezed his brother's shoulder and walked away.

Maggie went home, took the box straight out to her back porch and loaded a pile of pictures into the fireplace and set them aflame. It took her the better part of an hour to get it all burned, including her beautiful lingerie, which she tossed in with a broken branch from the yard. She sat back and watched the flames of a regular fire that was incidental to the immolation of her nasty relationship with Alex Parsons.

Two hours later, she drank Jack Daniel's straight out of the bottle as she looked up and saw Kyle standing at the back door.

"Hi," he said quietly, fighting a smile.

She got up a bit unsteadily to unlock the door and let him in. "Hi."

Taking the bottle from her hand he looked into her face and lost his battle to hide his grin. "Hmm, had a wee bit of whiskey I see."

"Just a bit," she said defensively but had to laugh when she heard how badly she slurred her words. 'Course once she started it was a bit hard to stop.

Continuing to grin, he led her to the couch and sat her down. "Feel any better?"

"I do now that you're here." Giggles finally dying, she climbed into his lap.

"Good answer, Red." He sounded amused. He stroked a hand over her hair. "Let's get something to eat, okay? Looks like you could use it."

"Okay. Your mother came by earlier and brought me three casseroles. Want some chicken noodle casserole, ham casserole or tuna?"

"I knew she couldn't stay away," he said with a snort.

"She didn't stay long. She just brought enough food to last me through a nuclear winter and left again. She's a good person."

"She likes you a whole lot." Which was an understatement.

"The feeling is entirely mutual." She stood up and held on to him as they walked into her kitchen and she put the casserole into the oven.

After eating a quiet dinner, they went up to bed. They didn't make love, instead, Kyle held her tight against him and she slept, feeling safe and protected.

Chapter Nine

Thanksgiving Day with the Chase family was quite an experience. There were the normal players, Matt, Marc, Shane, Kyle, Polly and Edward. But they were also joined by Polly's sister, Georgette, and her husband Paul. Kyle's maternal grandparents Ellen and Andrew were also there. Maggie was overwhelmed as she came through the door holding three pies, a platter of lemon tartlets and a container of brownies.

"Good lord, honey! You must have been baking all day yesterday!" Matt kissed her cheek as he took some of the goodies from her arms. She followed him into the dining room and put the food down.

"No big deal, I had yesterday off."

He hugged her and grabbed her arm. "You ready? Come on through, the family's in the living room and they're all dying to meet you."

Taking a fortifying breath she nodded and let him lead her through the door. Immediately, she was greeted by the din of a family at holiday. There was a football game on and plenty of arguing about politics and sports. The noise stopped totally as they noticed she'd walked in.

Kyle jumped up and came over to kiss her cheeks before

sliding his arm around her shoulders. He introduced her to his grandparents who took to her right away.

"Is that Maggie?" Polly called from the kitchen.

"Yeah, Momma!" Shane called back.

Maggie stood up. "Oh for goodness' sake, Shane, don't bellow at your mother." She looked down at their grandparents. "I'll just go in and say hello to Polly. I'll be back in a few minutes, I'm enjoying getting to know you."

Kyle walked with her down the hall to the kitchen. Polly was inside with her sister Georgette and lit up when she saw her. "Hi, honey! I'm glad you're here. This is my sister, Georgette."

A tall woman in purple stretch pants and a gold metallic sweater stepped from around the refrigerator and enfolded her into a bear hug. Maggie tried not to panic as her face got trapped between two enormous breasts.

"My goodness but you're a bitty thing! Just adorable. I'm glad to meet a woman who can take another Chase man off the bachelor market. You should have seen Edward when he first met Polly. He was the stuff around these parts, he and his brother. All the women of Petal wanted Edward Chase and he had his share of most of them. Until Polly let her hair grow and she suddenly got breasts."

Kyle looked as if he wanted the earth to swallow him whole but his aunt kept on with the story and Maggie struggled not to laugh.

"Oh my goodness, when we walked into the Grange for a dance, lordy he fell apart. Tripped over his feet to get to her. From that night there was no other woman in Petal that could get his eye again."

Maggie smiled, thinking about what a looker Polly must have been at twenty years old. Polly smiled back at her. "Oh, honey, they may take forever to fall, but when they do, it's hard and it's forever."

Kyle rolled his eyes discreetly and Maggie pinched him. "Okay, Momma, I'm in the room."

Polly reached up and patted his cheek. "I know, darlin'. Honey, your uncle and your daddy are out back, chipping balls. Get them in here please. It's time to eat."

Kyle nodded and went out the door looking relieved to escape.

"He's so cute when you're around." Polly's smile was bright.

"He's always cute, Polly. You and Edward sure do make gorgeous boys."

"Yes, we did, didn't we? Now, let's get this food out there!"

Maggie sat in between Marc and Kyle and the constant carping between the two of them made her laugh. Marc was a shameless, but totally harmless, flirt and he did it partly just to needle Kyle. Finally, Polly leaned over and rapped Marc across the knuckles with her fork and told him to stop harassing his brother and Maggie laughed even harder.

The family was so wonderful and welcoming, she felt like she'd never truly even had a holiday dinner before. She helped clear up the dishes but then the men took over, sending the women out to sit and drink coffee and brandy.

"Ah...this is the life," Polly said, kicking off her spike-heeled shoes and wriggling her toes. "Too bad they don't do this more often. Maggie, darlin', you must raise my grandsons to do the dishes. I came from a different generation, it wasn't done very often. I admit I spoiled them a bit."

"Just a bit," Maggie said dryly. "It is mighty difficult to not want to take care of Kyle. Luckily, he can cook and his condo is quite clean. As for grandchildren, well, let's just take this one step at a time."

Georgette laughed. "You're the sacrificial lamb, sugar. The first real woman who's caught a Chase boy this generation. Just think about how much easier it will be for the next three after she's broken you in."

Polly threw her sister a dirty look. "Don't you go scaring this little peach away! She's the best thing that ever happened to Kyle. Have you ever seen him so, I don't know, happy? Calm, satisfied-looking? No, this little girl, she's so wonderful that

Kyle's brothers can now see just how worthwhile love truly is. Not a sacrificial anything, an angel."

Maggie snorted. She wouldn't think Maggie was so angelic if she knew *why* her son looked so satisfied lately.

The doorbell rang and Polly started to put her shoes back on and groaned. Maggie put a staying hand on her knee and stood up. "I'll get it, just put those feet up."

She walked into the foyer and opened the door, only to come face-to-face with none other than Lyndsay Cole and her bimbo partner in crime, Stefanie Peterson. Maggie stared at them. "Yes?"

"We brought some pie by."

"That so?"

"We did it to be neighborly of course. We're very close to the Chase family, you know," Stefanie snapped.

"Oh really? Funny, no one's ever mentioned you."

"Lyndsay is close to the Chase family, or at least one of them in particular."

Maggie snorted and nearly jumped out of her skin when Polly came into the hallway, in her bare stocking feet. She turned and gestured to Lyndsay and Stefanie. "Apparently, they wanted to be *neighborly* and bring over a pie."

"Why would we want their pie when yours were so good?" Polly said with a smile that slid into a glare when she turned her gaze at Stefanie and Lyndsay. "Cut the crap, girls. What are you really doing here?"

"Hello, Mrs. Chase. How are you today? Momma just had an extra pie and wanted me to bring it over," Lyndsay cooed. Maggie had to admire the girl's steel for not quailing in the face of Polly's scorn.

Polly took the pie, looked at it and handed it back. She just stared at Lyndsay for some moments before speaking. "You say your momma made that pie?"

"Yes, ma'am."

"She working over at Kroger's bakery these days?" Polly

jerked her head, indicating the Kroger's stamp on the bottom of the pie tin.

Lyndsay's face colored and then she brightened. Kyle walked into the hall and approached, putting an arm around his mother and Maggie. "What's going on here?"

"Apparently, Kyle, Lyndsay's momma is working at Kroger's bakery now and wanted her to bring over a pie. Also, Stefanie thought she'd come by as well, to be neighborly and all," Maggie said sounding quite dangerous.

Polly, hearing a tone similar to her own in Maggie, smiled in her own dangerous way. "Apparently, honey, she forgot to wear a bra, too."

Maggie burst out laughing and Kyle smiled down at his mother and then looked at Lyndsay—from the neck up, he wasn't a fool. "You two need to go on home. My family is having a nice day and I don't want you to ruin it."

"She's not your family," Lyndsay said.

"Of course she is. You see, family is about more than genetics. It's about love," Polly said, taking Maggie's hand.

"And I love Maggie very much, as does the rest of my family," Kyle added.

"Yeah, well she's a home wrecker! You'll see! She doesn't deserve you!" Lyndsay spat out venomously.

"Go home, Lyndsay. You're embarrassing yourself. Kyle. Isn't. Interested." Maggie sounded bored but still looked dangerous.

"How do you know that? If he's not interested, where was he last night?" Lyndsay tossed that out with a smirk.

Maggie met that with a smug smirk of her own and leaned in close to the other woman. "With me. All night. Where he is *every* night. Believe me when I tell you he'd have been too tired to go anywhere else."

Kyle chuckled. "Very true, sugar."

"You broke up your own parents' marriage!" She looked around Maggie to Polly, who'd moved back a bit to lean against the doorjamb. "On top of that, do you know, Mrs. Chase, that she went out with Shane and dumped him to go out with Kyle? Kyle and I were in a relationship before she came along and wrecked it."

Kyle burst out laughing. "A what? I shared an ice cream cone with you. I kissed you a few times. That's not a relationship. As for the Wrights' marriage, the blame for that mess of a family lies at the feet of Cecelia and Tom. Lastly, I'd be pretty flattered if Maggie here dumped Shane for me but that's not what happened, not that it's any of your business. Now, Maggie is right, you're embarrassing yourself, go home and leave us alone."

Maggie waggled her fingers at them and Kyle slammed the door in their faces.

"You're perfect for this family, Maggie." Polly chuckled and walked into the living room.

"I'm really sorry about Lyndsay, sugar. Honestly, I never even took the girl out. I don't know what her deal is."

Maggie pulled him to her by the waist of his chinos. "Her deal is that you're the sexiest, most handsome man around and she lost her chance and can't deal. Too bad, 'cause I'm not letting you get away."

"Good." He kissed her quickly before anyone could come out.

By the time Christmas approached, Maggie had pretty much moved into Kyle's condo. Her house meant a lot to her but also held a lot of ugly childhood memories. The less time there, the easier it was to deal with the fact that her mother had pretty much never wanted her. She'd bought the place, thinking if she'd made it hers, she could finally put the memories in perspective. But she realized now she had to jettison that house and move forward, making new memories and accepting her childhood for what it was.

Thankfully, she slowly built a relationship with her father. They had dinner every once in a while and spoke on the phone often.

She'd become a regular in the Chase household. They treated her like one of their own and she truly felt like it. Winter had brought a bit of a lull in Kyle's business and Maggie was off school for winter break so they had a lot of time to spend together.

Kyle woke up one morning about two weeks before Christmas in a hyper mood. "Let's go and get a tree today," he begged. Maggie had decorated the condo but they'd held back on a tree until they both had the time off.

She stretched and pulled him back down to her. "Convince me."

"Gladly," he murmured and with a grin, disappeared beneath the covers.

"Oh, yes, that's the way to convince a girl of just about anything."

He chuckled as his mouth descended and sent shivers over her flesh.

They went to the Christmas tree farm and chose a nice noble fir for the living room. She made mulled cider while he put the tree up and got it watered. Afterward, they decorated it with ornaments of their own and a few they'd bought together.

When they finished, they sat on the couch together and watched the lights on the tree, drinking the cider. "This is the best Christmas I've ever had," Maggie said with a satisfied sigh.

"Me too, Red." He loved the way they were building a life together. Loved to watch her in his kitchen—*their* kitchen. Loved to see her shampoo in the bathroom. Loved the way that her side of the bed smelled of oranges. He'd always thought having a relationship would be another person taking up his life, taking away space from him. Instead she added to his life, made it bigger, brighter.

"I need to finish my shopping. I'm not quite done. I'm going to meet Dee at three and we're actually going to brave the mall in Crawford. I'll meet you at your parents' for dinner tonight."

He nodded and kissed her as she got up to leave. "I told Daddy that I'd help with the tree in the side yard. Not that he's old or anything but I don't want him up in a ladder with a saw. Shall I take the presents in the hall closet over with me?"

They were going to have Christmas at the Chase household. They'd spend Christmas Eve there with the rest of the family and then open presents the next day. Her father was even going to come over for the gift exchange. He and Edward had become fast friends since Tom was using Edward's firm to represent him in the divorce with Cecelia.

She hugged him and bit his ear gently. "Thanks, hon, I'd appreciate that."

Kyle and Matt worked in the yard, dealing with the tree together and laughing. Kyle felt so relaxed. More than he'd ever felt. He'd always had a good relationship with his family but having Maggie in his life made him feel settled in a way he'd never imagined.

"You pick up the ring yet?" Matt asked as they put away the tools in the shed out back.

Kyle had decided to ask Maggie to marry him on Christmas Day. He'd have the ring wrapped up and waiting for her under the tree. "Yep. It's in Mom's jewelry box. She's going to wrap it and put it in a larger box. I wrote out the card for the inside already."

"I can't believe you're going to ask someone to marry you. Not that Maggie isn't great—she really is and the two of you give me hope that someday I'll meet someone who I fall that hard for. But still, this is big, Kyle. Forever-and-ever big."

"She's my whole life, Matt," Kyle answered simply.

From his spot across the road and behind a hedge, Alex ground his teeth. Of course the bastard was laughing, he'd stolen Maggie right from under Alex's nose. This should have been *his* Christmas with Maggie. It was their tree that should have been decorated and presents piled beneath.

Instead, all he had was an empty house and his memories of their time together. But that was about to change.

Dee and Maggie had a great time shopping despite the horrible crowds at the mall just two weeks before Christmas. Maggie bought a beautiful watch for Kyle and the engraving was finished so she picked that up first. Dee bought some sexy silk boxers for Arthur and Maggie got the last item on her list for Kyle, the new golf club he'd been drooling over. She had everything wrapped and drove over to the Chases' for dinner.

"Hello, all!" she called out as she let herself in with the packages she'd purchased that day. She put them under the gigantic tree in the formal living room and saw that the mound of presents had mutated and wondered what it would look like by Christmas Day when everyone in the family had added theirs. She smiled when she saw that Polly had knitted her a stocking and it was hanging next to Kyle's over the fireplace. A rush of warmth stole over her, she felt like she truly belonged. She had a place for the first time in her life.

"Hi, baby," Kyle said as he came into the room.

"Mmmm. What did I do to deserve that?" she asked dreamily after he'd kissed her thoroughly.

"You simply exist, Red. There's plenty more where that came from after we get home." He waggled his eyebrows. "Did you buy me lots and lots of presents?" He grinned, looking around her at the boxes she'd just put under the tree.

"You're bad, Kyle Chase. Spoiled-rotten bad." She laughed. "By the way, speaking of always getting what you want—I must have bumped into a dozen women who all pretended to care about me in order to ask about you. Checking on your availability." She snorted.

"I'm taken. Too bad for them. They'll have to deal with it."

Kyle knew it'd been a hard thing to deal with how women looked at him every time they were out but she'd done it. He showed her every day how much he loved her and wanted her and her only. She was finally in a place where she felt secure. That made him proud. And glad she knew she could always trust his commitment to her.

"Maggie, honey? Did I hear you come in?" Polly called out as she came around the corner.

"Hey, Mom, what's happening?" Maggie asked, getting up to hug her.

Polly shot her son a huge grin. Kyle knew it tickled her no end that Maggie had started calling her Mom. She was also over the moon about Kyle's plans to ask Maggie to marry him. Edward had asked Polly to marry him on Christmas Day. In fact, several Chase and Landry marriages started with a Christmas Day proposal.

Polly told them of the complicated chess game of organization of who slept where on Christmas Eve and Maggie volunteered her air mattress and trundle bed to help. She also offered to sleep in separate rooms from Kyle but he vetoed it and Polly refused, saying she was just fine with them in together. Polly wanted them both there together to celebrate her first Christmas with them.

It would be a stretch, but everyone would fit somehow and it would be lovely to share the morning together.

On Christmas Eve morning, Maggie woke up and stretched. Taking her time, she looked at the long naked lines of Kyle's body with a lazy smile. He was all hers. She got up quietly to run down and turn on the coffee maker before coming back up to shower.

"Hey, I think you missed a spot," Kyle said, stepping into the shower stall behind her. He took the sponge from her and soaped her back and down over the curves of her ass. He licked the cinnamon freckles of her shoulders and up her neck to her ear. He brought the sponge around and abraded her nipples with it, while tonguing her ear. Her eyes closed and she leaned back into him.

In her life she'd never felt so cherished and loved. His hands on her, his words in her ear wrapped around her heart. To belong to someone like Kyle had just never entered her imagination. Being loved like that was the finest gift life had ever granted her.

Rinsing herself off, she moved him around into the spray so she could do a bit of pampering herself. Stepping on the edge of the tub so she could reach him well, she washed his hair, gently massaging his scalp as she did. He held an arm wrapped around her waist to keep her steady. Afterward she scrubbed his back and legs and everything in between. And the in-between seemed quite pleased with the attention.

Her soap-slicked hands wrapped around his cock. Gaze locked with his, she watched his lips part and his pupils dilate as he thrust unashamedly into her grip. His free and easy acceptance of his sexuality turned her on immensely. He never hesitated to voice what he wanted or take what he needed.

Hot water rushed over them both, over her hands and arms and his cock until suddenly he picked her up and plunged inside of her. She cried out at the slice of sensation as he filled her up. He placed a foot on the edge of the tub to support her ass. Needing more of him, Maggie wrapped her thighs around his waist, opening herself up for him.

He slid in and out of her and she lost words for long moments. Her body arched, hands clutched his shoulders.

"I. Love. You." He spoke each word succinctly with his thrusts.

"Ohmigod. Iloveyoutoo," she rushed out in a gust of breath.

She looked into the sea green depths of his eyes and he felt like he was falling into her whiskey-colored ones. She opened herself to him, made herself vulnerable. It was raw then, tender and ferocious and what she was to him clutched his insides. He snaked a hand between them to find her clit, pressing a thumb over it in the way he knew she liked so much.

"Oh yes," she moaned out, her hips arching, moving on him. While he watched her face, he saw her eyes glass over. Her pussy rippled then, clutched him in that slick-hot embrace and climax hit, quicksilver from the base of his spine. He thrust and thrust and thrust as he poured into her, his forehead resting against her collarbone.

He stood there, muscles twitching, breathing hard and not noticing the passage of time until he felt the water run cold. Reluctantly, he pulled out and put her down.

"Oh God." He realized why she'd felt so good, so hot and tight.

"What?" she asked, turning off the water and grabbing a towel and drying his skin.

"I didn't put a condom on. I forgot. I brought one in here. It's on the counter. It's just when you ran your slick, soapy hands over me, I just lost it. I'm so sorry." He searched her face expecting her to be upset.

She sighed and smiled at him, slapping his ass. "It's all right. I wanted to make it a Christmas present but I went on the pill three weeks ago. It takes two weeks to work so I didn't want to say anything until the time was up. We both got tested for STDs, it's okay."

He exhaled in relief. "Oh God, you feel so good without a condom. I'm so glad we won't have to use them anymore. I wasn't sure how I could bear to go back to being covered while inside of you once I'd been there bare."

She kissed his chest and quickly dried herself off. "You do say the most unique but wonderful stuff, baby."

Laughing, he took the lotion bottle from her hands and applied it to her skin himself. "I won't be able to share a shower with you until we come back home so let me do this to tide myself over."

"It's just one night, Kyle. Sheesh."

He backed her into their bedroom. "But not being able to hear you scream out my name is going to be hard to live without. Even for just one night." His eyebrow went up and a frisson of lust twisted through her.

They ended up back in their bed for another forty-five minutes before stumbling up to get dressed.

The crowd at Polly and Edward's was insane. Kyle took their bag upstairs to their room while she headed into the family room where people covered every possible surface. They were all going to a Christmas Eve service at church and then coming back for dinner.

Nan and Pop were gushing over their new great-grandbaby and looking at Maggie and Kyle with sly smiles of expectation. Nan and Pop were Edward's parents. Pop was something of a local legend. A war hero in the Pacific who lost an eye, there were no less than three buildings and a street named after him. They took to Maggie right away. Pop was a terrible flirt and Nan just grinned at her and made unsubtle hints about great-grandchildren until Kyle just burst out laughing.

After the service, they laid out a huge buffet dinner of cold cuts and salads and then got down to the very serious business of game playing.

They cleared the dining room and set up some card tables in the family room. Two fast and furious games of canasta started. Kyle and Maggie were partners and their unspoken communication enabled them to kick butt. She saw that the Chase boys were as competitive at cards as they were in billiards.

In the end, after Kyle and Maggie won every round, Shane and Matt made a rule that they weren't ever to be on the same team at cards again.

Christmas morning was total chaos. Despite the fact that everyone there was in their mid-twenties or older, the rush to the tree was reminiscent of a bunch of seven-year-olds. Maggie's dad came over and settled in on the couch while Pop played Santa and handed out presents. The process took well over three hours as they waited while each person opened their present until the next one got distributed.

"This one is for Maggie, from Kyle." He brought a large box and sat it before her.

She ripped it open only to find another, slightly smaller box inside. Unwrapping that one, she saw yet another smaller box inside that one. She did it five more times until a small box remained. She looked down at it and saw the card tied to it. "Open Me First." She read it to herself.

Maggie, my heart never truly beat until the first time I touched your lips with my own. You are my everything. The air I breathe, the blood in my veins. You are my heart and my soul and I love you.

With tears welling up in her eyes she unwrapped the final package and saw the black velvet ring box. Stilling for a moment, she cracked it open with trembling hands, exposing a pear-cut solitaire diamond that was at least a carat. Her eyes widened and the room remained totally silent.

Kyle, who was already sitting at her feet, came up on one knee and took her ring from the box and then her left hand. "Margaret Elizabeth Wright, my sweet Red, will you do me the honor of marrying me?"

Her hands shook as she looked into his face and saw everything she'd ever wanted and dreamed of, sitting right there.

She nodded, tears running down her face. "Yes. Oh definitely," she said and he slid the ring on her left ring finger and a whoop of joy sprang up from several people around the room. Kyle hugged her to him tight and she saw he was crying, too.

"I love you so much, Kyle," she said into his ear.

"Ditto, sugar," he answered with a grin.

"Hot damn!" Matt exclaimed, a goofy smile on his face. "I've got the loveliest sister-in-law-to-be in the entire state of Georgia."

"Polly and I couldn't ask for a better daughter-in-law. You make our boy the happiest we've ever seen him. Thank you, sugar." Edward kissed her cheek and Polly, who stood at his side, weepy, nodded mutely.

She was on cloud nine for the rest of the day. Kyle loved the watch as well as his new golf club and the clothes and music she'd gotten him. She couldn't stop looking at how her ring sparkled on her hand as she sat outside on the porch after dinner watching the guys play a very rough game of football in the yard.

Shane came and sat beside her on the glider swing. The game had gentled a bit as they all had a few aches and pains. Many of the others had gone for an after-dinner walk.

Shane reached out and squeezed her hand. "Hey, Maggie, congratulations. I hope you and Kyle will be very happy together. He's a very lucky man to have a woman like you. I'm jealous."

"I think she's out there. The one for you. Waiting for you. When you find her, I hope you can open your heart enough to let her in."

"You think?"

"I really do."

He smiled and kissed her cheek and then yelped when the football Kyle had been throwing hit him in the head. "Hey!" He came up off the glider and headed down the steps.

"Hey yourself, lover boy. Keep your lips off my woman," Kyle taunted and then got tackled.

"Excuse me! What am I? A chew toy or something? Shane, get up off of him. Kyle…oh never mind!" she snapped and turned and stomped back into the house.

"You're in trouble," Marc taunted and got tackled in turn.

She was shoving her clothes into the overnight bag when he came upstairs. "Hey, are you really mad at me?"

"Last night you made that crack to Shane when we were playing cards. And I know you and your brothers joke a lot but the whole history between Shane and me is uncomfortable enough. When you make comments like 'you had your chance' or you tell him to keep his lips off me—when, by the way, he was congratulating me on our engagement—it just makes me feel like a thing instead of a person. You guys are competitive enough. I don't want to feel like I'm something to be fought over. And I don't want you disregarding what I have to say because you feel like you need to get even. It's not fair and it's not respectful."

He was quiet for a few moments, thinking over what she'd said. "I'm sorry, Red, I hadn't thought of it that way. I don't mean it like that. Although I do suppose I like to rub his nose in the fact that I could see you for the fabulous woman you are when he acted like a dick. I'll try hard not to do it anymore."

She looked at him and let go of the smile she'd been holding back. It was nearly impossible to stay mad at him. "Fine. See that you don't. Now, I was thinking that I'd go and swing by my house. I haven't been there in a week or so and I want to make sure everything is all right. We've had such cold temperatures that I want to be sure the pipes are okay."

"Maggie, you and I need to have a discussion about the house and our living situation. I'd like to set a date for the wedding, too."

"Okay. But not here." She held up her hands to quiet him. "No, it's not negotiable. I love your family but this is something I want to talk with you about *alone*. Why don't we talk about it tonight at your place."

"*Our* place. Move in with me, Maggie. You're practically living with me now. Sell your house and we can buy a place together. It's silly to have that great big house just sitting there empty and my place is going to be too small for us in the long run. We could live in your house but you seem to be a lot happier when you don't live there."

"It's true. I suppose that house has a lot of bad memories lurking around inside of it. Let's talk about this later all right? Honestly, you know someone is bound to come in here within the next three minutes and I don't want this to be a discussion by committee."

"Okay, sugar. Take my car over to your place and come back by to get me when you're done. I've got a game to finish with my brothers. Unless you want me to come to your place with you?"

"No, it's no big deal. I'm three minutes away, for goodness' sake. I need to grab some more clothes and check the pipes. I'll be there and back in less than an hour."

"Okay, Red." He kissed her and they walked out to the car.

Chapter Ten

She whipped into her driveway and gave a quick look around the outside of the house. The pipes looked fine but she got the insulation out of the garage and wrapped them, anyway. Especially as she'd already made the decision to accept Kyle's invitation and move in to his place so she wouldn't be around.

That done, she went inside and ran upstairs to grab some more clothes. She was zipping the garment bag when she heard steps behind her.

"Jeez, it's only been half an hour, couldn't live without me?" she teased and turned around. Only it wasn't Kyle, it was Alex standing there and a chill of dread slid through her gut.

"I can't live without you, Maggie. You're mine and I'm yours. Can't you see that? Why aren't you home anymore?"

"What the hell are you doing here! Get out of my house now or I'll call the police." She tried to edge her way closer to the phone on the bedside table.

"I'm here to take back what's mine," he said in a strange sing-song voice, inching toward her. "What is that?" He grabbed her hand and stared at the ring. "No!" He pulled it off and threw it on the bed.

"Stop that!" She reached for her ring and the world went

black for a moment. When she came to he was dragging her out of the room. A surge of strength and will to survive surged through her and she grabbed the wall near the door and tried to hold on but he yanked her loose. He half dragged her, half carried her down the stairs. Reaching down he slapped her across her face, hard, when she kept grabbing the spindles on the banister to stop him. Her head hit each stair, and her world hovered gray as she fought to keep conscious. She tried to yell but all she could do was moan and hoarsely whisper at him to stop.

"I'm taking you away from here, away from those meddling Chase boys. Now be a good girl and walk out of here. I don't want anyone getting suspicious." He yanked her upright and held her by the hair and she tried to kick him but got the leg of the table instead and knocked it over. Weeping now, she tried to grab at the doorway to hold on but he elbowed her in the face and the darkness fell over her again.

After two hours Kyle began to really get worried. "What could be taking so long? She said she'd be back in less than an hour and it's been nearly two," Kyle grumbled to Matt and Shane. Most likely she'd bumped into Liv and they were chatting about the engagement and he was worrying over nothing. Still, he had a strange feeling about it that only got worse as the minutes passed.

"Why don't we take a drive over there? Maybe she had problems with the pipes. If so, you know how she is, she's probably trying to do it all herself," Matt said laughing.

"Yeah, let's. It's not like her to not call if she's going to be held up."

They pulled up and saw the Saturn in the drive. "She's still here."

"Stay here," Shane said and was out of the car before it had stopped. Kyle, sensing that something was wrong, got out too, following his brother. The front door was wide-open and the table near the entry was on its side, the glass vase and bowl that sat upon it broken, pieces all over the place.

There was blood on the doorjamb. A bloody handprint. "Jesus. Where is she?" Kyle meant to yell but it came out as a whisper. He was suddenly cold.

"Go back to Matt's car. Call the station on your cell phone and tell them I said to send out a car with two officers. On the double." Reaching back, he took his gun out of the shoulder holster he had on.

"No, I'm coming in."

Shane turned and shoved Kyle, hard. "No you are not, damn it. This is my job, Kyle. Do what I tell you and do it now. You're endangering me and her by not listening." He turned away, closing the discussion, and slowly walked into the house.

Matt approached and Kyle turned and ran to him. "Call the station now! Tell them that Shane said to send out a car with two officers, on the double." Matt nodded and got on his cell phone. Kyle began to pace.

Back in the house, Shane walked up the stairs. The sight of the blood on the light-colored carpet runner sped his heart. He crept along, listening for any sound but heard none. Entering Maggie's bedroom he saw the bedside table had been overturned and blood on the floor and then on the wall near the door, as if someone had grabbed it to hold on and pull away from someone dragging them. He walked in carefully, not wanting to disturb evidence, and he saw Maggie's engagement ring on the center of the bed. He swept the rest of the room and the upstairs but found nothing. By the time he came downstairs, the other officers had arrived and had gone through the first floor.

Kyle couldn't seem to stop shaking as he waited out on the front lawn. Matt was with him, an arm around his shoulder. Seeing Shane come out of the house broke Kyle's stillness and he ran over. "Where is she, Shane? Is she all right?"

"She's not here. Kyle, I'm going to tell you what I saw in

there but I need you to hold it together, okay?" Stunned, Kyle nodded and Shane exhaled before continuing. "There's blood in several places. Her ring is on the bed. There was a garment bag of clothes but it's on the floor like she dropped it. Kyle, it looks like there was a struggle. There's a blood trail from the bedroom, down the stairs and to the front door. The officers are taking blood samples so that we can run a match. Thank goodness we got that grant money to have better lab equipment here, but it will still take time to identify the blood and the bloody handprints at the doorway. Kyle, the handprints are very small though. I'm guessing they're Maggie's. I think she was attacked and taken."

Kyle's eyes went wild, his heart threatened to burst through his chest in terror for her. "No! Damn it, Shane, find her!"

Shane grabbed Kyle's upper arms and got in his face. "Keep it together, Kyle. She was still alive when he got her to the door. That handprint shows she tried to fight. She won't give up, Kyle, remember that."

"It's Alex, you know that! Find him."

"I think so, too. I've called the judge and asked for a warrant to search Alex's apartment and he granted it. We're going to go over there now."

"Okay, let's go."

"No, Kyle, you can't. This is police business. I can't take the risk of you losing it and messing with evidence. Go back to the condo or to Mom and Dad's. Heck, raise a search party. But *do not* go to Alex Parsons' house." He paused. "We will find her, Kyle."

He turned and stalked off, getting into the squad car he took with another officer recently arrived.

Matt hugged his brother tightly. "Let's go back to Mom and Dad's to get people out looking. We'll drive Nan and Pop to your place in case she shows up and Grammy and Gramps can stay at Mom's in case she comes there."

* * *

Polly was beside herself but Edward and Peter helped by organizing everyone. Polly stayed back with her parents and Nan and Pop went over to the condo to wait there. They split up and took opposite sides of town to search. They all had cell phones with them and a description of Alex's car.

Shane called in to tell Kyle that Alex had taken a suitcase and some clothes. Dee was at the bank, checking the records to see if he'd pulled any large amounts of cash out of his account recently.

"Kyle, it's bad. There are more pictures here. Of the two of you. His walls are covered with pictures of her and there are stacks of letters everywhere that he'd written to her but never sent. His obsession with her has grown."

Kyle hung up, shaking with rage, terror burning the backs of his eyes. He looked at Matt who was there with him. "If that bastard hurts her in any way, I'll kill him."

"I'll help you. But she's going to be all right," Matt said, hoping he wasn't lying.

Maggie woke up in a strange room, disoriented. Her head hurt like hell. Blinking to try and clear her vision so she could figure out where she was, she quailed when Alex came into her line of sight. Suddenly, memory of what happened earlier rushed back, filling her with terror.

"Alex, please, let me go. This is crazy. Let me go and I won't call the cops, I promise." She desperately tried to recall the advice from the self-defense course she'd taken the year before.

He laughed and kissed her forehead and she tried not to show her revulsion. "Oh sweetheart, I'm not letting you go. You're mine, silly. I'm sorry I had to hit you. Is your head all right?" Maggie tried not to panic as she listened to him. His voice was so odd, dreamy and high-pitched. It frightened her, filled her with dread. He was obviously insane.

"What do you think, Alex? Can you untie my hands at least? My shoulders really hurt and this angle is making my back twist."

"No, I can't risk it. But I'll help you sit up and get you some Tylenol for your head." He gently moved her into a sitting position and left the room, coming back with a glass of water and two tablets. "Here. Open your mouth and I'll help you."

She clamped her lips shut tight and shook her head. God only knew whether or not he'd drugged or poisoned the water or even if the pills were actually Tylenol.

"Maggie, why are you being so difficult? Look." He held the pill up so she could see the factory stamp and he brought the bottle in as well. "See, here's the bottle. The water is from the tap. It's well water. The cabin is on a well. I wouldn't hurt you, Maggie. You can trust me."

She narrowed her eyes at that ridiculous statement.

"Suit yourself, then," he said with a sigh. He set the glass and the pills down. "Let me know if you change your mind. Seems silly to hurt out of spite."

She snorted but didn't say anything else.

When he reached out to caress her face, she shrank back as far as she could go until she hit the wall. Nausea and revulsion roiled in her gut, fear threatened to drown her. She gave herself a mental slap. She had to keep it together if she was going to get out of this mess.

"I love you, Maggie. I just want to touch you."

"Alex, get away from me. This has gone far enough. Take me home."

"You are home. Our home." He smiled dreamily and got up.

"Where are we?"

"This is our cabin. Our honeymoon cabin," he answered and walked out of the room.

She felt woozy and her world became fuzzier and fuzzier until at last, she lost consciousness again.

* * *

It was three in the morning and many of the Chase household slept on couches and sitting up in chairs. Kyle, his brothers, father, his uncle and Maggie's father were in the dining room sitting at the table, looking at pictures.

"Damn it! Where is she!" Kyle raged. They'd stayed out searching for hours and had found nothing.

Shane had come back to report on the situation. They had surveillance camera footage from the ATM machine at the bank. Alex took the maximum two-thousand-dollar withdrawal. In the background, after they'd blown it up, Maggie was clearly lying against the front seat, her eyes closed, a bloody trickle from her scalp down her face.

"Kyle, this was at five twelve, about forty-five minutes after she'd left here. We've narrowed the time frame down considerably. At least we know roundabout when she was taken."

"But she could be d-dead by that time. Her eyes are closed," he replied, barely containing a sob. Edward moved to hold his son, bracing him with his arm around his shoulders, lending him strength.

"Son, if he'd killed her, he'd have gotten rid of the body. She was probably unconscious. She was alive then, we have every reason to think she's alive now. Alex is obsessed with her. He doesn't want to kill her. He wants to possess her. She's a smart cookie, she'll do what she has to to stay alive."

"And what will that be, Daddy? What will he do to my girl?" Kyle whispered. "We have to find her. Where could he have taken her? God, I never should have let her go over there alone. We were talking about buying a house together. About her moving into my condo and selling her place and buying our own."

"That's it," Shane said, looking up at Edward. "Daddy, can you run a title search? See if Alex has bought any property in this and the surrounding few counties since September?"

Peter stood up. "I can. Let me run into the office and check," he said, looking relieved to be able to help in some way and Shane followed him out the door.

Polly came into the room. "Honey, it's three in the morning, why don't you get some sleep? We'll wake you if anything changes." She stroked a hand over his hair, trying to comfort him.

Kyle stood up. "I can't sleep while Maggie is out there being held by that sick bastard!" he shouted and Edward hugged him tightly and Kyle broke down and wept.

Tom went to him. "Listen to me, son. My little girl has been on her own, out of necessity, for most of her life. She's independent and she will not quit. I promise you that. She's strong, my baby. She won't let herself be killed, boy. Not without a fight. You keep that ring for her because she will be back here and she'll want it back."

Pulling himself together, Kyle took a deep breath and looked at the engagement ring he'd been wearing on his pinkie finger. He locked eyes with his father-in-law-to-be and nodded.

When Maggie woke up again, the throbbing in her head had subsided to a dull ache. She opened her eyes carefully but it was still dark. Judging by the position of the moon that she could see through the window, it was sometime between midnight and about four a.m. Alex lay next to her on the bed, his arm curled around her thighs. She shuddered in disgust.

Think, Maggie! How can you get out of this? She tried pulling at the ropes that held her hands but that just made them tighter and her movement roused Alex.

"Maggie, honey? Are you all right?"

"I have to go to the bathroom."

"Oh of course! Let me help."

He got up and helped her to stand and led her to the bathroom. The cabin was large and modern. That was a hopeful sign that they weren't out too far into the middle of nowhere, Georgia. He opened the door and started to undo her pants.

"No! Jesus. Get off me. Untie my hands, Alex, and wait for me out there. The window in here is too small and too high up, I couldn't get through it even if I could get up there. Let me have some dignity."

Alex sighed. "I'll untie you, Maggie. But I have a gun and if you try anything funny I will shoot you. Do you understand?"

"Yes. Now untie me."

He did and stepped back, looking at his watch. "You have two minutes and I'm coming in."

She moved her fingers a bit, getting the blood back into them, and went to the bathroom quickly. Not knowing when he'd decide to barge in, she got re-dressed and washed her hands and then her face, which had bloodstains all down the left side. She had a bump the size of a softball on the back of her head and another smaller one on her upper forehead, just at the hairline.

She noticed that he seemed to take it all right when she was a bit bossy but she knew he wouldn't take too much. She had to bide her time. The longer that she was there, the more time she had to think and plan. And hopefully, the more time Kyle would have to find her. She decided to be extra obedient. She wouldn't try to run just yet, she had to get her bearings back but she needed him to let her stay untied. She called out to him. "I'm done and I'm going to open the door now."

She did, slowly, and held her hands up for Alex to see.

"You cleaned off your face. I'm sorry, I meant to do it for you but I fell asleep. Let's go back to bed. I'm tired and you need to rest your head."

"All right," she agreed meekly and hoped he forgot about the ropes.

He didn't. "Maggie, I need to retie you."

"Please don't. My wrists are all raw and it hurts my back, neck and shoulders to have to sit that way." She tried very hard not to beg.

"I can't trust you not to run."

"Then tie me in the front and wrap something around my wrists to go between my skin and the rope. Please."

She wanted to seem reasonable but not have a turnabout of behavior that would be unbelievable either. She had to gain control of the situation.

He studied her. "Fine." He got out some face cloths and put them around the abrasions on her wrists and then bound her wrists in front. The price was that she had to lie down beside him. It took every bit of her will to survive not to scream in terror and revulsion as he put his face in the nape of her neck and his breath skated across her skin.

Kyle, where are you?

"We got it!" Shane burst in through the door. "He bought a cabin about two hours east of here six weeks ago. I've called the judge. It's still in this county, and he's issued a warrant for arrest and a search warrant. It's in an unincorporated area, no local police force so I'm taking my men out with me. We'll meet the cops from the nearest jurisdiction to make a joint raid on the house."

"I'm coming, too," Kyle said and Shane started to disagree until he saw the set of Kyle's mouth.

"You may wait outside the police line if you promise not to get involved. I mean it, Kyle. You can't interfere, you could get her or yourself or one of my men killed if you don't obey me." Kyle nodded.

"I'll drive him," Matt said and Edward grabbed his keys and he and Tom got into the back seat of Matt's Bronco. Soon they all tore out of the driveway, heading east.

They drove at eighty miles an hour and made the two-hour drive in under an hour and a half. Shane and his officers met with the local sheriff. Kyle watched, tense as his brother and his men all donned body armor and began their silent creep through the woods. They'd stopped their vehicles about a mile away from the cabin so they could approach it unseen.

* * *

Maggie was lying in bed, trying to think up a plan. Her muscles ached from holding still but she didn't want any movement to wake him up. The sun was rising and Maggie figured it was about seven or seven thirty. She sighed without meaning to and Alex stirred.

His eyes opened and stared into hers with an eerie light. He brought his hand up and cupped her breast and she screamed.

He hit her in the face. "Shut up, you whore! Why are you acting so afraid? It's not like you haven't fucked half the town already. Everyone but me. You led me on and I can't have that. You're mine, Maggie." He squeezed her breast hard and she bit back a whimper.

"Get off me, you bastard. I don't want you, damn it! There are plenty of other women in town. Date them and leave me alone!" She looked around the room for a weapon, anything she could use to stop him.

"I don't think so," he snarled and ripped at her shirt, sending buttons flying and exposing her bra and her bare stomach. "I mean to have what's mine."

"No! *No, Alex!*" Struggling and screaming, she turned her head and saw a face in the window. He held his finger up to his lips, indicating she should stay quiet about his presence.

Alex ripped at the fastenings of her pants and she kicked at him and tried to raise her hands but her wrists were still bound and he had them pinned with one hand, while the other was pulling at her clothes.

"Get off me, you bastard!" She screamed. She screamed and she screamed and he slapped her again, so hard she tasted blood. He ripped at the front of her bra and it came open, baring her breasts, and she began to weep. "Stop it, damn it! I don't want this."

"Doesn't matter," he muttered and unzipped his pants and started to pull himself out.

Suddenly, the door slammed open and several large men in

body armor poured in pointing guns and screaming, "Get down! Get off the woman, now!"

Shane stepped forward and yanked Alex off of her and threw him across the room. Another officer came to her and gently pulled the sheet from the bed around her, covering her nakedness.

"Are you all right, ma'am?" the officer asked softly.

She started to tremble, shaking so hard her teeth chattered.

"Did he rape you?"

"N-n-no. He—he tried b-b-b-but you s-s-s-stopped h-h-him," she stuttered out.

Shane came forward and looked her over. "Maggie, honey? I just need to look at you. Make sure you aren't injured." He gently opened the sheet and winced as he saw the hand-and-finger-shaped bruise on her left breast but he felt relief seeing that her panties were still on. "Honey, we don't have any female officers here but I want to get pictures taken of you and your injuries. Will you let me do it? Officer Jeffries here will stay in the room but he won't look at you when I have to take the pictures of your breasts. I'm sorry to even ask it of you but it's necessary for the case."

Tears running down her face, she nodded, still trembling. She went into another place in her head as he took pictures of her face, neck and her wrists and then of her torn clothes and the bruise on her breast.

Shane did it as quickly and methodically as he could but he couldn't fight the rising bile, the anguish over what she'd gone through.

"All done, honey. I'm going to wrap you in this blanket here. It's a blanket from my car, not his. I'm going to take you out to where Kyle's waiting for you. He's been so worried. And then we're going to take you to a hospital." He spoke to her calmly and softly as he touched her carefully.

Sobs tore through her stomach. "Kyle's here?"

"Of course he is, Maggie. He threatened to kneecap me if

I didn't let him come with me. Come on, honey, let's get you taken care of."

Nodding, she stood still while he gently put the blanket around her and picked her up. He held her against his body and carried her the mile back to where the cars were.

Her eyes were closed but she heard Kyle say "thank you, God" and come moving toward her.

"Thank you for saving me," she said softly to Shane and he nodded and handed her over to Kyle.

"We need to get her to a hospital. Kyle, you ride in the back with her. Dad, you all follow us."

Maggie opened her eyes but one of them was pretty near swollen shut and she had to close that one. "Kyle, he...oh God," she whispered and began to cry.

"I'm here, Red. Always here. God, I love you so much. Hell, I'm so damned thankful you're okay. We'll get through this, baby." He stroked gentle fingers over her hair.

They checked her into the hospital. She had a concussion and they wanted to monitor her at least for the next twenty-four hours.

Alex had been transported to jail and awaited arraignment on kidnapping, false imprisonment, attempted rape and assault charges in addition to violating the two orders of no-contact.

Maggie slept but they woke her up every hour to check on the concussion. She was feeling loopy from the lack of REM sleep and the rush of adrenaline her body had produced over the last day.

Kyle never left her side and he looked almost as bad as she did. The whole Chase clan was splayed across every available surface in the waiting room as were Maggie's father and her friends. Maggie's father had called her mother to tell her what had happened but she'd expressed disinterest in the whole situation.

Finally, after twenty-four hours, the hospital discharged Maggie and Kyle carefully loaded her into Matt's Bronco and they drove back home.

She stared out the window and he looked at his father with a worried expression. When they neared Petal, Matt asked, "Where to, sweetheart? Momma wanted me to tell you that you're welcome to stay with her and Daddy until you felt better. I figure you and Kyle might like some time alone. I can take you to your house, too. Just tell me where and I'll go."

"Not my house, not ever," she said, panic at the edges of her voice. "Take me to the condo please, Matt. If that's okay with you, Kyle."

"Of course it is, Red. Whatever you want, baby." Kyle looked back at Edward and his father's eyes softened at the sound of anguish in Maggie's voice.

All three men helped her into the house, even though she was perfectly capable of walking. She let them fuss over her a bit and thanked Matt and Edward for their help. She turned to Edward as he was leaving. "They won't let him go will they?"

"Honey, I want you to know I am on the prosecutor's ass about this. He was denied bail at his arraignment. I don't foresee that changing. Alex will do time. They'll charge him with everything they can, I promise you. Oh baby, I'm sorry," he said and swept her into an embrace.

She nodded up at him and blinked back tears. "Thanks, Dad," she whispered and his heart nearly broke in half.

She looked at Kyle and kissed the hand holding hers. "I'm going to take a shower and change. I'll be down in a few minutes."

"Hey, Red, afterward we'll get tucked up on the couch. I'll order in Chinese and we'll get pay-per-view. Holler if you need me all right?" Kyle asked gently and she nodded and walked up the stairs.

"Daddy, I know Momma wants to come over but can we hold off for at least a day? I can't see that she's got much reserve left to go on right now."

"Yes, I'll talk to her. You take care of my future daughter-in-law you hear? And yourself, too. You look like hell. I love you, son." Edward hugged Kyle tightly.

"I want to kill him, Daddy. She has a bruise in the shape of his hand on her breast. He gave her a concussion. He tried to rape her. Damn it, I want his blood!"

Matt grabbed his brother's arm. "She needs you, Kyle. I know you're angry. We all are. But you have to deal with this so you can help her through. We'll do all we can to be sure he does time but you can't go off half-cocked because she needs you. Now, do you have to work tomorrow? Marc, Shane and I will do shifts here with her around your schedule if you need us."

"No, I don't have anything until next week. She's due back in class on the third, we'll see how it goes. I want to wait to talk with her until she's had a chance to settle in. Thank you, though."

"We'll go and leave you two be."

Kyle watched them drive away and then called and ordered dinner, built a fire and went to change his own clothes. Worried that she still wasn't out of the bathroom, he went and knocked softly on the door. "Honey? Can I help you with anything?"

"No." She sniffed and pulled herself together. She'd scrubbed her skin for the last fifteen minutes and she still couldn't get the feeling of his hands off her skin.

"Maggie, I'm going to come in now," Kyle said seriously and slowly opened the door to see her sitting in the shower, the water still on. "Honey, let's get you out of there," he said gently and turned the water off. He hadn't seen her naked and the sight of all of the bruises she bore made his stomach tighten with rage. He dried her carefully and helped her get her clothes on and led her downstairs.

They ate from the cartons and watched a comedy and he massaged her temples as she lay tucked into his body. She looked at her ring, back safely on her finger. "You know, you don't have to marry me if you don't want to."

He moved so that she was facing him. "What? Why on earth wouldn't I want to marry you?"

"Well, I mean, I'm trouble. I can sense that you feel differently about my body. You're angry with me. I swear that I didn't do anything to lead him on."

"Oh my God, Maggie, how could you think that I'd ever imagine that what happened to you was your fault? Of course you didn't do a damned thing to deserve what he did to you! No woman who's been raped ever does. And I don't feel differently about you or your body. I just want to kill him when I see what he's done to you. I love you—God, I love you so much. I thought I'd die when I saw the bloody handprint that you left on your front door. I failed you. Maybe you don't want me because I didn't protect you. I should have gone with you to your house that night. I could have protected you." He started crying.

"I want to kill him, too," she whispered and kissed his tears away. "You didn't fail me. You didn't give up. You saved me. I love you, too."

He led her upstairs and sheltered her with his body as they got into bed. For the first time in several days she felt safe enough to sleep.

Chapter Eleven

Maggie walked into the conference room at city hall and total silence fell. "Hi, everyone. I brought the spreadsheets from last year's auction, I thought they might be helpful," she said, trying to keep a professional tone in her voice.

Kyle took a seat away from the table and pulled out a book. He attempted to pretend he didn't want to run interference for her with the Historical Society members seated around the table. All of whom looked at her with shock and pity.

"I'm glad you're here, honey," Maude Sheckley said and got up to hug her. "I'm glad you're all right."

"Thank you, Maude. I am too," Maggie said softly.

In the following moments, every member of the Society got up and gave Maggie a hug and the tension was broken. People were laughing and joking around when the click-clack of high heels on the wood hallway greeted their ears. Suddenly, the talking stopped. Polly swept into the room, gave Maggie a quick kiss and went to her seat at the head of the table, gave her hair a fluff and threw her massive purse down.

"Evenin', all. Did Maggie tell you that she's now engaged to my son, Kyle?"

The room once again erupted in chatter and Maggie smiled

as she showed off the ring. Kyle gave them all a wave and went back to his book.

They discussed the auction and other Society business and finally adjourned at eight. Kyle accepted hugs and congratulations from everyone and finally reached Maggie and his mother. "You ladies hungry? I'd love to take my two best girls to dinner."

Maggie froze up. She hadn't been out of the condo much in the last two weeks. She worried about facing the townspeople.

"Honey, this is your home. People here love you. I'm starving, let's go to The Sands and get some food," Polly said gently.

"All right," Maggie said taking a bracing breath.

It was late enough that the place wasn't full to the seams with patrons but still had plenty of folks inside. Ronnie Sands, the owner, got them into a booth and squeezed Maggie's hand. "Hi, honey, good to see you." She looked down and saw the ring. "Oh my! Is this what I think it is?"

"Ronnie, this lovely woman has agreed to marry me. Am I lucky or what?"

"Isn't that wonderful! Congratulations, you two. When's the day?"

"He only asked me on Christmas and then...well, anyway. We haven't even discussed it yet," Maggie said and Ronnie's face softened.

"I was hoping that we could do it in late spring," Kyle said.

"Ooh! Good idea, the weather will be so pretty." Ronnie grinned and looked to Maggie. "Shall I get you all the usual?"

"Sounds good. Make my fries extra crispy, please."

"Of course, girl. I've been serving you fries for a long time. Be back in a bit with your food and teas." She winked and headed back to the kitchen.

"Where should we have the ceremony?" Kyle asked.

Maggie narrowed her eyes at Kyle. She did not want to do this with an audience. But he was just so damned excited about it, she couldn't really be mad at him. "If we do it in late spring, say after Mother's Day, we could easily do it outside." Maggie hoped Polly would rein in her impulse to take over.

"Hmm, yes that could be nice. We could do tents for the reception. Where though? We could use the park I suppose." He had the sense to look a bit chastened as he saw her narrowed eyes.

Oh well, in for a penny, may as well be in for a pound. Maggie took a deep breath. "Or your parents' backyard. It's over an acre." She looked to Polly. "That is, if it would be all right with them."

"Honey, you're too good to be true!" Polly exclaimed, clapping her hands.

"But, Momma, remember that this is *our* wedding, yeah? So we'd love your *help* and appreciate your *advice* but Maggie and I need to make a lot of decisions for ourselves." Kyle squeezed Maggie's hand beneath the table.

Polly snorted. "Of course! I won't try and take over."

It was Maggie's turn to snort and she tried to pretend she didn't and Polly just laughed. "Okay, so you know me well, dear heart, but I promise, I do know what it is like to be a bride and I'd never want to take that joy from you. But I do want to tell you that I consider you a daughter. And well, I know that your own momma is a fool so please come to me whenever you need a hand all right?"

"Thanks, Mom, I appreciate that so much."

"So the Saturday after Mother's Day at Mom and Dad's house. We have a date and a place," Kyle said.

"I'd like to get my dress made, which doesn't leave much time seeing as how it's already January. Dee's mom just finished making her dress and it's amazing. I wonder if she'd make mine? I'll have to talk to her about it. We need to talk guest lists and color schemes and flowers and food. We need to deal with the invitations and the rentals for the tents as well.

Oh my, so much to do." Maggie broke out a pad and a pen and Kyle watched smiling as she and his mother started talking all of the details over.

Kyle and his brothers moved all of Maggie's belongings out of her house and she put it on the market. In the meantime, he and Maggie looked for a place of their own and soon found a four-bedroom near the river that they fell in love with.

Maggie went to counseling both alone and with Kyle for a while to deal with what happened with Alex. It helped a great deal.

The invitations went out in March and Alex's trial approached. Maggie prepared her students for finals and decided on a caterer, she had dress fittings and chose flowers. Kyle converted the first-floor bedroom into an office space for both of them. He chose tuxedos with his brothers and asked Shane to be his best man. Maggie asked Edward to walk her down the aisle with her own father. She wanted them both to give her away. Cecelia and Janie were not invited.

The trial happened to fall on the week of spring break so Maggie planned to be there every day. Kyle also took time off and the entire Chase clan and Tom Wright were there to support her although Maggie couldn't attend until after she testified, the same with the others.

Testifying was awful. It was fine when the prosecution was examining her but when Alex's attorney got up it was just horrible. He tried to twist her words, to make it seem like she'd led Alex on and that she'd run away with him on her own instead of being kidnapped. He also tried to make it seem like the bruises were due to rough sex and not assault. Thank goodness Edward and Peter had helped her by doing a little role play and showing her what it would be like before the trial. She managed to keep on task and to not let herself get too riled up. The other women that Alex had stalked when he was a student at the University of Georgia testified to his behavior.

Alex did not testify in his own defense as Edward told her he probably wouldn't. The defense case was relatively short and was essentially an argument that everything that happened was consensual. Which—in light of the testimony from the women who'd been stalked by Alex, her own testimony, the pictures and medical testimony of her injuries, signs of struggle at her home, and the testimony of the police who came to the cabin and saw her screaming and trying to fight him off—seemed ridiculous.

It only took the jury forty-five minutes to come back with a guilty verdict and Maggie sobbed in relief. Liv and Dee and a great many other people from Petal had come out to the trial and they all burst into applause and the judge had to pound his gavel to shut them all up.

The sentencing phase would be decided by the judge and he scheduled a hearing the following week to hand down his decision. When they returned, Alex was sentenced to seven years in prison. Edward explained that was pretty good considering but Maggie snorted, wishing he'd be in prison for life.

Chapter Twelve

The morning of May twenty-third arrived and Maggie awoke smiling. It was her wedding day. She spent the night at Liv's place and Kyle was at his parents'. Dee came over first thing and brought breakfast while Liv did their hair.

"Phone for you, hon, it's your husband-to-be." Liv handed the phone to her and she went back to artfully pinning up her curls and lacing flowers and ribbon through it all.

"Hi, honey! Not having second thoughts are you?" she asked with a laugh.

"Hey, Red, no way. Although I just want to say, yet again, how stupid I think it was to make me sleep alone last night. I haven't slept alone since November. I don't like it."

"Stop whining. It's the last time you'll have to. I didn't want you to see my dress until the ceremony. I want it to be a surprise."

"Okay, I'm sure it'll be worth it. I sure do love you, Red."

"Me too, baby. I have to go. Liv's doing my hair and the phone is in the way. I'll see you in an hour."

"Can't wait."

Maggie hung up and sighed. "He's so wonderful."

"Oh lawd! I thought the weekly Arthur-is-wonderful updates were bad!" Liv joked.

"Are you talking about my boy?" Polly flounced into the room.

"Hey, Mom. Of course we were talking about Kyle. My, don't you look pretty!"

"Thanks, doll. What can I do?"

"I'm done here. Let's help her get into the dress."

Maggie's dress was antique white silk and satin. Sleeveless, with tiny embroidered French-blue flowers along the neckline. The back had a small V in it with the same embroidered flowers. It gathered into a pleat at the small of her back and the material flowed down and made a modest pool of silk as a train. She opted against a veil and chose to wind flowers and ribbon in her hair. Her bouquet was of silver roses and white magnolias. As a present for Kyle later, she had on a gorgeous cream-colored bustier-and-garter set underneath with pale silk stockings.

Dee and Liv wore French-blue dresses of mid-calf length and the groom was wearing a dove-gray morning coat with his tuxedo.

"Look at you, girl," Liv whispered as they got her all fastened inside of the dress and she stood before the mirror.

Maggie smiled as she looked at them all. "We sure do clean up nice."

"I almost forgot. Here." Polly handed a velvet jeweler's box to Maggie. "This is from Kyle."

She opened the box and softly gasped when she saw the pair of sapphire-and-diamond earrings inside. The note said, *something blue and something new.* She put them on and they sparkled in her ears.

"Now for something borrowed," Polly said, "as well as old." She handed her a velvet pouch and Maggie opened it and a diamond bracelet came out. "My mother let me borrow this on my wedding day and then she gave it to me when I had Shane. So today, you'll borrow it from me. And when you and Kyle have your first child, it'll be yours."

Maggie fanned her face. "Oh lord, you're going to make me cry and ruin Liv's makeup job! Thank you so much!"

Edward and Tom waited on the front porch as Liv, Dee, Polly and Maggie arrived.

"You look beautiful, hon," her father said.

Edward kissed her cheek and winked at Polly. "You sure do. Kyle is a lucky boy." He called for Matt and Marc who were going to walk with Dee and Liv. She'd asked Polly to be her matron of honor and Shane came to escort her. All three Chase brothers looked at her and cracked grins.

"Wow! You look amazing, Maggie. Absolutely gorgeous," Marc said.

"I'm an idiot," Shane grumbled and Polly nodded and patted his arm.

"You look beautiful, Liv," Matt said and Maggie smiled at the chemistry that always brewed between those two.

"Let's rock, people," she said and they all went to the back doors and the music started as Polly and Shane walked out, followed by Liv and Matt, Dee and Marc.

Suddenly the music changed and she put her hands in the arms of her escorts and stepped outside and everyone stood. She looked out at the gathered crowd of friends and neighbors and then, up to the arbor where Kyle stood, smiling at her.

Kyle's heart stopped when she stepped out onto the back porch. Her dress molded to her body, her hair pinned up in artfully reckless curls and filled with flowers. She looked fey and wholesome and yet earthy and sexy all at once. And she was all his. Her smile flashed at him and he began to breathe again.

Both Tom and Edward placed her hand in his and the rest of the ceremony went by in a haze. Kyle pushed the platinum band onto her finger until it slid home against the ring she already wore and spoke the words that bound their lives together under civil law. She spoke the same words back as she slid a matching band onto his finger.

The minister, who'd married Polly and Edward and presided at the baptisms of each of the Chase children, smiled at Maggie and Kyle and gently turned them to face the crowd of friends and family. "I'd like to introduce Kyle and Margaret Chase."

Kyle's arm encircled his wife's shoulders and he steered her back into the house for a few brief moments of silence and solitude. "I love you, wife," he said, kissing her lips.

"And I love you, husband," she murmured back.

Epilogue

Six months later

It was a Friday night and Maggie, Liv and Dee were all at their usual table at The Pumphouse. Dee was drinking a Perrier because she was six months pregnant with the child she and Arthur conceived the night of Maggie and Kyle's wedding.

Maggie watched Kyle as he bent over to take a shot, hooting as he made it and smacking Shane in the head with the tip of his pool cue. He turned around, feeling her gaze, and shot her a look of total unadulterated lust and longing. Her pulse quickened and she smiled wickedly, raising her glass to him in promise.

"Oh God, the two of you!" Liv muttered.

"What?" Maggie asked, laughing. "You expect me to have that in my bed and not have this look on my face?"

"Point taken. I should go, my sister is coming in from Crawford in an hour and I want to pick up my house a bit."

Liv's sister Bea was coming to stay with her for a while, licking her wounds from a bad breakup and a lost job. Maggie smiled when she saw Matt cock his head and give Liv a wave and Liv blush and wave back.

"Night then, Livvy. You know, Matt isn't dating Nancy anymore."

"That so? Huh. Perhaps you and Kyle should have a barbecue, you know, a Thanksgiving thing. Give Bea a chance to get back into the swing of things in Petal again."

"And you a chance to hang out with Matt?"

"Something like that."

"All right. I'll call you with the details."

Dee shoved herself out of the booth and Liv helped her stand up. "Arthur is here to pick me up, I'll see you later." She kissed them both and went to her husband who was waiting patiently at the door.

Maggie turned and walked through the crowd to where the pool tables were. She hopped up on a high stool, watching Kyle who tossed his cue to Matt and grabbed her. "Night, all. See you Sunday," he called out and pulled Maggie out the front door and practically shoved her into the car.

"Now, I was thinking, Red, that there was a back road with our name on it. I just happen to have the sleeping bags in the back, along with a picnic basket full of food and some sparkling cider. What do you say, wanna neck under the stars?"

She leaned in and caught his lips with her own, pulling his bottom lip between her teeth. "Mm hm. I'll follow you anywhere. I might even let you get to second base."

He threw his head back and laughed and they drove off, heading for that country road.

* * * * *

Taking Chase

Chapter One

For the first time in years Cassie Gambol felt as if she wasn't being watched. She couldn't remember the last time that had been true. But as she drove down Main Street in tiny, way off the map, Petal, Georgia, her muscles relaxed just a bit.

It was Friday night yet most of the businesses along the street were closed but for the restaurants and what looked to be a bar or tavern. The place was pretty quaint. Definitely not Los Angeles. But that was okay. It was off the beaten path and that was where she needed to be.

The last thing she needed or wanted was for Terry to find her. Ever. She planned to keep her head down and get on with her life. Because she *was* alive and that wasn't something she'd take for granted ever again.

While she was stopped at a red light, she looked down to check the address she'd written down. She had no clue that the giant Cadillac was heading right for her until it rear-ended her, slamming her car into the intersection.

Muzzy but rising back toward full consciousness, Cassie did a mental inventory of her body. Everything seemed to be in working order. She could move her fingers and her toes. Great, teach her to relax her muscles.

The airbag deploying kept her from getting her head split open by the steering wheel, a good thing because she was pretty sure her skull had taken all it possibly could. Still, as she began to regain her senses, she knew she'd be bruised and sore as hell in the morning.

Cassie opened her eyes. The bag lost air and she was able to turn her body enough to see the group of people running from the bar toward the intersection. Oh, *special*. One of them was a cop. She hoped like hell those new documents Brian had given her a week before would hold up. The social security card and driver's license were legit but the rental documents and that kind of stuff were based on faked information.

Get yourself together, Cassie, you've dealt with cops before. Just keep it simple. She gave herself a mini pep talk as she took in the freakishly tiny woman with the huge hair standing next to the car wringing her hands.

"Oh my lands! Honey, are you all right?"

Cassie blinked several times to see if she was hallucinating or not but the woman was apparently real.

"Momma! Damn it, I told you a hundred times to stop putting on makeup while you drive," the cop, a very big man, hissed at the tiny woman with giant hair and four-inch heels.

"Shane, we can deal with that later." One of the other bystanders, clearly related to the cop, peered into the car, opening the door carefully. "Miss? Are you all right?"

Could the situation be any more ridiculous? Twenty seconds after she'd driven into town and she got rear-ended by a pixie with aspirations to drive NASCAR. Of course the tiny woman in the giant car had to be related to the giant cop. And the giant cop was droolingly sexy. Yes, her libido, which had died years ago, chose to come back to life at that very moment. A strange giggle tried to escape her belly.

The guy standing at her car door smiled at her as he looked her over carefully. "I'm Matt Chase, a firefighter and paramedic here in town. I'm just going to look you over to check for injuries, all right?"

Blinking slowly, she licked her lips and nodded. Gentle hands felt her head and neck, flexed her fingers and arms. He turned her toward him and checked over her legs and ankles. The experience was far from unfamiliar and the old fear began to well up. She hoped he took her trembling hands as shock from the accident.

"I'm all right. Just a bit shaken up."

He looked up, as though startled by her voice. "Can you stand?"

"Let's see." She took the hand he offered and stood, unsteadily at first but it wasn't very long until she was much stronger and didn't need to lean on the car. "Yeah, apparently so."

"Do you know your name?"

Her old one and her new one. "Yes, I'm Cassie Gambol."

"I'm glad you're okay, Cassie. I'm afraid your car isn't so all right. I called a tow truck to take it to Art's. He's the mechanic here in Petal. He'll get to you first thing."

"No thanks to Mario Andretti there." Cassie turned her gaze toward the tiny woman.

"Oh honey, I'm so sorry. It's totally my fault." The woman at least had the decency to really look upset about it.

The giant groaned. "Ms. Gambol, can I get a statement and your insurance information for my report, please?"

"For cripe's sake, Shane. Let's at least get her into The Pumphouse so she can sit down and get a drink of water." Matt rolled his eyes.

"Why aren't you asking Crash there for her insurance info?" Cassie motioned at Big Hair.

"Believe me, miss, I know her information." The giant heaved a put-upon sigh.

The tow truck arrived.

"Can we get anything out of your car for you?" Cassie turned to find a smiling redhead. "I'm Maggie Chase." She pointed at the hottie firefighter and the giant. "Their sister-in-law."

"I'm supposed to meet my new landlord in about ten minutes. I need my purse and that bag on the floorboard on the front seat. Oh and I have a few suitcases in the trunk and my overnight case."

Maggie turned and waved at the assembled men. "Get to it. Put it all in my car. I'll run her where she needs to go." She looked back to Cassie.

"Well, isn't this a wonderful welcome to Petal. Where're you meeting your landlord? I'll get you there in time if he's here in town."

"I uh…" Cassie leafed through the papers in the bag someone handed her. "It's 1427 Riverwalk Drive. He said it was a fourplex just off Main Street."

"It is." Matt turned to Maggie momentarily. "It's my place, you know where to go." That bright, white smile moved back to Cassie. "You're going to be my neighbor. I live in apartment C. Chuck said he had a new tenant moving in to A. He's a good guy."

Maggie nodded and grabbed her purse from another bystander. "Okay, Shane, you can come by in half an hour and take her statement then. We can't have her be late."

The cop scowled but moved to the side to let them pass. "Fine. I'll be there in a few minutes." He crossed his arms over his chest, looking imposing and suddenly, Cassie found him far less attractive and a lot more scary.

"Don't mind him. His bark is worse than his bite." Maggie ushered Cassie to a sedan across the street.

On the quick ride over Cassie was aware that Maggie Chase was sizing her up. It annoyed her but she supposed it wasn't unusual. After all she was a stranger in town, it would be natural to be curious. Still, it made her nervous.

"I apologize for my mother-in-law. I hope you don't think poorly of her. She's really a very good person. She's just a terrible driver and she gets distracted. I think it's all the hair-spray she uses to keep her helmet hair lacquered. Anyway, I just wanted you to know she'll make it right. Heck, if I know her, she's already working on making you enough food to last you until Christmas."

Cassie just wanted the ride to be over so she could be alone again. She needed a shower, a cry and then a lot of sleep. "That isn't necessary. She doesn't need to do anything but be sure her insurance takes care of any repairs for my car."

"If it doesn't, she'll deal with the difference. So, where are you from? What brings you to Petal?" Maggie pulled her car into a driveway of a well-kept fourplex with a big oak in the front and brightly colored flowers in beds that hugged the walk.

"This is nice," Cassie murmured, avoiding Maggie's questions. The place felt friendly, open.

"Matt lives in the top apartment on the left. You're next to him on the right. Oh, there's Chuck." Maggie waved.

Thank goodness the woman was as ADD as her mother-in-law. Cassie knew she'd have to deal with the questions sooner or later but after the last two months, hell, after the last year, she was exhausted. It was hard for her to be rude but it was self-preservation at that point. If she didn't get rid of them and get some privacy, she'd lose her shit in front of her new neighbors. "Uh, thank you, Maggie. It's very nice of you to have brought me here."

"Oh no problem. I'll wait here for you. Kyle and Shane will be here and they can help you move your bags in."

Cassie couldn't figure out if Maggie was being purposely obtuse or was just really nice. "That's not necessary. I can move my own bags. It's not a big deal. Really." Cassie got out before Maggie could reply.

Not that that stopped the redhead from getting out. "Chuck! This is Cassie, your new tenant. Polly rear-ended her right in front of The Pumphouse. She's had a rough night."

Cassie ground her teeth and tried to remember that Maggie

meant well. But she'd had enough being managed. Stepping forward she held out her hand to the man walking toward her with a sympathetic smile. She'd had enough of those too.

"I'm Cassie Gambol, it's nice to meet you."

"I wish it was under better circumstances. That Polly." He chuckled and shook her hand. "Come on up. Your furniture was delivered earlier today. I didn't know where you wanted everything but I had them do the hump work and bring it upstairs." He led her up those very stairs as he spoke.

When he opened the door, Cassie knew immediately she'd be okay. The apartment was right. It felt safe. Second floor. One entrance. She'd put on all the window alarms after everyone left.

"You just let me know when and where you want this stuff moved, okay? You surely don't need to be hefting anything heavy after a car accident." He dropped a set of keys into her hand and pulled out an envelope. "Here's a copy of the lease you sent me last week. Rent is due the fifteenth. But as you paid the first two months, you're good until September."

She walked through the place in a daze. Her muscles were sore and she wanted everyone to leave her alone so she could shower and sleep for about twenty hours. He showed her the various highlights, where the circuit breaker was, the air conditioner and heating controls.

When they walked back into the living room, Shane and Kyle entered with Matt and each carried one of her bags.

"Do you want these in the bedroom?"

Numb, she just nodded. The giant looked at her with suspicious concern but took the big suitcase into the other room as she got rid of Chuck. Only four more to go.

Telling herself to just hold on a bit longer, she thrust her new insurance card and driver's license at Shane when he came back into the room. "I was at the light. Stopped. Because it was *red*. Your mother hit me and knocked me into the intersection. My airbag went off. She wasn't going super fast but fast enough." Her recital of events was delivered in a flat voice.

"Would you like to go to the hospital?" Maggie looked concerned.

"I'm fine. I'm just exhausted, so if you're done, you can all go and I'll sleep." Her nails dug into her palms, trying to stave off the shakes.

"You could have a concussion. You should go in just to be checked," Shane said, his voice rumbling along her spine, eyes flicking over her body.

She wanted to scream and shove them all out the door. If any woman knew what a concussion felt like it was her. Terry had given them to her more than once.

"I said I'm fine. Honestly. Now, are we done? Because I'm dead on my feet. I need a shower and to sleep. I've been driving for three days."

Shane looked the lush, raven-haired beauty over carefully. His mental alarm was blaring. There was something off about Cassie Gambol. He didn't like it when people hid things from him. Petal was his town, it made him nervous to wonder what sort of secrets this woman was bringing into it. And she was hiding something. He was sure of that much. Her hands shook and her voice trembled here and there.

There was also no denying she was the most beautiful thing he'd ever seen. Something about her drew him in. Made him feel protective as well as suspicious. He found himself gripping the insurance card to keep from touching her hair where it had fallen loose from the clip thing holding it away from her face.

Taking a step back and a deep breath, he handed her back the insurance card and license. He didn't miss the half-moon imprints on her palms from where her nails had dug in. "I'm done. Your account matches my mother's. You'll need to follow up with Art tomorrow about the car." She took the business card with the mechanic's information on it from him and put it in her wallet, nodding her thanks.

"He told me he'd get on it first thing. If you need a rental he can hook you up with that too. I can assure you my mom's insurance will cover the repairs." He sighed heavily, he was sure he'd end up having to take her license away if she didn't stop driving like a maniac.

Officially done with the small talk, Cassie crossed the living room to the front door, holding it open. "Thank you for carrying my bags in. I appreciate that. And Maggie, thank you for the ride."

"Any time. I'm in the book. Please give me a call when you get settled in. I know it's got to be hard to be in a new place. I'd love to introduce you around. Folks around here are pretty friendly." Maggie patted her arm as she left.

"Just pound on the wall if you need anything." Matt grinned at her. "You'll probably need a grocery run. I brought some milk, bread and eggs over from my place. They're in your fridge. A few cans of soup are on the counter there."

Something warm and long forgotten bloomed in her gut. She smiled past the lump in her throat and blinked back tears. "Thank you. That's very thoughtful of you."

"No problem. Neighbors help each other. The grocery is only two blocks west. But if you need a ride there or anywhere, just let me know. I have tomorrow and the next day off and I'd be happy to run you wherever you need to go."

Shane pushed his brother out the door but kept his eyes on Cassie. Perceptive cop eyes. They both knew she was hiding something. "I think Miss Gambol wants us to go." He nodded curtly in her direction.

"Thank you all again." She refused to let herself even look at his ass in those uniform pants as he retreated. Refused. Okay, okay so one peek before closing the door. To help calm her nerves.

And she closed the door. Locking it. Alone. Alone and safe.

Methodically, she went into her bedroom and pulled the window alarms out of one of her suitcases, installing them one by one, checking the locks as she went. It was a warm night but the air conditioner seemed to do a good job keeping the place cool enough.

Pulling the blinds tight, she made a final pass through the place, making sure it was secure, and then kicked off her shoes. She knew she should eat but the very thought made her nauseated. At that point, she was on autopilot, finishing all her safety tasks would be her sole thought until she could assure herself she was locked in and safe. That if someone did break in, the safeguards would be enough to wake her up. She knew you couldn't defend yourself if you were sleeping.

Getting a change of clothing, her toiletries and one last item, she headed into the bathroom, locking the door behind her. After putting the doorstop alarm down and in place, she hung her towels and put the washcloths in a drawer.

As always, Cassie avoided looking in the mirror as she undressed. The fear was enough, she didn't need to see the scars. Anyway, the scars on the inside were just as bad and she couldn't look away from those. She cursed Terry for making her this way. Creating a scared rabbit from a woman who'd been so confident and self-assured. And she'd let him.

The water heated quickly but she made sure the safety on her gun was off and that it was within reach before she stepped into the stall. Her breath came out in a long exhale. Alone at last. Safe to let the tears come.

"So how about my new neighbor, huh?" Matt winked at his brothers as they all sat in his living room.

Shane heard laughter from the kitchen. Maggie was in there with her best friend, Liv, making up some nachos and, he also suspected, gossiping about the evening.

"She's something else, huh? It's not like I haven't seen pretty women before but this one is up there in the top five. Did you get a load of her legs?" Matt laughed. "Biggest blue eyes I've ever seen. Pretty lips. And that voice. Holy shit that voice. Made me hard just hearing it."

"She's hiding something." Shane wanted Matt to shut up about Cassie's body.

Kyle and Matt looked at their oldest brother. "Yeah? What makes you say so?" Matt asked.

"I'm a cop. I know what it looks like when people have something to hide. Her hands shook. She avoided eye contact. She wanted us out of her house pretty darned bad."

Maggie walked in and put food down on the coffee table with a stack of paper plates. "Of course she was shaking, Shane. She'd just had a car accident. She didn't know any of you and hell, I know what she must have felt like with all these giant handsome men in her living room. Give the woman a break. But she was nervous. Really nervous. Could just be her nature, though." Maggie looked up at her brother-in-law. "But I don't think it's a prosecutable offense to be nervous."

"She had some considerable scarring on her scalp and the back of her neck. I felt it when I checked her over. It could be that she'd been in another bad accident before. I've seen victims at the scene with major trauma from past accidents," Matt said around his nachos.

"Maybe. But I'm gonna watch this woman. I don't trust her. I don't like people coming into my town carrying trouble."

"Jeez, Shane, cut the woman some slack. Do you need to go from zero to the Terminator in three seconds? Not all women are out to hurt people," Kyle said.

"It's my job to watch people and I never said all women were out to hurt people," Shane growled at his brother.

"Okay, this needs to stop before it gets started. Kyle, lay off. Shane, give her the benefit of the doubt. And anyway, I saw you watching her. Did you think she was hiding something in her bra? Maybe her back pocket?" Matt snorted.

"Okay, so she's easy on the eyes. But I don't know what she's bringing into my town and I'm not going to be comfortable until I figure it out."

Chapter Two

When Cassie opened her eyes the next morning, it almost felt like she was a new person as well as living in a new place. Sun streamed into her bedroom and she heard the birds singing just outside. Peace. How long had that been?

As she got dressed she contemplated the importance of where she was at right then. She wasn't on the verge of taking the first step into her future. She'd taken it. And she was still moving ahead. For so long it had been about just surviving. It seemed monumentally scary to have her life be about living again.

Cassie decided to walk to Main Street, have breakfast and then deal with the car situation. Get to know the town a bit better.

While she was out she'd also look for a place with wi-fi so she could email Brian and check in. Or at the very least call him on a payphone. She hadn't spoken with him since she left the hotel the morning before and she knew he'd be worried.

After she got some makeup on, she pulled her hair into a po- nytail and made sure her shirt collar hid the scars at the back of her neck. It wasn't until she'd locked the door that the heat hit her. Like a thick, wet blanket. If it was this bad now, she knew she needed to get out and finish her errands before noon.

The trees cast nice, cool shade as she began to walk. People out working in their yards actually waved hellos at her. And taking a deep breath, she waved back. She had to claim her life again.

Once on Main Street she crossed over to a little diner she'd seen the night before, The Sands. It was everything she'd imagined a small town diner to be when she walked inside. Crowded and full of people talking and laughing, waving to folks as they came and went. Steeling her nerves, Cassie slipped into a spot at the counter and grabbed a menu.

"Hiya, sug. You must be the pretty girl that Polly Chase ran into last night."

Surprised, Cassie looked up into the face of a woman behind the counter. Big brown eyes sparked with good humor. Cassie couldn't help but smile back.

"That's me. I suppose this is my introduction to how fast news travels in a small town?"

The woman laughed and patted Cassie's arm. "Now you're catching on. I'm Ronnie Sands. I own this place." She put a coffee cup in front of Cassie and filled it.

"I'm Cassie Gambol. Nice place you have here. I like it. Looks like I'm not the only one." She ordered the pancake special and complimented Ronnie on the fresh juice.

Ronnie grinned. "Be right back with your pancakes. Welcome to Petal, Cassie." Ronnie bustled off to help another customer.

"Well, you're looking a mite better today." Cassie turned to see Maggie Chase hop up into the chair next to her. "Although I don't like those dark circles under your eyes. How are you feeling after last night?"

"I just need a few good meals and some rest. Thanks." Cassie felt torn between the idea of actually making new friends and the vulnerability that created in her.

Damn it, she used to be so good at this. She had friends and a vibrant social life. She used to be a lot of things before Terry.

The woman who'd come in with Maggie leaned forward and smiled. "You must be the Cassie everyone is talking about. Hi, I'm Liv Davis. Nice to meet you."

Ronnie came by, put a heaping plate of food in front of Cassie, took Maggie's and Liv's orders and hurried away.

Cassie waved back at Liv before digging into her breakfast. She'd forgotten what this kind of cooking tasted like. Terry had insisted on a cook to prepare low-fat meals based on his menu plans and when she wasn't eating at home, she ate what she could grab at work. Hospital cafeterias weren't known for their delicious meals.

"What brings you to Petal, Cassie?" Maggie asked.

Cassie knew the question would be asked again and all the way out from her brother's she'd worked on the answer.

"I got tired of the big city. I wanted a change." She shrugged. "One of my friends was here a few years ago, on his way through to Atlanta and he's always gushed about it. So I checked it out on the internet and ended up talking to Chuck and rented the apartment."

"I admire that. You just up and moved? Changed your life because you wanted to, that's pretty amazing." Maggie's smile was genuine.

"Don't. It's not a big deal really. The city was killing me." Or rather, someone in the city wanted to.

Maggie frowned a little before brightening again. "Well it's most certainly admirable. What city did you come from?"

She and Brian decided it was good to keep close to the truth. Los Angeles was big enough that it shouldn't ring any alarm bells. "LA."

"And what are you going to do here? Do you have a job lined up?"

Well, she couldn't be a surgeon anymore. Two of the fingers in her right hand had had the bones shattered so severely she'd never have the range of fine motor skills she'd need. Hell, she could barely hold a fork in her right hand for nearly half a year after she'd gotten out of the hospital. On top of that, she couldn't practice under her new name without a whole lot of hassle and paperwork. Hassle and paperwork that would expose her. Futile rage swamped her for a moment. Terry had taken away her greatest love as well as her safety and nearly her life.

"No. I need to start looking." She shoved it all away, not allowing him to own her fear or her anger. Her days of letting him control her were over.

"Well, what can you do? Any special talents? Maybe we can give you suggestions." Maggie buttered her toast.

"Clerk, secretary, bookstore? Coffeeshop?" Cassie shrugged, trying not to resent Maggie's apparent ease with herself and her surroundings.

"You know, I think Penny is looking for someone over at Paperbacks and More. You should pop in. She's really nice, our age, I think it would probably be a really fun place to work. And wow—" Maggie leaned in close to Cassie "—where did you get those earrings? They're gorgeous."

Smiling, Cassie touched them. "Thank you. I made them."

"You made those? Well they're beautiful. You're pretty talented, Cassie. Have you ever thought about selling them?"

"Funny you should mention that, I was thinking about it on the way here. Is there a craft market or flea market around here? I have a supply of things I've made that I'd love to sell on the odd weekend here and there." At least she could still make jewelry with her hands.

"As a matter of fact, yes. There's a Sunday Market. This is the first year for it but it seems to be doing pretty well. They close down Fourth Avenue, which is just a few blocks down. As it happens, our friend Dee is on the organizing committee. Here." Maggie dug through her bag and pulled out a pen and paper. "This is her number. Give her a call and let me know because I'd love to buy some of your stuff." Maggie grinned.

"Thank you, Maggie. I appreciate this." Cassie paid for her breakfast, a little bit of hope in her belly along with the great food. "Ronnie, breakfast was excellent and the juice made me feel a lot better. I'll be seeing you."

"Wait, Cassie. Do you need a ride somewhere?" Maggie asked.

She'd had just about all the small talk she could take. Cassie just needed to be alone to think. "No, thanks. I noticed from the card that the mechanic is only a few blocks away. After I check in there I need to run errands. Nothing I can't walk to and I need the exercise anyway. Thanks for the tip about your friend and the Market. Oh and do you know if there's a place in town that has wireless internet access? My phone won't be in until Monday and I haven't even thought about internet service."

"The Honey Bear. It's a bakery at the other end of Main. We'd be happy to give you a lift." Maggie's friendly nature was earnest and unvarnished. Cassie had to admit to herself she liked that. There didn't seem to be anything fake about her. The gorgeous best friend seemed nice too. But she wasn't ready for hanging out with the girls just yet.

"Oh thanks, but I'd like to get to know the town a bit. I appreciate it." Cassie backed away toward the door. "Have a great Saturday afternoon."

And she was free again. Free to do whatever she wanted. The walk down Main Street was quite nice. There were a number of little businesses along the way. A few cafés and specialty shops dotted the sidewalk. The town seemed to be thriving.

The mechanic shop was busy but when she walked in one of the men stopped what he was doing and came over to help her. "You must be Cassie. I'd shake your hand but I don't want to get you dirty. I'm Art."

Okay, so it was odd but she was getting used to everyone knowing who she was. Definitely *not* something she experienced a lot back home. "Yep, I'm Cassie. Nice to meet you. Just came in to check on my car. How is it?"

"Well, that big old Caddy is a menace. She's whacked your rear axle out of alignment and it's cracked. I've called in an order for the parts but I won't see them until Monday. The rest isn't too bad. The body work shouldn't take too very long and we can do the paint job here. But I wouldn't count on having a vehicle for another week or so. Do you need a rental? We have two on site. Polly's insurance will cover it."

Cassie laughed. "Everyone in town seems to be familiar with her insurance and what it covers."

"Well yes." Art blushed. "She's gotten into a few fender benders. But she really is a nice woman."

"So I'm told. And yes, I'll need a car if I won't have one for at least another week."

He completed the paperwork and she drove off half an hour later to the grocery store. But when she parked, she saw the small bookstore just a few doors down and decided to head over and check out the job lead.

"Miss Gambol."

Shit. The giant hottie of a sheriff came walking toward her. Stalking, like something big and bad but graceful too.

"Sheriff."

His eyes didn't miss anything on their slow circuit of her body. She knew that he knew she was holding back. "Please, call me Shane. How are you doing today?"

She resisted the urge to shift from foot to foot. "I'm all right. Just a bit sore. But I've got a rental and Art is taking care of my car." She shrugged. Cassie tried not to think about how his skin was so work-hard and firm and nicely sunkissed. She smelled him from where she stood. A bit of cologne, man and clean sweat.

Cassie doubted she looked as good. The heat made her skin feel clammy and her hair most likely hung like a limp rag. She chewed her lip, knowing the lipstick she'd applied first thing was gone. And then she smacked herself for even thinking it. No way. No more controlling men with power issues. And clearly this one had that in spades. He took up far more of the sidewalk than he physically occupied. His presence was overwhelming. And certainly he'd be hot in bed, but she was not going to find out. Oh no. Not her. She wouldn't even think about how he'd look naked and laid out on her sheets waiting for her. *Damn. Were vibrators legal in Georgia?* Yeah, she'd need to look that up online.

He was talking and she blushed when she realized she'd lost half of what he'd said. "I'm sorry. I missed part of that."

He smiled, with white predator's teeth. Oh my. *Okay, thinking about sex again! Stop it!*

"I was saying that you should be on the lookout for a visit from my mother. She's still upset over what happened last night and she wants to make it right. Which means she'll hound you until you let her. I suggest you don't try to resist. It's pointless anyway. She might be small but she handles four very big sons with one hand tied behind her back."

Suddenly he was so charming he totally disarmed her and she laughed. "I see. Like the Borg? Only with big hair and a bigger handbag?"

He cocked his head and grinned. "You got it. You settling in all right? Can I help you with anything? You shouldn't move any of that furniture so soon after the accident. I'd be happy to help." Her heart sped up as his gaze pulled her in. He was thinking something naughty wasn't he? Or maybe she was projecting.

Wetting her lips nervously, she shrugged. "I'm sure I'll be all right. Thanks."

His long pause alarmed her until he blinked slowly and cleared his throat. "Uh, okay. Well, I have to go. It was nice seeing you again. You be sure to call me at the station or go and get Matt if you need anything, all right?"

"Thanks again." Stepping back from his body made her feel a bit better. She could breathe without smelling his skin. It had to be the heat that made her feel so lightheaded.

With a wave she steered around him and headed into the bookstore, leaving him standing there, watching her.

Shane unfisted his hands as he took in her sway before she

disappeared into Paperbacks and More. Nervous as a cat that one. Why? And where in hell did the persistent need to protect her come from? She was in his town carrying something she didn't want him to know about with her. That made her a threat. But he didn't see a threat when he looked at her.

He saw the shadow of fear in her eyes. He saw the lines of stress around her mouth. And what a mouth. That mouth of hers was made for kissing and other things he shouldn't be thinking about doing with a woman like Cassie Gambol.

He'd done a quick check on her that morning when he'd gotten to work. Not much to be found and that made him nervous. No one got to be their age without something. No speeding tickets, no fingerprints on file, he didn't find anything about her in any newspapers from Southern California either. It was like she just came into being a few weeks before. A woman built for a hell of a lot of naughty fantasies, made from smoke with fear in her eyes.

In his town. And if he had any say in it, he'd find out who the heck she was and what she carried so close to the vest.

Cool air hit her skin as Cassie walked into Paperbacks and More. Being away from Shane and out of the heat, she found she could finally breathe again. Wandering through the store, she noted the cozy seating areas in the different sections and a good variety of genres. It was bigger than she'd thought it would be. The kind of bookstore she'd have found herself in every payday back in college.

Finally, she sighted the counter and smiled at the woman standing behind it. "I'm looking for Penny."

"You found her." The woman, dressed smart in a lightweight summer skirt and blouse, looked Cassie up and down. "Hmm, you don't look like an IRS agent and my personal relationship with the Lord is my business."

Cassie laughed and put her hands up in surrender. "I'm Cassie Gambol and I'm not peddling anything. Well, that's not entirely true. I'm looking for a job. I'm new here in Petal and Maggie Chase said you might be looking for someone."

"You ever worked in a bookstore before?"

"Back when I was in high school and then later when I was in college."

"Who's your favorite author?"

"What a question. How can I just name one? That's impossible."

Penny grinned. "Well, I must say that's a very good answer to start with. Okay, who are your five favorite authors?"

"Margaret Atwood, Isaac Asimov, Frank Herbert, Nora Roberts—and I'll snag JD Robb while I'm at it since they're the same person—and Barbara Kingsolver."

Penny's eyebrow rose. "Nice group there. Okay then, so of those authors—give me your favorite book by each."

"Hmm, for Atwood it's a tie between *Handmaid's Tale* and *Cat's Eye*. Asimov would be *Foundation*. Frank Herbert? *Children of Dune*. Nora—and you know that's a hard one—but *Born in Fire*. JD Robb's *Naked in Death*. I just love the beginning of Eve and Roarke. And Barbara Kingsolver's *Bean Trees*."

Penny Garwood knew people. She could do a resume check on the woman standing in front of her. Would do. She may trust her gut but she wasn't a moron. Still, she knew it would be fine. Her gut told her that Cassie Gambol was a good woman and would be a darned good employee. And Penny always went with her intuition. It'd never proven her wrong. And there was no doubt that the men would be coming into the store in droves just to get a look at her.

"Okay. When can you start, Cassie Gambol?"

"Are you kidding me? Really? Just like that?"

Penny couldn't remember the last time anyone had looked that overjoyed to be offered a job in a bookstore. The woman didn't look hard up for money, but looks could be deceiving.

"I have a rule, I listen to my gut. My gut says to hire you so I will. We'll start you on a trial basis. I'll give you a week. If it works out, I'll make you permanent. If it doesn't, no harm done. Let's start you part-time for now. We're open from noon to five on Sundays. Why don't you come on in tomorrow and we'll set up your schedule?"

Cassie offered her hand and Penny took it. "Thank you so much. I'll be here tomorrow at noon. You won't be sorry for taking a chance on me."

"Make it eleven-thirty. Come around the back. We'll get your paperwork done first and I'll give you a bit of a run-through before we open."

"You got it. Thank you again." Heart light and a smile on her face, Cassie headed out and back across the street to the grocery store.

It wasn't that she needed the job. Brian had changed her trust to pay blind to an account that fed into Switzerland and then back to her new name. Her father would have been heartbroken to know what a mess her marriage to Terry had turned out to be. But the money he'd left her when he died enabled her to run. Enabled her to get into the program to change all her identification like her social security number and name. Gave her a chance at a new life.

But she wanted to work. Wanted to do something with her time. Yes, she grew up with money but she'd worked from a very early age and it felt uncomfortable to not have some kind of major activity in her life other than being afraid. Working at a bookstore and making her jewelry wasn't the intricate and lifesaving vascular surgery she'd performed for the last four years, but it was something to help her take a step to move on with her life. And that's what she meant to do.

Matt Chase unfolded himself from his place, lying in a hammock in the shade of the big oak tree in the yard, when she pulled up. He was a work of masculine art. They sure did grow them handsome down in Georgia.

"Hey there, Cassie. Need some help?"

He ambled over and it was impossible not to notice the long, tanned legs in the cutoff jeans and the flat, tight belly peeking from under the hem of his T-shirt.

Pulling out a few bags and balancing them she smiled, she knew it was just a bit thin at the edges. "Oh no, that's okay. It'll just take me two trips. Thank you, though."

But as she began to walk up the steps, she heard him grab the remaining bags and follow her up. "Now it won't take you another trip." He breezed past her into the apartment and put the bags on her kitchen counter before leaning a hip against it and watching her.

"Thank you. It really wasn't necessary."

"I know. It wouldn't have been neighborly if I'd been required to do it. I was just goofing off and taking a nap."

He seemed nice enough, he truly did. But having him in her apartment with the door closed began to make her feel queasy. She didn't know him. He could be anyone and scary often had a pretty face.

She took a step back and he noticed. Concern spread over his handsome face. "Cassie? You all right?"

"I...the heat, I need to cool down and rest." She went to the door and opened it up, gripping the jamb tight. She wanted to gulp the air, try to breathe in the calm but it wasn't working. "Thanks again for helping with my groceries, Matt. I appreciate it." The shaking was coming, she could feel it and she clenched her teeth.

"Are you all right, Cassie? Did I do something wrong?" Matt stopped very close to her but didn't touch her. Still, the fine tremors in her hands hit.

"Please. Just go. I'm not feeling well."

"I...just bang on the wall please if you need me." He backed out of the door and onto the landing. She slammed and locked it, sinking to the floor as her legs would no longer hold her up.

Her teeth began to chatter as the shakes came. Her breath exploded in sobs and she curled into a ball and closed her eyes, letting it wash over her. She knew it was useless to fight it once it got that far so she rode it out.

After a time, she sat up, her muscles still rubbery and slightly sore from the shaking and sobbing. Ordering herself to buck up, she stood up, bracing her weight on the door until she could stand on her own, and went to splash some water on her face.

Moving tentatively, she put her groceries away as her body and spirit regained control over itself. It was then that she remembered she hadn't gotten in contact with Brian and she knew he'd be climbing the walls with worry by then.

She didn't want to leave the house. She wanted to stay inside and hide. But she couldn't. She wouldn't. Instead, she grabbed her keys and her wallet, and headed out to the payphone she'd noticed earlier that day outside the grocery store.

But Shane Chase was waiting at the bottom of her stairs and she recoiled for a moment. *Damn!* He noticed that.

"Oh, Sheriff Chase. You surprised me." She tried to be nonchalant and force herself to go down the stairs but she froze three quarters of the way down because he remained standing at the bottom of the landing, effectively blocking her way. Making her feel trapped.

"Shane. Please. And you want to tell me why the very sight of me scared you?" His voice had an edge she couldn't quite place. "Matt said you had a panic attack earlier when he was at your place. Why don't you tell me what's going on? I can help you."

Anger replaced the fear and she pushed her way past him and down the walk. "I'm on my way out, Shane."

He moved his body to halt her progress and the fear was back at the edges of her anger. "What are you hiding?"

"Sheriff, you're blocking my way. And anyway, what's it to you? I haven't done anything wrong unless panic attacks are illegal in Georgia." Her voice shook a bit, mortifying her even more but thank goodness he stepped out of the way.

"I'm sorry I scared you. I don't know why you're afraid but I can't help you if you won't let me." Hands held loosely at his side, he kept his voice calm and low and she felt like an animal all of a sudden. A cat spooked in a treetop. When had her life become so out of her control?

Oh how she wanted to tell him. To give it all to someone else and let them fix it for her. But that wasn't possible. No one could protect her but herself. And the last thing she needed was another big, dominant man who thought he could run her life far more efficiently than she could.

"I'm fine. Now if you'll excuse me." She walked around him, got into the car and pulled away, leaving him standing there, watching her go.

Matt waited on his landing as Shane came up the stairs. "Something has spooked that woman big time." Matt waved his brother inside and handed him a soda.

"I'd wager it was a man. Some asshole who beat her up a time or two. Maybe a daddy." Shane took a sip and sat down on the couch. "Either that or she's running from the law. I checked her out and she's clean but it's not like fake identification is a foreign concept to criminals."

"I don't think so, Shane. She doesn't come off as the kind of woman who's hiding something from others because of what she's done."

Shane nodded at his brother. His stomach clenched as he remembered the look on her face when she'd looked down the steps at him. No, that wasn't the face of a woman hiding from a drug charge. That was the face of a woman who'd been hurt by someone and was afraid it would happen again. No woman had ever looked at him like that and it bothered him deeply that she would be afraid of him.

That nagging protective feeling was back. "I think you're right. I think it's an ex. She didn't seem to have a problem being alone with Maggie or when she was with us all in her apartment. But men alone? You should have seen her reaction when she walked out and saw me on my way up the stairs to

her place. She flinched. There's something bad there and I aim
to find out what it is."

"I told you, she started shaking when I was at her apartment. I could hear her sobbing for breath after I left. I'm worried about her."

"Are you now?" Shane's eyes narrowed at his brother. "Leave
that to me. It's my job and she's not going to tell us anything
at this point. I just need to show her we're the good guys and
hopefully she'll come to trust me...us, in time."

Matt raised a brow. "Oh, so that's how it is? You staking a
claim?"

"I just want to help. I'm a cop, it's what I do." Shane paused
and Matt made a rude noise.

"Puhleeze. Shane, I've known you my whole life. That look
on your face says there's a lot more than your cop-type duty
on the line here."

Shane started to argue but groaned instead, shaking his head.
"Damn it, there's something about her. You should have seen
how pissed off she got out there. First she's totally freaked and
then I say something that makes her mad and she's spitting and
hissing. She's..." Shane shrugged his shoulders. "But if you had
your eye on her...oh hell, even if, unless you want to have some
serious competition, you'd best back up and let me at her. That
juxtaposition of timid ferocity gets to me. I can't say I've ever
been this intrigued before."

Matt threw back his head and laughed. "Well, she's a looker.
And those big blue eyes are haunted. But I'm still stinging over
my breakup with Liv. I don't think I'm ready right now. But I
do want to help Cassie. So I'll keep an eye on her."

"I'm sorry things didn't work out between the two of you. I
thought Liv was the one."

"Yeah. Me too. But after nearly a year of dating, she wanted
to move to the next level and I just wasn't ready after all. I
can't blame her for moving on. I look at Kyle and Maggie and
I know that if I'd truly loved Liv, I'd have asked her to move in

or marry me long before a year passed." Matt cocked his head. "Cassie may be able to get spitting mad at you but I don't think she's the plaything type. Don't play with her. I don't think she can handle it. And she deserves more."

Shane's lips tightened as he stood up and began to pace. "Hey, fuck you, okay? I don't play with women, Matt. I'm just not serious about them. I've made mistakes, I grant you that. But I have no intentions of harming Cassie Gambol. She's different. She moves me and I want to know more. A lot more." He ran a hand through his hair. "I should be running for the door right now, looking to hook up with a woman who'll make me forget those eyes. But she makes me want to stick around. I think I'm in trouble."

Standing in the payphone she'd spied earlier that day in the grocery store parking lot, Cassie punched in the numbers and waited for Brian to pick up. The shaking had finally abated but the aftereffects of the attacks always left her feeling off balance.

"Hello?"

"Hey, B. I'm here safely."

"I was ready to get on a plane and come looking for you. Why didn't you call me last night? Is everything okay?"

"My phone won't be hooked up until Monday. And I got into a small fender bender and my car is in the shop but yeah, everything is okay. I got a job."

"Already? Great news. Doing what?"

She told him about the bookstore and the five favorite authors question. "She's giving me a week's trial and if she likes me, she'll make me permanent. Who'd have thought I'd be so excited about something like this?"

"You've been through an awful lot. Of course something like this job is exciting. You're claiming your life. Now, a fender bender? Did the new identification work?"

"I guess so. The sheriff hasn't arrested me yet. And it was his mother who hit me. Rear-ended me at a red light. I'm all right but my car needs some TLC. My furniture arrived and there are people coming out of the woodwork to offer me help. It's all very stereotypical Southern small town here. Lots of people calling me miss and ma'am and going out of their way to be nice. It's odd. Disconcerting and yet, it feels nice."

"Did you tell them?"

"Hell no. That's my past. I mean, they offer to drive me places and move my furniture, that sort of thing. The sheriff has taken it into his head to try and save me. He's like nine feet tall and four feet wide. I'm wagering he was the quarterback in high school. In any case, I'll have to disabuse him of the notion that I need saving."

Brian laughed. "Honey, you can let people in, you know. You haven't done anything wrong. There's nothing for you to be ashamed of and he won't find you. Maybe telling the sheriff is a good thing, he can keep an eye on you."

"You just said Terry won't find me so why do I need an eye kept on me?" And she was ashamed. She knew she shouldn't be but she was. She had graduated at the top of her class and yet she'd let a man in her life who'd estranged her from her family and had nearly killed her. He'd taken away one of her greatest passions when he used a hammer to shatter the bones in her fingers. How she let things get that far, and more than once, was still something she didn't understand. And if she didn't how could she expect others to?

"You going to see that doctor they recommended? The one in Shackleton?"

"Yes, she has evening hours and I have an appointment on Wednesday night. I suppose I'll need to clear it with my job."

"You promised you'd go. She's a specialist with domestic violence survivors, Car—Cassie. Don't break that promise."

Closing her eyes, Cassie leaned her head against the cool glass of the enclosure. "I won't. I promised and I'll see it through. Even though I don't need it."

"No one can live through what you did without needing some help."

"It was a year ago."

"Yes and you spent months in the hospital. You were in a coma for three weeks. They weren't even sure you'd be able to use your right arm again. And then the trial and the fuckups. You need someone who can help you process it all. You've just been existing for the last year. Hell for the last several years."

"Fat lot of good the trial did when they found him guilty and he's out there free." Free and filled with violence and the need for revenge. She shivered against the ninety plus degree heat. Fear made her cold.

"I know, Cassie. I know. It's wrong. But you're alive and safe and damn it, you need to claim your life again and live. Get a boyfriend, go on dates, neck at the movies. If you like this town, buy yourself a house and settle there. When they catch him, I won't have to hide when I come and see you. Or you can come back here."

The mere idea of a life where she could have those things mocked her. Could she? Could she be normal and have friends and a boyfriend? A life where she didn't weigh every word and action out of fear? It seemed like such a ridiculous fantasy, rage bubbled up within her. But she didn't want to unleash it on her brother, who'd been her rock through everything. "I have to go. I need to get home and get some dinner. I'll email you and call you with my new info once my phone gets hooked up on Monday. Thank you, Bri. I love you."

"Good. Then you won't be mad when the cell phone I just bought for you shows up at your place early next week. You need one and it drives me nuts that you don't have one."

Cassie sighed. "Fine. Thank you. You're pretty peachy keen as big brothers go."

"I should have done more. I should have seen it. I'm sorry."

"Stop. Damn it, stop! Hell, I *lived* it and I didn't see it. Not all the time. Not until it was too late. But it's over. And I'm alive and you're alive and we're okay."

"I love you. Take care of yourself. You'd better call me on Monday when you get that phone working."

"I promise."

Before she got in her car, she went into the store and bought a gallon of chocolate chip ice cream.

Chapter Three

At eleven-thirty on the dot, Cassie knocked on the back door of the bookstore and a smiling Penny Garwood opened it and waved her inside. Penny's short, stylish brown hair had a pretty barrette on one side, holding it back from her face. Cassie liked the woman's style.

"Well that's a good start, Cassie. Right on time." Penny handed her a stack of paperwork. "Have a cup of coffee and fill all this out. I'll be out front getting everything ready to open. Come on out when you're finished."

She settled in with her papers and took a sip of coffee. She tried not to look at her hands as she wrote. Tried not to think about how much her life had changed in the span of not even an hour. Cassie had had to learn to write with her left hand while the fingers on her right healed. Her victim advocate had encouraged her to keep writing that way. Another layer to her new life. It'd been strange to think constantly about how to become Cassie Gambol and keep Carly Sunderland dead.

Still, she'd gotten to the point where she answered to Cassie like it was the name she'd been born with. She wrote her new social security number with her left hand on that paperwork and listed the past jobs as those people she knew she could trust to keep her secrets and back up her cover.

Cover. She nearly snorted. Once a respected surgeon, now she had to deal with cover. And she didn't even get a cool car like James Bond had.

Finishing up, Cassie went out to the front of the store and handed the papers to Penny who looked through them quickly, tucked them into a folder and smiled.

"Okay, that's all done. Let's get you to work."

For the next several hours, Penny showed Cassie the ropes. How to work the cash register, how to find stock, what went where. It wasn't complicated but it was more detailed than she'd expected it to be and after a while, Cassie fell into the rhythm of it all.

At five Penny turned over the closed sign and locked up. "Good job. Especially for your first day. I'm impressed."

Cassie hadn't felt accomplished in a very long time. It was a simple thing but it felt damned good.

"Thanks."

"Are you busy tonight? We need to set up your schedule and it just so happens I have chicken marinating in my fridge. As an added bonus, I've got sangria that I started last night so it should be nice and ready to drink."

With a little bit of effort she could make an actual friend. The first new one in a few years. "You sure I wouldn't put you out?"

"I wouldn't have invited you if that was the case."

For some reason, Penny's mixture of formal Southern charm and blunt manner put Cassie at ease. She didn't feel pitied or suspected. "All right then, sounds good."

Cassie followed Penny a little way from the center of town and into a neighborhood that overlooked a lake. Penny pulled into the driveway of a large Tudor-style house with gorgeous landscaping. The front yard had a huge willow tree that shaded the entire front of the house including the large porch.

She got out and caught up with Penny at her door. "This is

some place you've got here." The inside of the house was gorgeous. Filled with period antiques but it still felt comfortable and homey.

"Thank you. I quite like it myself. It was my wedding present."

"Oh, I didn't even think to ask if you were married." Cassie blushed.

Penny said, "I was. He died two years ago."

"I'm sorry. About your husband, that is."

"Well thank you, honey. He and I had a lot of good years together. I miss him of course, but this house has a lot of good memories." Penny hung her bag on a hook on a gorgeous oak armoire near the front door and Cassie followed suit.

Penny gave her the quick tour and they ended up in the kitchen. "I'm going to put the chicken on the grill. Can you throw a salad together? All the greens are in the fridge."

Expertly—salads were the only thing she could really do well in the kitchen—Cassie chopped up vegetables and ripped lettuce, tossing them all together in a big bowl as Penny tended the grill.

"You ready in there? Come on out and bring the sangria," Penny called to her from the deck.

The pretty glass pitcher of fruited wine in hand, Cassie paused a moment in the doorway as the full impact of the view hit her. The back deck overlooked a lawn that sloped down to the water. It was shady and cool there with a breeze coming from the lake. Peaceful. The kind of place you'd want to come out and sit at the end of the day with a man who loved you. How wrong was it that a man who gave this to his wife for a present was dead while the man who tried to kill his was alive?

"This view is something else." Cassie came out and put the sangria down.

"One of life's greatest pleasures, sitting out here with a glass of wine and watching the sun go down. You hungry?"

Cassie nodded and for a few minutes they got down to the

business of filling plates and sipping sangria until the edge was off. They made small talk as they ate dinner. Penny warmed up, losing a bit of her formality, and Cassie began to remember what it was like to have friends and do normal things like have barbecued chicken on a summer evening.

"So why Petal, Cassie Gambol?" Deciding enough small talk had been expended, Penny cut to the chase. Perceptive eyes watched the woman seated across from her.

"A friend passed through a few years back and loved it here. I was sick of LA and wanted a change."

"Well, isn't that easy sounding? Somehow, I think it's more complicated than that. You married?" Cassie was a good person, Penny hadn't seen or sensed anything to make her believe otherwise. But she skirted around details, kept things broad and general. She was hiding something.

Cassie's mouth tightened. *Bingo.* There was a story there. "I was. We divorced."

Penny waited but Cassie didn't elaborate. "What did you do in LA?"

"All kinds of things. I worked for my brother. I ran his law office."

"You certainly do seem to be organized. I know a lawyer who needs some part-time help, actually. One of my dearest friends, Polly Chase, her husband, Edward, is looking. She was just talking about this a few days ago."

"Polly Chase?"

Penny looked askance at Cassie when her voice cracked. "Yes. Do you know her? She's a pistol."

"She barreled into the back of my car at a red light night before last."

Penny's eyes widened and then she began to laugh. "Oh my. I wish I could say I was surprised but I'm not. Frankly, I'm waiting for Shane to take her license away. I love her like my own mother but she is the worst driver in the history of ever. I trust you're all right? I haven't seen her since Wednesday and haven't been out of the store much. I can't believe I missed the gossip on that." Penny sighed with a rueful smile. "She really is a good person. She's just the type to always be thinking about twelve other things and putting lipstick on at the same time."

Cassie just shrugged. "I'll have to take your word for it. My small bit of experience with the woman hasn't been all that encouraging."

"She'll win you over. It's useless to try to resist her. She's special in her own indomitable way. Fiercely loyal and loving. When Ben died, that was my husband, she came over here every day and brought me food.

"Did my laundry. The entire family has been there for me. Kyle, her son, he took care of the lawns and Shane—that's the sheriff, you may have met him after the accident—he was at my side the entire trial. Edward made sure they prosecuted that rat bastard within an inch of his life."

"What happened to your husband? If you don't mind my asking."

"He was murdered. A hit-and-run. That scum had a record of drunk driving as long as my arm. He hit Ben when Ben was on his evening jog. Left him bleeding by the side of the road. Didn't even call the cops anonymously. By the time they found Ben, it was too late. He had massive internal injuries." Penny's shoulders fell. "Anyway, one of that murderer's co-workers saw the damage to his car and called to report him. They found Ben's blood on the bumper. He confessed. And then he tried to say it was allergy medication that went wrong. He's doing ten years. That bastard killed my husband and all he got was ten years."

Penny's smooth veneer slid away and behind it, Cassie saw something she recognized. Reaching out, she squeezed Penny's hand. She knew what it felt like to be failed by the legal system, even when most of the people involved had done all they possibly could for her.

"I'm sorry. I don't even have words so I won't try."

Penny sighed and shook it off. "I'm mostly past it. I have my days, but you have to move forward. I met Ben in my last year of high school. He and I had twelve years together, that's more than a lot of people ever have. Living in the past kills you and I know he'd hate it if I couldn't let go." Penny smoothed down the front of her skirt as she pulled herself together.

"If you decide you'd like the work, I'd be happy to introduce you to Edward. He's a very nice man. And if you haven't seen those Chase boys yet, well, you're in for a treat." Penny winked.

Not being able to help it, Cassie laughed. "Yeah, I've seen 'em. I live next door to Matt, and Shane took my accident report. I met Kyle and his wife, Maggie, too."

"All of them are single except for Kyle." Penny's face tried to stay innocent and nonchalant and Cassie snorted.

"Oh, well, I don't think I'm ready to date just yet. Maybe later."

The humor slid from Penny's face. "That bad, was it? Your ex?"

"Yes."

Penny let the one word answer go because it spoke volumes. Whoever Cassie's ex-husband was, he wasn't a nice man. She liked Cassie and hoped one day she could confide in her. Penny knew that every story had to be shared in its own way so she'd back off for the time being. She would ask Edward about the job too, though, because she wanted to help Cassie all she could.

The following Sunday, Shane pulled his truck into his parents' driveway and hopped out. It was just in time for the weekly family dinner. He cut it close but he'd had a call and had driven past Cassie's on his way back. Just to make sure everything looked all right.

Opening up the front door, he smiled as he was greeted by the hoots of his father and brothers watching baseball in the TV room. Moving toward the insanity of noise, his attention was snagged by the feminine laughter of his mother and sister-in-law across the hall in the sitting room.

Baseball was for suckers when you could grab some attention from two of your favorite women. And he wanted to talk to his mother about a few things anyway. Tossing his stuff on the bench in the hall, he joined them as they sat drinking lemonade and talking.

"Hey, Momma, Maggie." He bent and kissed their cheeks and tossed his long body on the couch.

"Hey, puddin'. How are you today?" Polly grinned at her oldest son.

He pretended to glower at the pet name and Maggie just laughed as she handed him a glass of lemonade.

"Be better if you didn't call me puddin'. You get out to talk to Cassie Gambol yet?"

"I do believe that girl is avoiding me. Not that I blame her. Some way to greet her, plowing into her and all. But she can't evade me forever."

Maggie snorted a laugh. "She'd be a fool to even try, Mom. But from what I've seen of her, the woman is very shy. There's a story lurking just below the surface but I doubt she'll part with it easily. Liv and I had breakfast with her last week and I've seen her at the bookstore. She's friendly enough but she reminds me a lot of an animal that's been abused. Her eyes..." Maggie paused, looking for the right words "...there's a shadow there." Maggie looked to Shane. "I thought you suspected her of being the leader of a drug cartel and smuggling through Petal."

"She's hiding something, but I'm willing to admit I think it's more of her running out of fear than running to hide a dark history as a master criminal." He rolled his eyes at his sister-in-law.

Shane told his mother all about how Cassie had reacted to Matt and then him the week before. "I think she needs someone to turn to, Momma. I want her to know she can trust us. Er, the people here in Petal, I mean."

Polly's very perceptive gaze took her son in. "Well, aren't you sweet? You are, aren't you? Sweet on this girl?"

Shane gave up trying not to smile and sighed. His mother was too damned smart for her own good. "Yeah. Okay so yeah, I like her. There's something about her that draws me. I don't know what about her makes me just want to scoop her up and wrap her in my arms to protect her. It's not that she's giving me a line or anything. Hell, I can barely get three words out of her. I've tried to talk to her here and there but she's so jumpy.

"And sometimes I see her and she's so afraid. I don't want her to be afraid of me. I hate that. I may have been a jerk a time or two—" he looked quickly at Maggie "—but I've never physically hurt a woman. I want her to trust me. I want—" he scrubbed his hands over his face "—I want her to look at me without fear. I want her to see me as a man and not a threat."

And he hated that she made him feel that way but he'd fought it since the moment he saw her and had given up. He was more than sweet on Cassie, he had a major jones on for her.

"Well, I'll talk to Penny about her. Maggie, you said she worked at the bookstore?"

"Yeah, a few days a week. And Shane, she's…you'll be careful with her, won't you?"

"I'm not a villain, damn it!" Frustrated anger coursed through him but the look on Maggie's face calmed him down. "Look, I know I was a jerk to you. But I'm trying to be better and I really do want to know Cassie. I won't hurt her if I can possibly help it."

Maggie nodded. "I don't think you're a villain, Shane. I think you're a good man who needs the right woman to love. So okay we'll reach out to her."

"My heart breaks to think about that woman all alone here and scared." Polly's face shadowed for a moment before she recovered herself.

Shane watched his mother's face and realized he had such wonderful examples of womanhood in his life. His mother cared so much about people and so did his sister-in-law. He could finally begin to see that his own woman could have a place there, in his family and his life. And he wanted to know if Cassie was that woman.

Cassie worked out on her front porch filling the pretty planters with bright flowers. She wanted to make the apartment her home. Each week she decided to do one more thing to claim the space. The flowers were the first step, the next week she planned to try and make some curtains for the windows in her bedroom.

"Hey there, Cassie."

She looked down the stairs and into the upturned face of Polly Chase. She'd been trying to avoid the woman for the last week and a half but Penny told her to give it up because Polly would eventually find her.

She couldn't help but smile back at the woman as she teetered up the stairs toward her on spiky heels. "Hello, Mrs. Chase. How are you today?" Time was up, she'd been caught like quarry. Cassie got up and poured water into the planters while she waited for Polly to reach her.

"Better now that I've finally found you home." Polly got to the landing and thrust two bags at her. Cassie took them with a puzzled look on her face.

"Would you like to come in? I've made some iced tea." Cassie may have been annoyed at Polly plowing into her but it was impossible not to respond to the tiny woman's smile.

"That would be lovely." Polly walked past Cassie into the apartment. "Have a seat, I'll bring it out. What's this?" Cassie held up the bags.

"Oh just some casseroles and a cobbler. Peach. I hope you like peach cobbler."

"Like it? I never had it before until I moved here and it's solely responsible for two extra pounds. It wasn't necessary for you to do this, you know." Cassie began to put the pans in her freezer and the cobbler on the counter. She filled two glasses with ice and tea and brought them to Polly.

"It wasn't necessary but it's neighborly. You're new to town and I got you into a car accident your very first day here. Lordy, I can't believe I did that. I hope you don't think worse of me." Polly blushed furiously.

Cassie had of course but found herself unable to hold her anger now that she was face-to-face with Polly. "Everyone in this town adores you, Mrs. Chase. I appreciate you coming by, I really do. And no, I don't think worse of you. Accidents happen." Especially if you were Polly Chase apparently.

Polly laughed and drank her tea. "Not bad for a Northerner." She winked.

"Northerner? I'm from Los Angeles."

"Exactly. If you're not a Southerner, what are you then?" Polly waved it away and Cassie just laughed and tried not to stare at how high Polly Chase's hair was. It was like an engineering marvel.

In the end, Polly stayed for an hour and wrangled a promise that Cassie would come to dinner sometime within the next month.

Bowled over, Cassie watched her whip away from the curb and nearly hit an oncoming car. The capper was the gay wave she sent to her near-victim as she drove away.

Chapter Four

As the days passed, Cassie began to truly live her new life. No one knew about her past and it was like a weight lifted from her. Most days she even forgot about Carly until some odd thing would remind her that a year ago she'd been someone else.

Three days a week Cassie worked at the bookstore, spending her spare time making jewelry. She'd spoken with Dee and would begin to sell her stuff at the Sunday Market that coming weekend. The detailed work took time and attention and she found it really good physical therapy for her fine motor skills. She wouldn't do surgery again, but she was able to hold the tools without shaking and manage all the finish work.

Her friendship with Penny had continued to deepen and damn if it didn't feel good to have a girlfriend again. Terry had never allowed her to go out with friends, wanting all her free time to be spent with him. He was always jealous of friends and family. Over time she'd pushed them all away rather than get into continual fights with him over it. In any case, her friends had all been pretty smart cookies, they'd seen his behavior, commenting on it, and it was just easier to not have to deal with the embarrassment.

She'd even begun to see a therapist twice a week and found

that talking about her time with Terry had started to help. Began to understand how it all happened and also that she wasn't a bad person. Still the guilt and shame were hard to part with.

Petal began to be home to her. Her residents like an extended family. Cassie got to know her neighbors in the fourplex, most especially Matt Chase. She certainly had no plans to complain that because of Matt she saw Shane Chase nearly as often. It seemed like he was at Matt's all the time. Truth was, she was beginning to like him too. He knew she was skittish and respected her space. He never rushed up on her or surprised her. For a big man, he was surprisingly gentle with her each time their paths crossed. There was something disarming about the way he treated her. Not so much like he felt sorry for her or pitied her but he was careful, respectful of her.

As a whole, every Chase family member she met she'd taken a liking to. Polly, as predicted, was impossible not to like. There was something irresistible about her. Maybe it was that Polly just sort of accepted Cassie, warts and nerves and all and didn't seem to notice. It just felt so *normal*. And normal felt good.

Three weeks after Cassie had started at the store, she and Penny were closing up when Maggie came in.

"Hiya, Penny. Hey, Cassie, I saw you had some pretty flowers on your front porch. Looks nice. Kyle was impressed when we stopped over at Matt's on the weekend."

Cassie just smiled. It wasn't like she could get a word in edgewise with Maggie Chase if she tried. But as it turned out, Maggie, like the rest of the Chase clan, was simply a nice person and fun to be around.

"It looked so forlorn, I wanted to make it more colorful. Just trying to make it a home, you know? What are you up to?"

"Well, I have an ulterior motive for being here. You and I haven't really hung out much and I'm on my way to The Pumphouse for some beer and staring at some Chase brothers. Tonight is their pool game and really, we just gossip and watch tight butts in faded jeans. Sounds good doesn't it? What do you say? You and Penny should come and hang out."

How long had it been since she'd gone out with girlfriends for beer and burgers? And pool? "Pool?" Cassie grinned. "Really?" She loved pool.

Before marrying Terry, she'd played several times a week at the tavern near the medical school. After they'd gotten married, he'd bought a table for the house. Of course he couldn't deal with losing so eventually she refused to play with him.

But as Brian was so fond of telling her, she had to start living her life again and who cared what Terry did or didn't do? He was long gone.

"From that slightly scary look in your face I take it you play? Those boys play every Friday night. I'm sure they'd love for you to join them."

"Shane would," Penny said as she locked up the back door and came toward them.

Cassie blushed and Penny chuckled. "Come on, Cassie. Anyone with eyes can see how he looks at you. He's smitten."

"I uh. Well, he's just being nice. And I think he suspects I'm up to no good. But yes, I love pool. Or I did. I haven't played in a few years. I used to be pretty good."

"Well then I think some beer, gossip and watching you play pool with some handsome boys is just the ticket." Maggie grinned and they all headed out.

Liv and Dee were already waiting at a table near the doors when they arrived. Once seated, Cassie tried to pretend that she wasn't watching every move Shane Chase made. The man was so big and bad but there wasn't anything threatening about him despite that. She loved the color of his hair, sort of coffee brown with a hint of blond. He had a savage kind of handsome that she found herself thinking of during the day. Many times during the day.

Forcing herself to focus on the women at the table, she tried to put him out of her mind. She did not need any more men.

As if he felt her gaze on his skin, Shane turned and noticed her there with Maggie and the others. So tall and striking. She stood out every time he saw her. The woman was seriously beautiful.

"Oh for cripes sake! Just go over there already." Kyle took his shot and rolled his eyes as he straightened. "You look like a starving man. It's pathetic."

"Yeah, the last time I saw that look *you* were wearing it." Marc chuckled. "Go on, Shane."

"I will, only because you three won't shut up until I do. Bunch of old women." He leaned his cue off to the side and headed toward their table.

"Hi, Cassie. Nice to see you here."

Cassie looked up at him and smiled hesitantly. She'd lost most of her fear with him but there was still a shadow of it in her eyes. He wanted to wipe it away.

"Hi, Shane. How are you all tonight? Who's winning?"

The sound of her voice, smoky sex and velvet seduction, stroked over his skin and made his gut tighten.

"Cassie here loves to play pool," Maggie said with a grin.

Shane adored his meddling sister-in-law at that moment. "That so? Well, show me what you've got, then." He held out his hand and Cassie scooted out of the booth, grabbing his forearm instead to help herself stand.

The shock of the cool, soft skin of her hand touching his arm shot through his body. As always, she seemed so many things at once. Strong and independent, yet vulnerable and scared. And he was seriously messed up if a woman's hand on his arm made him cow eyed. He was so pathetic he wanted to kick his own ass.

He motioned toward the table in the back and she walked ahead of him. Which was fine with him. He had no problem at all watching the delectable sway of her denim-clad ass. And it was a mighty fine ass, round and high and juicy. Did she wear a thong? Boyshort-type panties would look nice too, just a nice little slice of her cheeks showing out the bottom. Okay that had to stop or he'd be embarrassed in about a minute or so.

"Cassie's gonna play a game with us. She says she used to be pretty good. So let's take it easy on her." Shane cleared his throat and thought about the college football scores to get rid of the substantial hard-on she'd given him.

Rolling her eyes, she grabbed a cue and chalked the tip. All four men watched, rapt, as she blew off the excess. Annoyed, Shane elbowed Matt and glared daggers at Marc but both men just shrugged and Kyle laughed.

"Rack 'em up, boys."

Oh, the way she said that made his heart stutter. Didn't matter what she said, he was sure she'd sound drop dead sexy ordering a grilled cheese sandwich.

"Ante's ten bucks," Matt said with a wink.

Cassie snorted, pulled a ten out of her jeans and slapped it down on the side of the table.

"Ladies first," Shane said, motioning for her to go ahead.

"You sure about that?" She stood, hand on her hip.

"Of course. Guests and ladies first."

Cassie shrugged and took her first shot and proceeded to wipe the floor with them. Shot after shot, she'd call and sink it. She cleared the table without breaking a sweat.

Turning back to them, a sexy grin broke over her lips. Satisfied, she grabbed the money and tucked it into her pocket. "Thanks, boys. That was a very profitable few minutes."

"You're a pool shark!" Shane had been dumbfounded but now he found himself even more attracted by this mystery woman. Okay, so watching her bend over the table as she played helped a bit too.

"Nah, not anymore. See I could have played dumb and suckered you in until the pot was much bigger and then kicked your asses. But I played true from the first shot. I wasn't even sure I could still play this well. I'm glad I still have it." She smiled and Shane's cock sprang from hard to impossibly hard.

"You guys underestimated me." She patted her pocket. "The element of surprise, boys. Kept me in milk money." Her laugh was honeyed sexual heat.

"Another game?" Shane wanted her there longer.

"I need to be getting home. I have to be up early to get all of my stock ready for the Sunday Market day after tomorrow. It was a pleasure taking your money, though. Enjoy the evening." She waved back over her shoulder as she walked away.

"Totally devious." He shook his head in wonder. "She's the perfect woman." Shane watched her go to the table and say her goodbyes to the women there. "I'm going to be sure she gets home okay." Blindly, he shoved his cue at one of his brothers, heading toward the door that she'd just walked out of.

"Cassie." He'd noticed how prone to spooking she was so he made sure to always make a lot of noise when he approached her.

She turned, a bit startled but relaxed when she saw it was him. "Hello, Shane. What's wrong?" He looked good coming toward her. Handsome and masculine.

"I just thought I'd offer you a ride home. Police escort and everything."

"Oh, that's all right. I have my car just up in front of the bookstore."

"I'll walk you to it then."

He didn't give her much chance to run away when he fell into step next to her. The heat of his body rolled over her as they walked. The more she was around him, the less he scared her, but still, it was hard to not cringe when he walked so close to her. He just took the world for granted. Lived without fear of being assaulted or raped. Men his size could walk around any time without worry. She wished she knew what that felt like. For even just a few minutes.

He was patient as she unlocked her car but stopped her from getting in with a gentle hand at her shoulder. "Cassie, uh, would you like to get dinner sometime? Maybe go dancing?"

"I…well, I don't know if I'm ready to date just yet." Her words came out in a rush and the tenderness she brought out in him bloomed through his heart. Damn, what was it about this woman that got to him so deeply?

"Just yet? Are you with someone? I should have asked." He knew she was divorced of course. Nothing stayed a secret very long in Petal. Hell, her landlord shared that tidbit innocently enough the first night she'd landed in Petal and Shane had done a background check as well.

"Not anymore. I'm divorced."

He wasn't sure what emotion was in her voice as she'd said it. Sadness? Did she miss the ex? Pain? Was she afraid? It was petty of him but he far preferred that she hated her ex than her still wanting him. "Oh, it's still new. I'm sorry."

He tried to stay as patient as possible, watching as she took a deep breath and licked her lips before deciding to answer him. "It's not really new. I'm not pining away for him or anything. It's…complicated." Her voice trembled a bit at the end and he locked his knees to keep from moving to her.

The fear was there, unmistakable. "I know you're afraid of something. You can trust me, you know. I want to help. You can share your story with me. I like you, Cassie." His voice was soft and he had to grip the top of her car door to keep from reaching out to touch her.

Her big blue eyes looked up at him for long moments, wavering. But at the last minute she looked away for a split second and when she looked back, the moment had passed. "I'm…it's not something I like to talk about. Anyway, I should be getting home."

"Just come as my friend then. I won't rush you. I want to get to know you. Unless you're not attracted to me at all. In which case, I'll back off anything other than just being friends."

She sighed. "I'll think about it." She got into the car and then rolled down the window. "And any woman not attracted to you is blind or a damn fool."

Before he could respond, she'd pulled out and was driving away, leaving him wearing a goofy grin.

He took those words as a sign along with her pool game. Later that night in his bed he stopped pretending he wasn't totally gone for her and just accepted it. He'd never failed at pursuing a woman and he certainly didn't plan to start. He wanted Cassie Gambol and not just for a few nights in his bed. At first it had been a mild crush, then an interest and now he'd developed a serious fascination with Cassie. She made him think about her in ways he'd never thought about a woman before.

The very specter of the feelings that had sent him running out on Maggie two years before seemed totally right and he realized he was ready for Cassie. The issue was that he had to make her ready for him.

He'd take it slow even if it killed him.

He made himself promise to not rush up on her as he walked toward Fourth Street the next morning.

She sat there, ebony hair glossy in the sunshine, pretty blue eyes shaded by sporty black sunglasses and he was drawn to her immediately.

He'd thought she was gorgeous as he caught sight of her but the smile she gave him once she'd recognized him made her a goddess.

"Mornin', Cassie." He stuck his hands in the front pockets of his shorts to keep from touching her.

"Good morning, Sheriff. What brings you out here on such a sweltering Sunday?"

She did. He'd tossed and turned and finally had to take matters into his own hands in the shower. The woman drove him to distraction, turned him on, electrified him with her presence and it drove him wild. That she apparently had no idea she affected him that way was even more irresistible.

"Oh just looking." He motioned to her wares on the table.

"You made all this?" Her creativity was impressive. He admired her skill and the craftsmanship of the things she'd made.

"I did. What do you think?" Her voice had gone soft and shy.

Reaching out, he fingered a pretty beaded necklace that she'd hung on some sort of stylized branch thing. "I think you're amazingly talented. This is all beautiful. In fact, I think this would look good on Maggie, don't you? And this for my momma?"

Her smile returned, brighter than before. "This amber color would go really well with Maggie's hair, yes. I've seen her wear something similar to this before. But this—" she touched the necklace he'd indicated for his mother "—is too delicate for your mother. She's much bigger than this necklace. Her jewelry should be bolder."

"She's barely five feet tall." Shane chuckled.

"Ah yes, but your mother is ten feet tall in personality. That's what I mean. Her hair is very..." Cassie chewed on her lip and he grinned, waiting to see what she'd say. "It's so festive and her accessories are all very large."

She looked over the things on the table and shook her head. "I don't have anything that's right for her." Reaching down, she pulled out a plastic container and flipped it open, rustling through it for a few moments. "Aha!" She held up a pretty piece of glass swirled with blues of all hues and a thread of silver. "This. Let me make her something with it. I'll let you know when I've finished it. If you don't like it, no harm."

"You'd do that for me?"

"Sure. I was thinking of having it hang vertically, I think it would draw out her neck."

He smiled at her, not knowing what the hell she was talking about but it sounded good. And it gave him the chance to see her again. "Thank you. That's very nice of you. Her birthday is next month. Can I buy that necklace there for Maggie now though?"

"Oh." She blushed and he liked that the blush was for something innocent and sweet between them and not her usual shyness. "Sure. Thank you. Would you like me to wrap it up for her?"

He nodded, without words. He watched her graceful hands draw the necklace from where it was hanging and lay it in a box and then proceed to wrap it up so fancy he was sure he'd fuck it up by the time he got it to Kyle and Maggie's.

She handed it to him and he paid her. He didn't want to leave but people had come to her table and were browsing.

"Well, thank you again, Cassie. I'll see you around." She waved at him as he walked away.

Cassie watched him walk away, feeling giddy. Oh man, she had a crush on the sheriff. She wanted to put her head down and sigh wistfully. Wanted to write his name on her notebook and ask Maggie if Shane liked her.

This was bad. She couldn't have a crush on the damned sheriff. She didn't need the big goon, damn it. She—if and when she decided to ever date again—needed some nice, easygoing man about half a foot shorter. With like, a third the testosterone. Shane was a walking testosterone factory. He emanated masculinity. It disturbed and attracted her all at once. What she needed was a plumber, an accountant or a carpenter. She didn't need law enforcement or men with god complexes.

That made her wince. She was being unfair and she knew it. Shane Chase had been very sweet to her and while he was obviously arrogant in some ways, he didn't appear to have a god complex. Still, what the hell would she do with a man like him?

A smile crept back onto her face as she pondered the answers to that question.

Several days later, Shane walked into Paperbacks and More and held up a take-out bag when Cassie looked in his direction.

"Hi there, darlin'. Care to share a couple of sandwiches and some soft drinks with me?" This was just another step in the "get to know me" plan. He wanted to just sort of barge in and order her to come have lunch with him. It probably would have been how he'd have handled another woman. But this one needed special handling and he wasn't sure where his patience was coming from but he was thankful for it nonetheless.

"I don't know. I…"

Before Cassie could finish her sentence, Penny poked her head out of the back. "It's lunchtime anyway. You came in early and worked late day before yesterday. Flex out the time. That's a Honey Bear bag he's holding. Best sandwiches in town. I'll see you in an hour."

Cassie's mouth moved a few more times but Penny simply took over and pretty much pushed her into Shane. He'd have to thank her for that later on.

"I guess I can, yes. Thank you, Shane."

"There's a big ol' shady spot near the fountain at City Hall that's got our name on it." He held out his arm and after a brief hesitation, Cassie took it.

"Shady sounds very good."

They walked the few blocks to City Hall. He liked the way she felt next to him, her arm in his. Liked the way she fit against him even as she'd forget herself and lean a bit before pulling herself away.

Shane wasn't a fool, he wanted her to himself so he'd chosen a time after the lunch rush and had scoped out the bench earlier that day.

"This is nice. Thank you very much. How much do I owe you?"

He snorted, handed her a soda and unwrapped her straw, poking it in the top of the lid. "Please. It's not going to ding my retirement account to buy you a sandwich, a lemon bar and some soda."

"A lemon bar?"

He grinned, liking the sound of eagerness in her voice. "You like them, huh? Me too. Turkey okay? It was the special today." He handed her a sandwich wrapped in wax paper. While she unwrapped it, he flattened the bag between them and put a bag of potato chips there for them to share.

She toed off her shoes and dipped her feet into the cool water of the fountain, sighing. He wanted to groan aloud at the sight of her pretty red toenails.

"Uh oh. Are you gonna give me a ticket now?"

He nearly choked on his sandwich and looked up at her. "What?"

She gestured toward her feet. "You were staring at my feet in the water. I figured I was breaking the law somehow."

He laughed, if she only knew just what he'd been thinking. "Nah. I like your toenail polish. It's sexy. And if I didn't have work boots on, my feet would be in there too."

"This heat is spectacular. Thank goodness for the shade. I don't know how you all deal with it." She leaned her head back, her spine arched.

He coughed as the erotic carnival of delights returned to his head. "Uh, yeah, it's bad but you'll get used to it. How's the sandwich?" *Must not think of sex, must not think of sex...*

"It's as good as advertised. I didn't realize how hungry I was. Really, thank you for thinking of me." Her voice suddenly turned shy and he saw a delicate blush work up her neck.

"Well, it's not hard. Thinking of you, that is. So uh, what did you do back in Los Angeles?" Jeez, the woman had the power to make him babble. Him, Shane Chase, a man thought of as smooth and cool, turned into a mass of babbling, lovesick fool. His brothers would have a field day.

She blinked at him a few times and he wasn't sure if it was about his question or the comment about thinking about her.

"A little of this, a little of that. Nothing major really."

He may be a small town cop but he was still a cop. He knew when someone wasn't telling the whole truth and Cassie Gambol was not telling anywhere near the whole truth.

"Okay, if you say so. Do you have any family?"

"I have a brother." She smiled.

"Ah, progress! Older or younger? Parents?"

"He's older by three years. My mother died when I was twelve and my father nearly two years ago now."

"I'm sorry. It must have been hard to grow up without a mother. And then to lose your father at a young age too."

"It was, yes. But my brother was always there for me and my dad was a good man. He worked a lot but he was home every night for dinner. We survived as families do."

"Did you grow up in LA then?"

"Born and raised. My father too and his father before him."

He liked the way her voice changed when she talked about her family. There was a fondness there that appealed to him.

"Which high school did you go to?"

She snorted and balled up her wax paper as she finished the sandwich. "Where's my lemon bar?"

He laughed and handed it to her. Her eyes lit up with greed as she pulled the plastic wrap free, amusing him. The way her eyes slid half closed and she moaned as she took a bite did other things to him entirely. He had to put his napkin over his lap to hide the ridge of his cock pressing against his zipper.

"That's so good."

"You have a sweet tooth to go with that sweet voice, huh?" His voice was hoarse.

"I love sweet things. My big failing." She smiled sheepishly, avoiding the rest of his comment.

"You're doing well being friends with Maggie then. She's quite a hand in the baking department."

"You seem very close to her. To all your family."

"I have a great family. My parents are the best, they've supported me in everything I've ever done and Maggie is my family now too. She and Kyle are great together." He leaned forward and drew the pad of this thumb over her bottom lip. Her eyes widened and he saw the pulse at the base of her throat flutter. "You had a bit of powdered sugar there."

She brought her hand to her lips briefly and the moment between them stretched until she licked over the spot he'd just touched. The unwitting eroticism of it sent him reeling.

Clearing her throat she took a deep breath. "Uh thanks. That's lovely. About your family I mean. Oh, I'm nearly done with your mother's necklace. If you like, I can leave it at Matt's for you in a few days. Or I can bring it to work on Friday and you can get it then. When is her birthday? I didn't want to miss it."

Impulsively, he took her hand and held it in his own for a few moments. She turned, her gaze locked with his. Relief rushed through him to see there was no fear in her eyes.

Bringing her hand to his mouth, he brushed his lips across her knuckles ever-so-softly and laid her hand back in her lap. Her taste tingled on his lips.

"Her birthday is Labor Day. So you have three weeks. And I'll drop in the shop Friday. We can have lunch again."

She bristled. "I don't know. I told you before, I don't know if I'm ready to do this yet."

He turned to her, bending his knee between them. "Do I make you feel pressured?"

"No."

"You said you didn't have any feelings for your ex, right?"

She shuddered and he dug his fingers into his calf, wanting to demand she tell him about it. Instead he waited.

"No. God, no. Well, not any good ones. It's just, I don't know if I'm ready for a relationship or dating."

"We'll take it one step at a time. This is step one here, friendship. It's going pretty well, don't you think?"

She cocked her head and studied him carefully. "You're running a game on me, aren't you?"

"A game?" He fought a smile, liking her pluck. Sighing, she sat back.

"It's just lunch. Look, you know I'm interested in you, there's no pressure there at all. You know where I stand and I know you're interested in me too. You're the kind of woman who'd tell me to hit the road if I got too uppity."

"I used to be." Her voice was quiet, sad.

He paused a moment, not knowing how to approach and not wanting to put her off or make her upset. Aw, hell, he could only be who he was. "Cassie, you know you can tell me. You'll feel better for sharing it. Not as the sheriff, tell me as your friend."

She shook her head. "It doesn't matter. But you've won this round, Shane. Lunch Friday would be nice."

"Don't think I don't know you're changing the subject. But as it got me what I wanted I'll let it go. For now." He winked and she snorted.

The rest of their lunch was quiet and comfortable as they finished dessert. Standing after he'd tossed the trash into a nearby can, he reached down and offered her a hand up.

This time, instead of avoiding his grasp, she took it and let him help her. But he didn't let go and she didn't insist so they walked the few short blocks back to the bookstore hand-in-hand.

"Thank you very much for lunch, Shane. Why don't I deal with lunch Friday? I'll bring us something."

He grinned. "Nope. I got it. Friday is peach pie day at The Sands. We'll go there if you don't mind, sit in the air conditioned cool and have the special of the day while I pretend not to look at you a lot."

Her hand went to her throat. "I don't know what to say when you lay stuff like that on me. You're really good."

"Do I offend you?"

"No. It's flattering."

Quickly, he brushed a kiss across her forehead and stepped back. "Then my work here is done. For now. Go on back inside. I'll see you Friday." With that, he turned and headed down the sidewalk and she had to grab the door to keep from melting into a puddle.

"How was the sandwich?" Penny's mouth twitched as she hid a smile. "Pretty good if you're having trouble staying on the ground, I'd say." A single eyebrow rose as Cassie floated back into the bookstore.

"I don't know what to think about it. About him. He's so... big. He takes up so much space. He's overwhelming and charming and he knocks all good sense right out of my head every time he looks at me."

"Well, Cassie, I think you need to ask yourself why it's so necessary to think about it at all? I've grown up with Shane, he's a good man. Up to this point he's not always been so careful with women. He's been the kind of man who flits from flower to flower if you know what I mean. But with you? He's different. Not cautious so much as gentle. It's clear he's interested in you and he's being patient and letting you set the pace. And if you're going to dip a toe back in to the dating life, why not with a man like Shane? Let's be honest here, he's so hard and hot you just want to take a big bite."

Cassie froze for a moment in surprise at Penny's—for her—racy comment, and then laughed. "No kidding. But I don't know. He's so...big and in charge. I don't know if I need any of that."

Penny shrugged. "No doubt the man is one of those take charge kind of guys. Being in a relationship with Shane would take a lot of work. I think he'd want to protect his woman all the time."

"Well, I already had a man who thought he knew what was best and that didn't end very well at all."

Penny reached out and squeezed Cassie's shoulder. "I want you to know you can tell me how much you want whenever you're ready. I get the sense it was very, very bad. But despite being a big, bossy man, Shane is not like that. He's not the type to hurt a woman. I like seeing you with a carefree smile. Let him make you happy why don't you? If it turns in a direction you're uncomfortable with, you can always take a step back. You're young, Cassie. Let yourself live." With a final squeeze of Cassie's shoulder, Penny went into the office again and Cassie went to finish putting the new releases out on the shelves.

Chapter Five

Penny smiled and waved as Maggie and Polly walked into The Honey Bear and joined her.

"The tea and brownies are on the way."

Polly tossed her gargantuan bag on the floor and sat with a happy sigh. "Good. How are you, sugar?"

"I'm doing well, Mrs. Chase. Hey, Maggie, looking great as always. Thanks so much for meeting me here."

"An offer of blond brownies and planning for Cassie? What's not to like about that?" Maggie grinned and took out a pad of paper and a pen.

"I was thinking of something like a welcome barbecue. We can invite folks to come and spend the day mixing. She could get to know people and feel like a part of something." Penny sipped her tea.

"That's a great idea. We can do it over Labor Day weekend. We were going to do something for my birthday but we can make it a combination thing. That way she'd have to come or risk insulting me." Polly raised a smug eyebrow and the other two women laughed.

"It's a good thing your powers are harnessed for good, Mom. She's so shy sometimes that I agree she might turn down something that was just for her but if we link it to your birthday she'd come. Plus, Shane can have her for the whole day then." Maggie bit into the just delivered brownie and groaned in delight.

"He's shown up twice to bring her lunch this week. Just this afternoon he brought her flowers and escorted her like she was some precious object. She's bowled over. He's putting on the full court press with her. It's impressive to watch," Penny told them.

"I haven't seen him this interested in a woman since before Sandra. He talks about Cassie all the time. I like her a lot. She's a sweet girl and smart. I think she's good for him because it makes him think about someone else. Not that he's selfish but he's never really put a woman first before. Whatever it is she's hiding, it's not anything she's at fault for, I can tell that just from dealing with her. I worry for her but if anyone can help her, it's my Shane."

"Polly, I think it's about her ex-husband. She hasn't shared much but I think there was some bad stuff there. She's nervous as a cat about men but she's not a criminal. Hardworking. Kind."

Polly sighed sadly. "I hate to think that any man would do something bad to his wife. But I'm glad she's here and we'll just have to show her that."

They planned the party, deciding to have it at Penny's house, right on the water with food and drinks and lots of fun. They'd invite enough people for Cassie to mix and get to know but not so many she'd feel overwhelmed.

Cassie's thoughts were filled with Shane as she watched him approach her table at the Sunday Market. His jeans clung to his long, powerful-looking legs and his T-shirt fit snug over his upper body. His muscles positively rippled as he moved, blue-green eyes only for her. She loved the way his hair looked a bit messy but still soft and silky as it touched the top of his collar.

"Hi." She waved as he stopped. She wished she had something more articulate to say but the man sapped her IQ as all her blood moved away from her brain to her nipples. Shifting and squeezing her thighs together to ease the ache his presence brought, she smiled up at him.

"You look beautiful today. Well, you always do. How's business?" He reached out and touched the scarf she had around her neck. The scarf she used to hide the scars.

Still, it was a major victory for her that she'd stopped hiding so much of herself. Yes, she hid the physical reminders of her years with Terry, but she was opening up in ways she hadn't in years. She'd had beer and burgers with Penny and Maggie and the others on Friday night after a really lovely lunch with Shane where he made her blush with his love of the necklace she'd made his mother. She'd beaten the Chase brothers at pool again and Shane walked to her to her car. The kiss had been on her lips, brief but still made her all shaky.

She'd gone into her growing feelings for Shane with her therapist and her brother. Cassie was beginning to feel normal again. She had a life with friends and grocery shopping and a paycheck. Normal was a gift and she'd agreed with her therapist and her brother that she needed to grab it with both hands and live it.

Starting with letting Shane Chase catch her if he wanted to. Or, at least let him take her on a date.

"I'm all right. Apparently your mother and Penny have got some big party planned to welcome me to Petal. They're saying it's for your mother's birthday so I can't refuse."

He threw back his head and laughed. "You're right. They've got your number. Not that it matters, she's got you on the ropes. You're coming, right?"

She grinned. "Yes. I've been promised peach cobbler *and* lemon bars. You're a terrible man to expose my weakness so it can be used against me."

He'd never seen her so flirtatious. He liked it. Liked seeing her lighthearted and unafraid of him.

"Darlin', you've been in Petal nearly six weeks now. By now, your brand of toothpaste isn't a secret. That's the price of living in a small town."

She blushed and he decided to forge ahead. "Would you like to go to dinner with me? Dinner and maybe some dancing at The Tonk? Dinner would just be us two. Well, 'cause I want you all to myself. But dancing would be a group of folks. Kyle and Maggie, Matt and Marc will have dates, too, of course. Liv will be there with her new boyfriend, Brody."

"Okay."

He'd been readying his next line of attack when he realized she'd just agreed to a date. "Okay?"

"Yeah. When?"

"Tuesday? I have Wednesday and Thursday off this week."

"All right. I have Wednesday off too."

"Pick you up at seven then? Is Italian food okay with you?"

She nodded and he stood there grinning at her for several long moments.

"I'm gonna go now before I do something stupid and you change your mind. I'll see you tomorrow for lunch."

Before she could argue, he turned and headed off with a wave. Still didn't stop her from watching his ass as he left though.

As satisfied as she'd been with the profits from her Sunday Market, the best part was that she got to use her hands to create. Truth was, she ached to practice medicine again.

There had been very little in her life she'd been more passionate about than being a doctor. She loved it. Loved helping people, loved improving lives. She missed it and found herself thinking about starting again with a new practice specialty.

Oh, she knew she'd have to go back and get more training. That didn't seem as daunting as it might have before. Before she'd decided on her surgical residency, she'd been fascinated by family medicine and one of her old mentors was a family practitioner in Orange County. The thought of taking care of entire families had a lot of appeal.

At the same time, it scared the hell out of her to imagine risking herself over something and losing it again. She couldn't work at the bookstore forever but it was good for the immediate future and her creative side was nourished by the jewelry making.

At the close of the day, Cassie went to a movie with Penny and called Brian once she got home.

"So, the sheriff asked me out today again."

"Yeah?" She could sense his grin.

"I said yes. We're going to dinner and dancing afterward."

"Well it's about time. Go Sheriff Chase. Good for you, Cassie. I'm proud. So proud."

"You know what? I'm proud too. It feels good not to live in fear. He's a nice guy, Brian. I really like him. And his family, they're like a dream come true. Every last one of them is adorably sweet."

"They'd better be. You deserve it."

They spoke for a long time after that, sharing their lives in a way she'd been unable to do since before the last years with Terry. She finally had part of herself back. Even better, she was sharing it with people who mattered to her. It was a kind of connection she'd missed so much. It felt so good she wondered when the other shoe would drop and something bad would happen to mess it all up.

Chapter Six

Tuesday morning dawned and Cassie puttered around the house all day. To keep her mind off her first date in a year and a half, she'd painted one of the tables she'd bought at a yard sale. It sat drying on her deck as she realized it was longer than a year and a half. It was six because Terry didn't really count. Hell, the first time she felt lighthearted about a simple thing like dinner and dancing since the first year she and Terry were together. Gah! So much for not thinking about it.

To get away from the apartment, she splurged and went to the beauty salon to get her hair and nails done. On the way back, she bought a sexy pair of shoes. Which would of course go with the jungle of sexy shoes in her closet right now. She had a weakness for shoes. Okay, an addiction. But hey, as addictions went, it wasn't that bad.

After a brief nap she still had an hour to go before Shane showed up and she began to get nervous.

"This is stupid. I should not be going out." She began to pace, mumbling to herself.

A knock sounded on her door and she looked at the clock. No, still an hour away, it couldn't be Shane. She'd kill him if he showed up an hour early. What kind of man showed up an hour early?

Stomping over to the door she looked through the peephole, fingertips caressing the baseball bat leaning against the wall.

She opened it and Maggie, Penny and Liv all rushed in. "Afternoon, Cassie." Penny gave her a brief hug. "I do like your hair. I think I see Tate's handiwork. She's a genius with those scissors."

Before Cassie could answer, Maggie and Liv followed with hugs and all three simply strolled past her into her bedroom.

"What are you all doing here? I mean, sorry, that's terribly rude of me. Hello, how are you all? Now what the hell are you all doing here?"

Liv laughed and gestured to the endless rows of shoe trees and racks lining her closet floor. "You're a shoe whore! My word, I don't think I've ever seen so many shoes in one place. What size do you wear?"

Cassie narrowed her eyes. "I don't know if I've known you long enough to share shoes with you. That's a very intimate thing. I'll need to run a credit check and do a few home visits to see what sort of environment they'd be in."

Liv looked startled and then laughed. "You've got a sense of humor. I knew it was in there somewhere." Her eyes moved back to a pair of red patent leather slingbacks with open toes. "Oh my lands. Cassie, I don't care what you were going to wear, you will plan an outfit around these shoes."

"Wait, I think I know the dress for them." Cassie reached into the closet and pulled out a white dress with a big red O ring on the bodice where the fabric gathered. It was backless and tied around the neck. The skirt of it had a handkerchief hem. The perfect sexy summer dress.

Of course, she hadn't worn it since the…what the fuck could she call it? It sure wasn't an accident. Was your husband trying to kill you an incident? Whatever, maybe she'd write Miss

Manners to see. But for now, she'd have to choose something else because backless wasn't an option.

"Oh, no. Let's see what else there is." She moved to hang it back up but Liv grabbed it.

"This is perfect. Cassie, you've seen yourself in a mirror, right? You know you'll look like a sex goddess in this dress. Shane will be under your spell the minute you open that door."

"I don't feel comfortable showing so much skin on a first date."

Liv started to speak but Penny put a hand out and touched her arm. Instead, Liv nodded and hung it back up. "Okay. Well that's fair enough. What else do you have?"

In the end, they decided on a different white dress with a wide, red patent leather belt and tiny, heart-shaped buttons. The cuffs on the short sleeves were red where they folded up and the sweetheart collar was also lined in red. It hugged every curve and the shoes made her legs look ten miles long.

No one seemed to mind when she shooed them all out of the room to change, although she did laugh when Liv told her to leave off panties or they'd show a line.

After she got dressed, the four of them crowded into the bathroom while Cassie put on makeup and did her hair.

"Man, you're a knockout. I'd probably hate you if I didn't have such high self-esteem." Liv winked and Cassie laughed. "You do know you're going to stop traffic tonight, right? I don't know if The Tonk can take it. Shane is gonna freak."

"Oh puhleeze!" Cassie blushed and rolled her eyes.

The other women stared at her in disbelief. "Are you telling me you can't see how beautiful you are?" Penny asked.

"Gorgeous? I'm attractive enough, I'll give you that. But I'm just average looking. Not all siren sexy like Liv or athletic sexy like you, Penny, or that sweet, fey kind of sexy like Maggie. I'm too tall, too leggy and I have an ordinary face. I do have nice boobs though. I got those from my mom."

Maggie shook her head as she stared. "Don't take this the

wrong way or anything but I'm pretty sure I've never seen a more beautiful woman in person before. Cassie, you're long and curvy and your features are seriously perfectly proportioned. And your hair, who has Elvis blue-black hair all thick and shiny? And back to the not taking it the wrong way thing? Your voice is so sexy it kind of makes me all tingly and I'm as straight as they come. You were stunning without makeup and in jeans but now, all dressed up and polished—you're a knockout."

"Girl, you must have hit your head if you can't see it. You're like, 'Top Ten Most Gorgeous People' beautiful. So shaddup. And take a compliment. And look in the mirror without whatever the hell happened to you. Because it's robbing you of your life," Liv said seriously.

Cassie spun and looked at Liv, heart pounding. "I wish I could," she whispered. "You have no idea how much."

Liv went to Cassie, bringing her into a tight hug. "Honey, I'm sorry. I didn't mean to be flip. It's obvious whatever it was, it was bad and I shouldn't make light. I just don't want you to hide your light under a bushel. Even if you are big-time competition." Liv winked.

"Thank you. I appreciate all of you coming over here and being my friends. It means so much to me."

"Well, that's what friends are for. And now I have to get home and get ready. Kyle is making me dinner before we meet you guys at The Tonk. You look fabulous, Cassie." Maggie kissed her cheek quickly.

"And I have to meet Brody at his place, we're having…uh, okay, we're having sex before we meet you all at The Tonk."

Cassie grinned and shook her head.

"And I have dinner in the crock-pot. I will see you at The Tonk later on. You look beautiful, Cassie." Penny joined Maggie and Liv at the door and they all headed out, leaving Cassie in the quiet, alone with her thoughts and her racing nerves.

Luckily, they'd all eaten up so much time, it was just a few minutes until the doorbell sounded and after a peek through the peephole, she saw Shane standing there.

Taking a deep breath, she opened the door. It would be step one of the challenge to be comfortable with him alone in her apartment. She hadn't had a panic attack in a few weeks and the mental exercises her therapist had given her really seemed to help.

His smile fell off his face as he stared at her.

"What?" She smoothed down the front of her dress. "Do I look awful?"

He shook his head slowly. "No. You look fucking amazing." He blinked quickly. "Oh shit, I'm sorry. Oh." He grimaced. "Sorry, I tend to get a bit profane when I'm nervous or agitated. That outfit has me in both states. You look beautiful. Sexy. Outrageously hot."

His flattery washed over her, making her feel warm and tingly. She smiled, blushing. "What are you standing out there for?"

"I was waiting for you to invite me in. I know you've been uncomfortable alone with Matt, I didn't want to scare you."

Her euphoric mood was cut by the reality of her insane life. "Come on in, I'm sorry. My manners are bad. I'm all right. I didn't know Matt then, I do now. I'm really not crazy, I swear."

He caught her hand and raised it to his lips. "I don't think you're crazy, Cassie."

They stayed long enough for her to gather her wrap and a bag and they were on their way to the restaurant.

Vincent's was a small, family-owned Italian restaurant. The interior was beautifully intimate. Candles in pretty glass holders cast a golden glow about the room, bouncing off the sheen of the polished wood furniture. The place smelled of garlic, marinara and roses from the two large bouquets at the hostess stand at the front door.

The hostess smiled at Shane, her expression all but turning into a snarl when her eyes reached Cassie.

"I had reservations, Stella. For seven." Shane was crisp and efficient and kept his arm around Cassie's waist. It wasn't possessive, though, so Cassie relaxed a bit and walked ahead of him with his hand, warm and solid at the small of her back as they went to their table in a far back corner.

The hostess was ready to break her own neck as she vascillated between flirting and simpering at Shane, who did his best to ignore it, and shooting daggers at Cassie. At last, seeing she didn't have a chance, she flounced off.

Cassie smirked at Shane. "My. I think I've upset your admirer. Is she an ex?"

"Stella?" Shane's voice was shocked. "Cassie, the girl is barely twenty. I'm thirty-four years old. I assure you, I don't date women who are fourteen years my junior. I'm not a letch."

Cassie laughed then and he stilled, closing his eyes a moment. "You do know that your laugh should be a registered aphrodisiac, right? Your voice in general but your laugh…well, if I could bottle it, we'd make a million dollars."

"You're full of compliments tonight and I haven't even told you how handsome you look. I really like that color on you."

She did. The dark blue dress T-shirt he had on brought out the chocolate hues in his hair and the blue in his eyes. The Tommy jeans were a rust color and hugged a very nice ass and hard thighs. He was a seriously dreamy man. And he smelled good, too.

"What cologne are you wearing? I like it."

"Oh, it's Ralph Lauren Black. A birthday present from my momma, believe it or not." He blushed.

"Are you blushing? Don't tell me you aren't used to women falling over themselves to compliment you, Shane Chase."

"I'm not going to answer that. I've been a man long enough to know better than that. But I will say that what matters is that *you're* the one complimenting me."

They ate a leisurely dinner and got to know each other better. Cassie found herself more able to relax with him each time they got together. Those lunches had made a difference because he wasn't really a stranger.

"You ready to go grab a dance or five with me? I have to show you off. I bet you'll fit against me just right." He stood and they walked out to his car.

"Do you write all this stuff down? Seriously, you're smooth."

He laughed and avoided the answer as he navigated into a spot to park. "Wow, crowded tonight. It's not usually this bad on a Tuesday."

"We can do it another night if you like."

"Oh hell no. You owe me a dance. Come on now. Let's show 'em how it's done."

He sprang out and walked around but she'd gotten her door open. He frowned and she took his arm.

"I can open a door, Shane. Stop pouting. I already see you have nice lips."

"I don't pout. And I like to do things for you."

She stiffened and halted. "Let's get this straight before we go inside. I can do things for myself. I'm a grown woman. I am capable of opening doors, making phone calls, ordering my food, buying my clothes and generally living my day-to-day life without being managed and done for."

He narrowed his eyes, ready to argue, but saw her eyes and took a step back instead. Fear and anger. He'd pushed a button and his cop brain began to piece together whatever the hell her ex must have done.

But he wasn't going to be put in the same category as some control freak asshole who fucked her over either. "I never said you weren't capable of doing things and I didn't order your food or manage you. I just wanted to open your door. But if it bothers you, I won't."

She sighed and looked him up and down. "Listen, maybe you should just take me home."

He closed the distance between them slowly, careful not to spook her or frighten her with his body. Gently, he took her hands in his own. "Cassie, clearly I've struck a nerve. I didn't mean to upset you. And I didn't mean to sound pissy. You have a right to be treated how you want to be treated. It wasn't my intention to offend you. I am a bossy guy, it's just how I am, but I'm not trying to control you. Come on, let's go inside. Okay?" He brought her hand to his mouth and kissed the inside of her wrist.

Slowly, he felt the tension leave her body and she nodded.

Inside, the place was chaos. Cassie was thankful for his size when he plowed his way through the crowd and led her to the table where their friends had gathered.

Matt's eyes widened and he whistled when he saw her. "You look fantastic, Cassie."

Shane pulled a chair out and then indicated that she sit. She appreciated that he didn't do it all for her. Appreciated his control and the fact that he seemed to be trying hard to let her be.

She chatted with Maggie and the others and tried to ignore Matt teasing his brother.

Shane leaned over and spoke in a low voice. "Eyes back in your head, Matt. Don't let the fact that you're my baby brother stop you from understanding I'll hurt you if you continue staring at Cassie."

Matt threw back his head and laughed so loud and hard that everyone turned to look at him.

"Shall we dance, darlin'?" Shane murmured in Cassie's ear.

"Uh, sure. What was that all about?" She looked back at Matt, who was wiping his eyes, as they walked to the floor.

"He's just being Matt. A dumbass."

"Mmm hmmm. If you say so."

"I do, darlin', I do." He winked and pulled her against his body, resting his arm around her waist, holding her hand with the other. They fit together perfectly. He was a big, tall man but she was tall, too, and in her heels, it was softness to hardness in all the right ways.

So right, Cassie was pretty sure she'd need to think about

it. With her eyes closed. In the dark, in her bedroom, after he dropped her home that night.

Relaxing, she put her head on his chest and melted into his body, breathing him in.

Their rhythm matched. Both with such long legs they moved over the floor gracefully, sinuously. She was aware the music changed here and there but really, it was all about Shane holding her against his chest.

Until they got bumped into. First and then again. The floor got crowded and they had to stop moving and just sway. Which was all right to start. But the people began to press in.

Every few minutes she'd get jostled again and she felt the edges of the panic encroach. Her hands started to sweat and the trembling built up in her muscles as she tried to hold it back.

But she couldn't calm it with breathing or meditation.

Shane stopped and leaned in. "Cassie? Darlin', are you all right?"

She shook her head, lips tight. Breaking from him, she headed off the dance floor to their table but people kept getting in the way. And being Petal, she was handled over and over as the men kept saying "excuse me" and helping her past. They weren't manhandling her, it was all to help her and be neighborly but it wasn't good.

By the time she reached the table the panic was gray at the edges of her vision. She knew she had to get home fast.

"I have to go. Please." She grabbed her wrap and bag and ran out the door.

Shane looked at his brothers and tossed down money for the drinks and moved to follow her but Maggie, Liv and Penny stood up.

"Shane, let us. I don't know if a man is what she can deal with right now. I promise you, we're going to her house right now. She's just a few blocks away. I'll call you and let you know she got home all right. Let us help her." Maggie begged him with her eyes and Kyle looked worriedly between them.

"She's right, Shane. Let them go so she won't be alone very long." Kyle squeezed his brother's arm.

He sighed. "Fine. But call me. Promise. Tell her I'll see her soon. I'm not walking away from her."

Maggie tiptoed up and kissed his cheek quickly. "I promise." She gave Kyle a brief kiss and the three women rushed out to follow Cassie.

Cassie had finished throwing up when the knocking on the door started. Shakily, she rinsed her mouth out and wobbled back into the living room.

She tried to ignore the knocking, it wasn't pounding but it was insistent. "Cassie, it's us. Please, let us in. We're worried about you."

Penny. She'd expected Shane and she *so* wasn't ready to deal with him.

"I'm all right. I swear. I'll see you all later." Cassie leaned her head against the door she spoke through.

"No way. We aren't leaving until we've seen for ourselves," Maggie called out.

Sighing, Cassie opened the door, ready to shut it after they saw her in the flesh but they pushed their way into the room.

"Now, do you have any tequila? Because I think this calls for some margaritas." Penny went into the kitchen and began to look around.

"I'm fine. You see? Now you can go. I'm not up for company right now. I don't feel well." Cassie followed them into the kitchen where they had her blender out and were assembling ice, tequila, limes and salt.

"You even have mix."

"I don't want to have drinks. I want to go to bed."

"Too bad. You're going to talk to us and if some margaritas make that easier, great. If not, we're still drinking them and you can tell us all about whatever the hell has you so spooked." Penny began to assemble everything in the blender.

"Oh, Penny said hell, I'm telling," Liv teased.

Smiling and shaking her head, Maggie pulled out her cell phone. "I'm going to call Shane to let him know you're all right. He's worried about you. He didn't come here himself because we were concerned about how you'd react to a man right now."

"I..."

Maggie held a hand up to silence Cassie while she made the call and Cassie sighed heavily and went to sit on the couch. Liv laughed and plopped down next to her.

"We're your friends, sugar. You need this. You may not even know how much but you do. Friends will sit your ass down and give you the 'Come To Jesus' talk when you need it most. And girl, you need it."

Penny brought a tray with the pitcher of margaritas and glasses and even a bowl of snacks.

"You're a pretty good hostess with my stuff." Cassie snorted.

Penny laughed. "Why thank you, I do try. Now stop being so damned difficult. Drink up and tell us what the hell brought you here today. And see, you made me curse. Three times in twenty minutes and Liv is going to call my mother and tell on me. So you'd better make this worth it."

Cassie blinked a few times and couldn't help but smile. Penny didn't swear much and it was sort of funny and hell, why not? Why not just let part of it go?

Maggie and Penny moved the small coffee table out of the way and they all moved to the floor on pillows.

"I don't suppose I could just say I had a bad ex-husband and it makes me wary of all men, can I?"

Penny arched a brow at her and Cassie sighed.

"Okay, the truth is that I did...do have a bad ex-husband. Really bad. He didn't start out that way. I met him when I was nearly done with school. He was so sweet. Funny. Concerned about my well-being. He went out of his way to be sure I slept enough and ate well." She didn't want to talk about being a doctor, she wasn't ready to reveal that much just yet.

"At first, I thought it was wonderful. He brought me roses and took me to lovely places. He bought me clothes. Lots of clothes. I didn't think anything about it. But really, that's where it all started. They were not the kind of thing I'd normally wear. But slowly, he made me into another person. The person he wanted to marry."

Cassie shrugged and drank several gulps of the margarita. Of course she'd thrown up everything in her stomach so it hit pretty fast and she felt the alcohol began to work on her inhibitions.

"And we did of course. My father liked him well enough and I wanted him so that satisfied him. But my brother always disliked him. God, I should have listened to that.

"Over time, he took over every aspect of my life. Little by little. I didn't even notice it until it was too late. He controlled everything. Where I worked, what we ate—he even hired a cook to make things the way he wanted—we lived in a house he chose. My hair color was his choice, along with my hairstyle. I lost most of my friends because he thought they were unsuitable and many of them thought he was an arrogant ass and didn't want to be around him."

She closed her eyes and a tremor worked through her. While she'd been able to relate this to the therapist and even in court, it was not easy to talk about. Shame burned hot on her cheeks.

"Take it slow. We're all here as your friends, Cassie." Penny squeezed her hand.

"The hitting started. Well wait, back up a bit. The emotional and mental abuse started after the control. If I questioned anything he did, he'd grind me down. Make me think I was stupid or mean to him, that I didn't love him or appreciate what he did for me. I'm a smart woman, graduated at the top of my class, but he made me feel stupid. Worthless. Invisible. Ugly." She gulped the last of her margarita and winced as the icy drink made her head ache. Still, she held up her glass and Penny refilled it.

"He didn't hit me all the time. He didn't need to really. I was so afraid to do anything wrong, I had no life outside of my job and our marriage.

"Being his wife was a full-time job. He made me weigh in every Friday. If I gained a pound or lost more than two, he'd punish me."

The other women cringed but stayed quiet, letting her tell her story in her own way.

"He was a doctor. He knew just where to hit where it would hurt me but not do outward damage. Kidney punches so hard I urinated blood. He punched me in the head, no bruises that way but I developed a vision problem so he stopped that. All of the physical stuff was where it wouldn't show. On my stomach and lower back, my thighs were a favorite place." Her voice seemed so calm as she related it all. Almost like she was reading it, or even talking about someone else. It was the only way she could get through it.

"Anyway, it all started getting really bad two years ago. The physical abuse was getting severe enough that my co-workers began to suspect something was wrong. He was questioned by his boss, which only made things worse for me. Our sex life—" Cassie shuddered "—was awful. He raped me more often than I consented. It was like this one part of me I could control. He couldn't make me want him or even pretend to." Her voice became choked and tears welled up. Maggie moved closer and stroked a hand over her hair.

"I wanted to leave. I don't know why I didn't. I was afraid. He told me he'd find me and kill me. I believed him. I had every reason to. I took birth control shots and thank heaven I never got pregnant because he really wanted kids.

"And then my father died and he deteriorated because I had money. A lot of it. In his crazy mind, enough to leave him. He became paranoid. He'd weep, begging me to forgive him one day and beat me nearly bloody the next. I was missing work and I knew it was a matter of time before I lost my job or he killed me."

She got up and went into the kitchen and took two shots of the tequila, wiping her hand on the back of her mouth before coming back. "Okay, I think I'm better now." Her words were slurred a bit but she wanted to finish it. Or at least most of it.

"My boss was…is a wonderful woman. Really supportive. I love her to this day. Anyway, she cornered me in her office and demanded that I tell her the truth. I'd been lying so long, hiding it, that I started to deny it automatically but for some reason, I shook it off and told her the truth. Showed her the bruises on my back and stomach and she called the cops and my brother. The cops took my statement and pictures and my brother made me move out of the house and in with him.

"I filed for divorce and we started going through the process. It sucked but my ex couldn't do much. My brother is a hotshot family law attorney and he had my back. There were pictures and lots of evidence from people who'd seen my physical problems getting worse at work. I got my divorce but I gave him the house and the car and the vacation house and all the clothes he ever bought me. I wanted to be free, I didn't care about the stuff. I just took what I brought into that house and my books.

"But it wasn't enough. And he wouldn't stop. I thought I had my life back but he wasn't going to let me. He just pretended to and he attacked me. A little over year ago. Bad." She couldn't detail that night. Could not.

She shook her head hard and began to cry. "I can't say more."

The women, her friends, surrounded her and enveloped her into a hug as they murmured. Comforting her.

She cried a long time until she couldn't anymore and sat back, head on the couch.

"Girl, I don't know how you came out of that clusterfuck with such a good head on your shoulders. You're a strong woman, Cassie. I admire you."

Cassie moved her head enough to look at Liv in utter disbelief. "Strong? I let this asshole fuck me over and beat me up, *rape me*, for four years! I'm not strong. I'm a doormat. I was weak and stupid."

Penny moved, holding her upper arms. "You are not stupid, Cassie. Domestic violence happens to women across class lines, across educational backgrounds, across race and religion. It happens to all kinds of women. It's the frog-in-the-pot syndrome. You didn't know the water was boiling until it was too late. That makes you *human*, not stupid."

"And that's what these asshole abusers do. They make you believe you deserve it. It's a mindfuck. He worked you over physically as well as mentally. But you got out. That's the key here, Cassie. I can't believe what you've gone through. No wonder you get spooked by men. It's amazing to me how totally together you are." Liv's voice was tinged with anger.

"I'm not some charity case, you know. I heard all this at my group counseling. You must all think I'm such a flake. I thank God my father never lived to see how it ended."

Penny shook her head. "I think you're amazing. I've thought that since the first day you came into the store and I continue to think so. You're a *survivor*, Cassie. He took your life for four years but you took it back. You're here, working, living, dating even. This doesn't change the way I feel about you. You're my friend."

"You have nothing to be ashamed about. What happened was not your fault. It wasn't. He hurt you, that's on him. I hope that bastard got what was coming to him." Maggie's face held an emotion Cassie couldn't quite identify.

Cassie sighed. "He didn't. But I don't want to talk about it anymore. Thank you for listening to me. You don't know what it means to be able to share this with someone other than a therapist."

"That's what friends are for. Cassie, nearly two years ago now, I was kidnapped, assaulted and nearly raped by a stalker. It's not the same as what you endured but I understand the guilt and the shame. If you ever want to talk, please call me or come over. Anytime. I mean that." Unshed tears shined in Maggie's eyes.

And suddenly, a weight moved from Cassie's chest and she took a deep breath. Deeper and more relaxed than she'd taken in quite some time. Her brother and her therapist were right, it did feel better to share her burden with people.

They stayed a while longer and talked until Cassie was well enough to laugh again. Alone in her bed that night, she didn't feel the specter of Terry over her shoulder. It was just her.

Chapter Seven

After a long day at work, Cassie slumped into her superheated apartment, turned on the air conditioning and hit the shower before even considering what to make for dinner.

Shane had left her a phone message, checking on her earlier in the day. He'd wanted to come by for lunch but it was a big new release day and she'd been rushed off her feet and had worked several hours overtime.

She'd called and left him a voice mail that she couldn't do lunch but hoped to see him later on if he still wanted to. She hoped like hell she hadn't freaked him out. Gauging by his wanting to have lunch with her, she didn't think so but hell, he may have wanted to lay it all out that he thought she was a freak and to stay away from him. Maggie was his sister-in-law after all, she probably told him all about the craziness of the night before.

Standing in front of her open fridge, hair in a ponytail, feet bare, legs exposed by a pair of cutoff shorts, she jumped when someone knocked on the door.

A quick check showed Shane Chase waiting on her doorstep. Taking a deep breath, she opened the door, wincing at what a mess she must look.

He looked her up and down and shook his head. "Darlin',

how do you manage to look as gorgeous in cutoffs as you do in a dress that hugs every curve? You're magic."

Taken by surprise, she smiled and blushed. "Oh, well, thank you." He held up a bag. "Takeout from China Gate. You hungry?"

Stepping back she waved him inside. "Come on in, it's hot out there and I'd never say no to those spring rolls."

She put out plates and silverware as he opened all the containers and put spoons in them.

"I hope you like it spicy." He grinned and grabbed her wrist, pulling her to him carefully.

"I do." Her voice was low, sultry.

"I'm gonna kiss you now, Cassie Gambol."

"Why? I mean, why do you want me? I don't understand it. I can't lie and tell you I don't know you've been regarded as a player here in Petal. I like men, yes, but I'm afraid of being a casual indulgence to a man like you."

"There's not a damned thing about the way I feel about you that's casual. Now, I've been dying to do this for so long." He closed the last bit of distance between them and he brushed his mouth over hers. His lips were lush and delicious, spicy and masculine, just like the rest of him. They both groaned as he moved away.

"Cassie, you fascinate me. I'm shocked by how much I want you. I think I started wanting you when you kicked my ass at pool. No, I'm a damned liar. Since you stumbled out of your wrecked car and called my momma Crash." He put his face into her neck and inhaled deeply. "God, you smell good."

"Shampoo, sweat and a little bit of Delice," she breathed out, running her tongue over the lips he'd just touched with his own. A sense of unreality washed over her. The connection between them was warm and sticky. Lethargic with want, she let him hold her against his body. The heat of him blanketed her skin. Her nipples hardened against the wall of his chest and a libido that she'd thought had been beaten out of her roared back to life.

There was a moment where she wondered if she was dreaming. Hell, if she was, she sure didn't want to wake up.

"Mmm." He licked his lips as she'd just done and a shiver ran through her. "You taste good, too. Better than you should. I ought to be running out the door but damned if you don't make me want things I'd thought I'd never want with a woman again."

His hand rested at the small of her back, hot and inescapably present. The other rested on her shoulder. He held her in his orbit physically and mentally. His presence was so intense it boggled her mind. Things tightened low in her gut as her skin tingled everywhere he touched her. And yet, aside from general nervousness, she wasn't afraid.

She caught her lip in her teeth and he groaned softly. "I know you want me too." Leaning in, he pressed a hot, wet kiss to the hollow just below her ear. "I can feel your nipples against my chest," he murmured, breath stirring the wisps of hair around her ear. His tongue darted inside and then he caught the lobe between his teeth. She shivered, going weak in the knees. "But I want more than your physical need of me. Let's have dinner. Some snuggling on your couch. A liberal smattering of smooches. Let me get to know you as a woman."

"I...yes." She nodded, incapable of further speech. Especially when his grin widened and he looked like a predator.

They sat down and began to dish up the food, digging in. He watched her and she laughed. "What? Do I have a bean spout between my teeth?"

"No." He chuckled. "I just like the way you look here with me." He shrugged. "And I like that you eat. Not like some dainty thing who wants everyone to believe she survives on air and mist, but you eat like a real person."

"Is that your finessed way of telling me I eat like a pig?"

He threw his head back and laughed. "Oh the unwinnable guy question. Darlin', you do not eat like a pig. You eat like a human who likes to eat. I *like* that."

She narrowed her eyes at him for a moment and shrugged

before going back to her plate. She'd only just put the weight on she lost from the hospital and afterward in the last three months or so.

They kept a wide berth around what happened the night before but Cassie was pretty sure Maggie had told him about Terry. He didn't seem freaked, which made her more comfortable.

After they'd eaten, he helped her clean up and get the dishes in the dishwasher before they retired to the couch.

"Let's get comfortable here, shall we, darlin'? Because I have some serious smooching planned and we should do it right." He winked and pulled her into his lap, her body straddling his.

The hard ridge of his cock fit up against her and she undulated, grinding herself over him without even thinking of it. Little flares of pleasure played up her spine and the muscles inside her pussy fluttered and contracted.

One of his eyebrows rose slowly and his hands slid to rest at her waist. "So that's how it's gonna be, huh? Mmm. You feel so damned good, Cassie. I need to kiss you again." Arching his neck up, he brought his lips to hers with crushing intensity.

Her head swam as she drowned in him. In a myriad of ways he affected her, overwhelmed her, turned her on and turned her out. Helpless to do anything more than hang on, she slid her hands up his chest and neck and into his hair. The soft, cool silk of it flowed over her skin, his skull solid and sure beneath her palms.

Grunting in satisfaction, he slanted his mouth to get more of her. His tongue slipped in between her teeth and he tasted her, met her warmth with his own. Her elemental flavor rocked him, he couldn't get enough. When she sucked at his tongue, he pulled her to him tighter and delighted in the moan that came from her lips. Swallowed it down with the rest of her that he took from the kiss.

God he wanted more. The luscious flesh of her bottom lip seduced him as he sucked it into his mouth. Arching into him with a breathy sigh, she traced the outline of his upper lip with the tip of her tongue. Down over the seam of his mouth where her lip was captured, the wetness of her tongue, the tentative and yet utterly carnal way she responded, drew him in.

It'd never been like this with a woman before. Intense, sure. Really good, that too. But so good, so right that it made his chest ache with want and need of *this* woman in his arms? Never.

Damn, he was falling for Cassie. Scratch that—had *fallen* for Cassie and he wasn't running. No, he wanted more. Wanted to gorge himself on every drop of her he could get as long as he could get it. He wanted to see what kind of tomorrow he could build with this woman. Cassie Gambol wasn't a casual indulgence at all, she was big league addiction and instead of fear, there was only joy that he'd found it at last.

It took every bit of his self-control to keep his hands resting at her waist instead of sliding down to cup her ass. She was so soft against him, so warm and pliant—everything sexy and earthy, he wanted to take her in the grass under the moon, the dew on his naked skin as he watched her in the silvery light. She was a goddess come alive in his arms.

Her head tipped back as he kissed down her neck. To keep her balance, one of his hands, splayed open on her back, moved up to her neck. He gripped her, sure but not hard. Still, she stiffened and pushed away.

"Whoa! What's going on?" he asked as she scrambled off his lap and put some distance between them.

"I'm sorry. I...you touched a nerve. He did that to me when he...damn, what you must think. I don't know why you even came over here after Maggie told you."

"Told me?"

"About all the abuse, the..." her voice lowered "...rape. I don't know if I can be normal."

"Rape?"

Cassie paled. "Maggie didn't tell you?"

"She told me you had problems with your ex-husband. She

said she couldn't tell me any specifics because she didn't want you to not be able to trust her."

"Shit. Never mind. It was bad. It's over. But there are things that happen and I don't even see them coming and I don't know if I can be a normal person again. I seem to have a minefield of emotional shit because of him."

"Sit down." He pointed to the couch and went to retrieve a glass of iced tea. Coming back into the room, he pressed it into her hands and sat next to her. "Now I want you to tell me. Damn it, Cassie, trust me. Please. I can't help you if I don't know. We can work through the minefield together but I can't if I'm blind."

Closing her eyes a moment, she began to relate all that she'd told her friends the night before. She kept looking blankly out the windows as she did and Shane didn't interrupt her.

By the time she'd finished, the sun was down and her tea was empty.

"I don't even know what to say. Cassie, you're so strong. Why didn't you tell me before? Why hide this? Of course it freaked you out when I grabbed your neck like that. He must have when he hurt you, didn't he?"

She jumped up. "Yes! Yes, okay? I don't want to do this. I didn't tell you because I hate it. I hate that it happened to me and that I let it happen. I hate the person I was and I hate that anyone would know I allowed someone to do those sorts of things to me."

Gracefully, he stood and went to her. "You didn't allow it. It happened to you and you got out. And damn if you did all the right things but were failed. I'm sorry." A gentle hand moved to her cheek and his fingertips traced the line of her jaw.

"You're not disgusted? Freaked out?"

"Of course I'm disgusted. But not by you, Cassie. How can any man do that to the woman he's supposed to love and cherish? How can a man turn that love into something sick and twisted? Look at you. How can any man have had you at his side and perverted it instead of rejoiced in it? Fuck, I want to kill him for harming you!" Dropping his hand, he began to pace.

"Okay so here's what we'll do, you'll be sure to get me the order of no contact from LA. My father can help you and get you in to see a judge to get it extended to here. Does the bastard know where you are now? We should assume he's looking for you and take precautions. We'll get you some better locks, a security system too. One of the guys I work with does installation of security systems on the…"

"Whoa!" she yelled, making the time-out motion with her hands. "I'm fine. I'm dealing. I'm moving on. I am so fucking done with the legal system right now it's not funny. Let's talk about something else please."

"Hell no we won't talk about something else. Cassie, you can't just ignore this. You have to take care of the legalities so I can protect you better if he comes to town. In fact, why don't you give me the name and number of the cop you dealt with and I'll give him a call and he can fill me in and I can handle things for you that way."

Her eyes widened. "This is not going to happen. Do you understand me, Shane Chase? You will not manage me. I can take care of myself."

"Yeah, sure! That's why this guy hurt you so bad that when people bump into you in a nightclub you totally shut down."

"You think you can wish all that away? Step in and make it gone? Poof, Cassie was never beaten up and raped by her ex? Stalked, nearly fired because of the harassment at the workplace? You. Can't. Save. Me! It's done. It's over."

"I have some skill and expertise here. I'm willing to overlook the fact that you didn't even tell me until tonight about the years of abuse, but it's unacceptable that you won't let me help when I have the damned ability. I want to protect you. I know what you need."

"I have had *enough*, and I mean always and forever, of men thinking they can protect me and that they know what I need more than I do. I do not need another pushy, overbearing, control freak man in my life. I do not need to be taken care of. Never again. Never again, do you understand me? I will not ever let anyone take me over and make me feel like I deserve to be beaten and treated like nothing. I like you, Shane, but not enough to give you my soul."

"Are you comparing me to your ex-husband? Oh fuck no. You will not. I've made a lot of mistakes with people in my life. Trusted the wrong ones, didn't trust the right ones, hurt those who trusted me. But I am not that filth you were married to. I care about you, Cassie. More than I've cared about a woman in..." he shoved a hand through his hair "...damn it, I've never cared about a woman this much. Have I harmed you, Cassie? Have I used my size to intimidate you? Does my wanting to be a cop and help you and keep you safe begin to compare to a man who'd punch your head?" His eyes were vivid with emotion and it cut straight to her gut.

"I don't want your soul. I want your heart. I can wait for it and I want it of your own free will. But I'd never harm you to get it. If you'll let me, I'll cherish you, not control you. I can't promise not to be an arrogant ass. Hell, I *am* an arrogant ass. But I can't bear to think you'd class me with him. It's not fair of you."

Standing there, arms crossed defensively over her chest, she realized she'd just had a heated argument with him but he'd never jumped at her or menaced her. He'd raised his voice, yes, but not once did she feel afraid. Irritated, hell yes. The man irritated the heck out of her and it was clear he had white knight tendencies. But he was right, she wasn't being fair and he wasn't anything like Terry.

Sighing, she moved forward one step and then another until she reached him. She placed her palm over his heart and looked into his face. "You're right. It's not right. And I don't think you're like Terry. God, you're a million miles away from his zip code." She pulled back.

"But I don't know if I can promise not to react again to something like this. Or anything. The panic attacks happen less and less frequently but when they do, they're pretty bad. And I can't be managed. You're a very in-charge type, Shane. I have to make choices for myself. Even if it seems stupid to you, it's everything to me. You should move on. Find a normal woman without baggage."

"Are you dumping me?" A smile played at the corners of his mouth.

"Are you mocking me?" she asked.

"If you're dumping me, I'm mocking you, yes. Cassie, darlin', I knew you were hiding something that first night you came to town. I knew you had something that was eating at you. But I pursued you anyway. You know why?"

"My sparkling wit?"

He grinned. "Yeah. And your smile. And your intelligence and beauty and damned if you don't have the nicest tits I've ever seen on a woman and I would very much like to see them naked and in a bed very soon." He held up a hand to continue. "I know it won't happen tonight, we're both a bit ragged. I'm just saying."

His arms encircled her waist and he held her to him. "Are you interested in me? In a relationship? For me, this is getting serious. You said you knew my history, well, it's true. Not that I've been a womanizer, but I've played around a lot. I had one serious relationship but I never should have moved in with her much less asked her to marry me. Looking back, I thank my lucky stars that she cheated on me and got caught.

"I want you to know you mean something to me. I'm going to try to be totally up front here because I want this to work. I want us to be together. Let's work through your panic attacks. I'll try to curtail my need to take care of the people I…uh… care about. I can't promise to stop, it's who I am, but you can yell at me and I'll never, ever, raise my hand to you in anger. I might be an asshole from time to time but I'm not a thug or a bully. Let me in. Let's see where this can go."

Her forehead rested against the hard muscle of his chest as she thought. Thought about what a relationship with Shane would be like after the morass of messed up she'd been married to. He made her smile. He cared about her and wasn't afraid to say so. That touched her deeply. And without a doubt, he was the sexiest, handsomest and downright most wonderful man she'd ever met.

"Are you sure? I'm a mess, Shane."

"I'm totally sure, Cassie." The bass of his voice vibrated through his chest.

Taking a deep breath, she leaned out and looked into his face. "Okay. But don't manage me, Shane, or I will chew you up and spit you out. I mean it."

He grinned. "Promise?"

Startled laughter bubbled from her gut and she rolled her eyes. "Cassie, do you trust me to touch you? I know we won't sleep together tonight but I'd very much like to touch you."

To demonstrate, his hands slid down the curve of her back and down to cup her ass.

"Oh, *that* kind of touching." Cassie couldn't help but smile.

The tips of his fingers brushed against the satin of the exposed skin just below the frayed hem of her shorts. Shane felt the gooseflesh erupt there as he stroked that sweet spot where the curve of her ass met her inner thigh.

He watched her eyes, waiting for her to refuse before moving his hands anywhere else. He needed her terribly but he also knew he'd have to take it slow with her at first. She had some wounds and he intended to heal them. Okay, to *help* her heal them.

Step by step he moved her back to the door behind them. He stopped when her back met it. The eyes locked with his showed trust and no small amount of desire and curiosity.

His mouth moved down and took hers. Her lips called to him, her taste tantalized and seduced. Unable to resist, his teeth caught her bottom lip, giving it a sharp nip before sweeping his tongue along the sensual curve there, laving the sting.

She sighed and his mouth caught the sound, swallowing it, taking it into himself greedily. Her palms slid up the muscles of his forearms and biceps, up his neck and into his hair as he feasted on her lips.

Their tongues slid together, sinuous and sex laden. He knew that once they got into bed together it would be incredibly powerful. Their chemistry was off the charts. That knowledge helped him stay in control.

As much as he wanted to be inside her, he wanted to be inside her heart first. Wanted her to be totally sure she could trust him not to hurt her.

He brought a hand up to free her hair and it tumbled down, the scent of her shampoo filled his senses. "Everything about you smells good," he murmured as his lips moved to the column of her throat and ever-so-slowly, one palm slid up her stomach, beneath the hem of her T-shirt and found her breast.

Emboldened when she arched into his touch, he moved his other hand, slipping down into the front of her shorts. The skin of her belly was soft and warm. Fingertips traced over the front of her panties, against the silky fabric. He felt her heat, her wetness through the material.

A soft moan slid from her lips, vibrating against his mouth on her throat. The hand on her breast moved out of the way and he caught her nipple between his teeth through the cotton of her shirt. She cried out, rolling her hips forward.

Clever fingers moved the panties out of the way and slid through the heat of her pussy. Shane groaned at the same time Cassie did, finding her so wet, knowing she wanted him as much as he wanted her.

She tried to reach down to his cock but he held himself out of reach. "No, not right now. Let me love you, Cassie." She made a sound of disapproval until his fingertips found her clit and her head knocked on the door behind them. He only barely resisted chuckling, instead, he moved to the other nipple, his hand replacing his mouth on the one he'd just left behind.

Cassie hadn't had an orgasm given to her by another person in several years. Since the second year she and Terry were married. She'd wanted Shane for weeks now and her body was primed to his touch. There was no fear, only the roar of desire in her ears and the burn of want in her muscles.

The way he touched her was reverent. It made her want to weep. This big man treating her with such gentleness in the middle of his wicked carnal assault on her senses wrecked her.

She felt her orgasm coming, begin to burn in her muscles. He had two fingers inside her and his thumb applied just the right pressure to her clit. There was something to be said about a man who'd been with a lot of women. He certainly had experience.

Shane moved his mouth to her ear. "Let me have it, darlin'. Give me your orgasm. I want to feel you come around my fingers, I want to hear the sounds you make when you climax."

A cry, low and deep, broke from her lips as orgasm opened up around her and swallowed her deep. Pleasure soaked her, sapped her strength and she held on to him as it buffeted her over and over again.

Her parched cells filled up, replenished, and she began to feel whole after being broken for so long. Serotonin flooded her brain and lethargy, warm and heady, stole over her as a smile crept over her lips.

It was his chuckle that made her open her eyes finally. His face was flushed, eyes desire-dark as he put her shorts back to rights and planted a kiss on her lips.

"I do believe I have never seen a more beautiful sight. Your neck arched, lips parted, a flush on that gorgeous face. You're amazing, Cassie."

She felt the tears in her throat but she didn't free them. They were bittersweet tears but she felt like giving in to them would have let Terry win and continue to fuck with her head. Instead, she embraced happiness and the thought that she might be able to have a real life, a real future and that just maybe, Shane Chase would be a part of it.

"You're good with the compliments, Chase. Now, it's your turn." She raised a brow and he laughed and shook his head.

"Not tonight. I want this first time to about you. We have so much time, Cassie. We'll take our baby steps and when we end up in bed, it'll be right and incredible."

She must have had a distressed look on her face because he laughed and kissed her again. "That look is almost as good as sex, Cassie. I like that you want me too. But we're not ready to go there yet."

She wasn't? She didn't know. She didn't think it was a problem. She wanted him to fuck her right then. But she also didn't know if she'd freak out either and so close to their fight and the panic attack yesterday, he was probably right. She vowed to make it extra good when she did get her hands on him. She hoped she could.

Shane led her to the couch and pulled her down with him, pulling her into his side and snuggling with her. "A whole lot is going on in there." He tapped her head. "You wanna share?"

Terry had seriously eroded her confidence about sex. Not just about her own sexuality but her ability to please men. He'd always told her she was frigid and lousy in bed. What if he was right? What if she couldn't please Shane?

"Hey, no, get that look off your face right now. Talk to me, please. We can't move forward if you don't share with me."

"I'm fine. I'm working on getting past all this stuff with my therapist. Man, I never thought I'd say, *my therapist* in this context, you know? It's just something that Terry, my ex, made me feel like."

Shane took her hand and kissed her fingertips. "Like what, darlin'?"

"Unattractive. Frigid. Like I couldn't please a man." Her voice went quiet. She *knew* Terry was wrong, but what your mind knew and what your heart knew were sometimes very different.

"Cassie, your ex-husband is an asshole. You're the sexiest woman I've ever laid eyes on. I'm not lying. And the way you just flew apart in my arms? You telling me that's frigid? He's the one with problems. Any man who'd force a woman has big issues with sex and power. That is not about you. And I'd scare the bejesus out of you if I put your hand over my cock to show you just how pleased you make me. Trust me, you do."

With a soft sigh, she snuggled into his body and he held her tight while they watched a movie.

He waited until she'd fallen asleep in his arms and then carried her to her bedroom. Checking to be sure everything was locked up tight, he set the air conditioning and left her a note, telling her he'd call her the next day.

Outside, he double checked that the door had locked behind him and scanned the area for anything amiss. The lighting was good on her porch. He'd noticed she'd put in a higher watt bulb and made a note to himself to put some security lights out back for her. He was sure Chuck wouldn't mind him doing it. The added security was a plus for any future tenants anyway. He'd also put in a new dead bolt for her, after he figured out a way to make it seem like her idea.

Chapter Eight

"Is there anything I can do to help plan this shindig?"

Penny looked up at Cassie, who'd just come into the room, bearing the day's receipts.

"No. And you can give those to me and go meet Shane. I know he's out there flitting around, waiting for you."

"He can wait." Cassie sat down. "Penny, do you date at all?"

Penny pushed her glasses up her nose and paused. "It was hard, losing Ben. He was like the other half of my heart. For the longest time I couldn't even imagine being with anyone else. In the last year or so I've been on a few dates here and there. I haven't met anyone who could hold a candle to Ben's memory. Still, it hurts less and I feel like I'm waking after a long sleep. Why? You're not planning on fixing me up are you?"

Cassie laughed. "Hell, Penny, I don't know anyone other than you and the Chases. Matt's pretty hot. And Marc, well, a younger man could be just what the doctor ordered."

Penny burst out laughing. "I grew up with those boys. They're like my cousins so while I can appreciate all that handsome, I can't see them like that. And I am quite sure Marc would wear me into nothingness. His prowess is pretty legendary."

"I was just wondering. After being married and having it

not be the best experience, it's odd to be dating again and have it be so different. Better. I'm a bit giddy even but I'm not quite sure what to do. What to expect. I thought you might have some sage advice."

Penny patted her arm. "Honey, I'm no sage. All I can tell you is to go on and enjoy yourself. Anyone with eyes can see Shane thinks you hang the moon. You two are good people. The two of you can be good together if you just let go a bit."

Cassie stood. "We're headed out to The Pumphouse, you want to come with?"

"I have a date with a pedicure. I'll see you for brunch on Sunday."

"All right, come on over and show us your fancy new toes if you're up for it."

Shane nearly swallowed his tongue when Cassie emerged from the back of the store. She'd pulled her hair away from her face and was wearing shiny red lip gloss. Her sneakers had been replaced with sandals that showed off those sexy red toenails. The jeans and pretty T-shirt had been exchanged for a knee-length skirt that rippled like water when she walked and a tank top-like blouse with buttons down the front. The casual professional look had transformed into something ultra-feminine and sexy with the addition of the sandals and some jewelry.

"I just needed to freshen up a bit."

He smiled and kissed her forehead. "A bit, huh? You look gorgeous."

"And you smell good and look handsome. It's going to be a shame beating a man at pool who looks so good."

"You're awfully cocky."

"For good reason. Now come on."

Chuckling, he led her out the door where she locked up and they took the two-block stroll down to The Pumphouse.

"Go on and play with your brothers for a while. I'm going to have a few beers and gossip with Maggie, Liv and Dee. Then I'll be over to kick your ass."

One handed, he wrapped an arm around her waist and pulled her flush with his body. "If it wouldn't smear that sexy lip gloss, I'd lay a kiss or two on you," he murmured, eyes locked on hers.

"Go on ahead, Sheriff. It's kiss-proof. And even if it wasn't, it's cherry flavored and I have more in my purse."

Her eyes fluttered closed as his lips met hers in a soft, brief and yet bone-melting kiss. He didn't even use his tongue and she was nearly panting when he pulled back.

He licked his lips. "Mmmm, cherries. Very nice, darlin', very nice indeed. I'll see you in a while."

Cassie waved at him and stumbled into the booth where her friends waited.

"Uh, hello? The two of you have so much chemistry I'm all hot and bothered now. Sheesh, I'm going to jump on Brody the minute he gets off work tonight."

Blushing, Cassie grinned at Liv. "He'll thank me then, won't he?"

"I don't need to ask if you two had worked everything out from Tuesday night then." Maggie poured Cassie a beer and pushed it in her direction.

"He came over on Wednesday and we talked for hours. And kissed, a lot. He's a great kisser."

"He is. Not as good as Kyle, but definitely award winning."

Cassie stilled. "How do you know?"

Maggie blinked several times and stammered a bit. "I thought you knew."

"Knew what?"

"Shane and I dated before I got together with Kyle. It was just a few times and he dumped me and acted like a total ass. He's long since made up for it and has really grown. It was nothing, Cassie. God, he never looked at me with half the emotion he shows when he looks at you. I thought you knew."

"I can't believe no one told me!"

"Are you mad at me? It was nearly three years ago. I swear

to you, Cassie, it was nothing. He really cares about you. Talks about you all the time."

"Well, I don't know. I'm not used to being around people who've kissed my boyfriend. It's weird."

Liv sighed and leaned toward Cassie. "Cassie, I'm going to say this as your friend and I want you to listen and take this to heart, okay? Shane has been with a lot of women in this town. I'm not going to lie to you about it. In this bar alone I count at least eight he's dated and it's early yet. He wasn't a slut as much as a guy who loved a lot of women. He's thirty-four, that's a lot of dating years.

"I want you to also hear me when I tell you that he's never dated a single one of them, including Maggie, for more than two weeks at a time. Shane hasn't dated since the night you came to town. You're it for him, Cassie. When a man like that falls, he falls hard and all the way. There's no middle ground for a guy like Shane." Liv smiled.

"And you *will* have to deal with jealous women, Cassie. I'm sorry to tell you but I know from experience. Not that I'm jealous of you and Shane," Maggie added hurriedly, "but I've had to deal with a lot of it with Kyle. If you let them get to you, you're letting them win. Don't. I can tell you without a doubt that Shane is not interested in any woman on this planet other than you. And I'm sorry if finding out Shane and I dated a few years ago bothers you or caught you by surprise."

Cassie sighed and looked toward the pool table. When she did, she saw the interested glances of women trying to catch the eyes of the brothers there, including Shane. But when he looked up, it was she his eyes sought out, not anyone else.

He must have seen her distress because he handed his cue to Matt and came toward them.

Not wanting to have a conversation at the table with the other women listening, she got up and met him halfway, near the arches that separated the seating area from the games section with the pool tables, darts and pinball machines.

Stopping just a hair's breadth away from her body he lifted a hand to touch her face. "You okay, darlin'?"

"Why didn't you tell me you dated Maggie?"

He looked over her shoulder toward the table but Cassie's voice brought his gaze back to her face.

"That's the kind of sneaky thing that bugs me. Why look over there for clues if you didn't have anything to hide?"

"You looking for a reason to push me away, Cassie? Hmm? Because I am quite sure Maggie told you what it was between she and I—nothing. Two dates. I dumped her because she was nice and I was worried I may actually have feelings for her at some point. I was an asshole. But it was her and Kyle from day one. Once they got together it was forever.

"I didn't think to tell you. It happened years ago. You said you knew about my history. I've dated a lot of women, hell, a lot of women in this bar right now."

"Yes, so I've heard."

One of the corners of his mouth lifted and the furrows in his brow smoothed. "You're jealous, darlin'? Because flattering as it may be, it's unnecessary. I'm with you. You and no one else. Not ever again. But I can't change my past. I'm sorry if that hurts you. I really am."

"Jealous? Puhleeze."

He laughed out loud that that. "Darlin', you don't think it's hard for me to see the men watch you as you walk through any room you're in? I also have a history of being cheated on. It's hard to trust you. All I can do is take it on faith that you wouldn't do that to me. And all I ask is that you do the same."

"It's weird, knowing one of my friends has had sex with you."

"Maggie told you we had sex?" His voice rose a bit.

"No, not in so many words. You dated, you're a very…sexual man, I just put two and two together."

"We did not have sex. Do you want to know how far it went? If you do, I need another drink because it's kinda creepy now that I think of her like my little sister."

"Was there naked?"

He thought about it. "I can't remember. There wasn't orgasm. Nothing like what we shared in your apartment on Wednesday."

She shivered at the memory and he nearly purred in her ear. "Oh, darlin', seeing you react that way as you think about my hands on you, my mouth, your taste in my throat, it does me in."

"Wh-where do you get all this stuff?" Her voice was shaky. The way he affected her shook her to her core.

"That's not a line. I want to tell you all the things you do to me, all the things I *want* to do to you. You have no idea how you make me feel do you? Standing here in the middle of this crowded place, I want to back you against the wall and take you. I want to lay you on one of the pool tables and look down on your body as I thrust into it. I want you so much my hands are in my pocket because I'm afraid they'd shake."

A flush ran through her. "Oh. My."

"Oh my indeed, darlin'. I'm going to kiss you now, here in this bar, and I don't care who sees it."

"Oh, okay," she said faintly as her arms encircled his neck like they'd wanted to all along.

He kissed her, not with the raw sexuality he'd shown in her apartment but it was still a kiss that she felt all the way to the tips of her toes. Holy cow the man could kiss. He tasted of beer and the spearmint of his gum and Shane and everything in her body tightened in response.

When he released her, she dimly heard applause and some hooting from his brothers.

"Wow." She licked her lips.

"*Wow* isn't a big enough word for the way you make me feel, Cassie. There is no one else. There hasn't been since the first moment I clapped eyes on you."

"You make me weak in the knees, Shane Chase. And you make me think I may not be as broken as I'd feared."

He smiled. "That's the best compliment I've ever gotten."

"Yeah? Come on back to my apartment and I'll give you a few more."

His joyous smile turned wicked. "Is that so?"

She nodded.

"Give me ten minutes to finish up with my brothers. Why don't we go to my house? You haven't seen it yet and you can, if you want to, sleep over. In my bed or in my guest room. I'll let you decide that one, I'm rather biased on the subject."

"Got any food there?"

He grinned. "I just went grocery shopping earlier tonight. I have fresh peaches and strawberries. I can think of a few things to do with them before eating them."

"Oh?" Her voice was faint as she pondered the possibilities.

"I'll let you think on it. Be by in ten to grab you. You okay? Are *we* okay?"

She nodded. "I don't like being taken by surprise. I don't expect you to be a virgin. I knew you were a player and all. But that it was Maggie just surprised me. You haven't been with Penny, Liv or Dee have you?"

"No, darlin', I haven't."

"I'm going back to the table. See you in ten."

"Go on then, I'll just stand here and watch." She rolled her eyes.

"Is everything all right?" Maggie's voice sounded sad.

"I'm not mad at you, Maggie. I was just surprised. It's fine. I talked to Shane. He and I are fine. You and I are fine. It's all fine."

Maggie leaned back, sighing in relief. "Thank goodness."

"That was some kiss. I don't think I've seen him kiss a woman in public twice in one night and certainly not like that. Whew. I need to go home to Arthur. I'm sure Michael is in bed by now and I'm all hot and bothered." Dee shoved her way out of the booth and stood.

"I'll see you soon, Dee." Dee and Cassie hugged and Dee hurried out the door toward home and her husband.

"And I'll be going soon too. Shane and I are nipping out early."

"To do what?" A single eyebrow rose and Liv struggled not to smile. "To play Scrabble." Cassie's voice was deadpan.

"Naked Scrabble?" Liv asked, laughing.

"I've never thought of that. Dude, that's a great idea. Strip Scrabble. I'm so getting the board out tonight to see if I can't lose badly to Kyle." Maggie winked.

"Just wow. Man oh man, Shane. I don't think I've ever been jealous of you over a woman before but Cassie is sinfully beautiful. And incredibly sexy." Marc leaned his butt against the table next to theirs.

"What was that all about?" Matt interjected before his little brother could goad Shane any further.

"Maggie mentioned she and I dated a few times. Cassie was caught off guard. It's all fine now."

"I saw that. That was some 'all fine now' liplock there, Shane." Kyle took a shot and sank it. "You find out anything about this ex of hers? I'm looking forward to finding him and helping you kick the shit out of him."

"Nothing. I've done some snooping with her name and social security number but I can't find any records. Some domestic violence records shield the victim so that may be the case. All I have is that the husband's first name is Terry. I couldn't find anything on Terry Gambol but she may not have taken his name when they got married."

"Does she know you're doing this? Obviously not if you're having to piece it all together this way." Matt sighed uneasily. "I don't think she's going to be pleased if she finds out you're investigating without her knowledge."

"I know, I know. But I want to protect her. God help me, I am falling so fast for this woman I'm in a tailspin. The idea of anyone hurting her kills me. It's just a little bit of snooping. Just to help."

His brothers looked at him skeptically.

"I'm out of here. She and I are on our way to my house and if any of you losers calls me and interrupts me with a flat tire or any kind of police emergency, I'll kick your ass."

He heard their laughter as he turned and saw the woman he was well on his way to being in love with, waiting for him, wearing a smile.

Nervousness began to creep into her stomach as they drove. The sex, or foreplay she supposed, between them two nights past had been wonderful but Terry's words were still in her head.

Shane held her hand as he drove them to his place in his big truck. She watched the light of the streetlamps and then the moon, on his face.

"Oh hey, this is Penny's neighborhood. I didn't know you lived so close." Cassie didn't know why but the thought of Penny's nearness made her feel better.

"Yeah, she's just three houses down. Ben and I were good friends, went to school together along with Penny."

He pulled into his driveway. His house was built in the Craftsman style, not something she'd seen often around Petal. Two large oak trees dominated the front yard, providing shade to the front of the house. The entire front lawn was beautifully landscaped with wildflowers and roses.

"Wow, this is so not what I expected." She joined him and they walked up to the porch.

"What? You expected some two-room bachelor pad with potato chip bags strewn around?"

"No, not really. But this is truly beautiful. So well put together. I don't think I've seen a Craftsman-style home around these parts at all. And the landscaping is just gorgeous."

"The landscaping is all Kyle. Wait until you see the back. One of my friends, the faithless asshole who cheated with Sandra, my ex, was...is a builder. He helped me with the plans and then my brothers, father, uncle and cousins all came out here and did a lot of the work, from the framing to the paintwork. I love this place." He opened the door and motioned her inside.

She watched as he turned off and re-set the alarm system. "Just for the front of the house. I'll show you the back. I want you to know you're always safe here. Come on through."

He led her through a big, open living room with exposed wood beams, hardwood floors and large windows. Dark greens and brick reds accented the space. It was a very masculine space dominated by leather couches and deep club chairs. A large fireplace fronted with river rock took up most of one wall.

He opened up glass doors to a view that took her breath away. The large wooden deck overlooked a grassy lawn that sloped down to the lake's edge. Pretty citronella candles hung on stands around the railing and furniture surrounded a sizable, built-in outdoor grill.

The moon's light reflected from the glassy surface of the lake, illuminating the whole yard. Hedges lined the boundary of his property and she saw little seating areas dotted here and there. Roses climbed the trunk of an oak and she smelled the star jasmine in the air.

"You're full of surprises, aren't you, Sheriff?"

"I'm glad you like it here. It's an oasis for me. A place I can come home and leave all my work bullshit at the door. My family comes out and we barbecue and watch the sunset. It's a good life." He looked down into her face. "And now it's better."

He turned into her body and she rose to meet his kiss as he bent his head to hers.

Cassie's body melted into his embrace. Her heart beat in time with his, pounding reassuringly against her palm on his chest.

After he broke the kiss, he murmured against her lips, "Would you like to take a walk in the moonlight with me?"

She nodded, leaning down to kick off her sandals. The grass felt cool under her bare feet and his hand in hers felt anchoring and strong.

"You've really built a place for yourself here, Shane. It's beautiful. The inside and the outside."

"I'm glad you like it. I really am." And he was. Ridiculously so. That she approved made him happy. He realized he wanted her approval on the thing he cared about so much. His house was an extension of him and he'd worked hard on every last bit of it, had a hand in everything. He liked having her there with him. A lot.

"Wow, you even have a dock."

He chuckled. "I do. It's more to jump off for swimming than for a boat. The lake isn't that big or deep really."

"Do you sail?"

"I've done it from time to time. A friend of our family has a boat and I go out a few times a year with him. I take it you do? I can hear the affection in your voice."

They stopped and she bent to pick up a stone from the rocky lakeshore and skipped it. "I used to. When we were first married, we lived in an apartment in Newport Beach. Not very far from the marina. We had a boat for a while but Terry didn't like to sail and he sold it. I haven't been in some years now."

"Did you live near water too, then? I love hearing the sound of the shoreline, the water lapping against the rocks."

"Our house was in the hills overlooking the ocean. I gave it to him after the divorce. I just wanted to be free of him. I didn't care about the stuff."

"Do you miss it? Your house?"

She shook her head. "No. It was never mine anyway. He bought it. He decorated it. It was his. I was just another one of the things he owned."

Shane's jaw clenched and unclenched. "I hate hearing you talk that way."

"It's the truth, Shane. For years I was a thing. An accessory and at times, not even a very good one according to him. I know he was wrong. But that's what I was." She shrugged. "I'm working to be more than that now."

"You're not an accessory to me. I just can't wrap my head around it. How any man wouldn't cherish you with every fiber of his being."

"I don't want to talk about it anymore. I hate that it's this constant thing in my life." She turned her body away from him and looked out at the water. "Damn it, I'm more than the poor battered wife. Fuck, I feel like I should wear a nametag or something. It's why I didn't want to tell anyone about it. That's all you see. That's all anyone sees."

He moved to stand behind her, encircling her with his arms. "That's not true, Cassie. It's not all I see. It's part of your past, yes. It goes into making you who you are now—a strong woman. A survivor. You're smart, and competent and the most beautiful woman I've ever seen. Inside and out, I like you, Cassie. You. Not your past, not your zip code, but *you*. But I can't deny, and neither can you, that what happened to you shaped who you are now. Just like the things that happened to me shaped me. We don't have to talk about it anymore tonight. There are far better things to do with our time."

He brushed his lips over her neck where it met her shoulder and she lost the rigidity in her spine, relaxing into him. He felt good behind her. The water from the lake lapped against her toes over and over with the beat of her heart.

Silence stretched as he held her, kissed her neck and shoulders with soft heat. She asked herself if she could have sex with this man and her body agreed right off and soon enough, her mind agreed. It was something she'd been thinking over a lot. But she wasn't afraid of him. She trusted him to take care with her and if she was going to live beyond those years with Terry, she had to move on with her life. Build a future and that included sex. Or she hoped it would.

"Stay right here. I'll be back in a minute." Her back felt cool when he moved away and jogged up to the house, disappearing inside.

She wandered up a path lined with sweet-smelling flowers

and bushes. His steps sounded against the decking and down onto the grass. He hesitated and she called out softly, "I'm here on the path."

"Ah." He showed up around the corner and held up a blanket. "I thought we could lie under the stars. What do you think?"

"Lie?" One corner of her mouth quirked up.

"Well, uh, if you wanted to just lie, that would be fine. I'd be happy to hold you in my arms as we looked up at the stars. On the other hand, I'd be even happier to see your skin bathed in moonlight as I made love to you. I want you, Cassie. But I want you to be okay with that. I don't want you to feel rushed or pressured."

"Hmm. Well, why don't you spread it out in this little area here, it's totally walled off by the plants and no one could see us. You know, if we got up to something no one should see."

Moving around her body, he spread the blanket out and held his hand out to her.

Taking a deep breath, her brain and her body in accord, she grabbed his hand and let him draw her down onto the blanket.

On her back, she looked up into his face and smiled. A lock of his hair slid forward rakishly. She could tell he was being very careful but she was sick of it.

She put her hands on his shoulders. "Shane, don't be so careful with me. I won't break. I can't guarantee something weird won't trigger something but I don't want this thing between us to be so fragile. I wasn't always this fucked up."

A look so tender slid across his face it made her draw breath quickly. His mouth covered hers in an intense kiss. The kind of kiss that makes a woman forget to breathe.

Cassie's hands pulled at his shirt, as she gave in to her sudden need to feel his bare skin. Breaking the kiss quickly, he sat up and pulled the shirt off over his head and she put a hand on his chest to stay him.

Impossibly broad shoulders led to a wide chest, covered with just the right amount of the same brown-blond hair on his head.

The hand that had stayed him slid over the hard muscle of his pecs down to his flat, hard nipple and he sucked in a breath but remained still as she looked her fill and explored him with her hands.

Muscled arms held his upper body away from her as she traced down from his nipple to each ridge of his abdomen. One. Two. Three. Four. Five. Six. Dear sweet heaven, the man had a real six pack.

A trembling fingertip traced around his navel and south along the trail of hair that she was sure led to his cock but his jeans were in the way. She tapped the button. "This is a problem."

"I want to look at you, too." His voice was strangled. In it she heard how much control it took to hold himself still for her inspection.

She licked suddenly dry lips. "I…"

He watched her as he slid off the skirt and looked at her long legs and panties. Boy was she glad she wore the pair of pretty ones she'd bought a few weeks back on a whim.

"Your pants." She tipped her chin in his direction.

What should have been awkward for any regular person, he made graceful as he shimmied out of his jeans while still sitting. One eyebrow rose as he touched the waistband of his boxers, asking how far she wanted to go. At her nod he pulled them off and she widened her eyes and blinked a few times.

"Wow."

He stopped for a moment and then laughed. "Oh, Cassie, you're so good for me."

"Shane, you're beautiful. So big and muscled and, damn, I'm drowning in testosterone. I don't think I've ever seen a naked man who was more masculine and handsome. Hell, any man more masculine and handsome."

"Thank you. Now, I'm at a bit of a disadvantage here, Cassie. I'm buck naked and you are not."

Oh how she wished she didn't have fourteen scars on her upper back and neck from where Terry had stabbed her with the broken handle from the hammer he'd used to break her fingers. Wished she had a body she could show him without reservation. But her breasts weren't as high as they'd been when she was in her twenties and Terry always complained about the roundness of her thighs and the swell of her belly. She already felt overexposed with her skirt off, she really didn't know how she'd hide the scars if she didn't have her shirt on.

"That's some internal dialog you've got going on in there, darlin'." He tapped her forehead. "You want to stop?"

"No." She shook her head vehemently and to underline that, she took his cock in her fist and pumped. He was so hard she felt him throb in her palm.

He hissed. "Holy shit!"

"Do you have condoms?"

"Condoms? Plural? My, you're ambitious. I like that." He leaned over and pulled three foil packets out of the pocket of his pants and held them up for her to see. "Three. I know, it's very hopeful of me."

She laughed and slid her thumb over the head of his cock, smearing his come there.

"Okay, hold it back there, Ace. You keep doing that and we won't be needing a condom. I'll come in your fist like a freshman in the backseat of a Chevy and be so embarrassed I won't be able to face you in the morning. I keep telling you, we have time, Cassie. Let's take it. And yet, you still have your shirt on."

She lay back and pulled each button on the front of the camisole free and the two halves of the eyelet cotton slid apart, exposing her bra and her belly. She figured she'd leave it on and between that, the dark and her hair, her scars would stay hidden. And to further distract him, she hooked her thumbs in the waist of her panties and shimmied out of them.

"Now, where were we?" Eyes locked with his, she watched as his gaze broke free and slid down her body. The intensity of his attention had her drawing her knees together and trying to cover her breasts with her hands.

Shane moved to stop her, placing his hands over hers. "Shhh, don't hide yourself from me. Cassie, you're amazing. More beautiful than I could have imagined." Letting go of her hands, his fingertips grazed over the curve of each breast, popping the catch on the bra. "I want to see your breasts bathed in moonlight."

The tenderness of his words, of his touch, moved her deeply. Tears stung the back of her eyes. How long had it been since a man had touched her that way?

"Cassie? Honey?"

She shook her head, lips pressed together to hold back the tears. Her hands came up to put his on her again.

Leaning down he laid a kiss on her chest, just over her heart. "I hate seeing you in pain. We can stop, go inside, watch a movie on the couch. I can wait for you. You're worth it."

The tears slipped free then. "Shane, I don't want you to stop. I promise. I'm sorry I'm such a mess."

"You're not a mess, Cassie. You're working to get past something terrible. Why are you crying?"

"It's nothing bad. Please, I can't talk about it right now. Just touch me again. Make love to me. I need you."

His lips found her cheeks and he kissed away the salt of her tears and then back down to her chest. His movements were slow and gentle, giving her the time and space to stop him if she needed to.

Shane gloried in the beauty of her body, in the fragile shell that lay around her heart. But she kept on and didn't quit. His woman was everything. He stilled as he insinuated himself between her thighs.

The enormity of that statement hit him. She was his woman. She'd held his attention from the first moment but each time he thought of her it built in him, attention became attraction became something more intense.

There was no fear though. The shadow of worry passed. The moment when he'd run out the door on Maggie became clear to him. It wasn't that they could have had this thing he shared with Cassie. It was that Maggie wasn't Cassie. His heart knew what he needed and it was the woman stretched beneath him.

He wanted to heal every hurt she'd ever endured. Wanted to let her know that even broken women deserved passion and love.

And suddenly his need for her was so intense that his hands shook with it.

Sliding his palms up her ribs, he took the curve of her breasts into his hands, holding them so he could taste the hard nipples begging for his mouth.

Triumph roared through his system when she gasped and arched into him, her fingers digging into his upper arms.

The moment Shane's mouth closed around her nipple, Cassie's hesitancy was gone. Instead, desire coursed through her with each pull of lips and tongue against the sensitive flesh of her nipple. The edge of his teeth just barely skimmed over her and a deep, shuddering moan came from low in her gut.

Her squirms placed his cock against her pussy, pressing against her slick heat, and they both stilled on a gasp.

"Oh hell. Okay, let me move away a bit or I'm liable to just plunge into you without a condom. You feel so good." When he shimmied down her body he left a trail of kisses down her ribs and belly.

When he knelt between her thighs the sheer size of him held her legs apart. "You're so wet, I can see you glistening in the light." Two fingertips dipped into her and, eyes still locked with hers, he brought those fingers to his mouth.

The sheer carnality of the action rendered her utterly speechless. Instead, she opened her mouth but no sound came out as her eyes widened.

"So good. I need more. Are you ready for that, Cassie?" She nodded quickly. Oh hell yes she was ready for that!

He chuckled as he settled himself on his belly. His thumbs spread her open to his gaze just before leaning forward to take a long lick from her gate up and around her clit.

Her hands slid through the softness of his hair, thick and cool against her fingers. His tongue flicked up quickly over her clit until she began to see white lights against her closed eyelids, until she began to feel the burn in her thigh muscles and the flush working its way up her body.

He angled his hand, sliding two fingers up and into her pussy, twisting his wrist to find that sweet bump, the pressure against it feeling so good it nearly hurt.

There was no time to think about how Terry hadn't gone down on her in years and how he'd never made her feel good and delicious and sexy like Shane did at that moment. There was only the intense sensation of his mouth on her, his fingers inside her and the open sky above them.

When climax hit, an arc of pleasure shot up her spine with blinding intensity. Her back arched as she rolled her hips into him, helpless to do more than bite back the cry of joy, instead, whispering his name.

Shane remained there, nestled between her thighs, until her pussy stopped spasming around his fingers.

"You're very good at that," she gasped out, eyes still closed.

"Darlin', you're the tastiest thing this side of the Mason Dixon."

She laughed and he loved the sound. It wasn't one he heard that often from her so he treasured it all the more. So damned beautiful and sexy and she had no idea.

"It's my turn now. I want to taste you." She tried to sit up but he moved quickly, leaning over her, reaching for a condom.

"Darlin', if you do that, it'll all be over before it starts. I want to be inside you when I come. I've been dreaming of it. Later, I promise you can suck my cock all you want." One handed, he rolled the condom on while keeping his weight off her. "Are you still okay with this?"

She reached up and caressed his cheek. "Yes. So okay with it I'm shaking like it's my first time."

"Well, it's your first time with me. That's what counts."

She laughed then. "Of course."

Without breaking his gaze with hers, he reached down and guided himself to her gate and slowly began to push inside. She was slick from her recent climax and relaxed but still blindingly tight. Beads of sweat broke out over his forehead.

"Fuck...sorry. You're so tight. I don't want to hurt you." And he didn't want to come before he'd even got halfway inside her either.

Her legs slid up and around his waist, ankles locking at the small of his back, opening her up more fully to him. "It's been a while. Two years. Apparently I've been saving up for the good stuff."

He grinned and leaned down for a quick kiss. "You trying to get in my pants with all that flattery, Ms. Gambol?"

"I believe I'm already there, Sheriff Chase."

"Indeed you are." With one last grunt, he seated himself fully within her.

With slow intensity, he dragged nearly all the way out before sliding back into her. Before too long, she matched his movements with a roll of her hips, her body meeting his, swallowing him, pulling him back inside.

The thought that she was made for him, her body was a haven for his own, flashed through his mind. He cupped the back of her head in one palm, protecting her from the ground below.

He wished it was as easy to protect her from her ex, from the past that had her flinching in the presence of unknown men.

Cassie looked up into his face as her body met his in an easy rhythm. Their breath mingled, the scent of honeysuckle and star jasmine hung thick in the warm night air. The lap, lap, lap of the lake against the shore was like a metronome to their movements.

The way he sliced through her pussy as he thrust into her was so intense it rode up her spine. Her body just molded to his, made room for him like he was meant to be there.

His gaze tenderly roved over her features and there were moments when she felt like he saw straight to her soul.

"Are you with me, darlin'?" His voice was soft and he held his weight off her with his upper arms.

She nodded. "Yeah."

"You feel so good, Cassie. I want you to feel good too. Are you all right? Am I squishing you?"

Somehow, the tenderness, the concern in his voice just got to her. He wasn't coddling her, he *cared* about her. Part of her that she'd closed off because it had simply been crushed into nothing by Terry, sparked back to life. And when it did, she felt what she'd been missing for four years. Not the intensity of someone's attention that she'd mistaken for love and adoration from Terry in the early years. No, this was a man who truly wanted her to be okay. Thought about her feelings.

Tears blinded her as he changed his angle and his pelvic bone crushed into her mound and created friction over her clit. A deep moan broke from her lips.

"Baby? Those good tears or am I hurting you?"

She laughed through her tears and reached up to wipe them away with the back of her hand. "Good ones. Now shut up and fuck me."

Her thighs began to tremble as each press and grind of his body against her clit brought her closer to orgasm.

"Cassie, darlin', I'm really close. You with me?"

"I…" And it broke over her, shattering her into wordlessness, eyes blurring and back arching. She heard his muffled curse and felt his cock jerk and spasm deep within her as he came as well.

With a long, satisfied sigh, he rolled off her and to the side, quickly dealing with the condom and coming back to lie beside her. Panting, sweat cooling on their bodies, they both looked up into the night sky.

He reached out and linked fingers with her. "Thank you," she murmured.

He turned to his side and looked at her. "Darlin', the pleasure was all mine, I assure you. God, I can't believe I fucked you on the ground. You deserve a soft bed and candlelight. I just had this vision of you, bathed in moonlight, making love to you with the sweet smells of night against our skin. I hope you don't think I was disrespectful. I'm sorry."

"Shane, don't." Tears laced her voice. "I can't seem to stop crying. I hate that. You have nothing to be sorry for. It was beautiful. You were wonderful. Gentle and patient. I enjoyed myself, believe me. Twice."

He laughed. "I'm sorry about that. It should have been at least three times but I had to have you. I'm usually more finessed than that."

"Three times? Wow. Well, I'm quite pleased with two. Hell, I'm thrilled with one."

He looked at her, shocked. "Do you know how fucking beautiful you look when you come? Your neck arched, eyes desire-blind, mouth slightly open, your nipples hard and pretty—just thinking about it right now makes me hard. Any man should want to see that as much as possible. Your ex needs his ass kicked. But then I suppose if he'd taken care of you I wouldn't be here beside you now."

"They aren't very nice anymore. They used to be lovely. But time. Well you know."

He sat up on his elbow. "No. I don't have any idea what you're talking about."

Her hands moved to put her bra back in place but he stopped her, kissing each hand and putting them back at her sides.

"My breasts. They used to be higher. They're sort of saggy. I'm sure you're used to tight bodies and perky breasts. I've seen some of the women in town, the ones who give me the dirtiest looks, their bodies are nicer than mine."

Shane exhaled sharply. "Cassie, how old are you?"

"Thirty-three."

"And you think you have saggy breasts?"

She sat up and moved to fasten her bra and button up her camisole. "Yes. And my belly has this little pooch and my thighs are flabby."

"Cassie, I'm just telling you so as not to spook you, I'm picking you up now." And she found herself tossed over his shoulder as he walked her, bare assed, into his house.

"Hey! I don't have any panties on," she hissed.

"No one can see but me and I like your ass." He took her up the stairs and into his bedroom and set her down in front of mirrored sliding doors in his closet.

"Now, I want you to look at yourself." His hand smoothed over her hair. "Your hair is truly beautiful, thick, black, long, tousled from sex." A thumb traced her bottom lip. "Luscious. I want to nibble it every time I see you."

He moved behind her and unbuttoned her camisole and popped the catch on her bra in record time. He held her breasts in his hands. "Gorgeous." And let them go. "They do *not* sag. You have large breasts and they're not in a bra and you're not twenty-one, Cassie. But your breasts are fucking phenomenal." A finger traced the valley between them. "I'd very much like to put my cock here sometime in the future. I think about that. A lot."

She shivered.

His hand slid down her stomach. "This is not a pooch. It's your stomach. You are not flabby. You're beautiful. Your thighs are beautiful. Your calves are beautiful. Your pussy is pink and pretty and beautiful. Your eyes are beautiful."

He picked up her hand and kissed it. "Your hands are beautiful." And paused. "Did you break your fingers?" He held up his left hand and the index finger was slightly crooked. "I broke it when I was twenty-five."

In the year since the attack, she'd had time to heal. Time for physical therapy. But her middle and ring fingers still bore the scars of the break. Bore the odd bend of what she knew she was lucky to still have working fingers after he'd done so much damage.

"Yes."

His face hardened and he met her eyes in the mirror. "He did this to you." It wasn't a question.

Her eyes closed for a long moment and she nodded. Shane brought her hand to his lips and kissed the fingers. "Beautiful. Cassie, one of the things that surprises me the most about you is how you don't see your own beauty. You walk into The Pumphouse and men bump into things from staring at you. I believe book readership has skyrocketed in Petal since you started working at Paperbacks and More. You speak and I get hard. You breathe and I get hard. I get jealous. Even when I walked in and caught Sandra with my best friend, I wasn't jealous. I was just betrayed and hurt and then pissed off.

"And let me clarify the jealous thing because don't think I didn't see the fear flare in your eyes when I said it. Yes, it drives me a little crazy to see men watching you and practically drooling. But I'm not going to hurt you over it. I may want to whack 'em in the back of the head with my pool cue, but baby, I want to cherish you, not hurt you."

Gaze locked with his in the mirror she leaned back into his body. "If I try to talk about this right now, I'm going to cry. And I am sick of it. So, I'm not going to except to say thank you."

He bent and as she watched in the mirror, he took her neck between his teeth and she gasped. "You're so beautiful, I want you right now. Again. Show me, Cassie." One hand moved up to cup her breast and roll and tug a nipple between his fingers and the other slid down her belly to her pussy.

Automatically, she adjusted her legs, widening her stance, and he put his thigh between them, enabling her to lean back against his chest. Unable not to watch, her eyes caught his fingers parting her and sliding through the still very wet folds of her sex.

She watched the pull, roll, tug of his fingers on her nipple and then two of his fingers disappear into her pussy and his thumb sliding from side to side over her clit.

Her eyelids slid halfway shut as the lethargy of desire stole over her. His eyes watched his hands on her in the mirror. Watched his fingers fuck into her and she didn't miss the widening of his grin when she rolled her hips to meet his hand.

But she was past embarrassment. She wanted to come. She'd turned off her expectations of climax during sex with anyone else and the need came back, sharp edged and starving after so many years denied.

"Give it to me, Cassie. I can feel your pussy beginning to flutter around my fingers. I know you want to come, I can see it in your eyes." His words were whispered into her ear and she shivered. "Let go."

Even as she was getting ready to tell him she couldn't possibly come again, she did. Not the explosion of pleasure she'd felt on the grass outside but a muscle-deep series of contractions. Wave after wave of pleasure rolled through her until she was nothing more than a boneless heap of satisfied woman lying against him.

"Oh, I wish I had a camera." He chuckled and she raised her hand in a half-hearted one fingered salute.

They cleaned up. He refused to let her reciprocate for the moment and ran outside to retrieve her panties, skirt and shoes which, to his disappointment, she put back on.

They stood side by side in his kitchen, made sandwiches and ate them. Later they brought root beer to his couch, snuggled and watched a movie. The normalcy of the moment fed her heart.

When the movie ended he stood up and stretched. "So, darlin', you staying over?"

"I have an appointment in Shackleton at ten. I should probably go home so I won't disturb you."

"What do you have to run all the way over there on a Saturday for?"

"My therapist is there." It wasn't as hard as she'd thought, saying it aloud.

He sat again and nodded. "Good. Is it helping?"

It felt slightly odd to talk to him about it but at the same time, good.

"I think so. Sometimes I have all this stuff in my head and I can't say it to anyone. But I can to her. She doesn't know me or my family, she doesn't judge me. It's very freeing."

"I imagine so. You can always talk to me you know. I'm not going to judge you."

"No, but you get mad about stuff. And sometimes, having to deal with other people's emotions over it is more than I want to. Sometimes I want it to be about me just saying it and being rid of it."

He bit his lip against what he wanted to say. He *did* get mad at some of the things she told him. When he'd seen the damage to her fingers and she'd revealed it was her ex's doing, a wave of rage so deep and dark swallowed him for a moment he was quite sure he could have killed the man over it.

Instead he nodded. "I understand. I'd still like you to stay over. We can get up early and I'll run you home. You can shower here with me." He waggled his eyebrows at her lasciviously, making her laugh.

"All of my stuff is at home. I'm very particular about my hair products. I know it's terribly shallow of me. And I don't have any night clothes."

"Sleep naked. Or, I can loan you a T-shirt if you like. I'm sorry if I'm pressuring you. I just want to wake up with you in my arms tomorrow. But I do understand if you'd like to go home."

She still had dreams, she had the scars. The weight of the hiding she'd have to do lay on her heavily. It warred with her yearning to be held in Shane's arms all night.

"I can't. I'm sorry. There's…it's…" She shrugged her shoulders, not able to find words, not knowing if she could trust him or herself to reveal more. "It isn't you. I know that sounds like a cliché. But I can't. Not yet. And I really do have to get up early tomorrow. Please don't be angry."

He pulled her against his body and kissed her temple. "Darlin', I am not angry. I won't say I understand because I don't know all of it and I couldn't possibly be in your place. But I do understand your wanting to go home and I'm not hurt or upset. I keep telling you we have time. And we do." He moved to look into her face. "We do don't we? I suppose I've just assumed that we're in a relationship but I haven't really asked you."

"I told you, I'm not a casual person. But I don't know what I have to give anyone just now. If you're asking if I'd like to continue seeing you and that I have no interest in anyone else, yes. What I have to offer above that right now? I don't know."

He stood and helped her up. "That's all I need for now. We can work through the rest as we go."

The drive back to her place was quiet but comfortable. His hand lay gently on her thigh as he drove. When they got to her place he walked her to the door.

"Goodnight, darlin'. Would you like to come to dinner at my parents' house on Sunday night? My momma's been bugging me to bring you. I won't lie to you, I think she's got a bigger crush on you than I do. There's a running competition to see who can talk about you more. She also tells me you've promised to come to dinner sometime soon. And I'd love for you to get to know them all better. Maggie will be there too."

She smiled. "I did promise her. It wasn't like I could do anything else. She's called me twice about it. And I do like her, even if she's the world's worst driver and a total menace behind the wheel."

"Yeah? And what about me?"

Coyly, she cocked her head. "You? Hmm. Well, it appears that your driving is decent. Safe enough. Clearly you didn't learn to drive from your mother."

He laughed, the sound echoing through the quiet of the post midnight evening. "My dad taught me. And you know that's not what I was asking."

"I know, I just wanted to tease you. I happen to like you too, Shane Chase. More than is probably wise."

"Good. Wisdom is overrated. Now, let me come in just to be sure everything is okay." Her back went rigid and he sucked in his breath, making an agitated sound. "Okay, so I didn't really phrase that like a request. And I know I'm pushy and I know you don't want to hear that I just want to protect you. I'm trying you know. Would it be all right with you if I came in just to check the place out?"

Her posture relaxed and she put a hand to his cheek. "Thank you for that. It means a lot to me. And I'd appreciate that."

He did a quick check of the apartment and all was well. After kissing her goodnight, he told her he'd pick her up on Sunday and waited on her doorstep until he heard her locking all her locks.

Whistling softly, he jogged down the steps and to his car, entirely sure he'd not been that happy in a very long time.

Chapter Nine

When they pulled up to the curb in front of the Chases' beautiful home, nervousness clawed Cassie's insides. Sure, she knew Polly casually and she saw Matt pretty much every day, but this was like a meet the parents date. What if they didn't like her for their son?

Shane grabbed her hand and brought it to his lips to kiss across her knuckles. "Darlin', don't be nervous. They already know you except for my daddy and he's going to love you. Trust me. Now come on." He jerked his head and she laughed.

He had to put his hands in his pockets to keep from going to open her door but the smile she gave him for letting her do it herself was worth it.

She took his arm though as they walked up to the porch and he wanted to shout to the whole neighborhood that Cassie Gambol was his. Long, curvy and absolutely astonishingly beautiful, he couldn't believe this woman beside him trusted him as much as she did.

Before he could reach out and turn the knob, the door opened and Marc stood there, grinning. "Hey there, Cassie. My, that blue does only good things for you." He leaned in quickly and kissed her, just a friendly greeting. But Shane felt her startle and stiffen. Putting an arm around her waist, he shot Marc a look and his brother stood back quickly.

Marc seemed to understand, winking at her but backing off to let them both in. She relaxed and he kicked himself for not talking to Marc about how to approach her. Matt, he knew, understood and Kyle didn't hug up on any woman he wasn't related to after he'd gotten together with Maggie.

"I thought I heard someone arrive." Polly Chase came click-clacking into the hallway, wearing a big grin. "Hi there, honey. Welcome. Can I get you something to drink? Maggie and I were sneaking a beer in my sitting room. You want to come on in there after my Edward meets you? He's been dying to after hearing us all talk about you nonstop."

Shane tensed, not knowing how Cassie would react to his mother's stream of consciousness, mile a minute chatter but she smiled and let his mother enfold her into a hug.

"Mrs. Chase, this is just a beautiful home. I love the period pieces you have. Are they family antiques?"

Shane wanted to laugh out loud. Now Cassie was in for it. She'd hit on some of his mother's greatest loves. Antiques and the history of the house and the pieces in it.

"Polly. My mother-in-law is Mrs. Chase. I'll give you a tour. Let's go say hi to the boys in the family room. Dontcha know baseball is on and once the game starts you won't see any butts moving from seats until dinner." Polly took Cassie's hand and Maggie came out of the sitting room and after a quick hug for Shane, followed Polly and Cassie into the family room.

Shane watched his father's eyes widen when he saw Cassie. He'd told his father Cassie was beautiful but Shane saw his father really understand the full impact Cassie made. He waited for the voice.

"Well hello there. You must be Cassie." His father, ever the gentleman, took her hand, giving her a courtly kiss. Cassie blushed slightly. "I'm Edward Chase. It's very nice to meet you and see you in one piece after my wife welcomed you to Petal in her own special way."

Cassie's delighted laugh sounded through the room and Shane wanted to laugh himself as he saw his father's eyes widen again and he snuck a quick peek at Shane.

"It's nice to meet you too, Mr. Chase. My neck has recovered from your wife's welcome and my car is good as new. I'm sure your insurance company is less thrilled than I am though."

"Edward, please, sugar. And my goodness, aren't you just a bundle of gorgeous? Shane told me you were beautiful but he was right that I had to see you, and hear you, to get the full impact."

"Okay, Daddy, enough. You trying to steal my girl?"

"Oh no, my boy! Your momma is more than enough for me."

Matt approached and paused a moment, making sure Cassie saw him before giving her a hug and kiss on the cheek. "Hi there, sweetie. You ready to run out the door yet?"

Cassie grinned. "Nah. I hear there'll be cobbler. I can't leave until after that."

Kyle laughed and stood up to squeeze Cassie's hand and reach around and smooch Maggie. It was an easy movement and Shane realized, not for the first time, just how good his brother was at making people feel safe.

Shane loved seeing Cassie so at ease and relaxed and hoped she'd come to be comfortable with his family enough to be like that all the time.

"Okay, we're off for the tour. You boys behave. Dinner in thirty." Polly took Cassie's hand and they left the room.

Shane grabbed a beer from the mini-fridge in the corner and sat on the couch, grinning at his father.

"Go ahead on and grin, boy. She's something else. Your momma sure does seem to like her and I don't believe I've ever seen you this way with a woman before. You watched her, made sure she was all right. I like seeing you that way."

"I'm sorry I spooked her, Shane. I didn't mean to." Marc

might come off as cavalier in public but those who knew him, really knew him, understood he was a truly sensitive person.

Shane turned and patted Marc's arm. "It's okay. You didn't mean any harm. She'll get used to you in time. She's really easy around Matt since she sees him every day. Women don't seem to spook her at all."

"She's a totally different woman than the one who practically shoved me out the door when she first came to town. You're good for each other," Matt said.

At dinner, Cassie marveled at how close they all were. Such an ease of communication and friendly banter. It was clear they all loved each other very much.

And they all went out of their way to make her feel included and welcome. She missed that kind of connection to family. Terry had interfered so much she'd backed away from her father until the very end and she'd had to sneak around to see Brian. Sitting there at the table, listening to the joking and the teasing, a pang of longing cut through her, and a tiny ember of hope flared too. She wasn't so far gone that this wasn't possible.

It was a scary thought but not as scary as it would have been even three weeks before. Suddenly she could see herself at this table with these people. See herself as part of their family. See herself with Shane.

The danger of hope was the very real chance of losing it. She wasn't sure she could afford it but her therapist seemed very happy and sure Cassie had the strength to succeed in a relationship with a man like Shane. She just had to find the strength to keep on believing in herself. To let go of the Carly she'd been and embrace Cassie and her future.

"You ready to run for Florida yet?" Shane teased as he drove her home.

"I like your family, Shane. They're all very nice and worked to make me feel welcome."

"They like you too, darlin'. I'd ask you to dinner next Sunday but with the party on Monday, I think my momma will be cooking and getting ready. The woman loves to throw a party."

"But it's her birthday. Oh see, I'm putting her out. I'm going to call a caterer so she doesn't have to do all the work. I'd do it myself but I'm a terrible cook."

Shane laughed. "Cassie, my mother *loves* to plan parties. She does. She loves to cook and be with her family. She lives for this stuff. You'll see when Homecoming approaches. And I don't want you spending any money anyway. I know it must be tight with just being part-time at the bookstore. My dad wanted to talk to you about some work in his office but he didn't get the chance. You should call him about it."

"I don't need the job. I told Penny that. I really don't. I have some money set aside and with the jewelry beginning to take off, things are very comfortable."

"Comfortable? Come on, Cassie. I know you can't be making much more than your rent. Where is the money coming from for you to live?"

"I told you, I have some money set aside."

"From the divorce?"

Money was a sore subject. She'd fought over it with Terry many times as it was a chief way to control her movements. As a surgeon she'd made an excellent living but her checks were direct deposited and he kept a tight hold on their bank account.

"Shane, I told you all you need to know. I appreciate your concern but it's not necessary."

"You know, you have to give some too. It's not fair of you to expect me to do all the compromising."

"Do I ask you how you pay your bills, Shane? How is it a compromise on my part to tell you how much money is in my bank account and where it came from? I told you I had enough to pay my bills and be comfortable. I'm not sure how it's any business of yours where it comes from."

"I'm the sheriff; it's my business if it's from an illegal source." He pulled in front of her building and stopped the truck.

"Are you accusing me of breaking the law? All because I won't let you snoop in my finances?"

He knew he was in trouble when he saw the set of her jaw and anger flashing in her eyes. Put the way she'd said it, he saw her point. Still, it frustrated him that she kept trying to keep him out. He was a cop. He couldn't turn it off even if he was dealing with his girlfriend. He knew that bookstore job couldn't pay very much and even if her jewelry business was doing really well, it couldn't be doing much more than paying her rent. He truly didn't think she was involved in something illegal but he hated not knowing and hated her not sharing with him even more.

"I'm sorry. Yes, I did insinuate that but I don't mean it. I'm just agitated that you keep hiding from me."

"I am not hiding from you. I've let you in further than anyone else other than my brother. That doesn't mean I'm going to let you snoop in my checkbook. I think I need to go in before we say something we regret." She grabbed the door handle.

"Are you always going to run away when things get difficult?"

She turned to him, shock on her face. "You don't know a fucking thing about it, Shane."

He knew he should shut up but damn it, his mouth wouldn't listen. "Then tell me! How can I know if you won't tell me?"

"You don't get every part of me! I am the only person entitled to all of me. If you need to know every bit of me and what I do, I can't offer it to you. I won't. I've been there and I will not go back."

"I'm sick of you comparing me to him, Cassie."

"Well, let me make it easy for you then. I won't compare you to anyone. Goodnight, Shane."

She got out of the car and began to walk to her apartment. He sat in his car and watched until she got inside and drove off.

Chapter Ten

For the next several days, he tried to tell himself he didn't need the aggravation of such a difficult woman in his life. He needed a woman who'd share with him without reservation.

He avoided the side of town the bookstore was on. Tried not to think about her. Matt was annoyed as hell at him. Gave him a lecture about how of course Cassie got her back up when she'd been controlled all those years and how Shane had a tendency to steamroll people to get what he wanted. Made the infuriating comment that Cassie was as stubborn as Shane was and that he'd met his match in her.

On Thursday he walked past The Honey Bear and saw the familiar fall of ebony hair and that long tall body. Cassie sat inside having lunch with Marc of all people. Shane stood at the door for a while, watching his little brother laugh and flirt and cajole Cassie. Just when he was ready to go in there and snatch his brother bald headed for moving in on his woman, Shane realized Marc was trying to get her to eat.

Marc looked up, face darkening when he saw Shane in the doorway, before moving his eyes back to Cassie. A sick feeling gathered in Shane's stomach and he went inside.

"Hi, mind if I join you?" He kept his voice light until he

saw her face. Dark circles, impossible to cover completely with makeup, smudged the normally flawless skin below her eyes. Eyes that had lines of fatigue around them.

"I'm just leaving."

The caramel of her voice was flat.

"You haven't finished eating, sweetie. You promised me you'd finish half that sandwich. You wouldn't break a promise would you?" Marc cajoled her.

"I'll take it to go. I promise I'll eat it when I get home." She smiled at Marc.

"Cassie, please, can we talk?" Shane wanted to touch her, had burned to touch her since she'd walked away from him Sunday night but his pride had stopped him from calling her. Damn it.

"I think we've said all we needed to."

"I'm sorry. I've missed you. You look terrible. I'm sorry." He scrubbed hands over his face and took a deep breath. "Can I walk you to your car at least?"

"I'm going to go get this wrapped up for you, okay, Cassie?" Marc stood and grabbed her plate.

"Thank you, Marc." She turned back to Shane and met his eyes. Their connection sparked. "I didn't drive. I walked."

"Okay. Can I walk you home then?"

Marc brought her a bag and handed it to her, kissing her cheek. "You promised. Don't make me give you my pouty face. I'm told it's quite devastating."

Cassie laughed. "I promised. Thanks, Marc."

He shrugged and moved past his brother, shooting him a glare over her shoulder. "Of course, sweetie. That's what friends are for. Now I'll see you Monday. You promised that too."

"Okay, okay. I'll see you then."

She watched Marc go and then grabbed her handbag and the paper sack that held her leftovers.

Moving so she could see him coming, Shane reached out to touch her arm. He knew there was hope when her eyes closed a moment. "Darlin', I'm a pushy bastard. But damned if I don't just think you're the best thing that ever happened to me. I think we covered the arrogant ass part in an earlier conversation. I'd like to refer you back to that."

"You can walk me home," was all she said as she headed toward the door and out onto the sidewalk.

"Would you like me to drive you? It's awfully warm out here and you look tired."

"I can walk. It's five blocks. And I *am* tired."

"Okay. How about I carry your leftovers so you can hold my hand?" Without saying anything she handed him the paper sack after a block and he took her hand in his. Relief rushed through him.

They didn't speak much on the walk but she invited him in.

"Only if you'll finish eating. I haven't eaten either. You have any food inside?"

She rolled her eyes and jerked her head, ordering him inside.

He'd been unsure what to expect. His own place was a pit, he'd been eating out a lot and sleeping on the couch, but her apartment was clean enough.

"Sit down, I'll make you a sandwich." She looked him up and down. "Two. You want iced tea?"

He grinned and she made a soft sound, part annoyance, part affection. He watched her as she moved in the kitchen, making him sandwiches and putting her leftovers on a plate. Within moments she placed the plates on her small table and went back to grab the teas, sitting down with a sigh.

"You haven't called."

"Neither have you." It sounded petulant even to his own ears.

"No. Because I've told you I can't deal with feeling controlled. That may not have been your intention but I was up front with you from the start that I have hot-button issues. What's your excuse?"

Damn she was direct. He swallowed hard. "I don't have one. Pride I guess. I'm a damned fool."

She looked him up and down and nodded shortly. "Yeah. But you're well meaning."

Unable to hold back a smile, he gave her one and took her hand. She let him. "Okay, the deal is, you and I have some major chemistry. But we're both stubborn. I think this will lead to fights."

"You're brilliant. You should have pursued rocket science."

He snorted but laughed anyway. "Sarcasm doesn't suit you. But I think if we know this and you absolutely know I'll not raise my hand to you ever, we can be mad, take a few steps back for a few hours and work it through. No more three days without speaking."

"Four days, asshole."

"You're a hard woman. Yes, four days. No more, okay? We'll work it through? Because you're worth it to me. I've missed you like crazy. Matt isn't speaking to me and I'm pretty sure after Marc tells my momma what you look like, I'm in big trouble from her too. My arms have been empty without you."

She softened. "You know I'm nearly helpless when you say that stuff. All right. I've missed you too."

"You look like hell."

"I haven't been sleeping well."

"I'm sorry."

"Stop saying that. We're done with that now. I'm sorry too. And I've just had some bad dreams. My therapist called in some pills to help me sleep better. I picked them up yesterday."

"And are they helping?"

"I haven't taken them. I..." She didn't want to be that far under in case Terry found her. If he broke in, she'd be helpless and he'd kill her. She'd dreamt of it over and over since Sunday night.

"You?"

"I just don't like narcotic sleep. It makes me feel out of control."

He nodded. "You working tomorrow?"

"Yes. Every Friday."

"I'm on shift until six tonight. I'll be back here with Chinese food and some clothes by seven. Don't worry, I'll sleep on the couch if you like. But you're going to sleep tonight and I'll be here to make sure you're safe. You'll take those pills and start feeling better because you're the guest of honor at a big party in just a few days."

She started to refuse but she wanted him here. He did make her feel safe. She didn't have the strength to refuse him. And she didn't want to.

"Okay. Thank you, Shane."

He came to kneel before her. "Cassie, I care very deeply about you. I'm sorry you've felt unsafe all this time while we've both been stupid. But you don't know how happy it makes me that you'll let me help, in even such a small way. Now eat."

That night he'd slept beside her, her body in his arms, breath on the skin of his neck. They'd made love but she'd kept her shirt on and the lights off. He knew she had body image issues and he didn't push her but he wanted her to know how beautiful she was. He hoped she'd trust him enough to let him see all of her some day soon.

He'd gotten up and ready first. She was a bit groggy when her alarm had gone off but some coffee and toast helped her wake up. When he'd left for work she was already looking better for her full night's sleep.

Chapter Eleven

Labor Day morning dawned bright and warm. Cassie had deliberated on what to wear for the last several days until she finally decided on a pair of denim shorts and a deep red sleeveless shirt. The collar was enough to hide the edge of the scars and she was able to wear her hair in a high ponytail.

Shane had wanted her to sleep over at his house the evening before but then he'd gotten called out for work at nine-thirty and she'd just headed home. She wasn't comfortable enough in his house to be there alone just yet.

She'd headed to Penny's first thing but Shane was already there with his mother and brothers, setting everything up.

"I thought I'd be able to beat you here." Cassie smiled at Polly, her hands on her hips.

"Honey, you'd have to get up a lot earlier to beat me to it." Polly laughed and pulled her into a hug. "I'm glad to see you here. Come on out here and tell me what you think."

Penny's backyard had been transformed into the perfect place for a party. A canopy was set up near the big oak tree and several tables rested beneath it for shade. Several stations of tubs filled with ice and cans and bottles of soda dotted the area.

Penny's dock had several floats and donuts for the kids to play on lying around.

"Wow. It looks great."

Shane saw her and dropped what he was doing to come and swoop her up into a hug. He dropped a kiss on her lips. "Morning, gorgeous. Sorry to have to duck out on you last night."

"Well, I suppose it's one of the hazards of being a cop's girlfriend. Is everything all right?"

He smiled at her and Polly laughed. "You just said you were my girlfriend."

"I am aren't I? I thought we'd discussed it."

"We did. I just like hearing it."

Cassie rolled her eyes.

"I like hearing it too. It's about damned time." Polly harrumphed and moved back out into the yard to order people around.

Before too long, people began to show up and two very large barbecues began to fill up with burgers and chicken.

Shane heaped food on Cassie's plate and got up to get her another glass of tea. He'd been very careful to make sure she stayed hydrated and ate well after she'd scared him several days before. At first she'd been testy when he insisted she take care of herself and eat better but to his relief, she finally let him take care of her. She did appear to be sleeping better though and the dark circles were gone.

"You're good together." Liv patted his arm after he'd gotten the glass of tea. "I wish…well, I'm glad for you and Cassie. She's a good person. And she clearly makes you happy. Love is a good thing, Shane."

He saw the sadness on her face and her eyes moved to Matt and then away. "I'm real sorry things didn't work out with Matt. I hope you find what I've got with Cassie. You deserve it."

Liv shrugged. "I wish it had worked too. But you can't make someone love you. They do or they don't. It was a nice time. He was lovely to me. He just didn't love me and after a while

I couldn't deal with loving someone when they didn't love me back. Love changes you. Look at you. You were an asshole, Shane. God, you treated Maggie like shit. But you see now, you see in ways you couldn't then. That's good."

Brody called to her and she smiled and waved, moving to him after she'd said goodbye to Shane.

He stood there, thinking about the last thing Liv had said. That love changed how he saw things. Sure he'd been sorry he hurt Maggie because he liked her as a person. Liked her as a sister, even loved her as one. But loving Cassie had opened his eyes. He wasn't sure he liked what he saw of himself before. He'd closed himself off and it hadn't made him particularly nice to women. He hadn't been a cad, but he hadn't seen them in the way he should have.

He looked across the lawn at her as she laughed and talked with Penny, her back resting against the tree trunk. Damn she was beautiful. Yes, stunning on the outside, but her inner beauty shone like a beacon. He loved her. He didn't see her with love, he didn't love things about her, he loved her. Was *in* love with her.

"You love her, don't you?" Shane's father came to stand next to his son.

He looked at his father. "You're scary. I just realized it myself. I'm scared to death I'll fuck it up. I don't have the best track record with this stuff."

Edward chuckled. "That's love. Real love is scary. Because you know what you stand to lose. But she's damned strong, Shane. You need that. You didn't need some tough-as-nails woman to capture your heart. That's Marc. No, you needed a woman who was as strong as you but who engaged your ability to empathize. To show you what it meant to truly rise above and live. She's a fighter, our Cassie. She's your equal and your other half because she gives you the ability to see beyond yourself.

"You're a good man, Shane. But you've been selfish with women after Sandra. It's been hard to watch you wall your emotions off the way you did. All we could do was hope like hell

Cassie would come along and break your shell. And she did and you've broken hers too. Seeing you so gentle with her does my heart proud. I'm proud of *you*, son. You're a man now." Edward pressed a kiss to his son's cheek and squeezed his shoulder before Shane moved to walk down to his woman.

But before Shane got to her she was standing up and looking toward the water. She took off at a run and Matt ran the other way, toward the front of the house.

Shane yelled her name but she dove off the dock and he ran, balls out, to reach her. Dee was crying and, in what felt like slow motion, Cassie surfaced, holding eighteen-month-old Michael in her arms. He'd fallen from the dock into the water and at some point, he'd taken a knock to the head and a deep, ugly wound gashed into his forehead.

Matt shoved him out of the way and took Michael from Cassie. Breaking free of his trance, Shane reached out to help her scramble up onto the dock.

"Back up," she ordered and everyone did. Shane put his arm around Dee with Arthur on the other side of her.

Matt opened a medical bag and Shane watched in awe, as his Cassie melted away and a confident, in-charge woman replaced her. Her face was set in concentration as she tipped Michael's neck up and leaned in.

"Matt, I'm going to need something for this head wound but let's get him breathing first."

Matt took orders smoothly as she began to give CPR to Michael, who'd turned blue.

Dee sobbed and he heard his father yell out that an ambulance was on the way.

Cassie broke her lips from Michael's and turned him onto his side and he coughed, water gushing from his mouth. She continued to give orders to Matt while she alternately spoke to Michael in a soothing voice to keep him calm.

Without taking her eyes from Michael, Cassie addressed Dee. "Dee, honey, can you hold it together? Just kneel down and touch his legs. He's scared. I'm going to get this gash on his head cleaned up and the bleeding stopped. He'll probably need a few stitches. Ask when you get to the hospital for a surgeon to do it. Preferably a plastic surgeon if one is available. That should help with the scar. He's going to be all right, Dee."

Dee took a deep breath and fell to her knees. She reached out to rub Michael's legs while talking to him, reassuring him. Cassie continued to work and Matt handed her everything she asked for. The siren sounded as the ambulance neared.

The paramedics ran over with a board and Cassie spoke to them clearly and quietly, explaining what had happened and what had been done. Dee moved to go with them in the ambulance, Arthur would follow in the car. Cassie followed until they got loaded in and drove away.

As she returned to the yard, Shane looked to her, amazement on his face. Matt wore an identical look.

She held up a hand. "I need a drink. The story is long and I can't tell it with everyone here."

Polly had already begun to shoo people out of the yard and Edward put a tumbler filled with an amber liquid into her hand. One handed, he pressed her into a chair in the shade.

When everyone but the Chases, Penny and Liv had gone, Cassie took a deep breath, and the smoky scent of good scotch filled her nose. Two swallows and it was gone. The heat spread through her, warring with the adrenaline crash.

"My name is not Cassie Gambol. It's Carly Sunderland. Or rather, it used to be Carly Sunderland, it's been changed legally. A long time ago in a galaxy far away, I was a successful vascular surgeon at a private hospital in Orange County. You all know the story of my ex-husband.

"I divorced him. He wasn't happy. He harassed me and my family. Showed up at my job until they had to bar him from the hospital and he lost his position and ability to practice there and his own practice group tossed him out. I kept quiet and was careful when I went home so he couldn't follow me. I thought

I'd been successful. But I wasn't. Eight months later he found me. Broke into my condo while I was sleeping. I woke up with him on my chest and a hammer coming toward my face. I threw him off but I tripped leaving my bedroom and he landed on my back. He held me down while he used the hammer to shatter the bones in two of the fingers in my right hand. I tried to get free but he's a big man.

"Blood was everywhere, I was slipping in it as I tried to struggle. I'll never forget the smell. It wasn't like I'd never smelled blood before but it was different because I knew it was mine. I knew I was losing too much.

"He'd hit me so hard the handle of the hammer began to splinter, and it broke completely when he hit me on the back of the head with it. I worked to stay conscious as he began to stab me with the shattered handle. Repeatedly. In the back and neck. He left me for dead as I lay in a pool of my own blood. But I managed to reach my phone just as I passed out. Luckily 911 sends someone out when there's no response.

"I was in a coma for three weeks and then in the hospital for nearly another month. It's all more complicated than I want to dwell on but after that they found him and arrested him. Put him on trial.

"At first they thought he'd paralyzed me. The wounds really messed up some of my nerves in my right arm. But with physical therapy, and my good luck at having one of my colleagues work on me, they saved most of my movement and by the time the trial was midway through I could walk through the door on my own power.

"I testified. They convicted him. He was supposed to be remanded immediately, awaiting sentencing. But there was some sort of paperwork error and they let him go. By the time they realized their error he'd skipped town."

She held up her hand to silence Shane, as Edward handed her another drink. Penny pressed some crackers into her other hand, which she ate to stave off the nausea.

"He called and taunted me. Said he'd be back to finish the job. It wasn't like I could be a surgeon ever again. I don't have the fine motor skills in my hand to do it. I had a wonderful victim's advocate the court hooked me up with. She got me enrolled in a program to change my name and social security number. He'd tracked me to my new apartment with my social security information.

"My brother drove through Petal a few years ago on his way to Atlanta and he liked it here. I chose an apartment I saw on-line and Carly went away and Cassie moved to Petal."

"Jesus God." Maggie looked up at Cassie.

Cassie swallowed and turned to look at Shane, wincing as she saw him. "I'm sorry I lied. I'm a little messed up right now, but I'll go home and clear out of town as soon as I can. You must all hate me."

A deep, tortured sound came from Shane as he fell to his knees and pulled her into his arms. "How you survived that and had the courage to come here and start your life over I'll never know. Cassie, you're amazing and I love you so much it hurts."

Cassie blinked several times, trying to figure out if she'd heard him right. "What?"

Shane pulled back and kissed her and kissed her again for good measure. "I. Love. You. Cassie, you're so damned strong. I don't hate you. How could you think I'd hate you for not wanting to share that horrible fucking story?"

"I lied about my name."

"So what? Cassie Gambol is your legal name now isn't it? Honey, you must think I'm a grade-A prick if you think I'd be angry at you for having to give up everything to move here to protect yourself from a homicidal freak."

She put her face in her hands. "I don't know what I thought! You don't...you're all...shit. I don't know. I'm sorry."

He laughed. "You're sorry? Honey, let's get you to my house, okay? Get you tucked into bed for a rest. You just saved Michael's life and told us one hell of a story. That's got to take a lot out of a girl."

"I've got lake water all over me."

"Why don't I go to your place and get you some clothes? I'll bring them by Shane's." Penny squeezed Cassie's hand. "Honey, I knew you were good people the minute you walked into my shop and not a damned thing you've done has made me doubt that."

"I lied to you all!"

"Not about anything important. Your actions speak the truth, Cassie. You were in charge and strong out there on that dock today. Even though it exposed you, you did it. You saved Michael's life without even a thought. You've been a good friend to us and you've, well, you've saved Shane too." Maggie fought tears.

Cassie couldn't deal much longer. She needed to be away from them all before she lost it. She also knew she couldn't be alone in her apartment. "My keys are in my purse. It's in the front closet."

Marc jogged inside and brought her purse back out and Penny took her keys and handed the purse to Shane, who took one look at Cassie and picked her up. "We're going to go to my house. I'll talk to you all later."

He started toward the car and Cassie laid her head on his chest and closed her eyes.

As the car pulled out of the driveway, everyone else stood on the front porch watching Shane take her to his house just three doors down.

"Holy hell." Matt leaned back against the front porch rail.

"I'm going to go to Cassie's and get her clothes." Penny moved to her car.

"I'll stay here until you get back." Polly sat in the porch swing and Edward joined her.

Penny waved and left.

"I can't even imagine. I knew it was bad. When she told us

about the abuse I was horrified. I thought there was some big incident but she didn't say. I just had no idea it would be this." Maggie leaned back against Kyle.

Polly sighed. "I knew it would be a strong woman who'd finally captured Shane's heart. But she's braver than any woman I've ever met in my life. Imagine just up and leaving after suffering so much and starting over again halfway across the country."

"She won't be safe until this asshole is found." Kyle held his wife to him.

"Shane won't stop until he is." Matt spoke with absolute certainty.

Shane took her up to his bathroom and turned on the water in his shower. "You can use a T-shirt for the time being. Let's get you cleaned up now." He tried to hold on to the tasks to get her comfortable. Anger and fear warred within him but he didn't want her to see either. He needed to be strong for her right then. Later on he'd go into his weight room and beat the hell out of the bag.

Woodenly, she let him help her out of her shoes and pull her shorts and panties down. As gently as he could, he freed her hair from the ponytail. Reaching down to pull her shirt off, he steeled himself. He knew seeing the scars would be shocking but he also knew he had to control his rage at Terry Sunderland to not make her feel bad. Her hands came down to stop him.

"Let me see you, Cassie. I think you're beautiful. You've told me the hard part. It doesn't matter to me. The scars don't make you less beautiful."

"You don't know. The scars…"

"Is that why you've left your shirt on when we make love?"

She nodded slowly. "That and well, my stomach and stuff."

"Cassie, please trust me. Your body is gorgeous. I don't care about the scars. They only make me think you're more beautiful."

More beautiful? Was he out of his mind? Angrily she pulled the shirt up and over her head and yanked her bra off. She moved her hair away, giving him her back. "There! Still think I'm beautiful? Still think fourteen stab scars makes me more beautiful?"

She felt the press of his lips over each one of her scars until tears came from so deep she couldn't stand anymore. He was there though, taking her weight into his arms, pulling her into the shower with him.

She clung to him as he shampooed her hair and soaped her up the best he could with her arms wrapped around him.

"Come on, darlin'. Let's get you out of here and dried off." He helped her out of the shower and toweled her off after he'd wrapped up her hair.

Leading her into his bedroom he had her sit on his bed. "I'll be right back. I'm guessing Penny has been by and left your clothes downstairs."

And she had. Left a bag just inside his screen door without disturbing them further. There was a note that Cassie's keys were at Penny's house when she needed them.

He stood in his living room, a towel wrapped around his waist, thinking about her scars. Out of Cassie's presence he let the rage take him. The rage at seeing the pink skin of fourteen scars on her back and neck. Of knowing the man who'd done it to her was still out there, keeping her so afraid she didn't sleep at night. That the sick fuck had taken away her career and nearly killed her—all because she wanted a divorce. Took away her name and her home.

He needed to let it wash through him because the last thing Cassie needed was a pissed off man. He knew right then that he would track Terry Sunderland down and turn him over to the courts or kill him himself. Shane Chase was a man who lived by law and order, believed in the power of justice. But at the moment, he wanted to kill another man. Wanted it with a power he'd never felt before.

Forcibly unclenching his fists, he took several deep breaths and let it go. He picked up the bag to bring Cassie her clothes.

Cassie lay on his bed quietly, her hands folded over her abdomen. Totally naked. The shock of her beauty hit him in the gut like it always did but this time with greater force because she wasn't covering up. She was totally exposed to him emotionally as well as physically.

"Darlin'? I've got your clothes here."

"Do you want me to cover up? Do the scars creep you out?" She sat up, the wet strands of her hair moving over her shoulders and chest.

Putting the bag near the door he pulled off the towel and stood there, naked and hard. "Does it look like your scars creep me out, Cassie?"

She shook her head. "Shane?"

"Yes, darlin'?"

"Do you have condoms?"

"Yes."

"Will you come here and make love to me please?"

He froze a moment. "Are you sure, baby? I'd like nothing more than to do that but I don't want you to do it if you don't feel up to it. It's been a trying day for you."

"It has." She nodded. "But I... I need to feel alive and you make me feel alive. When you're inside me, with your hands on me, I feel alive and vibrant."

He crawled across the bed to get to her. "You... Cassie, you make me feel so much. I love you. I've said it to another woman but I didn't even know what love was until I met you."

She moved to her knees and touched his chest and encircled his neck with her arms. "I love you too." Her voice was small but he heard it and his heart skipped a beat. "I love you but I'm scared."

"Let's work on that, okay? Because I'd give my life for you, to protect you. I love you and that means you're mine. And not in the way he meant it. You're not a *thing* to me. You're *every-*

thing to me. I want you to be free from fear. Happy. You deserve that. Let's work to make sure I can help protect you."

She pushed him back on the bed and scrambled to straddle his body. "I love that you asked to protect me."

"I love this position." He grinned lasciviously. "And I'm trying. God knows I want to hide you and go to war for you, but I know that's not what you need so I'm trying to find a middle ground. Because I have to tell you, I want to find this bastard so you can live freely. I want you to be able to choose to be Carly or Cassie. As long as you're with me, I don't care what you call yourself."

Leaning down, she kissed his lips and then the cleft on his chin. Her hands skimmed over the hard, tight flesh of his shoulders and chest. Through the hair there and over the coppery nipples, his gasp of pleasure bringing her a smile.

"I like that you have hair on your chest. It makes you even more masculine. And my goodness are you masculine. It makes me all shivery."

His hands slid up her thighs and came to rest at her waist. "I'm glad. I like that I'm not the only one shivery all the time."

She brought her lips to the hollow of his throat and swirled her tongue there, tasting the salt of his skin. Over his collarbone and down, teeth grazing over each nipple. Scooting back, her ass rested on his thighs as her hands traveled over the flat muscle of his belly until she finally reached his cock.

"I like this too."

"I'm *really* glad. It likes you as well." His voice was strangled. "We can get to the making love stage soon, right? Because I really need to be inside you."

"In due time, Sheriff." With that, she bent down and took him into her mouth, bringing him off the bed with a hiss of pleasure.

She explored him slowly with her mouth, with lips and tongue. Around the head, tasting him, and then slowly taking him as far as she could before nearly pulling off him.

His hands gripped the sheets so tight she was surprised he

didn't rip them. But his control, all for her, to make sure he didn't spook her, touched her. And she yearned for a time when he'd take her wild and hot, when she could be taken without fear. A time she felt would come someday.

Shane looked down his body at Cassie. Her dark hair, slowly drying, played peek-a-boo with her face so he got carnal glimpses of her sucking his cock. What he didn't see was just as hot as what he did see. One of her hands wrapped around the base of his cock and the other did something naughty and really good with his balls.

The hot wet of her mouth surrounded him and he was awash in pleasure. He knew he had to stop her soon or he'd come and he'd already discovered just how much he liked being inside her when that happened.

"Baby? Cassie, honey? Stop now, I'm getting close."

She pulled off him with a slight pop and looked up. She looked so wicked and sexy at that moment his cock jumped in response. Her lips were wet and swollen, eyes half lidded, hair tousled.

"That's the point, Shane."

He laughed. "Ride me, Cassie. I'll come, but I want to be deep inside you when I do."

Pouting, she took the condom from him and rolled it on. He was fairly sure he'd never want to put his own condom on again, the way she did it, slow and precise, was damned sexy.

Crawling forward, she reached around her body to open herself and guide him to her gate. He took it all in as she slowly sank back onto his cock.

Hot. Fuck, she was hot and tight as her pussy took him in. Welcomed him. Each time she pulled her body up, he watched the flex of her thighs and her breasts swayed forward.

"You're amazing, Cassie. So pretty up there I don't have words. I could look at you for days."

A crooked smile slid over her mouth and she rolled her eyes. "I love that you're so full of shit."

"You know, you're snarky when you get warmed up."

"Ha! You should see me when I've known you a while."

And that little comeback settled around his heart. "Yeah." He smiled a moment, drawing a fingertip around her nipple, delighting in her pause and the way her lip caught between her teeth. "I can't wait."

She took a deep breath and added a swivel when she came back down on him. "That was very nice," he said, voice strained.

"I got the mad skills. I haven't used them in a few years, but I got 'em." She tapped her temple and he laughed.

It was important to her that he realize she was more than the sum of those years with Terry. There was a time when she'd loved sex and she was quickly back there. Something about the way he looked at her, touched her, made her whole, enabled her to think about a future.

"You got 'em all right." He continued to circle her nipple with one finger and drew another down her stomach, finding her clit. Gasping, she rolled her hips forward. At first it was a slow stroke, building the fire of her pleasure.

"Cassie, give it to me. Let me feel you come around my cock."

She shivered at his words and arched, putting her hands on his thighs.

"Oh that's a sight. I love the way that looks. Almost as good as how it feels."

His voice was strained as the new angle of entry dragged the head of his cock over her sweet spot. That, along with his finger slowly sliding back and forth over her clit, brought orgasm over her with a sharp shock.

Shane looked up at her, watched the arch of her beautiful body. As her pussy clutched and clasped around his cock, he pulled her down on him and came, her name a hoarse whisper on his lips.

Boneless, she fell to a sated heap on the bed. He murmured that he'd be right back, checked the house to be sure it was locked up and lay beside her, his arms around her body, until she was deeply asleep.

Tucking blankets around her body, he set the air conditioner to keep the room nice and cool and grabbed some shorts before heading downstairs.

In his weight room, he worked out for well over an hour, hitting the bag, imagining it was Cassie's ex. He pushed every last bit of his anger and grief for her through his fists until he was so exhausted he trembled.

He heard a tapping on the door and got rid of the gloves before going out to see who it was.

Matt stood there and held up a six pack and a bag of pretzels. Kyle held up a dish of chicken and Marc held a cobbler. Shane let them in and put his finger to his lips.

"Cassie is sleeping. Come on through."

They followed him into the television room and flopped down on the couch. No one said a word until beers were cracked open and the pretzels passed around and chicken tasted. Shane put the cobbler aside for Cassie.

"How is she?" Matt asked.

"She's exhausted but sleeping. I thought the nightmares were just about the abuse. Shit, he broke in while she was sleeping. It's a wonder she slept at all." Shane ran a hand through his hair.

"You'll find him, Shane. Tell us what we can do to help." Kyle sighed and sat back.

"I will. Now that I've got a name that's a start. I'll call the officer in charge of her case tomorrow and see what he'll tell me."

"How are *you*?" Marc asked. "I can't imagine it's easy for you to know the woman you love has gone through something so awful."

"I'm better now. I punched the bag for a while, did some judo. I'll get down to the range tomorrow and I want her to come too. She's a strong woman, I'm betting she'll feel even better with some basic proficiency with a weapon. She'll feel in charge and I'll be helping her. God knows how touchy she'd be if I just did it all for her."

"You really love her, don't you?" Kyle smiled. "I'm sorry she had to endure all of that. But she's a damned strong woman and she's good for you. Maggie wanted to come over but she's with Momma, holding her back."

Shane nodded, understanding. "Momma must be like a bumblebee in a jar right now."

The brothers laughed, thinking about their mother in protective mode but being unable to leave to come and comfort Cassie and her son.

"Thank you." Shane looked to each of his brothers, jerking his chin at the food on the table.

"You love her. She loves you. That makes her one of us now." Matt shrugged his shoulders matter-of-factly.

Chapter Twelve

The next week went by in a blur. Shane spent every moment he could with Cassie, getting to know her better, falling in love with her a bit more every day.

Holding a bag of sandwiches and cream sodas, he headed up the stairs to her apartment and froze as he saw her on the landing, hugging another man. She clung to him tightly, her face buried in his neck.

Shane saw red and then his heart broke into a million pieces. It was Sandra all over again. He'd fallen in love after so many years and it happened to him again. He wanted to fall to his knees and howl at the unfairness of losing a woman he'd thought cared about him as much as he did her.

"Fuck all if you didn't totally fool me with your act. I'm as damned as you're faithless apparently. If you're going to cheat on me, Cassie, you should do it out of the public eye."

Cassie froze and looked around the man. And when the man turned Shane saw three things. The look of horror and pain on Cassie's face; his brother Matt standing in the doorway of her apartment behind them and that the man looked a lot like Cassie. *Shit.*

He moved quickly toward her but she pulled back into the

apartment and shoved the man inside who looked about ready to punch Shane. Of course, judging from the look on Matt's face, he'd have to stand in line.

"Cassie, I'm…"

"Let me guess, you're sorry? Shane Chase, this is my brother, Brian. He's here to meet the man I fell in love with and to tell me that Terry has been sighted." She tried to slam the door but he put a hand out.

"Cassie, I'm sorry. I thought…when I saw you with another man…it just… I'm sorry. Please. Can't we talk about it?"

"No, I don't think we can." She put a hand on his chest, shoving him back, and slammed the door in his face. He leaned his forehead against the frame and let out a ragged breath.

"Oh honey, I don't know what to say." Matt sat down and watched Cassie as she fought back tears. He was so angry at Shane he held his hands together between his knees to keep from shaking. The man found this woman who loved him so much, who'd never do anything so bad, and he might have just thrown it all away.

"I appreciate you coming over, Matt, but I think my sister needs to be alone right now." Brian stood and went to the door.

Matt looked back at Cassie. "He loves you, Cassie. He tries to pretend like what Sandra did didn't hurt him that bad, but it wrecked him. He couldn't trust anyone for years. I'm not saying he was right, but I want you to try and understand why he jumped to conclusions the way he did." He went to the door. "We'll see you tomorrow night at dinner then."

"Oh no you won't."

He sighed. "Cassie, don't. Please don't shut him out. You're good for him and he's good for you."

"I can see how good he is for her. Accusing her of being a whore on her doorstep, making her cry. Fabulous." Brian crossed his arms over his chest.

"It was wrong, I'm not saying it wasn't. But my brother loves her. He's a good man and he deserves a second chance. Everybody makes mistakes, Cassie."

"Yes, and they always tell you they're sorry after they hurt you. Until they do it again. There's always an excuse. I'm not her anymore. I won't go back to being her."

Matt realized the depth of Shane's mistake then but didn't say anything further about it. "I'm next door if you need me. No matter what is going on between you two, I'm your friend. Okay?" He moved to hug her and she let him.

"Thank you, Matt."

"Please don't judge my brother too harshly, Brian." Matt raised his hand in a wave and left, hearing the locks click into place behind him.

Shane sat on the bottom step.

"What the fuck is wrong with you, Shane?"

Shane shook his head, Matt saw tears shining in his eyes. "Oh shit. I hurt her so badly. It's just…when I saw her there it made me think of Sandra. I forgot who she was for a moment. I spoke before I thought and oh, her face." Shane rested his forehead on his knees and Matt knelt there, touching his brother's arm.

"I know why you overreacted, Shane. I understand."

"I may have lost her forever."

Matt took a deep breath. "I hope not. But. I'm sorry to say this, Shane, but you attacked her and falsely accused her and your shit with Sandra pushed her buttons. Both of your emotional shit hit in the same place at the same time. She's really upset and her brother is pissed off."

"And the ex has been seen?"

"She didn't tell me much. She came home from work and saw me out front. Told me her brother was on the way and that she wanted us all to meet him and for him to meet us. Then she told me the brother had said the ex had been seen. She didn't know more than that and I came over to her place to watch over her."

"I need to go to her, work this out." Shane stood.

"Don't. Shane, not right now. Her brother is really angry and protective. She's a mess. Call her, leave a message. Go to her stall tomorrow. Let her know you're here but don't rush up on her. Give her some space. She's scared right now that you're like her ex. Hurt her and say you're sorry and hurt her again."

"Fuck. I'm an idiot."

Matt hugged his brother. "No you're not. You've been one in the past but you got scared tonight and reacted before thinking. You love her and you hurt her. But you're not her ex."

Looking back over his shoulder at her door, Shane let Matt drag him over to his apartment where he called and left her a message.

"Carly, what is going on, honey?" Brian sat next to her on the couch, brushing a hand over her hair. "I thought this guy was the one."

Cassie had successfully fought away her tears and now just felt numb. "I thought he was too, Brian."

"Who's Sandra?"

She told him the story of Shane's ex-fiancée who he'd found cheating with his best friend.

"So he saw you with me and he must have flashed back on that. He's already left you a phone message apologizing. He sounded sincere. What do you think?"

"I'm afraid, Brian. He's probably the most sincere person I've ever met. But I don't know if I can trust my own perceptions these days and I'm afraid if I take him back that it'll be like with Terry."

"I understand. Well, I don't, but I trust your feelings here. I don't know this guy well enough to say. Why don't you give it some time to see how he acts in the coming days? Because I'd hate to see you write him off if he's the one for you. But I'd hate to see you take him back and end up with another asshole."

She put her head on his shoulder and sighed. "Tell me about Terry."

Brian did. He told her about how her ex had been sighted in

San Francisco three times before dropping out of sight again. All the more troubling was that one person claimed Terry tried to get her to use her state job access to search information about Cassie.

"We don't have any reason to think he knows you've changed your name or that you're here. But I think you should be aware at all times. I can't see that you should move away from Petal. You're building a life here and that's important."

Lying in bed that night, Cassie stared at the ceiling and felt the emptiness next to her in bed. She'd gotten used to Shane's body there at night. Reaching out and touching him. Knowing she was safe and loved. And that was gone and her heart felt empty. Everything felt empty as she tried to figure out what the hell to do.

Chapter Thirteen

Brian stayed in Petal over the next several days to visit and keep in contact with the investigators on Terry's trail. Still, Cassie tried to keep to a schedule.

Shane had come to her table at the Sunday Market but she asked him to go. It hurt just seeing him.

He left messages on her voice mail every morning to tell her he loved her and every night to say goodnight. Her feelings were all over the map. She loved him. No doubt about that. Every time she saw him walk by the front of the bookstore, every time she heard his voice or found a note he left for her on her car, she missed him more than she had before.

Loving Shane and being with him had filled up her life. Not in an onerous way like being with Terry had been. Being with Shane hadn't weighed on her. It had been good, right. She felt like she'd belonged to something instead of to someone.

But it would hurt less to lose him now than to take him back and fall into the same traps she'd done before and lose herself in the process. She'd rather be alone than live in fear ever again.

Polly Chase parked her car on Main and got out for the short walk to Paperbacks and More. "Damn kids. I tell you, if you want something done..." she mumbled as she patted her hair into place and absentmindedly waved at someone who'd called out a hello.

She walked into the store and zeroed in on Cassie. Her heart ached for the girl her son loved so much. Men!

"Hello, Polly." Cassie smiled wanly.

Polly pulled Cassie into a hug and held her upper arms as she gave her a long up and down. "Honey, you look like hell. When you gonna forgive Shane so you can both get some sleep?"

"Polly, I appreciate you checking in on me, I really do. But this thing between your son and I is not only private but complicated."

"Oh that's a pretty way to tell an old woman to mind her business. I like you, honey." Polly chuckled as she sat in the chair behind the counter. "But I'm a nosy old woman, it's a perk of getting old. You can be annoying and people just call you *eccentric*." Polly laughed at that. "Anyway, I know Shane messed up. I know what he did and how he reacted must have made you wonder if he'd be like your wretched sonofabitch ex. But you and I both know after a day or two, that's not the case. My son is a good man and that bitch gave him, how do you kids say, *issues* or baggage. I'm not excusing his actions, you best believe I tore a strip off him a mile wide and his father has too. But no one is punishing him harder than he is himself."

Polly leaned in, peering intently at Cassie. "You've made mistakes before in your life. I know part of that is what makes you hesitate now. But also, can't you see your way to giving my boy another chance? Let's face it, you two are going to fight. A lot. There's enough chemistry between the two of you to make an old woman sweat."

Cassie blushed crimson and looked at the paperback in her hands to keep from looking at Polly.

"You two have chemistry and heat but you're both stubborn, headstrong people. Lord knows this won't be your last fight. But you can fight with your man and know it's going to be all right the next day. Edward is the kind of man that butter wouldn't melt. I like that. It suits me. But Shane isn't that man. He's got my disposition. We're a tad hot headed. We love fierce. Shane loves you and I know you love him."

Polly hopped down from the chair, grabbing the bag she'd put near the register stand. "Two things. This has a cherry and a peach cobbler. Eat them both, you look pale. The second thing is I already think of you as my daughter-in-law so I love you too. Please give Shane another chance, for both your sakes. Oh, okay a third thing. You call Matty or Marc or me and Edward if you feel spooked, all right? We worry."

With that she thrust the bag at Cassie, hugged her again and click-clacked out of the store.

From there she headed over to the police station.

"Shane Edward Chase! You hold up right there, boy," Polly thundered as she stormed down the hall toward where he stood with the county prosecutor.

"Mrs. Chase, ma'am." The prosecutor, a boy she babysat many a time, bowed and got the hell out of there.

"Coward," Shane muttered and then waved his mother into his office. "Have a seat, let me get some soda because I can see from the look of you this will be a long lecture."

With narrowed eyes, Polly sat as she glared at her eldest's impertinence. "You look here, boy, I brought you into this world, I will not hesitate to take your dumb ass right out of it."

Shane laughed as he handed her a soda. "Of course, Momma, I'm sorry. I imagine this is about Cassie and I know, it's my fault and I'm trying to get her to talk to me. I told you that yesterday and the day before and before that too."

"I just went to see her, girl looks like she hasn't slept in a week. She's on the fence about you. But she loves you. She must 'cause I didn't let her get a word in edgewise." Pleased with herself, Polly chuckled again. "I made a good case for you, I hope. You know you and her are gonna butt heads a lot, right? Makes it more interesting in the bedroom I imagine."

Shane winced and got a sour look. "I don't want to have that line of conversation with you, Momma."

Polly waved him away. "Pshaw. Boy, you'll have any line of conversation with me I tell you to. Your daddy and I have four children, you think we don't have some chemistry ourselves? Now listen here, you've got to let her know that you love her and won't hurt her, even though you'll be fighting with her regular-like. And don't deny it, you two are just that way. But Maggie and I made her some cobbler and you know how your sweetie loves cobbler. Sweeten her up a bit hopefully."

Standing she raised the soda. "Thank you, Shane. You've turned out to be quite a decent man. I'm pretty proud of myself for not tossing your butt in the lake all the times I wanted to when you were a kid."

Shane grinned and kissed her cheek. "You're the best, Momma."

"Yeah, yeah. Boy, you better work on this girl harder because if she's not at dinner on Sunday you're eating a tuna sandwich."

With a last wave, she headed out while he chuckled.

Brian walked out of the apartment and saw Shane talking with his brother. Making his mind up, he stalked over to them.

Shane looked up and saw him approach and nodded. "I've wanted to talk to you for a few days now. Clear the air."

"I'm going to speak now. You have no idea what my sister told me every time I spoke to her. About how wonderful you were, how gentle and kind and loving you were. How you chased away her demons and made her feel not only protected but capable of protecting herself. She was so proud of you, proud of herself for finding a man who was worthy of her." Brian looked him up and down.

"And so I get this information about that fucking bastard surfacing, trying to find her, and I think I can come here, meet you. Instead, I get to listen to her cry every night. You tell me, Shane Chase, why the hell you think you're worthy of my sister."

Shane took a deep breath. "You don't know me so I can see why you'd be suspicious. It must have been hard to watch your sister go through what she did. I love her. Cassie means everything to me. You don't know what it was like…what I was like before. She changed me." He shrugged.

"I fucked up. I'm sorry. I have this old stuff and seeing her brought it to the surface. I was wrong. I've told her that. I made a mistake. I want to make it up to her. I'm not that bastard. I'm nothing like him. You can be mad at the person you love and not try to kill them. I don't know how to communicate that to her. But I'm going to keep trying until she listens to me.

"And I want to protect her. Yeah, yeah, I know she doesn't want that. But I love her and I'll be damned if that freak gets another shot at her. I'm trying to respect her need to do things herself. I want her to learn to shoot a weapon and take self-defense courses."

Brian looked at him funny and then chuckled. "I take it you haven't talked to her about this plan."

"Well, no. She just told me about the attack two weeks ago. I'd wanted to talk to her about going to the range and then we got into this fight. Why? Is she afraid of guns?"

"God help you, Shane." Brian shook his head and started to laugh. "She's not afraid of guns. After the attack, after she got out of the hospital she went to the range every day and learned how to shoot. At first with her left hand because the right hand was so damaged. She's a pretty damned good shot. She's got a license to carry, I took care of that. She's got a 9 mm. The self-defense classes would be good. She didn't have enough mobility yet after the physical therapy to really get proficient but she started to take martial arts classes just before she decided to up and move here."

Shane smiled wryly. "Okay, so the fact is that I'm *not* worthy of your sister. I can't think of anyone who is. She's just that special. But I love her and I'll keep loving her. And she makes me a better person, but I'm not perfect and yeah, I have buttons but so does she. So if I'm willing to work around hers, she should be willing to work around mine. Not that I think I handled it well. I didn't. But damn it, I deserve a second chance."

Brian looked at him silently for long moments and nodded shortly. "Yeah, I think you probably do. I have it on good authority that she's having dinner with Maggie, Penny and Liv tonight at Dee's. She told me she'd be home by nine. I'll be out then if you think you might want to talk to her."

Without saying anything else, Brian turned and walked away but not before looking back over his shoulder and tossing back, "If you hurt my sister again, I'll make it my business, Shane."

Matt watched as the man drove away in his rental before turning to his brother. "I like him."

Cassie spent the evening with her friends, enjoying the time with Michael and the easy communication with people. She began to know them and they her. Mostly they didn't talk about Shane but in their own way, each of them encouraged her to at least talk things over with him.

And she began to think they were right. Oh who was she kidding? She'd wanted to talk to him for days but was afraid. Afraid that if she did she'd lose him. Indecision had frozen her.

She'd talk to him the next time he called, she resolved as she walked from her car toward her stairs. Stairs that Shane sat on, holding a bouquet of roses, a gold box of chocolates at his feet.

"Those will melt out here in this heat," she said, walking past him and up the steps to her door.

"I should probably get them inside then, huh?"

"The roses need water too or they'll wilt."

He stood but stayed down at the bottom of the stairs, looking up at her. "Can we talk?"

"The lives of roses are at stake." She unlocked her door and walked in, leaving it open.

When he got inside, she'd pulled out a vase and was filling

it with water. He locked up behind himself and came into the kitchen, handing her the roses.

"So talk."

And he did. He sat at her kitchen table and laid it all on the line. "Do you remember our first real fight? We promised each other that we'd step back and then work it through. We said no more not talking for days. So I called you every day. Twice a day. I kept my end of the bargain.

"I was an asshole. Stupid. I got caught off guard and when I saw you there it wasn't you, it was her for just a brief second. But I didn't let it process, I just spoke out of pain and I hurt you and I'm so sorry. I didn't mean to hurt you and I did but I'd like the chance to make it up to you."

"I'm not her! I would never do that to you! How could you even think that of me? I love you. I trusted you with my heart and you hurt me."

"And I'm not him! Come on, Cassie, give me a break here. I said some not very nice stuff, yes. I take responsibility for it. It was wrong but I didn't hit you, I didn't blame it on you. I made a mistake, a stupid mistake. I love you, but we both know it won't be the last mistake I make. I'll make more because I'm a clumsy guy and I do clumsy guy stuff. I'm a tool. But I love you more than words can say. I want you to be with me forever. I'm serious about you, about this, us. I want us to move forward and build something. Please let's move past this. Please forgive me."

She exhaled and looked into his face. A face she loved. She didn't see arrogance there, not anger or calculation. His words seemed genuine. She wanted to believe him so badly.

"Okay. We both have our buttons and I realize what Sandra did to you changed you and made you gun-shy. I'm sorry she hurt you so much and I wish you hadn't been so devastated. Honestly, the woman is out of her damn mind. So in the offing, after all is said and done, you have baggage and you unloaded it on me. Problem is, you heaped a lot of nasty on me. Even for just a moment. And that intersected with six years of my life that I don't care to repeat, even as a sick, vague memory caused by your behavior.

"You can be a tool and do stupid guy shit, that's normal. But derision like that is another story. I can't deal with it. I won't ever again. I won't." Reaching out she took his other hand in hers as well. "I know. I know what it feels like to have that shadow of who you used to be come up and surprise you."

He closed his eyes a moment and let out the tension that'd built up in his muscles. "I love you so much, Cassie."

She smiled. "Yeah, yeah. I love you too, Shane."

Standing up, he pulled her to him, hugging her tight. "We'll just work it through. You and me, we're it, right? I've missed you this week. My bed has been empty, my arms, my life. I was getting used to your presence in my life and then you were gone and I didn't know quite what to do. Don't tell anyone that last bit."

She laughed. "Yeah, wouldn't want to blow your cred as a hard-ass or anything. I missed you too."

He moved slowly, bringing his lips to hers, and kissed her. Relief, joy, reconnection, desire, love—all rushed through him at once at having her back. "Bedroom?" he asked, breathless as he broke the kiss.

"Can't. Brian is due home any minute."

"I'd say I'll be quick but that's not really a good thing in this situation. Can I stay over? And you and Brian can fill me in on everything about your ex too. I want to know not just as the sheriff but as the man who loves you. Share your life with me."

"You hate my bed. You think the mattress is too soft," she said.

He grinned. "It'll absorb the sound of the makeup sex."

"Uh." She blushed. "Well go on home and get some clothes and bring back some cobbler from The Sands, it's still open. And then I'll let you have the side closest to the door."

He brought his lips back to hers, brushing his mouth over hers softly and nipping her bottom lip between his teeth for a moment. "When you put it like that, how can I refuse? Peach or berry?"

"I had peach yesterday so berry."

"You ate an entire cobbler?" he asked, not entirely shocked.

"So sue me. Your mother and Maggie made me some but I get hungry when I don't get sex regularly. You were an ass. I needed the comfort."

"I'll help you burn the calories." He waggled his eyebrows.

"You saying I'm fat?" she teased.

"Oh, you're just torturing me for fun now, aren't you?" Shane groaned.

She laughed and tiptoed up to kiss his chin quickly. "Yeah. G'wan then. I'll see you back here in a bit."

The minute Shane walked into The Sands and asked for a berry cobbler, Ronnie smiled at him for the first time in a week. She also followed up with an exclamation of pleasure that he and Cassie were back together.

When Shane returned, Brian had gotten back and Cassie had a pot of decaf brewed to drink with the cobbler.

Shane relayed the story to Cassie and Brian. "The whole damned town took your side, I'll have you know. They didn't even know what the hell happened and still they took your side. My mother hasn't spoken three words to me other than how I had to fix it between us. My brothers wouldn't play pool with me. At dinner last Sunday you should have seen it. My brothers all got these big juicy steaks and I got this tiny piece of gristle."

Unsuccessfully stifling a laugh, Cassie put a plate with cobbler and ice cream in front of him and then filled his coffee cup. "Your mother came over on Tuesday. She called every day this week too. Came into the bookstore every day I worked as well. Brought me cobbler to sweeten me up on your behalf. She's Machiavellian, that woman."

Cassie got her brother and herself a cup of coffee and joined them at the table. "She likes Brian. Maggie even baked tartlets for us. Lemon because it's his favorite."

Brian started to laugh, pleased to see his sister so lighthearted and silly. His reservations about Shane had faded over the week as he watched the man continue to reassure Cassie that he loved her but also didn't crowd her. And his family was just what Cassie needed. Brian didn't like the heartache she'd endured but he did like the fact that the man owned up to it and made it better. It was more than Terry had ever done.

"Tell me about him. Give me the details." Shane continued to eat but his expression darkened and by the end of the story, his eyes were narrowed and his mouth set in a tight line.

"Here's what we're going to do...with your permission." He looked quickly at Cassie who'd tensed up and then relaxed. "I hear you're a crack shot, we'll keep you going to the range, we can both go together so neither of us gets rusty. I'd like to put in a full security system here. We talked about it a little bit a while ago. I've got a list of available options and one of our contractors can put it in as soon as you decide on which you want. I even spoke with Chuck and he said he'd pay for half of it and not raise the rent if you paid the other half. If it's more than you can afford right now, we can work out a payment plan."

Brian looked at his sister from under his lashes. "Don't worry about the money. It's not a problem. Carly... Cassie, I'm with Shane on this. Please put in the system. I can't be here, you can't come back to California and live with me at my place, it's hard enough having you so far away. If you have this system, I'll feel so much better."

"Don't think I don't know you're both working me," Cassie said, eyes narrowed. "But I'd be stupid not to do it. Shane, if your friend can do it on a Tuesday, Thursday or Saturday, let's get him scheduled."

"If he can't, I can be here or Matt can or someone. I'd like to do it as soon as possible. If that's okay with you of course."

"Fine, fine. Thank you. And I'm not a crack shot. I just know my way around a gun. I've got a license for it."

They finished up the coffee and cobbler as it got late. Brian stood up and stretched. "I'm going to go to bed. I've got a plane to catch tomorrow afternoon."

They said their goodnights and Shane and Cassie went into her room and shut the door.

Cassie sure hoped Shane was right and the softness of her mattress drowned out the sounds of their reunion or they probably kept Matt and Brian up all night long.

Chapter Fourteen

Petal was filled with activity as Homecoming Week activities took over the town. Cassie loved the pretty banners that went up on Main Street with the school colors.

Nervously, Cassie tried to figure out what to wear to the picnic she'd been invited to attend with Shane and his family. Terry didn't have any family and she'd rarely attended events like the picnic when growing up. She'd been to the Governor's Ball a few times, swanky restaurants and parties but none of them had her as excited or nervous as the picnic did.

She wasn't expected to bring anything. There'd be food at the picnic. Shane told her they had big tables of barbecue and peach pie with homemade ice cream—and she was sure he smirked slightly as he said it—and all sorts of other goodies. That was a relief as she was a terrible cook. Anything more complicated than salad, grilled cheese and soup and she was lost.

She had an appointment with her therapist in the early part of the day so she told Shane she'd meet the Chases at the park after she got back to town.

After running home, she changed out of her jeans and into capri pants and a T-shirt. Early fall was still warm but she tossed a sweater into her bag as she left.

The park was already filled up with people when she arrived. Shane had told her the Chases always sat beneath a big oak tree on a rolling hill just as the park sprawled toward the lake shore. There'd be fireworks after dark and he'd promised the view there was the best around.

She should have known she'd be able to find their patch of ground by the sheer population of women gathered nearby and clustered around the blanket.

She knew she really didn't like the way one tall blonde was looking at Shane like he was a piece of pie with ice cream on it. What Cassie did like was the hostile look on Polly's face and the way Shane kept moving away from blondie.

"Hey, Cassie." Maggie waved and grinned as she approached them. "Come and sit, Shane's been saving you a place."

Cassie winked at Maggie.

Shane turned and when he saw her, the annoyed look on his face melted away. His features lightened and a smile tugged at the corners of the lips she loved to feel over every part of her body. He held his hand out to her and helped her sit down. Leaning in, he gave her a quick, but solid kiss. "Hi, darlin'. I've missed you today. You look beautiful."

Cassie rested against him for a moment and waved at the whole Chase family, sprawled out on the series of blankets there under the tree. "Hi, Shane. Hey everyone."

"I just brought back a whole bunch of food, Cassie. Eat up." Edward indicated the pile of food in the middle of the blankets.

"And here, honey, iced tea." Polly put a cup in Cassie's hand before shooting another dirty look at blondie.

"You want to tell me who your fan club president is?" Cassie murmured into Shane's ear.

He barked a startled laugh and kissed her again. "You taste good." He winked. "I thought you were the president of my fan club."

"Mmmm hmm. So?" But before he could answer, blondie moved in closer on his other side.

"Hello, I'm Kendra. And you are?"

"This is my girlfriend, Cassie Gambol. Cassie, darlin', this is Kendra." Cassie just tipped her chin and waited for blondie to move back.

"Your girlfriend?"

"Yes, that's what he said. I take it you're a friend of Shane's?"

"You could call it that." Blondie smirked.

"Ooookay." Cassie raised a brow at Shane and he moved closer to her. "Kendra, you really don't need to be in our laps. We get it. Everyone within a mile gets it. You dated Shane before he met me. Oh, snap. Okay now, point is made."

Shane tried not to smile but the corner of his mouth trembled a bit. He turned to blondie and said quietly, "Kendra, I've asked you to move back. You're being disrespectful to Cassie and me and my family too. Come on now, don't embarrass yourself."

Maggie sighed and Cassie craned her neck to see her around blondie. "How are you today, Cassie? I really like your hair that way."

Out of the corner of her eye she saw Kendra get up and storm off. "I'm glad you tried not to embarrass her, Shane."

He looked surprised. "You keep doing things I don't expect. I like that. And I like that you've got a big heart, even for people who don't necessarily deserve it."

She shrugged. "She's got a thing for you. How can I not understand that? Plus, I've been told that I'll have to deal with stuff like that all the time. They should suck it up now while I still have patience."

Polly laughed in the background.

"You sure you want to keep her, Shane? Because I'd be glad to take this fine young thing off your hands for you." Marc waggled his brows at them both and the tension was broken.

"Punk. You'll see when it happens to you, Marc. And then we're all going to tease the hell out of you." Shane put his arm around Cassie and squeezed her against him.

* * *

And that night was what solidified Cassie's entrance into the Chase family. Every Sunday she sat at their dining room table and shared dinner with them. Every Friday night she had beer and junk food with her friends while Shane played pool with his brothers. Toward the end of the night, she'd wander back and play a game or two with them.

The awful heat of summer cooled into the more moderate temperatures of autumn and Cassie realized that for the first time in nearly six years she was leading a normal life.

Penny hired her on to work full-time at the bookstore, which came with healthcare benefits, which was very nice. She kept busy and worked hard and began to feel like Petal was really her home and not just a place to wait until Terry got caught.

"Go ahead on and lock up, Cassie. It's nearly closing and I know you'll want to go and get ready for the Grange." Penny smiled as she came out to the front of the store where Cassie was rearranging the front tables.

"Thank goodness for you, Penny. Every time I asked Shane about what to wear he'd do that guy thing and shrug. *Oh you know, it's just the Grange. Wear some skirt or something.*"

Penny burst out laughing. "You do a great Shane impression."

"Well, I do think it's nice to have the community doing something like this for the local charities. I used to be more involved in charity work but I haven't done much since…well anyway. I've spoken with Polly and she's put me in touch with the woman who does the holiday drive for the soup kitchen and food pantry so I'm excited about that. *And*, I can't wait to meet this mystery date of yours."

Penny blushed. "I told you, he's an old friend of my family's. He went to school with all of us here. No big deal, he's just visiting from Atlanta for the weekend and I bumped into him."

"Yeah, old family friends always make me blush like a schoolgirl. I'll see you tonight." Laughing, Cassie squeezed Penny's hand and headed out after locking up.

Cassie's nervousness had been making her slightly nauseated all day. This Grange thing was a big community event and the Chases would all be there in force and it was like some big step for Shane to have her there with him. She'd gotten used to the stares in town of the jealous women but from what she understood taking a date to this event was a big deal for a Chase. None of them did it until Kyle brought Maggie.

Things had gotten very serious between her and Shane. As she put on her makeup, she realized that. Realized that she either spent the night at his house or him at hers at least five nights a week. They went out every weekend and saw each other or spoke on the phone every day.

In truth, she'd never expected to find love after her divorce and the attack. She certainly didn't figure she'd end up with a man like Shane, strong and protective who also gave so much. He respected her space and continued to be nothing but gentle and kind toward her. They'd had some minor disagreements but she'd never felt threatened or worried about them. And he simply put up with her skittishness. How he did was beyond her. She knew she brought a lot of issues with her but he never made a big deal of it. He accepted and loved all of her, warts and all.

She also realized that the holiday season was upon them. Brian was coming back for Christmas but they'd been invited to celebrate with the Chases at their home. It warmed her heart to be included and thought of as one of them.

Shane showed up right on time looking and smelling positively fabulous. She'd never seen him so dressed up.

"Wow. You sure clean up nice, Shane Chase."

He spun her in his arms and kissed her neck. "I have to keep up with you. It's hard when a man's woman is the most beautiful woman in town. You set a tough example. I love red on you, by the way. That dress is hot."

She laughed, pleased by this compliments. "I don't think I've been called hot since college."

"Ah, there's more where that came from. I'm a silver-tongued devil."

Her eyes slid halfway closed at that. "Yes. Yes you are."

He stilled and then looked toward the front windows. Reaching back, he hit the lights, leaving them both in the dark.

"What are you up to?"

"Oh, well. Just proving you right. Do you have panties on under that dress?"

"What?" She laughed nervously. "Of course!"

He moved toward her and she stepped back until she bumped against the kitchen island. He dropped to his knees and a soft moan came from her lips.

"No matter, I'm good with my hands too." He slid his palms up her calves and stopped when he got to her thighs.

"Surprise."

"You're wearing stockings and garters."

"I know."

"We should be at the Grange in fifteen minutes."

"You'd better be quick then, huh?"

His chuckle brought the brush of his warm breath against her thighs as he pushed her dress up. "You'll be showing them to me later. In my bedroom with the lights on. I think you should leave the shoes on too."

Her hands dropped to his shoulders as her upper body leaned against the island behind her.

He pulled the panties out of the way and she widened her stance as his fingers slid through her pussy, hissing when he found her hot and wet.

Leaning in, his mouth found her ready for him, her clit already swollen and sensitive. Her taste seduced him. He loved the way she felt on his tongue, loved the scent of her body, of her skin and the honey that rained on his tongue. Loved the long, lean flanks of her legs.

Two of his fingers pressed up and inside her as he took quick, whisper-light licks over her clit. A gasp tore from her lips and her fingers dug into his shoulders.

This was an appetizer, something to whet his appetite for her and get him through the next hours. When he got her back to his place he planned to get a better look at those sexy stockings as her legs wrapped around him.

He recognized the change in her taste, the tremble in her thigh muscles and the quickening of her breathing and knew her orgasm was on the way. He loved to give her a hard, fast climax, leaving her for a few hours, knowing he'd be back for more later on. Knew she'd be wet for him for the rest of the night and it was only fair because he'd be hard for her all night long too.

With a soft intake of breath and a long moan, she came with his name on her lips. He loved hearing it that way. Often thought of how it sounded during his day.

After her pussy had stopped fluttering around his fingers he withdrew them slowly and rearranged her panties before standing and kissing her. Hard and possessive.

He was glad they'd reached the stage where he could be a bit more dominant with her and it didn't spook her. Just thinking about her made him want to grab her and head for the hills. She brought out something very primal in him and he liked it. No one else ever affected him on that level.

"You ready to go?"

Eyes opening slowly, she brought her fingertips to her lips. "I…uh yeah. What about you?"

He was glad she couldn't see how predatory his grin must have looked there in the dark, as he thought about once they were back at his place. "Believe me, darlin', I'll collect later on."

At the Grange, Cassie was sure everyone would know Shane went down on her with the drapes open in her kitchen in the dark. But if they did, none of them seemed too bothered by it.

That's when she noticed Penny walk in with a tall, handsome man about their age.

"Ryan Betts. How are you?" Shane stood up and clapped the man on his shoulder.

"I'm good. Just squiring Penny around for the evening. It's only taken fifteen years to get a third date with her. You look well, Shane." He turned his green eyes to Cassie. "You must be Cassie. Penny talks about you all the time. I'm Ryan, it's nice to meet you."

Cassie took his proffered hand and shook it before turning her eyes to a very pink-faced Penny. "Nice to meet the mystery date. I've been bugging Penny for the last week but she kept telling me I'd meet you when I met you."

"And you did. It's a good thing you're such a good employee because you're a pest." Penny's laugh sounded different than Cassie had ever heard. It was nearly a giggle.

There were long minutes of back slapping and drink getting and a few toasts as Cassie watched them all. She hadn't felt like an outsider for a few months but realized that's what it looked like when you had lifelong friends.

She felt the edge of that divide rather sharply although she knew none of them intended it. Cassie didn't have friends she'd known all her life. People left a lot. Her mother died, she went to boarding school for several years until high school. She did stay in LA to go to college at UC Irvine and then medical school at UCLA. The only permanence had been Brian.

"Why the long face, gorgeous?" Matt sat down next to her and put a mug of steaming cider in front of her.

"Oh nothing. I was just thinking about how I didn't really have lifelong friends like all of you. I suppose I was just feeling a bit sorry for myself."

Matt took her hand and squeezed it. "You have us now. And once you're a Chase, you don't want for company. Of course, that also means we're always up in your business too."

"You making a play for my girl?" Shane turned and smiled.

"In a perfect world, Shane, your lovely woman would realize what a tool you are and run away with me. But alas, the world

is a flawed place and for some crazy reason, she loves you."
Matt put a hand over his heart dramatically.

"Come on, darlin'. Let's grab a dance or two before dinner
gets started."

Cassie stood, taking Shane's hand, and let him draw her onto
the floor and against his body.

"You were meant to be here against me. You know?" he murmured into her ear.

"It feels that way, yeah."

"God it makes me happy when you accept all of this. This
thing between us."

"It makes me happy too. I was just thinking tonight as I got
ready about how lucky I am in you. You're so good to me."

Dinner was the usual Chase affair—organized chaos of arms
and hands and talking in all directions. Cassie watched, amused
as Penny and Ryan flirted and grew smitten with the other.
She knew she'd be demanding the full story from her friend
on Monday.

"You're staying over at my place tonight, right?" Shane
leaned into her and kissed her temple.

"I have to get up and out early. I haven't done a damn bit of
shopping for Thanksgiving yet. I'll invite Penny I think."

"Shopping for what?"

"Uh, food. I imagine you'll be at Chase central all day. You
can come over afterwards."

"I can come to your apartment after I spend the day with my
entire family eating turkey, ham and roast beef? Just stroll on
in and say hey after I've done that?"

She drew back, looking at him. "What's with the attitude?"

"I've got an attitude? Cassie, did you really think you weren't
invited to Thanksgiving at my parents' house? And if you
weren't invited, did you really think I'd be with them and just
come on over to your apartment after you ate by yourself? Is
that how little you think of me and my family?"

"I didn't want to presume."

"Presume? And they say I'm the dumbass. My momma told me to invite you weeks ago but I assured her you knew you were invited. My manners are bad apparently. Well okay, that's not a surprise. Anyway, you're eating dinner with me at my parents' house on Thanksgiving. Afterwards, we play cards and then you all sit on the porch and talk about us while we play football. It's a tradition. You can't buck tradition, Cassie."

"Oh. All right then."

He looked at her askance and then chuckled. "I wish you'd agree to everything that easily."

"I do to all the important stuff."

The way he looked at her made her all tingly.

"So you're staying over then? Now that the Thanksgiving situation is all cleared up and all."

She leaned in and put her lips to his ear. "I've been waiting for a while for you to take me. I feel how much you control yourself to keep from scaring me. Show me, Shane. I want it all."

He sat very still, she wasn't even sure if he breathed for long moments. Slowly, he turned to look her in the eye. His pupils were so wide it was hard to see the color. He turned to his family.

"Folks, Cassie and I are going to cut out early. I have a headache. We'll see you Sunday for dinner."

He stood and helped her up, grabbing her wrap and putting an arm around her, steering her toward the door.

"Goodnight, everyone." She waved as they moved to leave. Everyone just looked at them, amused.

Shane didn't say much as they drove to his house. Cassie watched the scenery pass through her window, smiling.

"What are you smiling about, darlin'?"

"I love the sound of your voice. It's deep and masculine and so sexy. Sometimes it's almost a growl. If you weren't mine I'd be working to grab you every day."

He pulled into his driveway and turned to her. "I...when you say stuff like that it does something to me. You held yourself away from me for so long and now to see you like this, saying I'm yours, it…" He took a deep breath as he shook his head, unable to find words.

"I'm sorry if I don't say it enough. I'm smiling because my life is normal. Because I trust you. I'm smiling because I know you're going to take me into that house and make love to me."

"You got that right." Leaning over, his upper body pressed her gently to the seat. Lips just above hers, his eyes stared deeply into hers. "I want you to tell me if I go too far or scare you. You have no idea how much I want to take you a dozen times a day against every conceivable surface just to know I'm the one making you feel the pleasure, just to hear the sound of you coming in my ears. But we need to go slow with this. I know that. All you need to do is tell me to stop or slow down, all right?"

Moving just a bit, her lips brushed up against his. "All right." Quickly, they got out of the car and went into the house. "Bedroom."

Cassie looked back over her shoulder at him and then took the stairs with a sexy sway.

"You're playing with fire, darlin'."

"Mmm, good. You'll have to make me wet to put it out."

He chuckled and she found herself tossed on the bed, his body above hers on his hands and knees.

Lifting her hands to his chest, she worked the buttons on his shirt and exposed his chest. His heart beat reassuringly against her palm as she slid it over the hard muscle of his pectoral muscles.

Sitting back, he pulled his shirt off, tossing it to the side, and moved to her again. This time he undid the tie at her hip and pulled the dress apart, exposing her body that way.

He sat there looking at her for a long time, quietly taking her in. A month ago she'd have felt embarrassed at his close perusal but he'd made her realize that he thought she was beautiful. Her scars did not matter to him. If her thighs were an issue, he hid it well and so she just let him look, loving that he wanted to.

Reaching out, he traced a fingertip along the scalloped lace of her bra, skimming just over her nipple.

"I like this. Red looks good on you with all items of clothing I see."

The catch on the front was a black rose and he popped it with one-handed ease. Her breasts spilled into his hands, his thumbs coming up to flick back and forth over her nipples. Each movement of his fingers against her sent an answering pulse to her clit.

Her fingers dug into the muscle of his upper back as he leaned in, the heat of his mouth closing over the pulse-point at the hollow just below her ear.

Moving her hands, she pushed him back and scrambled atop his prone body, wriggling out of her dress and bra.

"Now that's a reward for a long hard day. A beautiful woman sitting over my cock in nothing more than garters, stockings, a wisp of red lace pretending to be panties and some very sexy shoes."

"There's that silver tongue, I see." Her hands made quick work of his belt and the button and zipper of his trousers and she kissed down his neck, over his chest and belly. The way his hands felt on her, so large and warm, confident and gentle, always made her want to cry.

"Pants off!" She struggled to get his trousers off and he laughed, setting her aside and standing to do it himself.

"Well, lookit you." He moved toward the bed, his cock so hard it pressed against his stomach.

When he'd stopped, his cock was right at eye level. She looked up at him, up his body and saw the look on his face. He waited there, making sure her comment at the Grange wasn't just made in the heat of the moment.

"I do want you to take me, Shane."

One of his hands caressed her face, down her neck. He watched her face until he appeared to be sure.

"Well then, I think there's a little rain check to be collected and then I'm going to fuck you with those garters on."

She grabbed him and angled his cock to slowly take him into her mouth. Loving this, loving how much pleasure it gave him, she took it slow, doing all the things she'd learned he liked so much.

Her tongue swirled around the head, digging into that sweet spot just beneath the ridge of the crown. The salt of his skin, of his essence, sprang on her tongue, filled her with desire, made her feel like a goddess that he wanted her so much.

Shane looked down at her, watched his cock disappear between her lips and pull out again. He loved the way her eyelashes swept over her cheeks.

His fingertips traced over the raised marks of her scars on her back. He'd found it reassured her that he thought she was beautiful. As if anyone could look at her and think anything else. Her scars were as much a part of her as her eyes or those long-as-sin legs. So he loved them too, even as he wanted to take the man down who'd given them to her.

When she'd told him she wanted him to take her, he'd nearly come on the spot. He dreamed of being able to show her the depth of intensity of his desire for her but kept it in check to keep from scaring her. He wanted to take her hard and fast but he'd watch her, especially this first time, to be sure she was all right with everything.

"Cassie, stop. Lie back, leave your legs over the side of the bed."

She did as he told her to and he marveled at her, lying there on his bed. Her dark hair spread around her head like midnight. Her breasts, breasts she thought were sagging, were capped with puckered pink nipples, just begging for his mouth. Her belly, with no pooch he ever could divine, led to the neatly trimmed patch of hair that shielded her pussy. Only right then the pretty red panties covered her.

"Next time, put the panties on after the stockings."

She laughed, a slow, sexy sound that never failed to make him crazy. Reaching down, she pulled at the sides of the panties and they untied. Lifting her ass, she pulled them off and threw them over his shoulder.

"Oh. Very nice. Very nice indeed. You know, I wanted to see these legs wrapped around me but I'm thinking we can save that for another time."

He pulled out a condom and sheathed himself quickly before flipping her over with relative ease. He did sense her stiffen and he drew a fingertip down her spine. "Shhhh. I want to take you from behind, Cassie. Feel you from this angle, be able to reach around and touch your body, have your clit right where I want it."

He paused, giving her time to stop if she was freaked but she relaxed. Pulling her body toward him, he brought her feet to the ground and bent her just so, moving to check her readiness.

When Shane touched her pussy and found her so wet she was slightly embarrassed by how much he turned her on, he made a low sound.

"Fuck. Cassie, how do you do this to me? Make me want you even more when I feel the evidence of how much you want me?" As he finished the last word, the blunt, fat head of his cock pressed against her, nudging his way into her gate.

She pushed back into him and they both grunted in satisfaction as he seated himself fully inside her.

Losing herself a bit as he began to thrust, her hands gripped his comforter, cool against her heated skin. He felt so good as he filled her up over and over. Her body molded itself to him, took him in and made itself his.

"I want to feel you come around me," he murmured, leaning down and kissing her shoulder. One of his hands found her clit, fingertips strumming through the wet flesh, bringing the skin of the hood to stroke against the clit. The friction was delicious, right on the edge of just enough but not quite there.

His lips pressed over each one of her scars as the fingers of his free hand stroked lightly over her arms and back and down over the curve of her ass and thighs.

"More."

In answer, he began to thrust into her hard and fast in deep digs. He gave up the slow tease of her clit and squeezed it gently between slick fingers over and over until she came, screaming into his mattress. All the while he continued to fuck her.

"Damn, you're so fucking sexy I don't know what to do. I just want to spread you on a cracker and eat you up. I want to kiss every inch of you. You walk past the front window of the bookstore as I drive past and my cock throbs. You've bewitched me, Cassie."

His voice was slightly breathless, staccato even, as he continued to move within her. She felt, for the first time, the full power of his thighs as his muscles flexed against the back of her thighs. Felt the strength in his arms as he held her, the uncoiled desire in his movements and heard it in his voice.

And there was no fear. This wasn't how Terry used her. He'd used this strength *against* her to hurt her. Shane used his strength for her, on her to bring her pleasure. Even with the strength he had, he did not abuse it, he kept it under control and she gave in to her need to moan and cry out as he built the pleasure within her.

"Pleasepleaseplease," she whispered.

"Please what?" His voice wavered a bit, she knew he was close and she wanted him to come deep inside her. More than she'd ever wanted anything and she wasn't quite sure why. She just knew she wanted him to find pleasure inside her, to know her body gave him safe haven when he needed it. When he wanted it.

"Please come inside of me, Shane. I want that so much."

Her words escaped her mouth in a quick flow before she could worry that he'd be disgusted by her brazenness.

"Hell…" His word was stuttered as he pressed once and then once again, deep into her, his fingers holding her hips tight as he pressed deep, his cock jerking within her as he came.

Long moments later, he kissed her neck and left the room. Returning quickly, he helped her into bed after he'd taken her shoes off and removed her garter belt and stockings.

"You'll wear those again, right?"

"I couldn't deny you the chance to see my legs wrapped around your waist with them on."

"I don't know what I did to deserve you. I haven't always been the nicest man to women, you know. But you're the best thing that's ever happened to me. I love you, Cassie." He kissed her deeply, pulling her against his body.

Chapter Fifteen

Cassie paused as she picked up the cashmere sweater from the table where it'd been stacked in a pile of folded luxury. The hair on the back of her neck stood on end and a chill settled at the base of her spine.

She turned and looked around the area but nothing seemed amiss. "Cassie? Honey, are you all right?"

Shaking off the dread, Cassie turned and found herself looking into the face of Edward Chase.

"Edward, hello." She kissed his cheek and he gave her a hug.

"You looked upset just then. Is everything okay?" He looked around the area much as she had.

"It just felt like someone was watching me. Probably because I'm here buying Shane's Christmas present." She tried to believe the lighthearted laugh she gave but couldn't.

"Sugar, you should tell Shane. Do you think your ex has found you?"

"I don't have any reason to think that, Edward. My brother is keeping in regular contact with the investigators and they're all in contact with me and Shane. He hasn't surfaced since the summer. Maybe he's given up."

Edward looked at the charcoal-colored sweater she held in her hands. "Shane will like that. Can I take you to lunch?"

Cassie really liked Edward Chase. She definitely enjoyed Polly but Edward was quiet and insightful and Cassie treasured their conversations on everything from post modernism to baseball.

"Sure, why don't I meet you at El Cid in fifteen minutes? I just need to pay for this."

He kissed her cheek and agreed, heading out while she went to the cashier to pay for the sweater and the shirt she'd found. With the assistance of a local artisan, she'd made Shane a bracelet of pounded copper and silver that she hoped he liked. The sweater and shirt were nice and all, but the bracelet had taken her a lot of time and effort. She'd never done anything like it before and wanted to create something that fit his personality perfectly. But now she had a new skill and had taken to working with silver to create earrings and necklaces that did very well.

Edward was waiting with fresh chips and salsa and waved as she caught sight of him.

After they'd ordered and the food arrived, Edward told her that he'd been looking into how she could go about practicing under her new name with her medical license.

"I don't want you to think I'm presumptuous but I'm asking around. The state board is going to want to have the ability for your patients to know who you are. This name change project has been around for several years but it's still hard to get professional licenses in the new name for many women."

"I appreciate that, Edward. I've been thinking on it long and hard. I miss medicine a lot. I know I'll have to go back to get more training but if I mean to make my life here, I'll need to figure out what I want to do. I like working at the bookstore and all, but it's not what I'll do forever."

"So you plan on making Petal your home then? Pardon my nosiness but my son loves you very much. The change in him is remarkable. I'd hate to see his heart broken."

Cassie reached across the table and squeezed his hand. "I never thought I'd want to be with anyone else again. I swore the last thing I needed was a big, domineering man and look who I went and fell for. I want to be where Shane is. He gets me. Like no one ever has. He understands me and makes room for my quirks and works around my crazy stuff. I adore him."

"Good. That's good to hear. I like you, Cassie. I like you being in my family an awful lot."

After lunch, Cassie went home and wrapped the presents and checked to be sure Brian's flight was on time. He was flying in for the weekend to celebrate Christmas with her and the Chases.

Shane managed to convince her that she and Brian should stay at his house because it was bigger and more comfortable for everyone. In truth she spent seventy percent of her time there anyway, and Brian knew they were a couple and was very happy about that fact.

Even though she had a key, she knocked on Shane's door and ignored his annoyed look.

"Hi, baby, take these will you?" She thrust the packages at him and bent to pick up a bag of extra clothes she'd packed.

"Darlin', use your key. You're not a guest. And let me get that." He held the door and then went to put the packages under the tree they'd both picked out the weekend before.

"It feels weird just letting myself in."

He grabbed her and pulled her down onto the couch with him. "Move in here and it won't feel weird."

"What?"

"I'd ask you to marry me but I know that would be rushing you. But I want you here with me. I want to wake up with you every morning. I like that my bathroom has your stuff in it. I want to build a life together."

"I... I don't know if I'm ready for that."

His face lost a bit of its light and seeing that she'd caused him pain sliced through her. But she was afraid of making another Terry-sized mistake.

She put her hand to his face. "I love you, Shane. But it's only been five months since I met you."

"Almost six and I love you too. You're here or I'm at your place almost every night. What's the difference?"

"Shane, I don't want to hurt you but I need the haven of my own place right now."

Kissing her he nodded. "Okay, fair enough. But you know how I hate it when you treat me like I'm him."

"This argument is really old, Shane. I don't want to have it again. I promise you that's not what I'm doing."

"Bull. If it hadn't been for him you'd move in here. How is that not making me pay for his behavior?"

"If it hadn't been for him I wouldn't be here so that's a moot point. Stop making this about you! I am not wanting to take this slow because I think you're Terry. I *know* you're not Terry. I'm taking this slow because the last man I lived with nearly killed me after beating the hell out of my body and soul for years. The difference is pretty major, Shane."

"It feels the same to me."

She stepped back, out of his embrace. "I'm sorry. All I can do is feel what I feel and tell you the truth of it. I'm being honest and trying my damndest to explain the inexplicable to you. This is about me. If you choose to make it about you, I can't stop you."

"Why are you so difficult? Why don't you let me love you?"

"I do. I've given myself to you, heart and body. I'm not giving anyone my soul, Shane. I love you, more than anyone I've ever loved but that's not going to stop me from using my common sense. I'm sorry it offends you that I want to wait to move in together. I'm not doing it because I don't trust you or want to be with you. I'm asking you to respect my feelings and to give me time. But I can't make you what you aren't any more than I'll let you make me into what I'm not. So if you can't live with that, tell me now so I can walk away. I'm in deep enough with you and your family, if you're going to break it off, do it now."

Pacing, he shoved a hand through his hair. "I'm not going to break it off. I love you. Things would be so much easier if you just agreed with everything I said."

Cassie snorted a laugh and he moved to where she was standing to pull her close. "You're a very complicated, difficult woman."

"You're a very arrogant, difficult man."

"Perfect match." He grinned.

"So you say."

"I do. Wanna get lucky? I'll let you open a present early."

"Oh you think I'll fall for that one twice?"

Laughing, he took her down to the carpet.

"I can't believe you gave me rug burn on my ass," Cassie murmured in Shane's ear as they had Christmas Eve dinner around a table filled with only about four hundred of his family members.

He chuckled. "It was worth it."

"For you! I was on the bottom."

"Next time roll me over, darlin', I'm quite happy to have you on top."

She fought off laughter. "As if I'm not nervous enough meeting all these people, I have rug burn."

"And a bit of beard burn on your inner thighs too, I'd wager."

The charming devil had the audacity to leer at her and she burst out laughing. Luckily, everyone seemed to find their interaction wonderful and amusing and his grandparents only dropped marriage and great-grandchild hints about every twenty minutes.

"Did you tell Shane about how you felt like you were being watched at the department store earlier?" Edward's voice was casual but Cassie heard steel there and fought annoyance as her brother and Shane both rounded on her.

"I just felt weird, not necessarily watched. And no, I hadn't had the chance to tell either my brother or Shane about it.

Thanks for that, though." She rolled her eyes at Edward and Polly sighed and smacked her husband on the arm.

"Cassie, you promised to tell me!" Shane glared at her.

"And me," Brian echoed.

"Look, as much as I'd *love* having this conversation here with the family of my boyfriend looking on, I'm not going to. I hadn't had the chance to tell either one of you. Brian, your plane was late and Shane, you waylaid me when I got to your house. I appreciate your concern but it was nothing. And that's all I'm going to say right now."

"Cassie…"

"Shane Edward Chase, let it go. Your daddy made a big enough mistake, don't compound it. She'll talk to you about it later." Polly narrowed her eyes at him and he backed off with an annoyed shrug.

Maggie changed the subject quickly to the trip she and Kyle were taking in the spring to Italy and Cassie sent her a grateful look. Penny was there with Ryan, he'd come to town once or twice since the Grange night and had spent quite a bit of time on the phone and email with her. Cassie approved, she'd never seen Penny so glowing before.

After dessert and a game of cards so cutthroat that Cassie just watched in awe, they made their way back to Shane's. They'd promised to be back at seven the next morning in exchange for not sleeping over. Cassie felt self-conscious enough, she really didn't want to sleep with Shane at his parents' house.

On the way out, Edward took her aside. "I do apologize, honey. I didn't mean to put you on the spot like that. I just spoke while thinking about it and then realized that you must have felt nervous with all those new people and all. I know it seemed nosy of me, but I care about you like one of my own. I was just concerned. I hope you're not mad at me."

She kissed his cheek. "Thank you for explaining. I feel a lot better now. I do appreciate you caring about me, honestly. I'm not angry. It takes a bit of getting used to, being part of your circle, I'm trying."

"You're not part of our circle, honey, you're part of our family. You're one of us. Even if it was only that Shane loved you we'd think of you that way. But we love you too. You're an eminently lovable woman. Now go on, Shane's going to want to hear all the details along with your brother. We'll see you first thing."

All she could do was nod. It was a simple thing, the acceptance and love from the Chases, but it meant so much more than she could ever begin to put into words. Swallowing back her tears, she smiled and walked out, garnering hugs and kisses from a whole host of Chases before she reached Shane who waited for her on the porch.

In the car she got belted in and held up a hand as they pulled away from the curb. "I will tell you everything. I was shopping and felt odd. Like a cold chill. I looked around but there wasn't a damned thing wrong. Your father bumped right into me, asked if I was all right. I assured him it was and we had lunch. That's it."

Shane sighed hard. "All right. But I want you to tell me this stuff right away. Call me from the restaurant."

"Me too! Damn it, Carly—Cassie, I can't be here, the only way I can keep from worrying to death over you is your assurance that you'll tell me what's going on."

"Brian, you were on a plane. And Shane, I wasn't going to call you from the restaurant over a funny feeling. I was with your father and you know why I was a bit busy later on. If it had been important I would have called you immediately. Now it's Christmas Eve, let's talk about something else, please."

Chapter Sixteen

The beginning of February had Penny and Cassie heading to Atlanta to pick up more supplies for Cassie's blooming jewelry business. With Valentine's Day approaching, Cassie found herself nearly out of the findings she needed for earrings and she wanted to pop in to a little bead shop she'd ordered from online.

Ryan joined them for lunch after they'd spent too much money on beads and clothes. The roads were a bit slick but not icy so they wanted to get back before it got too dark and cold.

Cassie had a sense of foreboding all day. She'd attributed it to the anniversary of her divorce from Terry and the news from a week before that Terry had been sighted in New York City and that it appeared his family had been helping him financially.

Shane had insisted on their driving his giant truck and in retrospect later on, it probably saved their lives. Halfway between Atlanta and Petal, Cassie noticed the lights of an SUV that had been with them for the last ten miles. It stayed right on her tailgate and felt aggressive. Not so unusual really, people drove like idiots all the time but she couldn't ignore her increasing nervousness. On top of that, Penny was in the car and Cassie didn't want to ignore something that could hurt her friend.

Swallowing back fear and nausea, Cassie reached out and

touched Penny's arm. "Penny, I want you to get on that cell phone and call Shane. There's a car following us. A big SUV, Georgia plates. It's probably nothing but it makes me nervous. Crossed a few lanes to keep up with us several times." Putting her hands firmly on the wheel, she wrestled the demon of her terror and read the plate number to Penny, who calmly made the call.

Shane stayed on the line with her and patched a call into the state patrol to check the plates. He urged Penny to tell Cassie to stay watchful. They'd entered a more rural part of the drive back to Petal and there weren't many off ramps. So rural that even at most of the few off ramps there weren't any services or places to go for help.

The SUV backed way off and Cassie breathed a sigh of relief and wanted to kick herself for her paranoia. She turned to tell Penny everything was all right when she caught the lights moving toward them from the next lane at a high rate of speed.

The truck skidded on the rainy road and flipped over twice into a ditch on the side of the road finally landing right side up.

Cassie returned to full awareness as the paramedics were cutting her free of the seatbelt and pulling her out of the car.

They spoke to her, asking if she was all right and what hurt where.

All she could think about was her friend. Sick dread coursed through her. "Penny! Is she all right?"

"Your friend? She's fine." One of the paramedics pointed over to the side. "She's there. Some cuts and bruises but she's conscious and alert. She said you might have some prior head wounds?"

Numb, Cassie recited her past history. They took her vitals and were discussing the need for hospitalization when she caught sight of the huge body of her man moving purposefully toward them. The lights of the ambulance and police cars glinted off the bracelet she'd made him for Christmas that, much to her relief, he seemed to love. Two state police officers stood in his way, speaking to him.

"That's my girlfriend and I'm going to her. Period."

The deep bass of his voice echoed up her spine and she felt safe then. So safe that the fear came over her in a wave so shocking she began to tremble violently.

"Ma'am?" The female paramedic touched Cassie's forehead. Cassie heard them speaking to her but the panic attack took over. Her teeth chattered and in moments Shane's voice vibrated off her skin as he reached her, kneeling at her side. Strong, gentle arms pulled her to him, encircling her with his body as he rocked her slowly back and forth. The prick of a needle and then the sting of medication hit her as she fell into the dark calm of unconsciousness.

It wasn't until he'd brought Cassie back to his house afterwards that it all began to hit him. The terror of what could have happened felt clammy on his skin.

Running a hand through his hair and over his face, Shane hung up after speaking with Brian for nearly half an hour. Cassie's brother was understandably upset and feeling helpless. He was grabbing the next flight out to Atlanta and would be arriving the next afternoon.

He'd also spoken with the state police at the hospital while he waited for Cassie. The car that Cassie had given him the license plate for had been stolen. They'd done a fingerprinting check but the investigating officer felt that the prints they'd found were the owners' but would let them know once they heard back officially.

The hospital waiting room had filled up with Chases as they'd all waited to hear back. Kyle held on to Maggie tight—the scene was scarily reminiscent of the one several years before when Maggie had been kidnapped and assaulted by a stalker.

Polly click-clacked over and hugged her son tight around the waist, Edward held on to the other side. "She's going to be all right, Shane."

Shane had felt five years old again as he'd slumped into a chair and his mother stroked his hair away from his forehead and kissed his temple, speaking softly to him. His father's strong hand at his shoulder, Shane realized once again how important his family was to him and how much they meant to his life. They'd refused to leave his side at the hospital, knowing he needed the support.

Even at that moment Matt was downstairs, camped out on one sofa, Marc on the other. Both had refused to leave. Penny was recuperating in one of the Chases' guest rooms with Ryan in another. Family meant more than just being there when things were good.

After they'd examined Cassie at the hospital and watched her for a few hours, they'd sent her home in his care. There hadn't been any sign of a concussion but her therapist had come to the hospital and had advised them to sedate her. She'd also told Shane to expect some flashback behavior and perhaps some greater occurrence of panic attacks and jumpiness that Cassie had shown when she'd first come to Petal.

Standing in the doorway to his bedroom, he watched her, reassuring himself she was indeed all right. She lay in his bed sleeping soundly, a bruise marring the left side of her neck and face where the seatbelt had dug into her. He thanked her quick thinking and his insistence that she take his truck. The other car had struck just behind the passenger seat. The scene investigators told him the other car had to be going at least seventy miles an hour to cause that much damage and the rollover.

His fingers dug into the doorjamb. It could have been a co-incidence. Punk kids stole cars and caused accidents in them on joyrides every day. The car was stolen in an area of Atlanta that had suffered a rash of car thefts in the last week. Still, it was hard not to think Terry was behind this.

Truth was, Shane was pretty sure that it was his presence on the scene that lent credence to Cassie's story and not her history. The state police were looking into it more carefully than they would have if it had been a clear-cut joyriding case. He didn't like it but the fact was, it was just all a coincidence and she hadn't received any threats and there wasn't a reason to believe that Terry had found her.

The way he'd felt when Penny had called hit him. He closed his eyes against the helplessness he'd felt, knowing Cassie was in danger and he was too far away to help. It had taken all of his strength to keep his voice level and talk Penny through as he'd called the state police on his other line. He'd wanted to hear Cassie's voice himself but he knew it was more important for her to keep focused on driving and being safe.

And then the screams and the dead air after the crunch. The phone line had remained open, the call never broke so he heard the shattering glass, the groan of metal, the screams and the sobs of pain. He'd stood up, yelling Cassie's name. The state dispatcher assured him the ambulance and response cars were on the way as he'd run to his city vehicle and headed toward the scene with the sirens on.

And when he'd arrived, seeing the glitter of broken glass on the pavement and the flashing red and blue against the bent metal, it was nothing compared to the feeling in his gut as he'd caught sight of her being treated on the gurney.

Single-mindedly, he'd moved to her, the staties let him move past. He could see her trembling start from all the way back where the staties had stopped him. He needed to get to her to help. Seeing her that way again, the panic attack sending her so deep into herself that she could barely register what people said to her, sent protective feelings warring with anger through him.

No, not anger. Anger was too mild a word. Murderous. Rage washed over him, made him see red until he clenched his fists imagining Terry Sunderland's neck there. It was war and there was not a fucking chance in hell Shane would walk away the

loser. His woman's life was at stake for real and he would not
stop until Terry Sunderland was in prison or dead.

He went to her quietly, brushing his lips across her temple,
tucking the blanket around her. Her pulse was normal and her
breathing was calm. Blinking back hot tears of impotent rage,
he backed out of the room and headed downstairs.

Neither brother was sleeping and Kyle and Maggie had joined
the group. Everyone looked up as he entered the living room.

"You all can go home, she's sleeping soundly. Her doctor said
the sedatives would keep her sleeping deeply for several more
hours. There's nothing anyone can do right now. I'm going to
go to sleep in a bit too."

Maggie handed him a cup of hot tea and pushed him down
onto the couch. "Nothing anyone can do but be there. Drink
that. It's chamomile, it'll help you sleep. I imagine you're pretty
wound up."

"Not every day your woman almost dies." Kyle watched
Shane through knowing eyes. Leaning over, he poured a liberal helping of whiskey into the tea. "That'll help more than
chamomile I expect."

Maggie sighed. "Why don't I go up and sit with her for a
while? I've got a good book with me and you three can plot and
not worry." She kissed his cheek. "I promised Mom I would.
She wanted to be here so badly but Penny needed some TLC
too. I'm her stand-in."

Shane squeezed her hand. "Thank you so much, honey. I'll
be up shortly, I promise. I'm just keyed up right now. I don't
want to disturb her. But you must be tired…"

Maggie shook her head. "I slept already. I have tomorrow,
or today I suppose, off. Kyle is going to make me brunch later
on. Now go on, wind down and let me help. She's my friend,
you know, I love her too."

Shane nodded. "Thank you. Really."

After she'd gone upstairs the brothers all looked at each other
with perfect understanding. One of their own was threatened,

no one hurt a Chase and got away with it. Cassie was Shane's therefore she was theirs too.

"Brian's plane comes in at two. He's driving straight here. I spoke with him a few minutes ago. Terry hasn't been sighted since last week in New York but his mother admitted to a friend that she'd seen him and given him a significant amount of money. More than enough to move around the country."

"How did he find her? She changed her social security number and name." Matt punched the arm of the couch.

"Money talks, Matt. You know that. If he knew where she was getting her domestic violence victim advocacy, he had a way of getting to people. I don't know anything for sure, but I do know that this is not a coincidence. He's found her."

"She can't stay here. We have to get her to another city and right away." Marc looked to his brothers.

Shane chuckled ruefully. "I wish she would go for that. But if you think Cassie would agree to it, you don't know her very well. She's not going to let him chase her away. And he'd just find her again anyway. No. We need to draw him in and take him down before he gets her."

"Her apartment isn't safe." Matt watched Shane through serious eyes.

"Nope. She's moving in here. I've asked her, hell I've *been* asking her for months now. I've got a great security system here. I'm going to do all I can to protect her and she's going to have to deal with that or I'll sic Momma on her."

"You aren't going to get married? Momma's gonna be hot." Kyle chuckled.

"What? *You* and Maggie lived together! And anyway, if I thought she'd say yes, I'd marry Cassie tomorrow. She's gunshy, you know that. We'll live together and then I'll ask her to marry me. I'm charming, she won't be able to resist me."

"You let us know what to do and we'll do it. Nothing is going to happen to her." Matt looked to his brothers who all nodded solemnly.

"We're taking Terry Sunderland down. It has to happen. Scum like him has to be taken out. What kind of man beats his woman? What kind of man hurts the person he should be cherishing? He had the best thing in the universe and he threw it away. He tried to kill my woman and I am not having it. It's her or him and I know how it's going to end."

Cassie awoke, sore and disoriented, mouth dry. Within moments, the night before came back to her in disturbing clarity. Terry found her and tried to kill her. *Again.*

The trembling started in her hands and she gripped the sheets to stop it. She was not going to fall apart.

"Darlin', I'm here."

A hand cupped her cheek and she turned to face those green eyes. She let herself fall into his warmth, allowing herself to feel safe with him, to relax. The shaking in her hands subsided a bit.

"Nothing is going to happen to you. I'm here and the alarm is on. You know where the handgun is on your side of the bed, right?"

Cassie opened her eyes and looked at him again. "You're very calm for a cop telling me where my handgun is."

"Cassie, if he breaks in to this house you will shoot him before he can shoot you. Or beat you with something, he seems to like the up close and personal, fucking bastard. It is you or him now, I have no qualms about wanting it to be you and telling you so. Do *you* have qualms about that?"

"About what? How would you feel about me if I told you I wouldn't feel bad if I killed him? He's making it me or him." She sat up with a wince and he put pillows behind her. Carefully, he reached across her body to get her pills and a glass of water.

"I'd feel reassured that you're willing to protect yourself. Now, the doctor said you'd be sore. There's no major injury. You're bruised. Your therapist said you may have some panic attacks for a while and to take medication if you need it to sleep and keep calm."

She shook her head and pushed away the pills but drank the water. "No. I don't want that. I need to be clear headed now."

"There's no shame in it, Cassie."

"Don't you tell me what there's shame in, Shane Chase! I will not be sedated right now. My life is at stake. This man wants to kill me. He's tried and he almost succeeded. He's been controlling my life all these years. Making me afraid to even live. No more. Damn it! No more. I will not. If I need to sleep, I'll take the pills but I will go to work and live my life and I swear to you right now that if he tries to hurt me I will make sure he can never harm me, ever again. However I have to."

Shane nodded and put the pills back on the tray. "There you go. You don't forget that, either. Take that fury and hold it close, use it. It is you or him and damned if I want you to apologize for wanting it to be you. If you're in pain, take the damned pills. I have ibuprofen for that if you'd rather. If you get to a point where you can't function through the panic attacks, take the damned pills. But yes, defend yourself and your life. I will too. We can do it together but, Cassie, please, I'm begging you right now, please move in here."

"I will not be a burden or a charity case!"

"Oh shaddup. Seriously. I want to fuck you on demand. It's a lot easier if you're here. I wake up, roll over and bang, you're right there. Easy access. What more can a man want? Plus, honey, you are a shitty cook, I can keep you from wasting away after all that strenuous sex."

She rolled her eyes at him but at the same time, she realized she was an idiot to resist what she wanted anyway.

"I've been asking you for months now. It's not like this is a last-minute pity request."

"Are you sure? Because I'm still going to be a pain in the ass you know. I won't be managed just because I live here."

"Darlin', perish the thought of you being managed in any way." He grinned and she swatted him playfully.

"I'd like that. Thank you."

He let out a long breath. "Whew. That's a relief. My brothers offered to help pack your stuff and get it over here. With your permission of course," he added with a sexy wink.

"Heaven save me. You're some smooth operator, Shane."

"Cassie, I was empty before you came along. You fill me up. I love you."

Tears stung Cassie's eyes. "Me too. When I saw you last night, I knew it was okay. I knew I was safe. Even there on the side of the road with broken glass in my hair I felt safe. Thank you."

"You wreck me, darlin'." Gently, he pulled her down to snuggle against his side.

Chapter Seventeen

Brian came and went back to Los Angeles after he helped with the move. He wanted to stay longer but he had to get back for a case and there wasn't much he could do anyway.

There'd been no conclusive evidence that the person in the SUV had been Terry. No witnesses to the accident or the theft to begin with and it remained quiet with no contact.

Spring came and heated up the landscape. Cassie realized she didn't miss much about LA except for the ocean and they could drive down to the Gulf for that if they wanted to.

Cassie's life became Cassie and Shane's life and it wasn't scary anymore. She loved him and loved waking up to his body next to hers each morning. Loved coming home to their big house every evening. They'd sit out on the back deck and look at the water or have friends and family over for barbecues.

As May approached, Cassie began to believe that the accident in February was just that, an accident. Nothing more than a stupid coincidence. Still, she set the house alarm every time she came and left, went shooting at the range twice a week with Shane and took judo classes with him. She was moving forward and arming herself for the eventuality where Terry did find her. It gave her a measure of control in some sense.

Walking into Penny's backyard on June first, Cassie halted at the unexpected sight of thirty people clapping and cheering. Brian stood next to Shane, and Penny beamed as she stood in Ryan's arms.

"Happy birthday, Cassie." Shane approached her and pulled her into his arms.

"Oh my goodness. A surprise party? Where did everyone park? I can't believe you did this and I didn't know it."

Brian pushed Shane out of the way and hugged his sister, kissing her cheek. "Shane's been planning this since the end of February. We all parked at the Chases' and came over in just a few cars that are tucked all around the neighborhood. Now come on in, there's cobbler and cake and food galore."

"And presents?"

Brian laughed. "Yes, doofus, lots of presents."

Shane watched, a wide smile on his face, as Cassie accepted hugs from everyone with ease. Gone was the woman who winced or trembled if someone she didn't know well hugged her. She still got spooked from time to time but she'd grown into an effusive person who loved to touch as much as be touched. It gladdened his heart to know he had a part in that.

Once seated at the head of a large table, she dug into the pile of presents. He'd noticed that she loved presents. Big or small, cheap or expensive, it didn't matter. It was the ripping of paper and ribbons, the surprise that she loved.

The day was a good one. The kind of day that memories were made of. Cassie wouldn't forget the smell of the cobbler and the sound of the salt and ice crunching in the old-fashioned ice cream maker or the taste of fresh, homemade vanilla ice cream. She wouldn't forget the way it felt when she'd seen all her friends and the people who'd become her family stood there, smiles on their faces as they shouted *Happy Birthday!*

The sun shone on the water, the day was warm and clear and absolutely perfect. Shane had given her something wonderful yet again, a memory to replace the bad ones.

They all cleaned up as the sun went down and Cassie looked up when Brian called out to her.

"What?"

"Your phone is ringing."

She trotted over to her bag and dug through it, wondering who the heck it could be since everyone she knew had been at the party.

"Hello?"

"Happy birthday, Carly."

Nausea bolted through her as she lost her legs, her knees hitting the ground as she heard Terry's voice.

Brian's eyes widened. "Cassie? What is it?"

"Are you having a good day? I hope so. This is the last birthday you'll ever see." With that same laugh he used as he'd berated her, the line went dead.

She looked up at her brother as he went to his knees. Dimly she heard someone call for Shane and then his feet pounding the earth as he came to where she was.

"Cassie? What is it?" He looked confused at Brian and then her.

"It was him." The phone dropped from her nerveless fingers.

"Him? Terry? Terry just called you? What did he say?" Brian demanded.

Shane grabbed up the phone and flipped it open. "Caller ID? There's a number here."

Cassie watched numbly as Shane went into cop mode and called the number on the phone and then hung up shortly. He then called into the state police and spoke to some people who told him within moments that the number was one from a disposable cell phone that could be purchased anywhere.

"Cassie, darlin', what did he say?" Matt helped Brian get her into a chair and Shane knelt before her, touching her face.

She told them.

"How did he get the number? It's…"

"What?" Shane looked up sharply at Brian.

"It's in my name. I didn't want to chance putting it in hers when I bought it for her last year. I'm an idiot. I've put her in danger."

Shane squeezed his shoulder as Cassie shook her head vehemently. "Brian, you didn't. Don't you see? He doesn't have to know her new name if you had this phone in yours. All he had to do was find out your phone information. He doesn't necessarily know she's here. You kept her safe by doing that."

"He called me Carly."

Shane looked back to her. "Okay, that's a good sign. He probably doesn't know your new name."

"He would have used it if he did, just to fuck with me. He doesn't know my new name and I'm betting he doesn't know I'm here. Don't you see, that means it probably wasn't him on the road in February."

"Oh honey, one step at a time. Could you tell where he was? Think carefully, any details at all could be important."

She shook her head. "No. It was loud here, people talking and laughing. All I heard on his end was his voice and that laugh."

"Okay, sweetie, let's get you home, all right? I bet you'd like a stiff drink and a shower." Penny put her arm around Cassie's shoulders and looked worriedly at Shane.

Once home Cassie stood on the top step and looked down at Shane and Brian and Shane's brothers. "Do not talk about me when I'm gone. We'll plan together. I won't let this happen *to* me. I will have a hand in this or I'll go crazy. Please."

"Of course we're going to talk about you when you're in the shower. But I promise to have you in on the plans when you come back down here," Shane negotiated back.

She exhaled and narrowed her eyes at him. "I will not be handled, Sheriff."

He rolled his eyes. "Go and shower, woman. I need to talk about you while you're gone."

"Honestly!" Throwing up her hands she walked toward their bedroom, mumbling.

"She's going to be okay if she can still get pissy about being managed," Shane murmured to Brian who chuckled.

"You two know each other pretty well. Now, what the hell are we going to do to protect her?"

"We don't know that he knows where she is. She seems to think he doesn't and she knows him better than I do. Only that he's tracked down this number." Shane held up the phone. "I need to call the California authorities to get a warrant so we can set up a trace on this phone. That'll be complicated, we'll have to get a warrant for her own company and then one for whatever company that handles the phone he calls from next. That means it may be a matter of days or even weeks once we find out who he's used on his next call and he'll have time to jump to a new location. But it's something. I also want to get someone to keep a watch on the house here."

"I'll hire someone to bodyguard her."

"Don't you think you should ask her?" Maggie walked in with Liv and Penny, and an agitated-looking Cassie brought up the rear.

"Yeah, I hear she gets really pissed off when people try to manage her life the minute she steps out of the damned room." Cassie put her hands on her hips and glared at the men in her life.

"Of course I was going to ask you. It doesn't have to be invasive, I know you'd hate that. But I can hire someone to drive by the house here a few times a night. Nothing major." Brian's tone was calm but firm.

"And you know as well as I do that a trace on the phone is a good idea." Shane's jaw was set in a hard line.

"Look, I'm not arguing. But I am not a piece of furniture either. You can't just make plans about my life and my safety without including me."

"You're not arguing?" Brian looked surprised and Cassie sat on the couch beside him.

"I'm not an idiot, Brian. I just don't want other people making my decisions and choices."

And so they planned. Shane worked with the California authorities to get a warrant in place for a tap on her cell phone and they'd be ready to move on a warrant for the records from that company when and if Terry called again. That done, Brian arranged with Shane to have a local security company drive by the house every hour each evening after Cassie got home from work.

It wasn't foolproof, there was a lot left up to chance and it made Shane uncomfortable but it was all he could do short of keeping her with him every moment of the day and neither one of them would survive that.

Later that night in bed after everyone had left or gone to sleep, Shane turned to Cassie. "Are you all right?"

"At first I lost it. I couldn't deal with hearing him, with him being a reality in my life again. But I have a plan to focus on and I feel better. I feel safe with the precautions you and Brian have set up."

"I'm not going to let anything happen to you, Cassie. I love you."

"I know. But you should show me. You know, just in case I forgot."

"Are you sure? I'm…well, I'm not sure I can be gentle right now. I'm so damned angry and worried for you. I hate seeing him do this to you. I hate not being able to stop it."

"I don't need you to be gentle right now. I need you to make me feel alive, Shane. And you *can* do something for me, you can touch me."

With a deep groan, Shane moved his lips to hers, crushing them in a kiss filled with desperate need to make everything all right.

Feverishly, his hands roamed her body and pushed her tank top up and out of the way, work-roughened palms finding her nipples hard and begging for his touch. His mouth swallowed her gasp as he pinched the nipples between thumb and fore-finger.

Her fingers sifted through his hair, holding him to her, drinking in his kisses, the passionate need in him. She was his refuge more than he could ever tell her. She often said he gave her so much but in truth, she gave him more. Gave of herself and made him whole.

He would *not* lose her. Would not lose this battle with her psycho ex.

She writhed restlessly beneath him as he rolled onto her body after getting rid of her panties one handed. Her thighs slid up his rib cage, keeping his torso nestled there against her. His hands moved to bracket her body as he rolled his cock, the heat of her pussy nearly scalding him even through his boxers. Her hands were cool as she reached around their legs and bodies to pull his cock out and stroke him.

He loved the way her thumb slid through the slick of pre-come on the head. She knew him, knew how to touch him in small ways that totally devastated him.

With a gasp of his own, he broke the kiss and looked into her eyes. "I love you, Cassie. So much."

She nodded. "I love you too."

"Are you wet for me?"

He noted the catch in her breath, loved it. Loved it even more when she nodded, wordless.

Putting his weight on one elbow, he reached down and slid a fingertip through her pussy, finding her ready. Superheated, slick and desire swollen. For him. He pressed two fingers up into her and she moaned, her grip tightening slightly around his cock.

"Let's get this party started, shall we?" he murmured. "First the appetizers and then the main course."

Latching on to a nipple with his mouth, he slowly thrust his cock into her fist while he moved his thumb up and over her clit in time with his fingers sliding in and out of her body. Her clit bloomed beneath the pad of his thumb and he knew it wouldn't be long before she came. And oh how he loved to make her come! It was like her body was tuned to his own, her responsiveness made him crazy with need.

Her back arched, pressing her nipple deeper into his mouth as she gasped. The muscles inside her clenched around his fingers and he felt her climax.

Without pause, he extracted himself from her grip and pressed deep into her pussy in one thrust. Back straight, he looked down at her, spread out below him, her hair a spill of midnight around her head, gaze locked with his. "So beautiful. You're so amazingly beautiful."

A smile curved the corner of her lips as her palms slid up his abdomen and the wall of his chest.

"You're one to talk. Look at you, all big and bad and masculine. So damned tall and broad-chested. I've never seen a more handsome man. That first night when I looked up from the steering wheel and deflated airbag and I saw you walking up my heart stopped for a moment. Part of me was screaming, *cop!* But the rest of me was like, *hello there!*"

His chuckle vibrated through them both. "Okay, the talking portion of the show that doesn't include, *oh fuck me harder* is now over." With that, he dragged out and pressed back into her, delighting in the flutter of those inner muscles around his cock.

"Oh fuck me harder!"

Laughing together, he set a rhythm as he thrust into her body, her hips rolling to meet him, take him back inside her as deeply as possible. The smooth skin on the inside of her thighs stroked against the hard muscle of his hips as she wrapped her legs around his waist, locking her feet at the small of his back. Each time he was inside her like this, the hot flesh of her pussy pulling at him as if she couldn't bear to let him go, her body there laid out before him as she gave of herself, he knew he was home.

Cassie still had trouble believing this man was hers but he proved it to her every day. She hadn't exaggerated, he was the most handsome man she'd ever clapped eyes on. His size had been daunting at first, Terry was very tall as well. The similarities were scary in the beginning until she realized Shane would never use his size against her, not physically and not mentally to threaten her. They'd been in some heated arguments and he'd never made a move that scared her even when he was clearly losing his temper.

But this? His size dominating her as he sliced into her body with his cock? It was delicious and touched parts of her she was sure were long dead. She loved it when he took her hard and all she could do was hold on. Loved it that he desired her so much his eyes glazed over and his muscles bunched as he wrestled for control. It made her feel beautiful and special.

She'd never loved sex so much in her life. Simply put, she could not get enough of Shane. Except for those rare times when one didn't feel well, they made love at least once a day in some way. All he had to do was look at her and her body responded.

He'd chased away the demons and helped her slay them. Yes, the threat was still there but her response was different. When she'd first heard Terry's voice she'd lost it but by just a few minutes later she'd recovered and had a plan. The old Cassie—no, Carly—would have hidden and fallen apart because she didn't know what else to do or experience, Terry had taken all emotion and response from her but fear. But Shane had pushed that away and helped her remember love and hope and courage and she'd be damned if Carly would come back now.

"You're thinking. Is that good or bad?"

His voice was low, nearly a growl and it caressed her skin. "Good. But it wasn't a fuck me harder thought so I'll save it for later." She grinned.

He rolled his eyes and lifted her ass, changing his angle and she gasped as the wide head of his cock stroked over her sweet spot. "Ah, I found it."

"Yes, ohgodyes you did. More. More, please."

"My hands are full of your luscious ass, darlin'. I think I need you to make yourself come."

Months ago it would have embarrassed her but now he'd freed her, made her feel so sexy that it didn't bother her. She did it not only because it felt wonderful but because she knew he loved to see it.

Eyes locked with his, her hand slid down her stomach to her clit. Still sensitive from the climax he'd given her just minutes before, she kept an easy touch while watching his face. His gaze broke from hers and moved to watch her hand on herself.

"I've never seen anything sexier than you making yourself come. The way you feel around me, when you start to get close, it's heaven. So hot and wet, your sweet pussy hugs me. Even right now I can feel it coming. I love that."

Her teeth caught her lip at the carnality of his words even as her body began to move toward orgasm. Each thrust brought a stroke over her sweet spot, lit up the nerve endings as he filled her and withdrew.

A low moan broke from her lips as a rolling, deep orgasm spread through her. Her head moved back and her eyes closed as she heard his muttered curse, felt his rhythm speed and deepen. As her body calmed from climax she opened her eyes to find him watching her with such an intensity that she wanted to sob with it. That look said so much, how much he loved and desired her, what she meant to him. It was utterly unguarded and a gift like none she'd ever received before.

Unable to find words she put her fingers over his lips and smiled, tears in her eyes.

"I almost hate to come, you feel so good. I want to feel this forever, right here on the edge…" he murmured against her fingers as he pressed deep one last time and came.

After a shower, they snuggled back in bed as they waited for sleep to come. "You want to tell me what the non *oh fuck me harder* thought was?" He nuzzled her neck.

"I was just thinking about how much I love and trust you. How you've helped me be a person I was pretty sure would never exist again."

She felt his smile against her skin. "That's a good one. You know, you've done that for me as well. For the last years I haven't trusted anyone, least of all myself. I kept my heart walled off and only allowed myself to love my family. I had this missing piece of myself, turns out that piece was you."

"You know I saw her. Sandra."

He stiffened and moved so he could look into her face. "When?"

"Last week. Penny and I were in Riverton, shoe shopping, and she walked past. Penny pointed her out."

"She's nothing to me. You know that right?"

Cassie laughed. "Shane, you were going to marry her at one point in time. You two lived together. She hurt and betrayed you with your best friend. Of course she's something to you. But I'm not threatened by that. I know it's in your past but I don't expect that not to have made a dent in your heart. It's okay to have feelings about her."

"I used to hate her. I don't even have that anymore. I just feel bad. We weren't right for each other, I should have seen it sooner. Hell, I miss Ron, my old best friend, more than I do her. Anyway, I hope it didn't upset you and I don't know why you didn't tell me."

"It upset me because she hurt you."

"She's married now, to Ron. It's all in the past." Shane shrugged. "If it had worked out with her and me, there'd be no you and I. So I can't be sad about it. Everything happens for a reason."

"She's sorry you know."

He raised a brow. "And you know that how?"

"She told me."

He sat up and pushed a hand through his hair in that way he did when he was agitated. It made her smile.

"You talked to her?"

"Of course I did." She snorted. "She fucked you over. I walked right out of that shoe store, Penny ran behind me trying to stop me. I called out Sandra's name and she turned and when she saw Penny she paled but waited. That took guts. Anyway, I told her who I was and she looked me up and down and nodded her head. Congratulated me, told me what a bitch she'd been and how sorry she was for breaking up two best friends and for hurting you so much. She's happy now with your old friend but he misses you too, talks about you all the time according to Sandra. He apparently stood in the back at the last two swearing in ceremonies when you were re-elected. By the way, even with saggy boobs and stab scars, I am way hotter."

He burst into laughter and pulled her against him, kissing the top of her head. "You are indeed way hotter, darlin'. I can't believe you confronted my ex on the street." He snorted. "Thanks for defending my honor."

"I was ready to smack the spit out of that woman but I have to say, after talking to her, I believe that she is sorry and while she hurt you and that can't be taken back, she did me a favor. But I'll tell you if I ever see Maggie's mother or sister on the street? Oh it's going down!"

"Look at you, like a gorgeous badger. If I weren't a man, I'd have smacked the crap out of Maggie's mother and sister too. Two more callous women I've yet to meet. But you'd have to stand in line behind my momma."

"Oh I know. I talked to her about the Sandra thing. She was hopping mad at me for a bit. It's okay now, she still hates Sandra and I can't blame her but she knows why I did it and I hope you do too. I want you to have closure on this. I want you to let it go because she's not worth it."

"A smart badger too." He kissed her upturned lips. "I have to admit that it does feel good to know she's sorry and also that Ron came to my swearing in. I can't say that I'd ever share a beer with him again but it hurts a little bit less now. No more going all Terminator on my ex-girlfriends though."

"Worried about your fan club president? Man does she hate me."

"Kendra? She does? Honestly, Cassie, I dated her a few times. I haven't in several years now."

"Shane, if I were threatened by every woman in this town with a torch burning for you, I'd be miserable. I trust you. That's all I can do." She shrugged.

"Well, if I get face-to-face with your ex things won't be so nice."

"Good."

Summer broke with ridiculous fury. Cassie was pretty sure that she'd never been so damned hot in her life. It was only late June and she felt like melting candle wax every time she walked out onto the street.

But things were going well otherwise. No more contact from Terry, her job at the bookstore made her happy and she'd expanded her jewelry business to include several local stores as well as her booming market stall.

Shane's house was hers now. She no longer felt like a guest but comfortable enough to change around furniture and hang pictures on the walls.

"I'm out of here, Penny," Cassie called back to her friend as she got ready to leave for the day.

"Okay, see you later tonight at The Pumphouse." Penny was seeing Ryan every weekend now and he'd looked at houses in a town that was halfway between Atlanta and Petal so he could see her more often. He drove out every Friday night after work or she would stay with him while Cassie handled the store.

Just as she rounded the corner to the courthouse where Shane's office was, her phone rang. Moving fast now, she saw that the number wasn't one she recognized.

Picking up, she waved to Shane and pointed to her phone when he saw her. He ran to her as she said, "Hello?"

"And how are you, Carly?"

She took a deep breath and Shane moved the phone so he could hear as well. "I was fine until you called, Terry. Don't you have somewhere to hide?"

"Oh ho! I see my little mouse has found her roar. Talking tough when you think I don't know where you are, aren't you? I can find you. I did before, remember that night?"

Shane's arm tightened around her and she focused on the people milling around and tried to keep from losing it. She would not let him win.

"Which night, Terry? The one where you were convicted of attempted murder but then you scurried off like a coward? That night?"

"You fucking bitch! I told you you were mine, don't you forget it. I made you, you whore! I'll tell you when you can walk away, I'm not ready yet. When I kill you at last I'll be ready."

The line went dead and Cassie let Shane take her phone and lead her into the alcove outside his office. His secretary took one look and helped her sit down, pressing a glass of water into her hand. Shane grabbed the phone and went to work.

An hour later, the office had filled with Chases and Penny as well. Polly held one of Cassie's hands and Edward was on the phone with Brian. Shane came back and shook his head when she looked up.

"Disposable again. Your cell phone company told us who his cell phone company was. I've forwarded the info to your California guy and he's working on the warrant now. Because we don't know how long these companies keep records on what cell towers were accessed when a call is made, I'm hoping the warrant will go through quickly. I hate this waiting, damn it!" He pounded the wall with his fist and Cassie jumped.

Seeing it he closed his eyes. "I'm sorry, darlin'. I didn't mean to scare you."

"You didn't scare me. It startled me. I'm not worried you'd do that to me. But here's the deal, we know we're not going to find him with the phone tracing thing. So even if you get a warrant tonight and they get it to the cell phone company and they give the records quickly and trace it to Topanga Canyon or Boston or wherever, he'll be gone. He's been on the run for over a year, he's not a stupid man. So why not get rid of the damned phone? I don't want to take calls from him again and if he can't find me and can't call me, I don't have to hear it."

"She's right, son. Why put her through it?" Edward shrugged. "You need a phone. It's a basic safety issue."

"Fine, but Cassie can get a phone. I don't need this one in Brian's name." Cassie's voice was tired but steady.

They agreed that she'd get a new cell phone but also keep the other phone. Shane felt it was a way to keep track of Terry and in the end, Cassie agreed.

The warrant took a day and a half to go through and they locked the call location to Daytona Beach, Florida. He wasn't in Petal and that was at least one happy thing.

They sent out police to the area but found nothing. Terry was on the run again.

In July, another call came as they celebrated at the Chases' house. Celebrated the one year anniversary of her arrival in Petal and at the same time, the one year anniversary of her crush on Shane Chase which was now a full-out jones.

She danced with him under the stars in the backyard, surrounded by the people who'd become fixtures in her life. Happiness soared through her until she heard the ring of the phone, the old one.

"That's him."

Shane stood next to her as she flipped it open and answered it. "Hello, Terry. Don't you have anything better to do than ruin my Saturday evening?"

"You think you're so clever, don't you? I hear music in the

background. You're whoring it up with some man? You're mine, Carly. I made you! Don't ever forget that. You'd be nothing without me."

"I was nothing with you, Terry. Move on. You have your freedom, why don't you get the hell out of my life and make your own better?"

"You and I have unfinished business, Carly."

The talking and laughing in the background began to die down bit by bit as people began to realize what was going on.

"We have nothing, Terry. You're nothing to me but a horrible period in my life. You tried to kill me and you sucked in bed so you had to rape me. Fuck off." She clicked the phone shut and Shane looked at her, surprise on his face.

"Bet that felt good."

She appreciated his simple response. "Yeah." He pulled her into his arms.

This time the warrant came more quickly because he bought the disposable cell phone from the same company. He was in St. Louis. Again police went out to the general location, the area around Washington University. They found nothing.

Chapter Eighteen

The anniversary of Cassie and Shane's first date came and went without any further calls from Terry. Homecoming arrived and Cassie cheered on Petal at the game like she was a lifelong fan.

She'd looked into medical school again, she'd found out she had to go back and get more training to change specialties and there was still worry about her hand. And she would have to deal with her name change no matter what. Laws that allowed patients to know who their doctors were and to be able to file complaints were important, she realized that, but they also held her back. But she'd been discussing some possible avenues with her therapist and was really excited about one of them in particular.

In the meantime, Penny came to her with an offer.

Waltzing into the shop on a Monday morning, she put a cup of coffee in front of Cassie and said without preamble, "Ryan's asked me to marry him and I've accepted."

Cassie looked up from the inventory screen and laughed. "Oh my lands. What wonderful news. I'm so happy for you!" Moving around the desk she hugged Penny tight. "Congratulations. When's the date?"

"He'd like to do it as soon as possible. I'd be fine with living together but his family wouldn't be pleased and he loves me and wants to start a family soon. We're thinking November fifteenth."

"Wow, honey, that's a month away. Okay, it's doable. Let's get to work. What can I do? Obviously I can be here at the shop for you so you can take more time off. But I can help with other things, call around, make reservations, that kind of thing."

"You're such a good friend to me. You know, I always thought the idea of an adult woman having a best friend was sort of silly, the thing you only saw in books. But you're that to me. And I want you to be my maid of honor, or matron or whatever the hell, your marriage to Terry does not count." Tears ran down Penny's face as she laughed. "I never thought I'd feel this way after Ben. He was the great love of my life. This second chance is so special."

"It is, Penny. Ryan loves you so much. I'm so happy for you and of course I'll be your maid doodad."

"Doodad sounds just fine and I promise I won't make you wear anything with tulle or a bow on the ass. It'll be simple, we want it that way."

"Fine, sweetie. It's your day. Where are you going to have it?"

"We just bought a house yesterday. It's an hour and a half from here. It has this grand stairway that leads into a formal living room with floor to ceiling windows. I want it there."

"Well, you're full of good news aren't you?"

"It's a wonderful house. As much as I love my house here, it'll always hold my life with Ben. I have to let go of that now. Take the memories with me as I build my new life. Which leads to my next thing. You interested in a bookstore?"

"What? You're selling this place?"

"Not all of it unless I have to. But I can't be here every day like I am now. I'll live far enough away that more than two days a week would be a pain to drive. I was thinking of breaking it down fairly, like seventy-five percent yours, twenty-five percent mine? We can talk to Edward about it and have him draw up the sales agreement. That is if you're interested.

"I know you want to practice medicine again but I also know it'll be a while before you can if you can at all. I'd like this place to belong to someone who loves it as much as I do."

"I'll need to talk to Shane and my brother but I can tell you I'm very interested. Truly, I don't think I can go back into medicine the way I was before. I was thinking about going into victim's advocacy. My therapist and I were talking about the difficulties in going back into medicine with my hand being so messed up and the name issue and what I want to do is help people heal. I can do that in other ways. She works with a doctor in Shackleton and has suggested that I speak with Doctor Wallace here in town to see what he'd think about me working with him on a volunteer basis. I'd need training obviously. But it solves some problems for me and gives me a way to help people."

"Oh my, Cassie, that's a wonderful idea. You'd be so good at it."

"Thanks. Okay, let me talk to Shane tonight and see what he thinks. I don't need his permission or anything but I want to run it by him. Brian is the person who deals with my trust and he'll need to handle payment. I suppose we'll have to get the store appraised too."

"I'll get on that today and talk to Edward as well."

Cassie left the shop with a bounce in her step, things were going well. The more she thought about victim's advocacy and counseling, the more she liked the idea. She could use the bad stuff she'd survived to help other people. And she loved the bookstore, it would be hers, something to hold her to town in another way.

At home, Shane was delighted with all her good news. They cooked dinner, Polly was giving her cooking lessons and she'd achieved at least a basic level of competency.

Of course, as it happened from time to time, Shane got a call after nine and had to run out. With a sigh, she accepted his kiss and went into her workroom to finish up some jewelry. As the holidays fast approached, she wanted to build up her inventory.

She'd lost track of time when she heard Shane come in. "I'm in the back here, honey. I'll be out in a sec."

Putting away her equipment, she turned to leave the room and saw not Shane standing in the doorway, but Terry.

Sick dread hit her, replaced by fear and then by fury. "What the hell are you doing here?" Backing up a bit, she reached behind her and hit the 911 button on the phone.

"Oh Carly, or should I say Cassie, why ask questions you know the answer to?"

"How did you find me?"

He laughed and it crawled over her skin like an insect. "The second time I called I heard someone say Chase. And the last time I heard someone yell out Polly and then Shane. What do you know? When I did a search for Polly Chase I saw a newspaper clipping and a picture of an event in small town Petal, Georgia. A drive for the local food bank and who did I see in the background but my faithless wife. Only her name was not Carly Sunderland anymore, it was Cassie Gambol. So unimaginative." He waved around. "I take it this is where you and Shane live? Nice. Not as nice as our house in the hills but for a small town backwater like this one, I expected shacks and hound dogs on the porch."

"Go away, Terry. I don't want you anymore!" In her pocket, she realized she'd dropped a pair of needle-nosed pliers she used to tie off findings on a necklace she'd been working on. She slipped her hand inside and held on.

"It's not what you want, bitch! You fucked my life up. I gave you everything and you threw it back at me. You took my reputation and dragged it through the mud. I can't practice medicine anymore and it's all your fault." He came toward her and she stabbed at him with the pliers, felt them dig into the flesh just below his shoulder.

He bellowed in pain and rage and she ran past him, hoping the call had gone through, hoping the security guard would drive past and see something amiss, hoping Shane would come home. For that moment though, she was on her own and she needed to get to the table next to the couch to get her gun.

A hand, slick with blood but with a sure grip, closed around her upper arm and the weight of him rode her body to the ground. She tasted blood as her lip split open when he punched her in the face.

"You bitch! You won't make it this time. I'll make sure you're not breathing when I walk away." His fingers moved to her throat and began to squeeze.

The world began to narrow as she lost oxygen. Desperately, she reached with both hands, trying to find something, anything to hit him with. Shane's coffee mug! Grabbing it with the tip of her fingers she put all her remaining strength into it and hit Terry upside the head as hard as she could.

Air rushed into her lungs as she coughed when he fell to the side, losing his grip on her.

She began to scream over and over as she scrambled around the coffee table and got to the drawer where her gun was. Fumbling, she heard him right behind her as her fingers touched the cool metal and pulled it toward her.

Her head yanked back as she continued to scream. She couldn't get to the safety to turn it off! Pain seared her as he bent one arm back so hard she felt the shoulder dislocate which probably numbed her enough not to feel the full impact when he broke her wrist. All she could think was thank goodness she knew enough to learn to shoot with her left hand. He hadn't seen the gun she'd been holding in it just yet.

"You can't have my life, you bastard. You got enough from me!" she screamed.

"I'm going to fuck you one last time, you whore, and then I'm going to kill you. Leave you for your loverboy to find." His voice was in her ear, right behind her, and she pulled her head forward and threw it back as hard as she could, hearing the crunch of his nose.

His pain-filled scream gurgled as she realized she'd broken his nose. Time slowed as she rolled, flicking off the safety and pointing the gun, steadying herself as best she could one handed.

She came to peace with the fact that she was ready to take his life, breathing out as her finger squeezed. Just before her arm took the brunt of the shot, a red bloom covered his chest.

Confused, she watched as he hit the floor, her ears ringing as the shot deafened her. Blinking back the sweat, she saw Shane running toward her and one of his officers going to Terry's slumped over body, checking for a pulse.

"Honey? Oh God, are you all right?" Cassie watched his lips more than heard him ask. Her hearing was still gone as Shane gently took the gun from her hand, wincing as he saw her other arm hanging at an odd angle.

"He's dead?"

"He can't hurt you ever again, Cassie. He's dead," the other officer told her as he stood up.

"Good. God damn it, good. My arm hurts now, Shane, I need to go to the hospital."

Cassie related it in a matter-of-fact voice right before she passed out in his arms.

Hours later, at the hospital, he paced back and forth through the waiting room. Another officer came in and took over the investigation. Obviously Shane did not have the ability to judge the situation without bias. Looking at her history and Terry's past and that they'd come in as he was attacking Cassie, Shane was sure his shooting would be justified. Still, he was placed on administrative leave while the shooting was investigated and that was all right with him.

Cassie's weapon was discharged but had missed. They found the bullet in the wall behind where Terry had been standing.

She would have hit him in the chest if he hadn't begun to fall after Shane shot him. There wasn't any reason to do anything but see her as a victim in the situation.

Another officer was questioning her as they patched up her arm. Shane wanted to be there but as he was the person who shot the suspect he couldn't. So one of his father's law partners was in with her and her therapist was on the way.

Chapter Nineteen

The months passed. Shane was cleared and came back to work right before Penny and Ryan's wedding. Cassie bought a three quarters share in Paperbacks and More and began to take classes to pursue becoming a victim's advocate.

Penny announced a week before Christmas that she was pregnant.

"Wow, you said you wanted to start on a family right away, you weren't kidding." Cassie laughed as she hugged her friend.

"We started a while before the wedding, don't tell his mother. Anyway, it's still new so don't tell anyone just yet, okay? I had to tell someone and I couldn't tell you over the phone."

"I can't wait to shop for baby clothes with you. Ryan must be over the moon."

"He is. He's already looking for a crib and I swear has a college fund started. I'm so happy, Cassie."

"Oh, honey, you deserve it. I'm happy for you too."

They agreed that Penny would tell everyone in Petal after New Year's when the first trimester had safely passed. It was a delicious little gift for Cassie though, knowing that life continued even in the shadow of such ugliness.

Her cast came off three days before Christmas. "Thank goodness. I can only deal with so much. It's stressful enough spending the night at the Chases'. I don't want to think about doing it with a cast on too."

Shane chuckled. "Honey, my mother loves you. My father loves you and my single brothers would steal you in a minute if I didn't keep an eye on them every second. It's no big deal. We live together, they know we sleep in the same bed."

"I'm only agreeing to this because of presents you know."

"I do know, you're very easy. I like that in a girl."

Cassie rolled her eyes.

Even being used to the Chases for a year and a half did not prepare her for the insanity of Christmas morning in their household. Last year they'd driven over in the morning but waking up there was a whole different story. While they'd had a bedroom to themselves along with Maggie and Kyle, relatives slept everywhere. The pleasing picture of people young and old in pajamas around the eight-foot high Christmas tree did her heart good. This was family. This was wonderful and normal and special all at once.

Brian smiled at her as she came and sat on the floor, resting her arms on Shane's thighs.

Shane's paternal grandfather handed out presents and the process took several hours as everyone ooohed and aaahed over each present from mundane to fabulous. The diamond bracelet Kyle gave Maggie was positively gorgeous and Cassie was proud that her jewelry was thoroughly loved by all recipients.

Still, she had to admit that her favorite moment was when Edward unwrapped the first edition *Black's Law Dictionary* she'd found in an old bookstore in downtown Los Angeles when she'd visited Brian the month before.

"Holy cow! Girl, you're too good to be true. Shane, boy, you'd better keep this one around." Edward stroked the leather spine and beamed.

"She grabbed it before I could, Edward. Even with a broken arm and a bum shoulder she beat me to it." Brian laughed.

"That's my girl." Edward winked.

"Oops, I didn't see this last one. It's for you, Cassie." Pop handed the long, flat box to Cassie.

"From Shane, oooh!" Cassie set to unwrapping it. It was a card with a key attached. *Use me.* was written on it. She pulled the key off. The key to Shane's truck.

Everyone followed her out to the driveway, standing back as she opened the truck. "You giving me this monster, Shane?"

"My truck?" He sounded horrified. "No! Follow the clues, darlin'."

She saw a bow on the glove box and another note stuck there. *I need a key.*

Sliding the key into the lock she opened it and saw the light blue box. "Oh lordy! A blue box." Delighted, she pulled it out and opened it up. It wasn't until she saw the black velvet box inside the blue box that she realized what it was.

With trembling hands she cracked it open and a pear-shaped sapphire sat nestled in the velvet, diamonds on either side of the deep blue stone. She turned to face Shane but he was on one knee. Tears began to run down her face.

"Cassie, will you marry me?"

"Holy cripes! Hell yes, I'll marry you." She jumped into his arms and they toppled onto the cold, wet grass, laughing.

Reaching around her, he grabbed the box and slid the ring on her finger. "Perfect. I knew you'd look better in something other than a diamond. I saw it and had to get it for you."

"You rock."

He laughed again. "Thanks, darlin', you do too. How about a Valentine's Day wedding? In that little chapel just outside town? You seem to really like it."

"Oh the one with the pretty stained glass? Do you think it would be available on such short notice?"

"Probably not but I booked it last year this time."

She stopped. "You did? Oh my. Awfully sure of yourself."

"We all know I'm an arrogant man, we established that early on. I wanted to ask you to marry me last Christmas but I knew you wouldn't be ready. But I wanted that little chapel for you when you were ready. Just in case."

"You're a giant marshmallow, you know that?"

"Don't tell anyone."

* * * * *

About the Author

Lauren Dane is a *New York Times* and *USA TODAY* bestselling author of over fifty novels and novellas across several genres. She lives in the Northwest with her patient husband and three wild children.
Visit Lauren on the web at www.laurendane.com

E-mail laurendane@laurendane.com

Twitter: @laurendane

You can write to her at: PO BOX 45175, Seattle, WA 98145

Keep reading for an excerpt of
A Man You Can Trust
by Jo McNally.
Find it in the
Spring Blockbuster 2024 anthology,
out now!

CHAPTER ONE

THE RESORT PARKING lot was quiet.

That was hardly surprising, since it was seven o'clock on a Monday morning.

But Cassandra Smith didn't take chances.

Ever.

She backed into her reserved spot but didn't turn the car off right away. She didn't even put it in Park. First, she looked around—checking the mirrors, making sure she was going to stay. Pete Carter was walking from his car toward the Gallant Lake Resort. He waved as he passed her, and she waved back, then pretended to look at something on the passenger seat as she turned off the ignition. Pete worked at the front desk, and he was a nice enough guy. He'd offer to walk her inside if she got out now. And maybe that would be a good idea. Or maybe not. How well did she really know him?

Her fingers tightened on the steering wheel. She was being ridiculous—Pete was thirty years her senior and happily married. But some habits were hard to shake, and really—why take the chance? By the time she finished arguing with herself, Pete was gone.

She checked the mirrors one last time before getting out of the car, threading the keys through her fingers in a move as natural to her as breathing. As she closed the door, a warm breeze brushed a tangle of auburn hair across her face. She tucked it back behind her ear and took a moment to appreciate the morning. Beyond the sprawling 200-room fieldstone-and-timber resort where Cassie worked, Gallant Lake shimmered like polished blue steel. It was encircled by the Catskill Mountains, which were just beginning to show a blush of green in the trees. The air was brisk but smelled like spring, earthy and fresh. It reminded her of new beginnings.

It had been six months since Aunt Cathy offered her sanctuary in this small resort town nestled in the Catskills. Gallant Lake was beginning to feel like home, and she was grateful for it. The sound of car tires crunching on the driveway behind her propelled her out of her thoughts and into the building. Other employees were starting to arrive.

Cassie crossed the lobby, doing her best to avoid making eye contact with the few guests wandering around at this hour. As usual, she opted for the stairs instead of dealing with the close confines of the elevator. The towering spiral staircase in the center of the lobby looked like a giant tree growing up toward the ceiling three stories above, complete with stylized copper leaves draping from the ceiling. The offices of Randall Resorts International were located on the second floor, overlooking the wide lawn that stretched to the lakeshore. Cassie's desk was centered between four small offices. Or rather, three smaller offices and one huge one, which belonged to the boss. That boss was in earlier than usual today.

"G'morning, Cassie! Once you get settled, stop in, okay?"

Ugh. No employee wanted to be called into the boss's office first thing on a Monday.

Blake Randall managed not only this resort from Gallant Lake, but half a dozen others around the world. It hadn't taken long for Cassie to understand that Blake was one of those rare—at least in her world—men who wore their honor like a mantle. He took pride in protecting the people he cared for. Tall, with a swath of black hair that was constantly falling across his forehead, the man was ridiculously good-looking. His wife, Amanda, really hit the jackpot with this guy, and he adored her and their children.

Blake was all business in the office, though. Focused and driven, he'd intimidated the daylights out of Cassie at first. Amanda teasingly called him Tall, Dark and Broody, and the nickname fit. But Cassie had come to appreciate his steady leadership. He had high expectations, and he frowned on drama in the workplace.

He'd offered her a job at the resort's front desk when she first arrived in Gallant Lake. It was a charity job—a favor to Cathy—and Cassie knew it. It took only one irate male guest venting at her during check-in for everyone to realize she wasn't ready to be working with an unpredictable public. She'd frozen like a deer in headlights. Once she moved up here to the private offices, she'd found her footing and had impressed Blake with her problem-solving skills. Because Blake hated problems.

She tossed her purse into the bottom drawer of her desk and checked her computer quickly to make sure there weren't any urgent issues to deal with. Then she made herself a cup of hot tea, loaded it with sugar and poured Blake a mug of black coffee before heading into his office.

He looked up from behind his massive desk and gave her a quick nod of thanks as she set his coffee down in front of him. Everyone knew to stay out of Blake's way until they saw a cup of coffee in his hand. He was well-known for not being a morning person. He took a sip and sighed.

"I was ready to book a flight to Barbados after hearing about the wedding disaster down there this weekend, but then I heard that apparently *I*—" he emphasized the one-letter word with air quotes "—already resolved everything by flying some photographer in to take wedding photos yesterday, along with discounting some rooms. Not at *our* resort, but at a *competitor*. I hear I'm quite the hero to the bride's mother, but I'll be damned if I remember doing any of it."

Blake's dark brows furrowed as he studied her over the rim of his coffee cup, but she could see a smile tugging at the corner of his mouth. The tension in her shoulders eased. Despite his tone, he wasn't really angry.

"The manager called Saturday looking for you," she explained. "Monique was in a panic, so I made a few calls. The bride's mother used the son of a 'dear family friend' to organize the wedding, instead of using our concierge service. The idiot didn't book the rooms until the last minute, and we didn't have enough available, which he neglected to mention to the bride's mom. Then he booked the photographer for the wrong date." She smiled at the look of horror on Blake's face. "We're talking wrong by a full month. It was quite a melodrama—none of which was our fault—but the bride is some internet fashion icon with half a million followers on Instagram. So we found rooms at the neighboring resort for the guests we couldn't handle, and convinced the wedding party to get back into their gowns and tuxes for a full photo shoot the day *after* the wedding, which was the fastest we could get the photographer there. Mom's happy. Bride's happy. Social media is flooded with great photos and stories with the resort as a backdrop. I assumed you'd approve."

Blake chuckled. "Approve? It was freaking brilliant, Cassie. That kind of problem-solving is more along the lines of a VP than an executive assistant. You should have an office of your own."

She still wasn't used to receiving compliments, and her cheeks warmed. When she'd first arrived, she'd barely been able to handle answering calls and emails, always afraid of doing something wrong, of disappointing someone. But as the months went by, she'd started to polish her rusty professional skills and found she was pretty good at getting things done, especially over the phone. Face-to-face confrontation was a different story.

This wasn't the first time Blake had mentioned a promotion, but she wasn't ready. Oh, she was plenty qualified, with a bachelor's degree in business admin. But if things went bad back in Milwaukee, she'd have to change her name again and vanish, so it didn't make sense to put down roots anywhere. She let Blake's comment hang in the air without responding. He finally shook his head.

"Fine. Keep whatever job title you want, but I need your help with something."

Cassie frowned when Blake hesitated. "What is it?"

"You know I hired a new director of security." Cassie nodded. She was going to miss Ken Taylor, who was retiring to the Carolinas with his wife, Dianne. Ken had taken the job on a temporary basis after Blake's last security guy left for a job in Boston. Ken was soft-spoken and kind, and he looked like Mr. Rogers, right down to the cardigan sweaters. He was aware of Cassie's situation, and he'd made every effort to make sure she felt safe here, including arranging her reserved parking space.

"Nick West starts today. I'd like you to work with him."

"Me? Why?" Cassie blurted the words without thinking. She laughed nervously. "I don't know anything about security!"

But she knew all about *needing* security.

Blake held up his hand. "Relax. I'm not putting you on the security team. He'll need help with putting data together and learning our processes. I need someone I can trust to make sure he has a smooth transition."

"So… I'm going to be *his* executive assistant instead of yours?" Her palms went clammy at the thought of working for a stranger.

"First, we've already established you're a hell of a lot more than my EA. And this is just temporary, to help him get settled in the office." Blake drained his coffee mug and set it down with a thunk, not noticing the way Cassie flinched at the sound. "He's a good guy. Talented. Educated. He's got a master's in criminal justice, and he was literally a hero cop in LA—recognized by the mayor, the whole deal."

A shiver traced its way down Cassie's spine. Her ex had been a "hero cop," too. Blake's next words barely registered.

"I'm a little worried about him making the shift from the hustle of LA to quiet Gallant Lake, but he says he's looking for a change of pace. His thesis was on predictive policing—using data to spot trouble before it reaches a critical point." That explained why Blake hired the guy. Blake was all about preventing problems before they happened. He did *not* like surprises. "It'll be interesting to see how he applies that to facility security. His approach requires a ton of data to build predictive models, and that's where you come in. You create reports faster than anyone else here."

Cassie loved crunching numbers and analyzing results. She started to relax. If Blake wanted her to do some research for the new guy, she could handle that.

"I also want you to mentor him a bit, help him get acclimated."

"Meaning...?"

"Amanda and I are headed to Vegas this week for that conference and a little vacation time. Nick's going to need someone to show him around, make introductions and answer any questions that come up. He just got to town this weekend, and he doesn't know anyone or anything in Gallant Lake."

"So what, I'm supposed to be his babysitter?"

Blake's brow rose at the uncharacteristically bold question.

"Uh, no. Just walk him around the resort so he's familiar with it, and be a friendly face for the guy." He leaned forward. "Look, I get why you might be anxious, but he's the director of security. That's about as safe as it gets."

Her emotions roiled around in her chest. She hated that her employer felt he had to constantly reassure her about her safety. Yes, the guy in charge of security *should* be safe. All men should be.

"Cassie? Is this going to be a problem?" The worry in Blake's eyes made her sit straighter in her chair. What was it Sun Tzu wrote in *The Art of War*? The latest in a long line of self-help books she'd picked up was based on quotes from the ancient Chinese tome.

Appear strong when you are weak...

"No, I'm sure it will be fine. And the data analysis sounds interesting. Does he know...?"

"About your situation? No. I wouldn't do that without your permission. I only told Ken because you'd just arrived and..."

She was hardly strong now, but she'd been a complete basket case back then.

"I understand. I don't think the new guy needs to know. I don't want to be treated differently."

Blake frowned. "I don't want that, either. But I do want you to feel safe here."

"I know, Blake. And thank you. If I change my mind, I'll tell him myself." She was getting tired of people having conversations about her as if she was a problem to be solved, no matter how well-meaning they were. "When will I meet him?"

"He's getting his rental house situated this morning, then he'll be in. I'm planning on having lunch with him, then giving him a quick tour. He dropped some boxes off yesterday. Can you make sure he has a functioning office? You know, computer, phone, internet access and all that? I told Brad to set it up, but you know how scattered that kid can be."

Two hours later, Cassie was finishing the last touches in West's office. The computer and voice mail were set up with temporary passwords. The security team had delivered his passes and key cards—his master key would open any door in the resort. Brad, their IT whiz, had been busy over the weekend, and a huge flat-screen hung on one wall. On it, twelve different feeds from the security surveillance room downstairs were scrolling in black and white. It looked like a scene straight out of some crime-fighter TV show.

A familiar voice rang out in the office. "Hel-lo? Damn, no one's here."

Cassie stepped to the doorway and waved to Blake's wife. "I'm here!"

Amanda Randall rushed to give Cassie a tight hug. Cassie *hated* hugs, but Amanda got a free pass. The woman simply couldn't help herself—she was a serial hugger. She was also Cassie's best friend in Gallant Lake. They'd bonded one night over a bottle of wine and the discovery they shared similar ghosts from their pasts. Other than that, the two women couldn't be any more different. Amanda was petite, with curves everywhere a woman wanted curves. Cassie was average height and definitely not curvy—her nervous energy left her with a lean build. Amanda had long golden curls, while Cassie's straight auburn hair was usually pulled back and under control. Amanda was a bouncing bundle of laughing, loving, hugging energy. Cassie was much more reserved, and sometimes found her friend's enthusiasm overwhelming.

"I brought chocolate chip cookies for everyone, but I guess you and I will have to eat them all." Amanda held up a basket that smelled like heaven.

"You won't have to twist my arm. Come on in and keep me company."

Amanda followed her into the new guy's office.

"Wow—this is some pretty high-tech stuff, huh?" Amanda walked over to the flat-screen and watched the video feeds change from camera to camera. One feed was from a camera in front of Blake and Amanda's stone mansion next door to the resort. The private drive was visible in the view from above their front door. "I really need to talk to Blake about those cameras. I don't like the feeds popping up in some stranger's office."

"Hasn't resort security always been responsible for the house, too?"

"I was never crazy about that, but Blake insisted. And it was different when it was Paul, whom I'd known from the first week

I was here. And then Ken. I mean, he's like having a favorite uncle watching over the house. But some hotshot ex-cop from LA watching me and the kids coming and going?" Amanda shuddered. "I don't think so. Have you met him yet?"

"Who?"

"The new guy? Superhero cop coming to save us all? The one who has my husband drooling?"

"No, I haven't met him yet." Cassie set a stack of legal pads on the corner of the desk, opposite the corner Amanda now occupied as she devoured a cookie. "What do you know about him?"

"What *don't* I know? He's all Blake talked about this weekend. 'Nick is so brave!' 'Nick is so brilliant!' 'Oh, no! What if Nick doesn't like it here?' 'What if Nick leaves?'" Amanda acted out each comment dramatically, and Cassie couldn't help laughing. "But seriously, he *really* wants this guy to work out. You know Blake—he believes in preventing problems before they happen, and that wasn't Ken's strong suit. He's so anxious for this guy to be happy here that he actually suggested we skip our trip to Vegas so he could be here all week for *Nick*! That was a 'hell no' from me. We haven't been away together without the kids in ages." Amanda finished off the last of her cookie, licking her fingers. "And this girl is ready to par-tay in Vegas, baby! Whatcha doin'?"

"Blake said Nick dropped off these boxes. I'll unpack them, and he can organize later." Cassie pulled the top off one of the boxes on the credenza. It was filled with books on criminal science and forensics. She put them on the bookshelves in the order they were packed. Police work was usually a life's calling. What made this guy walk away from it?

She stopped after pulling the cover off the second box. It contained more books and binders, but sitting on top was a framed photo. She lifted it out and Amanda came around the desk to study it with her.

It was a wedding portrait. The tall man in the image looked

damned fine in a tuxedo, like a real-life James Bond. His hair was dark and cropped short, military style. His features were angular and sharp, softened only by the affectionate smile he was giving the bride. Her skin was dark and her wedding gown was the color of champagne. Her close-cropped Afro high-lighted her high cheekbones and long, graceful neck. She was looking up at the man proudly, exuding confidence and joy. Cassie felt a sting of regret. When was the last time anyone thought that about her?

"Wow—are those two gorgeous or what?" Amanda took the silver frame from Cassie and whistled softly. "I wonder who it is." She turned the frame over as if there might be an answer on the back.

"I'm assuming it's Nick West and his wife."

"No. Blake told me he's single."

"Maybe she's an ex?"

Amanda rolled her eyes. "Who keeps photos like this of their ex? Maybe it's not him at all—could be a brother or a friend. But if it is Nick, he's hot as hell, isn't he?"

Cassie took the picture back and set it on a shelf. "I hadn't noticed."

"Yeah, I call BS on that. There isn't a woman under the age of eighty who wouldn't notice how hot *that* guy is. You'd better be careful, especially now that you're living in the love shack."

"The *what*?"

"Nora's apartment—we call it the love shack. First it was her and Asher. Then Mel moved in there and met Shane. And now *you're* there, so…"

Cassie's aunt had sold her coffee shop in the village to Aman-da's cousin Nora a few years ago but still worked there part-time. The apartment above the Gallant Brew had been a godsend when it came vacant shortly after Cassie's arrival. But a *love shack*?

"I don't believe in fairy tales. And even if Nora's place *did* have magic powers, they'd be wasted on me." She started to pull more books out of the box, but Amanda stopped her.

"Hey, I'm sorry. I don't mean to push you. Sometimes my mouth gets ahead of my brain. But someday you're going to find someone…"

Cassie shook her head abruptly. "That ship has sailed, Amanda. I have zero interest in any kind of…whatever." She glanced back to the photo and studied the man's dark eyes, sparkling with love for the bride. Her heart squeezed just a little, but she ignored it. "I can't take the chance. Not again."

"Not every guy is Don. In fact, there are millions of guys who *aren't* Don."

Amanda meant well, but they were straying onto thin and dangerous ice here. Cassie had wedding photos, too. They were packed away somewhere, and they showed a smiling couple just like this one. She'd been so innocent back then. And stupid. She was never going to be either again.

"Look, I have a ton of work to do, and this guy—my *coworker*—is going to be here any time now. No more talk about love shacks and hotness, okay?"

Amanda stared at her long and hard, her blue eyes darkening in concern. But thankfully, she decided to let it go. She picked up the basket of cookies. "Fine. I have to finish packing for the trip anyway. I'll leave these out on the coffee counter." She started to walk away, then spun suddenly and threw her arms around Cassie in an attack hug. "We leave in the morning, but we'll be back next week. If you need anything at all—*anything*—you call Nora or Mel and they'll be there in a heartbeat."

Cassie bit back the surprising rebuke that sat on the tip of her tongue. She was fed up with everyone hovering and fretting, but she knew it was her own damn fault. How many times had she called Amanda those first few months, crying and terror-stricken because of a bad dream or some random noise she heard? Sure, she'd changed her name and moved about as far away from Milwaukee as she could get, but Don was an ex-cop with all the right connections. That's why she kept a "go-bag" packed and ready at her door. She took a deep breath, nodded and wished Amanda a safe and fun trip. But after she left, Cassie was too agitated to sit at her desk. She ended up back in Nick West's office, unpacking the last box.

A little flicker of anger flared deep inside. It had been nudging at her more and more lately, first as an occasional spark of frustration, but now it was turning into a steady flame. She wanted her life back. She wanted a life where she could rely on herself and stand up for herself. She looked at the wedding photo again. She wanted a life where she smiled more. Where she didn't jump every time someone…

A shadow filled the doorway.

"Hey! Whatcha doin' in here?"